MW00715897

LOST
IN
TIME

Next Time Book 1

... UNTIL NEXT TIME

LOST
IN
TIME

Next Time Book 1

W.M. WILTSHIRE

NEXT TIME SERIES: LOST IN TIME
First Edition

Book Cover Design and Interior Formatting by Melissa Williams Design

Edited by Hugh Willis and Susan Strecker

ISBN: 978-1-9991134-0-7

To my Dad, who taught me the meaning of hard work and perseverance.

As a fellow pilot I think you would have enjoyed this book.

I miss you.

Foreword

TIME IS LIKE a river or stream; while it may move at different speeds, it always moves in the same direction—relentlessly forward. From the day we are born, time moves us along a predetermined course to our finality—to our death.

But, what if we could control time? What would happen if we could change the course of that river? What if time no longer had any meaning when we refer to the past, present or future?

Time, while still poorly understood, has fascinated physicists for hundreds of years. Recently, this fascination has extended to the notion of travelling through time.

In 1843, Charles Dickens wrote a story involving time travel using spectral transportation. Some sixty years later, in 1905, Albert Einstein's *special theory of relativity* proved that time travel to the future is possible.

Having accepted the possibility of travelling into the *future*, modern debate between physicists, mathematicians, cosmologists and philosophers began to centre on travelling into the *past*.

By 1915, Einstein's *general theory of relativity* proved that travel to the past is also possible. Even the renowned theoretical physicist and cosmologist, Stephen Hawking, admitted that there is nothing in known physics today that actually prohibits travelling to the past. Amazingly, time travel to the past violates none of the known laws of physics.

So isn't it unbelievable then that H. G. Wells wrote the first contemporary time travel story, based on "plausible" science in 1895? Wells's story refers to four dimensional space-time, which theoretically, allowed for travel into the future. Wells wrote his story ten years ahead of Albert Einstein's special theory of relativity and twenty years before Einstein's general theory. Did Wells have some foreknowledge of time travel, maybe from a visitor from the future?

What if you could build a time machine like the one in H. G. Wells's story and travel to the future? Just think of it! You could get next week's winning lottery numbers, return to the present day, buy a ticket and in one week's time become a multi-millionaire.

Or you could travel even further into the future: years, decades or centuries, but what would you find? Would you find a unified world, living in peace and harmony, as in John Lennon's song *Imagine*? Wouldn't that be wondrous? Or would you find a world where today's known species are either extinct or have become altered mutations of their earlier selves? Would it be a result of natural evolution or due to some unknown element? Or would the pollution and toxic levels in the atmosphere be so unbearable that they threaten all life as we know it today? Or would you find a world at war, where humankind, still bent on its own self-destruction, is now getting closer to succeeding.

Then, upon your return to the present, with this foresight, what would you do? Would you alter the present to prevent or change the foreseen future?

There are endless variables associated with time travel to the future. But what about travelling to the past? Would you travel to a specific period of time where you could save a loved one from a future tragedy? Could you prevent the terrorist attacks of September 11th which put the world into a spiralling tailspin and changed our way of life forever? Could you warn the people of Sri Lanka of the 2004 Boxing Day tsunami and prevent the senseless deaths of over 250,000 people?

Would you become a part of history by changing the events of the past and altering history as we know it today? Or would you be merely an observer of the past, becoming part of the events as they unfold?

We know Einstein's *special and general theories of relativity* clearly indicate that time travel is possible. So it's now not a question of *whether* you can travel into the future or the past. Maybe it's now a question of **should** you?

Part I

Time Began When . . .

1

ONLY HE COULD hear the soft groans from the varnished oak staircase, as his weight shifted from one step to another, during his slow descent. A tantalizing aroma pulled him toward the kitchen, relentlessly drawing him closer. He was a slave to his growling stomach, helpless to resist the pull.

He made his way quietly through the living room where the warmth radiating from the stone fireplace removed the dampness hanging in the early spring air. Soft music emanated from the surround sound system, wirelessly linked to the television mounted above the fireplace's mantel. He crossed the hardwood floor, drawn by his persistent need to satiate his hunger.

The kitchen was a spacious, open-concept design with slate-grey granite countertops and walnut cabinetry, with two islands. One partitioned out a casual eating area with a maple table and upholstered benches. The other provided additional counter space directly behind the sink. Large windows above the counter overlooked the manicured lawn and provided a panoramic view of the water.

Daric took a spoon from the counter and quietly crept up behind the lone figure stirring the contents of a steaming pot. He reached around and quickly plunged his spoon into the homemade marinara sauce.

"Jesus, Daric, you scared the living crap out of me," Sandra scolded, placing her left hand over her rapidly beating heart.

"Sorry, Mom," Daric said half-heartedly, licking sauce from his spoon. He'd always been a bit of a prankster and took great delight in trying to scare his mom.

"Smells great. When's dinner?" Daric asked, eagerly.

Sandra Delaney was putting the finishing touches on the family's traditional Friday night spaghetti dinner. Meals nowadays aren't as messy as they were when the kids were two years old. "Dinner will be ready in about thirty minutes. Where's your sister?" she asked.

"I saw her down at the lake earlier, trying to teach Bear how to swim . . . again," Daric said laughingly, as he hoisted himself up to sit on the center island. "She should give up. It's a waste of time. Bear will never learn to swim."

"You know your sister, she'll never give up." Pride resonated in her voice. "One of these days, Bear will actually like the water. Now, go do something useful," Sandra said curtly, gently shoving Daric off the counter so she could finish making the salad. She was still annoyed with his prank. "Go tell Dani to get ready for dinner. And while you're at it, see if you can track down your dad. He's probably in his lab, as usual."

As an afterthought Sandra asked, "Do you remember the access code?"

"How could I forget?" he said dejectedly, walking out the kitchen door.

Sandra watched her son through the window as he made his way to the water. She noticed his slumped shoulders and his slower-than-usual gait. She couldn't help but wonder what was plaguing his thoughts.

She also felt a great sense of pride at how well he had grown into the young man she saw before her. He stood six-foot-one; his broad shoulders and narrow waist clearly reflected a swimmer's physique. Being raised around water, he was naturally drawn to it. He could swim before he could even walk. She had a devil of a time trying to get him out of the water back then.

Now as captain of his varsity swim team, he pushed himself harder than anyone else, determined to set an example for others. He trained harder than anyone else on the team, too. So, with all his hard work, it was no small wonder he was crushed when he failed to make the Olympic swim team last year.

But Sandra knew not qualifying for the Olympics wasn't what was bothering her son. Even with her gentle prodding, he wasn't ready to share it with her.

2

DARIC SLOWLY MADE his way to the water's edge. His parents had already raked the yard, as they wanted the short time the kids were home on spring break spent visiting, not doing chores. With the number and the wide variety of trees on the 720-acre estate, it was difficult to keep the grounds pristine. Thank goodness most of it was left in its natural state. The peninsula was mostly forested, providing much-needed shade in the heat of the summer and additional tranquil privacy for its residents. Only the immediate area around the house opened to reveal the manicured lawns.

Daric reflected on the last time he was home from university; it was Christmas vacation. There was really no excuse for not coming home more often. He loved his family, but, at times, they made him feel like a real screw-up. He'd never been as 'perfect' as his sister, Dani. Lord knows he'd tried.

Just because Dani was twenty-three minutes older than he, didn't mean she was smarter or, for that matter, in charge! She'd always told him what to do growing up, ordering him around. Even his parents seemed to give her more responsibility.

Whenever he offered a suggestion, she would quickly shoot it down saying he wasn't thinking things through before speaking, making him feel insignificant. Even though she was right most of the time, it did nothing for his self-esteem.

And then there were his parents—how could anyone measure up to their expectations or compete with their well-established reputations?

Dr. Sandra Delaney was the head of Emergency Services at Mount Albert Hospital. She also conducted classes at the local medical college on a part-time basis, sharing her years of expertise with undergraduates.

Professor Quinn Delaney went to Princeton, then later to Harvard, getting his Ph.D. in physics. He also had a major in history. After graduating, he held a position as a physics professor at Stanford for five years and still conducted the odd lecture. He was currently on the faculty at Perimeter Institute, a cutting-edge scientific research and theoretical physics institution.

How can anyone compete with all that? Daric thought. He knew his playful nature was usually misinterpreted; probably the reason people didn't take him seriously. He used his sense of humor to mask his insecurities.

Daric was actually keenly intelligent and quick-witted. He radiated an easygoing friendliness with everyone he met. His ripped body, piercing blue eyes, even features, framed by wavy, sandy-colored hair, drew the attention of both sexes.

Daric glanced farther down the shoreline and spotted Dani still trying to coax Bear into the water. Even he had to admit that his sister was a looker. She was five-foot-eight, with a slim athletic physique enhanced by her delicate features. Her sun-kissed skin, honey blond hair and azure eyes, in another era, she could have passed as a Greek goddess.

Daric caught a movement in his peripheral vision along the tree line, past Dani, toward the end of the peninsula. By the time he focused on that area, there was nothing to see. *Probably a deer,* he assumed.

Then his attention was drawn to the boat in the water, tied to the Bauhaus dock a short distance away. He quickly detoured to check on his boat; his pride and joy.

Daric painstakingly built the twenty-four-foot fiberglass speed-boat from forms he had designed and manufactured himself. He also rebuilt the 150-horsepower inboard Mercury engine. His dad must have put it in the water, knowing Daric would be eager to take her out for a spin during his short visit home.

"Thanks, Dad," Daric whispered as he caressed the boat's polished surface.

He'd always enjoyed tinkering with anything power-driven. When he was five years old, he took the mixer from the kitchen, pulled it completely apart and then reassembled it. There were no leftover pieces, and it looked just as it did before he started; he was so proud of himself. It wasn't until his mom went to use it that she realized someone had tampered with it. When she turned it on slow, batter flew all over the kitchen, including all over her. How she knew it was his fault, he had no idea. She made him take it apart to get it working correctly again even if it took him all night. He needed only two attempts. It was so simple once he recognized the speeds were reversed.

Ever since then, he'd loved working on engines of any kind. He has a Pratt & Whitney R-985 Wasp Junior aircraft engine from 1950; a 1948 Harley-Davidson Panhead vintage motorcycle he rebuilt and the 150 Mercury inboard engine in his boat.

He knew computers too; circuit boards, processors, microchips and programming. He even built the security system for his parents' home.

Having decided on going for a joy-ride after dinner, he got back to the business at hand, after his stomach made it known again that it was feeding time.

3

DANI FELT IT was important to teach Bear how to swim, considering their home was surrounded by water. But it would seem that Bear was just as determined not to venture any deeper than past her elbows and knees.

Bear was the family pet; a four-year-old Shiba Inu. She looked more like a fox with a curly tail than a bear. When she first arrived at her new home as a puppy, her stubby black muzzle, rounded ears, and short tail made her look like a little bear cub, hence the name Bear. When she started to mature, her muzzle grew out and lightened in color, her ears perked up, and her tail bushed out and curled. Now she looked nothing at all like a bear.

Bear had never had a fondness for the water. She didn't even like to go outside when it was raining. Now snow, that's an entirely different story. Sometimes you'd swear she was part Husky. Except for her sesame coloring, she could pass for a miniature Husky.

Bear was a loyal, faithful, and good-natured dog. Her "country-girl beauty" was simple, yet elegant and poised. Bear had a spirited boldness, combined with a keen sense of awareness. She wouldn't shy away from a threat; nor would she act with unwarranted aggression. She wouldn't start a fight, but she'd be happy to finish one. And when it came to her family, Bear stood her ground to defend them.

"Come on Bear, do it for me, please?" Dani pleaded, standing in the cool water just over her knees, still trying to coax Bear to come out to her.

Upon hearing her name, Bear tilted her head to the right, but did not budge. The Westminster Dog Show introduced the Shiba Inu as a tenacious breed that constantly provided challenges to their owners. They weren't kidding!

Bear had several ways of expressing herself. Her facial expressions were mostly defined by the positioning of her ears. In their natural forward perked position, she was alert and attentive. When her ears were lying almost against the side of her head, she was smiling and happy to see people. When her ears were sloped sideways at a forty-five-degree angle, she was anxious. And then there was her tail: up and curled was the natural, happy position; uncurled or down meant she was restless or nervous.

"Give up Dani, it'll never happen," Daric jeered.

Hearing Daric's voice, Bear raced out of the shallow water to greet him.

"Hi, Bear. Don't like the water, eh?" Daric teased as he gave her a pat on the head in passing. Bear eagerly wagged her tail in response and then raced back to the beach where she continued to bite at the waves as they rolled onto the beach.

"Come on, even you have to admit knowing how to swim could save Bear's life some day. What would happen if she ever fell out of the boat?" Dani asked irritably as she walked toward the beach.

"Why don't you get her a life jacket," Daric offered. "They make them for dogs, you know."

"You know damn well Bear doesn't like wearing even a collar. How am I supposed to get a life jacket on her?" Dani retorted.

"That's your problem," Daric said dismissively. "Mom said dinner is almost ready, so go get changed, I'm starved."

"Then where are you going, the house is that way," Dani said, stating the obvious while pointing in the opposite direction.

"I have to get Dad. Mom thinks he's at the lab," Daric replied over his shoulder as he continued toward the end of the peninsula and Professor Quinn Delaney's laboratory.

"Hey, wait up," Dani yelled. "We'll come with you. It'll give Bear and me a chance to dry off before going into the house. Come on, Bear, let's go find Dad."

Dani caught up and matched strides with her brother, Bear anxiously leading the way.

4

UNDER THE VEIL of approaching dusk, a lone figure crept through the large estate, hiding in the shadows of the trees, slowly and quietly making his way toward the end of the peninsula.

Richard suspected Quinn was working on something big, otherwise he wouldn't have turned down the next semester of lectures at Stanford. Instead, Quinn took a leave of absence. That wasn't like him. Quinn had been a workaholic since their first meeting back in grade school.

Richard and Quinn couldn't have been more different in their work ethics. Quinn was diligent, resourceful and committed, whereas Richard preferred to let others do all the work and then take the credit for himself. He'd been riding on Quinn's coat-tails for years. And Quinn was always so willing to assist Richard, to a point where Quinn was doing the work for him.

Quinn was incessantly working on some project or other. Never idle, persistently inquiring, trying new theories or sometimes trying to prove old ones. He stubbornly used the same process: testing, evaluating, retesting, re-evaluating and testing again, until he was satisfied with the results and had covered all eventualities. The same endless set of procedures, never deviating. It drove most of his colleagues to the brink of despair from sheer frustration. Never had Richard known Quinn to take a shortcut.

Exactly what Quinn was working on now was a mystery. Quinn had been distant and secretive about his work, even keeping Richard at arm's length. This recent behaviour was odd, considering they had been lab partners and colleagues for years.

Richard had to know the reason behind Quinn's request for a leave and the only way to do that was to get into Quinn's lab on the Delaney estate, undetected of course. He couldn't risk jeopardizing his relationship with Quinn or his family; their relationship went back to their high school days.

Richard took a quick look around before moving from cover. He spotted Daric checking out his boat and saw Dani and Bear farther down the shore at the beach. He decided he could make it to the lab without detection, so slipping from the shelter of the trees he quickly made his way to the lab's front door.

Quinn had installed a security system that required an access code to gain entry. Fortunately for Richard, Quinn used the same code for everything: the date his children were born and the number of minutes apart. Quinn may have had a high I.Q., but, when it came to security, he was inept. Richard punched in 031723 and the door silently opened. Richard slipped inside and quickly closed it behind him.

From the exterior, to anyone passing by, the lab looked like a gazebo, in the well-treed end of the private peninsula, overlooking the glistening waters of Lake Ontario. The windows were a specially treated glass, concealing the interior, but mostly used for regulating the temperature inside.

Richard noticed there were only two items in the room: a six-by-eight-foot computing island in the middle of the spacious room; and on the rear wall, a tinted projection surface. Quinn conducted his quantum physics lectures from there via satellite for the University of Stanford, Richard reasoned.

"This doesn't look like a lab; it looks more like a projection room. There has to be more to this place," Richard surmised. While impressed with the set-up, Richard was there for a specific reason and what he currently saw wasn't telling him what he needed to know.

After examining the computer island and finding nothing out of the ordinary, he searched along the walls, running his hands over the surface, looking for any irregularities. After what seemed like hours, but was in fact only minutes, his hand ran over a small bump on the wall. Upon closer examination, he found a small, rectangular-shaped port, behind the projection area. It was covered with a plate, which was painted the same color as the wall. If he hadn't been running his hand over the wall surface, he never would have found it.

Richard had found what he was looking for, he hoped. It had to be an access point to another part of Quinn's lab. *What else could it be?* he thought. Now all he had to do was get it open.

Prior to venturing out to the Delaney Estate, Richard's experience told him he would come across some very sophisticated technology. So he called in a favor from a hacker he had caught and failed to turn in to the authorities, anticipating that someday this young man's talents would come in handy. The lad was quite clever with breaking security codes. He used viruses to infiltrate and override the existing security systems, before they even knew what was happening, so no warnings or alarms were triggered. It was brilliant, really. And in a few seconds he'd see whether his hunch paid off.

Richard inserted a USB device into the port. A red light immediately flashed on, followed a few seconds later by a green light and then a clicking sound. Part of the wall and the floor receded: a three foot wide piece of the wall rose from the floor three-feet in height, while the same width of floor pulled back from the wall three feet, both combined created an opening which led downward.

Clever, he thought. It was the only way to conceal another doorway in a gazebo that had windows all the way around.

The opening revealed a set of stairs going down to a second level. "Yes," he muttered as he hunched down and entered the opening.

He groped the inner wall looking for a light switch. He found one just inside the doorway and flipped it on. Richard quickly descended the stairs. His breath caught as he beheld what lied in front of him. He took a minute as his eyes scanned the entire room. If he could have designed a lab, this was exactly what he would have created. It was magnificent.

A central computer station, similar to the one on the upper level, sat in the center of the room. It appeared to be the control center for a bank of display screens that ran the entire length of one wall. In the far left corner stood a five-by-five-foot square platform; its purpose eluded him and but he didn't have time to figure it out.

There wasn't a single piece of paper anywhere; nothing like a regular lab. No notes, no pens, no pencils, not even reference material; everything was electronic.

The only thing in the lab that seemed a little out of place was to the left of the island. There, sat a small metal table, on which were three open jewellery cases, each lined with blue velvet and containing what appeared to be bracelets. Two held one bracelet each: the third held two, smaller than the others.

Richard spotted a shelf underneath the table that contained a small metal chest, which he picked up. It was much heavier than he thought it should have been. He was eager to see what was inside that made the chest so heavy. He tried the latch, but it was locked. He looked under the table again for something that might open it, but there was nothing. He inspected the locking mechanism. He'd never seen anything like it; he was intrigued, his curiosity piqued. He might have to call on the special services of his 'friend' again, if he wanted to get a look at the contents.

Bear's yowl and the echo of distant voices abruptly interrupted his pondering. He had run out of time and still hadn't discovered what Quinn was working on.

Richard knew he couldn't go out the same way he came in. Frantically looking around, he needed to find an alternate exit. He spotted a smaller door at the far end of the room. "Hope this leads out of here," he prayed.

Unconsciously clutching the chest, Richard headed for the

small door. Halting suddenly, Richard realized he had left the door open to the lower level. *Too late,* he thought. *Besides what could be the harm.*

5

THE SHOWER FAUCETS were turned off; the sound of running water ceased. An arm snaked out from behind the frosted glass door to retrieve a towel. Professor Quinn Delaney felt it was a fairly successful day. He'd achieved more today than he thought he would. Then he hit a roadblock.

Quinn frequently appeared to be slightly disheveled, unless of course, he had just emerged from a shower. He didn't spend a lot of time on his appearance, especially when he was immersed in a project.

By all outward appearances, he looked like a nerd. But don't let that fool you; he's no slouch. Quinn's six-foot-one-inch muscular physique, hidden beneath his lab coat, was a result of a lot of hard physical work. Even with his busy academic schedule, Quinn found time for his labour of love—his family's estate. By building docks, cutting down trees, splitting firewood, and hauling rocks, Quinn had maintained his youthful build.

Quinn decided he needed an early break from his work and his stomach applauded that decision. He planned on returning to his lab after dinner, to see if he could move his project along. He was so close now; just a little further.

After his refreshing shower, he put on a pale blue golf shirt and denim shorts, and then headed downstairs for dinner. He could tell Sandra was in the kitchen preparing dinner from the aroma that was wafting up the staircase.

Quinn sidled up behind Sandra, who was stirring spaghetti in the boiling water so it wouldn't stick together.

Quinn reflected on when they first met and marveled at how Sandra still looked as beautiful now as she did then. She had developed into a self-assured beauty, in her five-foot-six-inch statuesque form with the no-nonsense personality her position at the hospital demanded. Except of course when it came to Quinn; she still kept that playful side that he had first fallen so deeply in love with.

Quinn quietly slipped his arms around his wife's waist and nibbled on her neck. "I thought I smelt something good. It tastes even better," he said tenderly.

"Where have you been?" Sandra asked softly, enjoying the attention.

"I hit a roadblock today, so I decided I'd take a break and go back at it again after dinner. Speaking of which, when's dinner? I'm starved." Quinn plucked the spoon from the sauce and stole a quick taste. "Mmmm. Perfect, as usual."

Sandra, with a gentle scold, grabbed the spoon from Quinn's hand and placed it back in the sauce. "Where're Daric and Dani? Aren't they with you?"

"No. I haven't seen them since lunch," Quinn answered nonchalantly.

"I sent Daric to get you and Dani for dinner over half an hour ago," Sandra stated, slightly annoyed, knowing dinner was about to be spoiled. "Why can't he follow a simple request?"

"When?" Quinn questioned uneasily, uncertain he heard correctly.

"Daric went looking for you over half an hour ago," Sandra restated, still stirring the contents of the pot.

Quinn grabbed Sandra's arms and spun her around to face him. "Did you send him to the lab?" Quinn asked anxiously.

"Where else? You've been spending every day there for weeks

now. It was the first place I thought he should look," Sandra stated matter-of-factly.

"He should have been back by now." Quinn dashed from the kitchen, throwing open the back door as he raced across the lawn toward his lab.

"Wait, Quinn! What's wrong? Where are you going?" Sandra yelled.

Not sure what had Quinn in such a panic, Sandra turned off the burners on the stove and raced out the back door, calling him as she desperately tried to narrow the growing gap between them.

Quinn knew that, given enough time, Daric could discover the access port to the lower level, and this terrified him. Even with the separate access system, Daric was a genius when it came to anything technical. He would eventually figure it out.

6

DARIC REACHED THE lab just behind Bear, who was anxiously waiting to enter.

"Give me a sec, Bear. I have to unlock the door first," Daric said.

He entered the access code, grabbed the door handle, and pulled open the door to the lab. Bear raced in, followed by Dani and Daric.

Bear ran around the lab in search of Quinn. She stopped in the center of the lab and sniffed the floor, then moved toward the back of the lab.

"Dad's not here. Let's go back to the house; he's probably already there," Dani said flatly.

"Come on, Bear," she ordered as she turned to leave.

Daric noticed Bear slowly making her way to the back of the lab, her nose to the ground, as if she were following a scent or trail. "Hang on," Daric directed toward his impatient sister.

"Bear, what is it?" Daric followed Bear to the back of the lab.

"Come on, Daric, dinner's ready. You know Mom will be annoyed if we're late," Dani cautioned.

"Dani, come here and look at this. There's something back here," Daric said excitedly.

"What?" Dani's curiosity was getting the better of her as she made her way over to Daric and Bear.

There, hidden behind the projection panel, was an opening in the wall and floor that created an entranceway, with a set of stairs heading toward a brighter light source. Bear raced, with abandon, through the opening into the unknown below.

Daric realized they had discovered a hidden entrance. *Why would dad have to hide his work, especially from us?* Daric thought. *One way to find out.*

"Come on," Daric said excitedly, making his way through the door, following Bear's lead.

"Wait, Daric," Dani warned. "I don't think we should go down there."

"Why? What could happen? It's Dad's lab, not Dracula's lair," Daric retorted.

Dani nervously followed her brother to the lower level. She was still apprehensive about their intrusion into their father's inner sanctum. When she emerged from the stairwell, she was astounded by what she saw.

"Hey, Dani, look at these." Daric drew Dani's attention to the table to the left of the central console.

Daric reached for one of the objects in the velvet-lined cases and examined it. The metal band was a little heavier than he thought it would be. The inside and outer edges of the band were gold in color. The inner portion was black, looking very much like onyx. On the black surface on either side of the clasp, was a golden symbol; the caduceus—a short staff entwined by two serpents, topped with a pair of wings. It was the symbol of the staff carried by Hermes in Greek mythology. The clasp was a gold letter 'H'.

"Cool. Wonder if these are gifts for us from Dad," he murmured. Daric, taking no time to figure out how to open the clasp, twisted the 'H' sideways, opening the band, and placed it on his right wrist.

Dani walked up behind Daric. "Hey, you shouldn't be doing that."

Daric lifted the second band from its resting place, grabbed Dani's wrist and put the second band on his sister.

"Daric, these aren't ours. We need to take them off," she admonished.

"Look." Daric held both of their wrists together to compare the bracelets. There was a faint click and then everything went black.

Bear looked around the lab, but couldn't see Daric or Dani. Not sure where they went, she sniffed around the entire lower level. After several minutes of searching and finding no trail, Bear lay on the floor in the exact place where Daric and Dani were last standing. Her front paws stretched out in front of her. She placed her chin on top of her outstretched limbs. "Roo," Bear moaned sorrowfully.

7

QUINN, REACHING THE front door of his lab, quickly punched in the access code—nothing. "Damn," he muttered. He tried again. Nothing. "Slow down," he scoffed. Quinn entered the code for the third time—click, the door unlatched. "Finally!"

Quinn flew through the door; everything looked as it had when he left earlier that day. There was also no sign of Daric. A faint light from the back of the lab caught his attention, and he immediately realized the hatchway to the lower level was open. "Damn," he muttered, running to the back of the lab. He raced down the stairs, taking two at a time.

Sandra will never forgive me, he thought.

When the lab was originally built, Quinn had a second, lower level created thirty feet below the water level for his special research projects. He promised Sandra that their two young children would never have access to this lower level. So he installed two separate security systems. The main door was a simple key code entry. Once the children were old enough, they could get access to the main level if they ever needed to reach him.

However, access to the lower level was next to impossible, or so he believed. Quinn had installed an automatic sensory system, which could be activated only by Quinn's personal command. The entrance to the lower level was cleverly concealed, too; if you didn't know it was there, you'd never find it.

The lower level had state-of-the-art technology; some that had never been seen before and that Quinn had developed personally. There were computer glass surfaces everywhere, again accessible only upon Quinn's command. The system was so intelligent that it would open to the precise place where he had last finished his work prior to leaving the lab. It was an efficiency tool, really: he hated wasting time.

Quinn quickly scanned the lab. Behind the table, he found Bear lying on the floor with her head on her outstretched paws.

"Hey, Bear, what are you doing down here? I thought you were with Dani." Quinn walked to Bear, bending down to scratch behind her ears. Bear raised her head briefly to lick Quinn's hand and sadly put it back down on her paws. This was unusual behaviour for her, Quinn reflected. Bear was usually excited to see all the members of her family.

Quinn stood up and took a more detailed look around his lab. Right in front of him, on the table, were two empty cases. Quinn grabbed the cases, frantically looking all around the table, hoping that his worst nightmare wasn't about to become a reality.

Too late, the bands were gone.

"NO!!"

Still on the lab's upper level, Sandra heard a guttural moan resonating from the bowels of Quinn's lab. She ran down the stairs and saw Quinn on his knees, sobbing, clutching two empty blue velvet cases.

8

RICHARD MADE A hasty ascent up the steep back staircase of Quinn's lab. The stairs were narrow and set close together, almost like a step ladder perched at a sixty-five-degree angle. Handrails were set into the walls on either side to aid in the climb. The walls, cold and damp, felt as if they were carved out of rough-cut stone. The passageway itself could not have been more than three-and-a-half feet in diameter.

Richard had previously tucked the small metal chest inside his shirt. He needed both hands to make the climb. He was determined not to leave the chest behind; after all, he wanted something for his efforts today.

Richard could hear Bear's claws coming down the other set of stairs and now he could clearly make out Daric's voice egging Dani on. Richard had to put more distance between himself and the lower lab. Bear may be small, but she could be a real problem, if she suspected something was out of place and tried to investigate.

Wait, did I close the lower door? he thought, trying to remember whether he had pulled the small door closed behind him. He took a quick look over his shoulder; everything was in darkness. He relaxed; he had remembered to close 'this' door. Bear couldn't follow him. He quickly continued up the narrow steps.

Richard's head suddenly struck something hard. "Ouch," he exclaimed, quickly biting his tongue, so he wouldn't be heard.

Richard reached up, groping in the dark. He felt the outline of a circular metal hatch. He felt for a handle or knob that would open it, but what he found felt like a small wheel instead. Spinning it counterclockwise, he unlocked the hatch. He moved up the ladder. Crouching, he put his shoulder to the hatch and pushed up until it fell back and rested against a wall.

He climbed the remaining few stairs and stepped onto the floor of a dark tunnel. Before closing the hatch, he felt along the tunnel walls for a light switch. Once he found one, he lowered the hatch into place and spun the wheel to lock it. He was conscious now of not leaving any evidence of his visit or his retreat.

Once the hatch was secure, Richard turned on the light. A string of overhead lights revealed a small tunnel carved out of stone, about thirty feet long, running horizontally toward the lake. On the wall above the light switch, hung a dive mask and snorkel. *Odd,* he thought.

Richard walked to the end of the tunnel. He came to what appeared to be a small metal door, which he assumed was the exit, but he could find no way of opening it; he could see no latch, key hole or release switch.

Richard retraced his steps back to where he had entered the tunnel to examine that area more closely. "There has to be a way out of here," he reasoned. Right next to the light switch, under the mask and snorkel, was a red button. "This must be it," he surmised. Then he pushed it.

There was a mechanical creaking sound, followed by a tremendous roar. Richard spun around in time to watch a wall of water thundering down the tunnel. Panic quickly ensued.

"Crap." Richard frantically reached up and grabbed the mask, pulling it on. He took a couple of deep breaths, hyperventilating, before he became totally submerged underwater.

Richard tried to pull his way along the tunnel against the force of the incoming water, but it was useless. He would have to wait until the tunnel filled with water, before he could swim out. Thankfully, the tunnel was filling quickly. He calculated he would have enough time to swim out before his lungs started to scream for lack of oxygen.

As the tunnel continued to fill, it occurred to him that Quinn must have designed the tunnel to act, not only as an emergency exit but also as a fire extinguisher. All he'd have to do is leave the hatch open and allow the lower level of the lab to flood.

Once the tunnel filled sufficiently for the rush of incoming water to diminish, Richard pulled himself along the wall. Upon reaching the end, Richard surfaced quickly to get some much-needed air into his starving lungs and to get his bearings. Deciding on a stealthy retreat, Richard submerged again and swam toward the eastern edge of the estate, where he had left his car hidden among the trees.

Richard pulled himself out of the cool water and, running among the trees, out of sight, headed for his car. Just as he reached for the door handle, he heard a hideous wail.

"Was that Quinn?" Richard muttered. "He must have noticed his metal chest is gone . . ."

Pulling the chest out of his shirt, he held it up in front of him. Richard wondered, "What could be in this small chest to cause Quinn such anguish?"

9

"QUINN, WHAT IS IT?" Sandra asked while bending down next to her distraught husband.

"What have I done?" Quinn moaned, kneeling on the floor below the table, still clutching the two small cases.

"Quinn, what is it?" Sandra pleaded. "Talk to me, Quinn. What's going on?" Sandra had never seen her husband, in their thirty-two years together, so distressed.

"Professor, we have a problem," said a voice from out of nowhere.

"Awroooo," Bear yowled as she sprang from her prone position, scanning the area for the source of the intruder.

"I know, I know," Quinn countered. Quickly realizing sobbing wouldn't solve his problem, he pulled himself up off the floor. He placed his hand on the security scanner which brought the computer to life. He flipped through several screens, looking for specific data, and then threw them up on the projection screens on the wall.

"Who was that?" Sandra asked, referring to the disembodied voice. Still kneeling on the floor where Quinn had been, she slowly got to her feet, looking earnestly at Quinn.

"I am so sorry, Dr. Delaney. Allow me to introduce myself," the voice added.

Sandra spun in the sound's direction. She noticed a thin vertical string of pale blue light emanating from a five-by-five-foot platform in a vacant corner of Quinn's laboratory. The light grew in mass. Sandra took a glance over her shoulder in Quinn's direction to see whether he was watching this, but his attention was completely focussed on the stream of data flowing across the numerous screens projected on the wall.

"Awrooo," Bear repeated, as she cautiously made her way to the corner to investigate.

"My name is Hermes. I am the professor's so-called sparring partner." The light slowly dissolved, revealing a three-dimensional hologram of a man.

Quinn had created an artificial intelligence, a second generation cognitive computer; he called him HERMES, named after the messenger of the gods, also known as the god of travellers. Hermes was a 3-D hologram, programmed with every scrap of information related to time travel, quantum physics, and quantum theory. It was the first computer of its kind that had the ability to learn and to adapt. Quinn enhanced the program so that Hermes could also simulate human emotions.

"What took you so long?" Quinn agitatedly asked, never relinquishing his concentration from the screens in front of him.

"I didn't want to pop in here, like a genie from a bottle, and startle Dr. Delaney," Hermes retorted.

When Bear stuck her nose close to Hermes, the image wavered and distorted, startling her which resulted in another vocal protest.

"Well, you can cut the dramatic entrance. I need your help," Quinn demanded, still focussing on the data projected on the walls.

"So you're an A.I.," Sandra concluded, staring at the apparition in front of her.

"I assure you, Dr. Delaney, there is nothing artificial about my intelligence. My database contains a complete history of the world, every known fact and theory regarding the laws of physics, quantum mechanics, every assertion on wormholes, cosmic stings, black holes and I am just getting my introduction to the medical aspects of homo sapiens."

"Wait, you said your name is Hermes," Sandra restated.

"That is correct, Dr. Delaney," Hermes replied.

"Then why do you look like Albert Einstein?" Sandra asked.

"The professor found it a little frustrating discussing the laws of physics and quantum theory with a toga-clad Greek god and decided to give me a second alter ego, one he felt he could realistically interact with on his level."

"If you two are finished with your introductions, I could use a little help over here," Quinn interjected.

"Excuse me, Dr. Delaney, the professor appears to need my help. He could use a little help with his manners, too." Hermes apologised for Quinn's abruptness.

Hermes vanished, startling Bear again, and re-materialized beside Quinn. "Yes, Professor, how may I be of assistance?"

"Tell me what's happening. Where is he?" Quinn demanded.

"What?" Sandra interjected, walking up behind Quinn. "Where is who?"

Bear had trotted over beside Quinn to continue her investigation of this intruder. But since no one else seemed concerned with the stranger among them, Bear lost interest and went back to her previous duty; to guard what she believed to be a hole in the floor.

"As I started to say when you first came in, Dr. Delaney, we have a problem." Hermes started to explain to Sandra before he was cut off again by Quinn.

"Do you mind?" Quinn interjected, exasperated at Hermes. "Sandra, sit down, please. This will be a little hard to digest."

Sandra pulled out a chair from behind Quinn's computer console and sat down, crossing her arms over her chest. "Okay, shoot, I'm all ears."

"As you know, the door to this level automatically closes and seals when I leave. When I came in just now, it was open. How, I don't know."

Quinn stared at Sandra, trying to judge her reaction to this news. It was the one stipulation Sandra made when he was planning to build his lab: his children were never to know about this level, nor would they ever gain access to it. Quinn had installed a state-of-the-art security system to ensure that his promise to Sandra would never be broken.

Sandra took a breath and was about to remind Quinn of his promise when Quinn held up his hand.

"Please, Sandra, let me finish, then you can lecture me," Quinn pleaded, knowing there would be hell to pay when he finished his story. Sandra crossed her legs and sat back in her chair, waiting for Quinn to continue.

"When I went back to the house to shower before dinner, I went in the side door. Not knowing I was already in the house, you sent Daric to find me."

"That's because dinner was almost ready," Sandra reflected. "I suppose it's ruined by now."

"If you had sent Dani, I think none of this would have happened," Quinn reasoned.

"What wouldn't have happened? Quinn what's going on?" Sandra asked, moving forward in her chair, quickly losing patience with Quinn.

"I can only assume what happened next." Quinn held up two blue velvet-lined cases. "In these two cases were two bracelets. Now they're gone. The only thing I can think of, that could have happened, is that Daric got in here somehow and put the bracelets on."

"So?" Sandra responded curtly.

"You know what I've been working on for years. Finally, after all that time, I'm extremely close to making a significant breakthrough," Quinn said rather proudly. "Sandra, I . . ." Quinn's next sentence was cut short abruptly.

"Excuse me, Professor," Hermes interrupted.

"What is it?" Quinn said exasperatedly.

"It would appear that we have two sets of vital signs," Hermes replied, pointing at the display screen he had been reviewing.

"That can't be!" Quinn ran over to the display screens. "That's not possible!" After a brief review, the screens confirmed his worst nightmare.

"Oh, my God. Both of them?"

10

"QUINN, WHAT'S GOING on?" Sandra was out of her chair and standing beside Quinn, looking at the screens. The displays showed blood pressure, heart rate, respiratory rate, body temperature, and body mass for two people.

"What's that?" Sandra asked, pointing at the vital sign readouts.

"That, Sandra, is Dani and Daric," Quinn said sadly. "And that would explain why Bear is down here too. She must have come in here with Dani."

"Explain yourself now, Quinn! What's going on?" Sandra insisted angrily. She was terrified of what Quinn was about to tell her.

"As I started to explain a minute ago, you know I've been working on my special project for years," Quinn began, taking a deep breath before explaining the most unbelievable thing she would ever hear.

"Sandra, I have finally made a significant breakthrough. I built a prototype which was in those two blue cases. It would seem that the kids have tested my prototype."

"Go on," Sandra ordered.

"I have built what I call travel bands. You put one on each wrist. The wearer of these bands will *eventually* have the ability to travel through time," Quinn explained cautiously, allowing Sandra to fully comprehend what he was saying.

"Are you saying you built a time machine?" Sandra said incredulously.

"No, mine is quite unique," Quinn swaggered. "It's not like the big bulky ones they persist on using in Hollywood science fiction movies and that, of course, never work. Mine works."

"Professor," Hermes warned.

Quinn noticed Sandra's face going pale as the information sank in. He quickly grabbed the chair, positioning it behind Sandra just as her knees buckled, catching her gently. He walked around, kneeling to face her.

"Are you trying to tell me that my children are somewhere in another time period? That they have actually travelled through time?" Sandra was having difficulty even hearing what she was saying, let alone comprehending it.

"Yes, I am."

"Fine, now bring them back," Sandra demanded coldly. She was quite finished with this experiment and wanted her children home–now!

"Well, therein lies the problem?" Quinn said sheepishly.

"What problem?"

"I haven't finished my calculations yet. The travel bands weren't ready for testing," Quinn continued. "I built two sets. Once I was satisfied they would work, I was going to test them on Bear first. That's what the small set is for."

Bear raised her head from the floor upon hearing her name and looked in the direction of Quinn's voice.

"You were going to experiment using Bear?" Sandra asked incredulously, looking at the despondent family pet lying at the base of the table.

"Please, Sandra. Only once I was certain it would work. Believe me, I would never put Bear in harm's way," Quinn said imploringly.

Bear finally got up after hearing her name a third time. She left the spot she was so vigilantly guarding since Dani and Daric vanished. She walked over to Sandra, curling up on the floor, resting her chin on Sandra's foot. Sandra reached down and gave Bear a gentle pat on the head, then scratched her behind her ear.

"Okay, so now they've been tested and they work. Great, now get my children back," Sandra repeated in earnest.

"As I said before, Sandra, I haven't finished my work. The travel bands weren't ready for testing yet."

"What's that supposed to mean? You've seen for yourself that they work, so get them back!"

"Sandra, I can't get them back."

"What?" Sandra couldn't believe what she was hearing.

"The travel bands are currently configured only to move the traveller into the past," Hermes said. "We haven't finished the computations to allow the traveller to come forward in time," he finished, hoping his explanation would assist with Sandra's comprehension.

From the confused expression on Sandra's face, Quinn realized she wasn't quite getting the whole picture.

"To get them back, they will have to move forward, from their current time period," Quinn stated uneasily.

Part II

Lost Somewhere in Time

Unknown

11

BLACK SLOWLY DISSOLVED into grey and the immediate surroundings gradually came into focus. The grass still held the early morning dew.

"What happened?" a dazed female voice uttered.

"Oh my God! He did it. He actually did it!" Daric cried excitedly, like a child on Christmas morning.

"Where are we?" Dani asked, slowly getting to her feet.

Daric had already sprung from his prone position and was spinning around, taking in his new surroundings, not quite believing what he was seeing.

"I think the better question is 'When are we?'" Daric replied cryptically.

They were standing in the middle of a field. The grass to the north of them was cut short and ran in a straight path approximately three-thousand feet long and seventy-five feet wide. The air held a cool, crisp, freshness of early spring. The sun was slowly rising in the east and the clear blue sky was a sure indication it was going to turn into a beautiful day.

"Daric, what's going on? Last thing I remember, we were in Dad's lab. How did we get here?" Dani asked.

"Don't you get it?" Daric taunted.

"Get what?" Dani replied irritably. She wanted answers, now. She was very much like her mother in that regard.

"Dad finally did it," Daric stated excitedly, still taking in his new surroundings.

"Will you quit dancing around and just spit it out!"

Daric, being more accepting and in tune with their situation, heard a faint noise in the distance. It was rapidly increasing in volume. He recognized the sound instinctively. He didn't need to look to verify that he was right and that time was of the essence. He spun around and launched himself at his sister, taking them both to the ground.

"Stay down," he yelled over the roar of engines, while trying to keep his protesting sister down and as low to the ground as possible.

A twin-engine airplane was coming in for a landing on the grass airstrip. Because of the nose attitude and low wings of the aircraft, the pilot wouldn't have been able to see them on his final approach to the airfield.

The airplane touched down a mere fifteen feet from where they had been standing. It continued to roll down the grass runway before coming to rest in front a building that looked like an aircraft hangar.

From that same direction, Daric could see two figures, a man and a woman, running toward them. *Odd*, he thought. The two had the running gait, like graceful gazelles running across the Serengeti, in sync with each other.

Daric slowly got to his feet, pulling his sister up with him. Still holding onto her arms, Daric looked directly into her eyes and pleaded, "Dani, you need to trust me here. Please! You have to trust me, this one time. Just follow my lead, okay? I'll explain everything to you first chance we get to be alone. I promise."

"Daric . . ." Dani's sentence was cut short.

"Are you two all right? You almost got run down by that airplane." The words were coming from the figure that Daric had thought was a man, but he could now clearly see was a woman, as she checked Dani over for injuries. His mistake was understandable, considering she was wearing pants with a brown leather bomber jacket, with her short-cut hair giving her a tomboyish appearance. She had wavy blond hair, warm blue-grey eyes and a smattering of freckles across her nose. She also had a model's tall, willowy figure and was the same height as Dani.

"That was so close. You two are really lucky," the second lady stated while checking Daric over carefully, touching his arms, legs and chest, while staring into his indigo-blue eyes. She was a few inches shorter than the other lady and also appeared a few years younger. She had long curly auburn hair and sea-green eyes. She carried a smaller frame than her companion and seemed more reserved and polished in her demeanour. She also dressed more like a lady, in a printed dress under a long trench coat, cinched at the waist, accentuating her curvy female figure.

"Yes, we're both fine, thank you," Daric said.

"What are you doing out here? This is a restricted area of the Union Air Terminal; for authorized personnel only. You're trespassing," the first lady stated matter-of-factly.

"Sorry. We wandered out here last night by mistake. When we realized our error, we left immediately," said Daric. Thinking quickly on his feet, he continued, "But then I noticed I was missing my pocket knife, so we came back to look for it during the day. I thought, if we were here early enough, no one would be the wiser," Daric finished, hoping his story would be convincing enough. A quick glance at his sister revealed a look of disbelief.

"As long as you're both okay, no harm done," said the first woman. "My name is Millie." She extended her hand to Dani and then Daric. "And this here is my sister, Pidge."

That explained the similarity in their strides, Daric concluded.

"I'm Daric and this is my sister, Dani," Daric explained as he returned the handshakes.

"I don't know about you two, but we've been up since before dawn and with only a couple of cups of coffee to keep us going. We were just about to grab some breakfast. Join us, please? It's the least we can do for almost running you down," Millie declared.

"But, you didn't . . ." Dani started, before being interrupted.

"You haven't eaten already, have you?" Pidge asked, hoping the handsome young Daric would continue to grace her with his presence.

"Actually, no, we haven't," Daric replied, accompanied by his growling stomach.

"It's settled then. Come on," Pidge said. She grabbed Daric's arm and placed it over hers, as they made their way down the run-way toward the airplane that had come to rest outside the United Air Services hangar, adjacent to the Union Air Terminal.

"Did you find it?" Pidge inquired.

"Find what?" Daric asked, not sure what she was referring to.

"Your pocket knife; did you find it?" Pidge repeated.

"No," Daric answered, knowing he couldn't produce one if they asked him to.

12

"SO, WHERE ARE you from?" Millie asked Dani as they continued toward the hangar. "There aren't any homes close to this airport, just miles upon miles of vineyards." She had noticed the strange clothes they were wearing, but was far too polite to say anything.

Taking her cue from Daric, Dani started to fabricate her own story. She and Millie were a few paces behind Daric and the clingy and overly attentive Pidge.

"We don't actually have a home; we're orphans," Dani stammered. "My brother and I have been on our own for years," Dani finished, looking forlornly at the ground, hoping to add to the believability of her story.

Daric peered over his shoulder and looked at his sister with an understanding smile, realizing she had picked up on his ruse.

"That's terrible. I'm so sorry," Millie said, empathetic of the young siblings' plight. "How do you manage to live, especially during such hard times?"

"We get odd jobs along the way, where we can," Dani explained. "Actually, Daric is excellent with any type of engine," she continued. "He's a real genius when it comes to anything mechanical. I mostly cook or wait tables at diners for what cash we actually need.

But I have also done some office work, too." She was hoping to seize what could turn out to be a very fortunate set of circumstances. She had no idea what might present itself later down the line or how long they'd be here.

Pidge was listening carefully to the conversation and thought there had to be some way she and Millie could help these two. She knew what it was like to grow up without any money. Their father, Edwin, had consistently struggled to find and keep a job. His struggles had resulted in the family moving around a lot during her early years. She and her sister had been sent to live with their grandparents for a while until their father got back on his feet. It wasn't until Millie was ten-years-old and Pidge eight, that the family had finally been reunited.

"Millie, weren't you saying the other day that you could use a little extra help?" Pidge remarked, hoping Millie would take the bait.

Pidge strongly believed their upbringing had led to Millie's independence. Millie had learned early on how to take care of herself and her sister.

"She's right, I did say that. But I can't pay you much." It embarrassed Millie to admit she was feeling the pinch during the depression and what little money she did have was funding her latest goal.

"Why not let them work for their room and board?" Pidge suggested. "They said they don't have a place to stay and I can hear Daric's stomach growling from here."

"That would be great," Daric jumped in, before they could rescind the offer. "We don't need much, just a bite to eat and a roof over our heads at night. And we travel real light. We have only what we're carrying on our backs," Daric added.

"Oh my," Pidge whispered, astounded at what the two siblings endured simply to get by. Neither of them was dressed very well. Daric had an old faded denim shirt and faded blue jeans, with loafers on his feet. Dani had what looked like a cut-off pair of jeans, a long-sleeved plaid shirt, and sandals. She noticed that Dani was about the same height as Millie and could use some of her clothes;

Daric, however, was another story. She would have to work out something.

"I would love to get my hands on that," Daric said, pointing at the airplane now sitting only twenty feet away.

"That, my dear Daric, is a . . ."

"Lockheed Electra," Daric blurted out.

"That's right." Millie was taken aback. "How could you possibly know that?" Millie asked, amazed at the young man's knowledge of a relatively new aircraft.

"Uh, uh," Daric stuttered, thinking quickly. "My dad used to work for Lockheed, in their design department. I have–or I guess I should say, I had a Pratt & Whitney engine I used to take apart at home. As Dani said earlier, I have a way with engines," Daric acknowledged as humbly as he could, hoping his near-disastrous slip was buried in his plausible lie.

"Really? That's great. Then I could definitely use your help. Because I'm going to fly this airplane around the world," Millie stated proudly.

Daric's jaw suddenly dropped open. Millie smiled at his reaction; she thought it was because he didn't think a woman could fly an airplane, let alone fly around the world. In fact, Daric simply couldn't believe in whose presence he was standing.

Pointing to the men gathered outside the airplane, Millie continued. "They were just out testing the equipment and the radios on board. The test flights are going to help us determine the best speeds, altitudes, and power settings to obtain optimal performance during our long journey. Come, I'll introduce you to my team." Millie motioned for them to follow her as she closed the distance between the two groups.

13

"GENTLEMEN, I'D LIKE to introduce you to the newest members of our team." Millie began the introductions. "This is Daric and Dani . . ." Millie cut her sentence short and turned to the twins. "I didn't get your last name."

"It's Delaney," Dani supplied.

"As I was saying, our two newest members, Daric and Dani Delaney," Millie finished.

The three gentlemen were hard-pressed not to stare at the two strangely dressed newcomers in front of them, especially the scantily clad beautiful young woman. But before an uncomfortably long silence became embarrassing, one of them broke the uneasiness and began the introductions.

The first gentleman stepped forward, extending his hand. "Nice to meet you. My name is Paul Mantz. I'm the technical advisor."

Paul Mantz evoked the image of a dashing aviator often seen in the movies. He was shorter than Daric, but carried a compact muscular form, with brown hair combed off the forehead revealing a slightly receding hairline. He had soft brown eyes, shielded by long bedroom eyelashes that any woman would have envied. He also sported a well-trimmed mustache.

"I'm Harry Manning," the next gent offered, when Paul had

finished with his introduction. "I'm the navigator and radio operator." He was the same height as Millie, slim build, brown curly hair, clean shaven and weighing about one-hundred and sixty pounds.

"Nice to meet you," Daric said in awe. He couldn't believe with whom he was shaking hands and, more importantly, with whom he was standing. He took a quick glance over at Millie, then at Dani to see whether any of this was registering with her. Apparently not.

"And I'm Joe Gurr, from United Airlines here in Burbank. I was just aboard to test some radio equipment. I'm not part of this team, only on loan as a courtesy." He was shorter than the other two men at five-feet-six. His small build afforded him easier access to the small confines of the airplane's cockpit.

All three men were in various stages of peeling off their khaki flight jumpsuits. Underneath, each was dressed in a business suit: jacket, pants, pressed white shirt and narrow neck tie. *Somewhat formal attire, for an early morning test flight,* Daric thought.

"I don't know about you guys, but I'm starving. I've been up since 2:00 A.M. and I've only had coffee. Let's grab something to eat," Paul urged as he made his way over to the Union Air Terminal entrance.

"That's just where we were going too," Pidge stated, grabbing Daric's arm and dragging him along. "I'm famished."

The rest of the party fell in behind and covered the short distance to the terminal and a decent hot meal.

14

THE GROUP ENTERED the spacious well-kept terminal. A floor-to-ceiling, unfinished, wooden wall separated the office/lounge area from the adjacent hangar section, which was large enough to accommodate three aircraft. In the area where the group gathered, there was a small glass-enclosed office to the right of the entrance. Opposite, was a waiting lounge, with a sofa, two tub chairs and an end table covered with old, well-used magazines, as you might see in a doctor's office. Toward the back, there was a small kitchen with a pass-through to a Formica-topped serving counter, complete with red padded stools for patrons. There were also two round tables with wooden folding chairs that could accommodate groups of up to six people. Over the doorway to the hangar section, a sign pointed to a restroom.

As soon as Dani saw the sign, she realized it offered her a chance to get Daric alone. She was going to seize the opportunity, not knowing when another would present itself. She had questions that needed to be answered, sooner rather than later.

"If you would excuse us," Dani said to the group as they entered the hangar. "Daric and I need to freshen up before we eat." Dani pulled Daric from Pidge's tight grip. "We'll be right back," she finished as they made their way toward the hangar door.

"Yeah, don't wait for us, go ahead and order, we won't be long. Need to get some of this grime off first," Daric yelled over his shoulder, trailing behind his sister. She still had a firm grip on his arm and was hauling him through the doorway as a mother would a defiant child.

Daric knew Dani was at her wits end and needed to know what was going on. He feared she wouldn't take the news very well. He just hoped she didn't make a scene, or worse.

Dani and Daric proceeded in silence to the restroom. The room proved to be small, with a toilet and sink; both had been white once upon a time. Neither Dani nor Daric said anything until the door had closed behind them.

Dani wheeled around and confronted Daric. "What the hell is going on?"

They were well out of the hearing range of the others. Daric knew it was time to share what he knew with his sister. He took a moment to compose himself. He wanted to break the news as gently as possible.

"You know Dad's been working on his special project for years, right?" Daric eased into his story.

"Yeah, so? What's that got to do with us?" Dani's frustration was evident in her tone.

"These bands we have on, I believe they brought us here, somehow." Daric wasn't explaining things very well.

"What are you talking about?" Dani asked, confused.

"When we put these on, we were in Dad's lab, like you said." Daric held his arm up to show Dani the band on his wrist. "Next thing we know, we're in the middle of an airstrip. And as near as I can figure, we're somewhere between late 1936 and early 1937."

"What?" Dani was trying to digest what she thought she'd just heard.

"Think about it a minute. Dad's been working on Einstein's theories of relativity. Think back to your basic physics classes. Einstein's theories proved that time travel was possible. And it would appear that Dad has built the first-ever working time machine. Or should I say bands?" Daric was looking in awe at the metallic band on his wrist.

"You can't be serious?" Dani still didn't believe what she just heard.

"Look around you, Dani. Didn't you notice the cars parked outside the hangar? The blue one is a Buick Century sedan. The brown one is an Auburn Speedster. And the black one is a Plymouth Model coupe. They were all built in the 1930s," Daric pointed out, clearly proud of his knowledge of classic cars.

"And the airplane out there, the one that almost ran us down, it's *the* Lockheed Electra 10-E." Daric paused. He took a deep breath before finishing the whole picture with the final piece of the puzzle. "That airplane was flown around the world by the one and only Amelia Earhart, a. k. a. Millie. And as you well know, she never completed her world flight." Daric finished and waited for a reaction.

Dani just stared at her brother, her mouth hanging open in disbelief. Then she uttered only three words: "Oh my God."

15

"HEY, YOU TWO, breakfast is getting cold." There was a knock at the door. "We took the liberty of ordering for you, so come on." Pidge had been sent to hurry the new team members along.

"Daric, we need to finish this . . ." Dani whispered anxiously, holding onto her brother's arm.

"Later, I promise," Daric assured her as he pulled the door open and left the restroom.

"Lead the way, Pidge, I'm starved," Daric said. He draped Pidge's arm over his and the two of them walked in step as they left the hangar section. Dani followed behind them. As she passed the Formica counter, she casually glanced at a newspaper perched on the corner. The date read March 7, 1937. Her jaw dropped.

The three approached the table where the rest of the group was in the midst of finishing their meals. A rather heated conversation was underway. Paul looked up as the threesome approached; he stood up and pulled out a chair for Dani. "What took you guys so long?"

"Sorry, we were talking about how lucky we are to have a roof over our heads for a little while," Daric quickly explained. "It may be trivial to you, but it means a lot to us."

Millie leaned toward Dani. "Are you all right? You look a little pale."

Dani, still feeling a little off balance, looked into Millie's concerned face. "Yes, I'm fine, just hungry, I guess," she responded quickly. "I'll feel better after I eat something, I'm sure."

Actually, Dani had lost her appetite in the restroom, but she had to put up a good front. So she picked up her fork and slowly moved her scrambled eggs around her plate before taking a small mouthful. Daric, on the other hand, was having no trouble putting away his meal.

"This is fantastic," Daric enthused around a mouthful of food.

"The way you're inhaling that, you'd think you hadn't eaten in days," Pidge said. "I'm so sorry," she added quickly. "I wasn't thinking. I didn't consider that maybe you hadn't eaten in a while."

"That's okay, not to worry," Daric reassured her, turning his charming smile on Pidge, who couldn't help but smile in return.

Paul, trying to get the group to focus on the business at hand, said anxiously, "Good, glad you're enjoying your meal. Now, can we get back to business?"

"Relax, Paul, and enjoy your coffee. I'd rather wait for G.P. to get here before we discuss the results of the test flight from this morning," Millie admonished gently.

Sometimes Paul was no fun at all, just strictly business. He took his role as technical advisor seriously. They had a big job ahead of them, with what seemed like a thousand details still to be ironed out. And time wasn't on their side if they wanted to start the flight around the world on March 17 . . . just ten days away.

Sunday, March 7, 1937

16

OUTSIDE THE TERMINAL, a dark blue 1935 Cadillac 400 series automobile pulled up and parked beside the front door. It appeared that this particular parking spot was reserved specifically for the lone occupant of this car. A tall man emerged from behind the wheel. He made his way to the front door and peered through the small window into the lounge area. He saw a group at a large table. More notably, he saw two strangers among the familiar faces.

The man opened the door, snagged a chair as he passed a table and placed it between Millie and Harry, directly across from the two newcomers. As he sat, he removed his fedora, which had been rakishly tipped over one eye.

"Great timing, G.P. We were waiting for you to join us before we went through our debriefing from this morning," Paul said.

"First things first," G.P. countered. "Amelia, who are these two young people?"

Grabbing G.P.'s hand, Millie began, "G.P., may I introduce Dani and Daric Delaney, the two newest members of our team. And this is George Palmer Putman, preferring to be addressed as simply G.P. He's also my husband."

Millie and G.P. were never ones for public displays of affection, not even a simple peck on the cheek in greeting. G.P. was a tall, slender man at six-feet-two. He was clean shaven and impeccably dressed in a double-breasted suit. His brown, wavy hair was parted just left of center and was greying slightly at the temples. Perched on his nose were a pair of wire-rimmed glasses. He carried himself confidently, projecting a commanding presence.

"Our two newest members?" G.P. repeated quizzically, standing to firmly shake hands with Daric across the table. Turning to Dani, he gently squeezed her hand. He was totally captivated by the beautiful young woman standing in front of him. Her strange attire, which revealed a substantial amount of sun-kissed skin, had him mesmerized.

"Yes," Millie said firmly, drawing G.P. out of his trance. He abruptly dropped Dani's hand, and the three resumed their seats. "Daric is a genius when it comes to engines and Dani can help us with the overwhelming number of travel arrangements and time-tables. We have too many details that still need to be finalized if we want to get this show off the ground as planned. We could use the extra help. The best part is, they'll work for free."

G.P.'s brows pinched together. "Really?" he asked skeptically.

Dani, Daric, Millie and Pidge all nodded enthusiastically.

"Well then, welcome aboard," G.P. conceded.

"Thank you." Dani spoke softly, punctuated with an appreciative smile.

G.P. cleared his throat, then asked no one in particular, "Now that all the introductions are over, would someone bring me up to date with this morning's test flight?"

"Aside from almost running these two down, everything went . . ." Paul started.

"What?" G.P. grimaced.

"It's okay, G.P., no one got hurt," Paul said, as he continued with the business at hand. "As I was saying, everything went as planned, no changes from the previous test flight results. The airplane is performing as expected. We'll get the flight data over to Kelly so he can get started on calculating the flight procedures."

Everyone's head turned toward the open door as a tall, barrel-chested man in a grey pinstriped suit entered the building and made his way over to their table.

"Well, speak of the devil," Paul observed. "We were just talking about you."

"All good, I hope," he quipped.

"Daric, Dani, this is Clarence "Kelly" Johnson," Millie offered by way of introductions. "He's Lockheed's performance engineer. We've asked for his help in providing the best flight altitude, airspeed, and amount of fuel required throughout the various stages of the world flight."

Daric stood and shook hands with Kelly.

"Nice to meet you," Dani said. Kelly had the warmest hazel eyes Dani had ever.

"We just finished the last test flight," Millie said wearily. "Paul will give you all the details."

"Uh . . . it will take me a few days to analyse the data and produce the optimum performance charts," Kelly said, expressing regret. "I know you need this as soon as possible."

"As soon as you can, Kelly; by Thursday will be fine," G.P. needled, conveying his expectations. "Now, I think that's enough for today. Harry and Joe can get the airplane back into the hangar and secure her for the day."

Millie looked at G.P., her eyes reflecting a level of exhaustion G.P. had never seen before.

"We're going to head back to the hotel with our newest members and get them settled in. We'll meet you guys for dinner, say, around 6:00 P.M.," G.P. directed, while rising and pulling out Millie's chair.

G.P., Millie, Pidge, Dani and Daric left the hangar and loaded themselves into G.P.'s beautifully appointed antique car. But then again, it was an antique only to Daric and Dani.

The Cadillac left the airport and turned right onto San Fernando Road. The sun was rising toward its zenith; it was going to be a beautiful warm spring day, which Millie was unfortunately going to miss. She had already fallen asleep in the front seat of the car as it headed back to the hotel, her head resting on G.P.'s shoulder.

"Pidge, why did Amelia introduce herself as Millie?" Dani whispered, not wanting to disturb Millie.

"Millie and Pidge are our childhood nicknames. It seems that whenever we get together, we still use them," Pidge explained. "We grew up in a little town called Atchison, Kansas. We were inseparable; we did everything together."

"Our mother's name is Amy," Pidge continued, "which could be confused with a shorter version of Amelia. So, our parents gave Amelia her nickname Millie. Being the younger sister, I always wanted to be like my big sister; so, of course, I had to have a nickname, too. They gave me Pidge. My real name is Muriel."

"So, what are we supposed to call you now?" Daric interjected, turning his gaze from the miles of farmland to the two women beside him in the back seat.

"Come Tuesday, I'll be on my way back to West Medford. Millie will go back to being called Amelia. So, you might as well start calling her by her proper name now. I've only ever called her Millie, so I'll never change," Pidge grinned shyly.

"Where's West Medford?" Dani asked.

"It's a small town just north of Boston," Pidge provided. "Most people have never heard of it. I guess I should have just said Boston."

The Cadillac eventually turned into the circular driveway in front of the Hollywood Roosevelt Hotel. The Spanish-style hotel, built only ten years before, catered to the show business elite. Its magnificent architecture and luxury set the hospitality standard, against which other hotels were measured. Its twelve storeys made it one of the tallest buildings in the area and allowed it to overlook the famous Hollywood sign.

A valet attendant, dressed in a dark green uniform with polished brass buttons, opened the driver's door. Gently pushing Millie off his shoulder, G.P. handed over the keys to the car upon exiting. G.P. walked around the car and opened the front passenger door. He reached in and carefully pulled Amelia into his arms.

Making his way through the opened front door, into the lobby, G.P. asked, "Pidge, could you see to our guests? Daric can bunk with Harry and if you don't mind . . ."

"Dani can stay with me. It'll be fun having company," Pidge interrupted enthusiastically. "I'll get the keys from the front desk. We'll see you guys later for dinner."

Pidge started to make her way across the highly polished marble floor to the large mahogany reception desk when a thought hit her.

"Oh, G.P., Daric and Dani need some clothes to wear. This is all they have," Pidge said sadly.

"Some of Millie's clothes should fit Dani," Pidge asserted. "Do you think Harry and you could pull something together for Daric? They don't need much."

"We'll work something out. Now, if you'll excuse me, I'm going to put Amelia to bed; she's exhausted," G.P. finished. He made his way through the thin haze of tobacco smoke hanging in the lobby and took one of the three lifts up to their suite on the twelfth floor.

Monday, March 8, 1937

17

AMELIA WAS SITTING on the large three-seater sofa in their suite, studying some maps and sipping a cup of coffee. G.P. was talking on the phone, gazing out the window onto Hollywood Boulevard and the famous sign beyond. Cars were coming into the main entrance below. From this height they looked like small die-cast Dinky toys moving non-stop along a toy factory's conveyer belt.

The hotel suite was just over one-thousand square feet and featured chocolate and creamy white hues that created a bold yet soothing atmosphere. In front of a brown leather sofa in the separate living/dining area was an oblong, dark walnut coffee table. To the left of the sofa was a white leather tub chair in whose cushioned depths a person could get totally lost. A walnut dining table and six chairs, padded with cream-colored leather cushions, filled most of the remaining space. The bedroom was set apart from the rest of the room, behind white French doors. The king-sized bed had white custom-made linens, with a goose down duvet, and two large over-stuffed pillows. The bathroom had a combination of cream and brown marble, with a plush bathmat in front of the four-legged bathtub.

Amelia had had a good night's sleep last night, but still looked tired to G.P. He was concerned about her. Was this world flight too much for her? After a rare heated discussion this morning and with tremendous cunning on his part, he had convinced Amelia to spend the day resting at the hotel. It was a cold, rainy, dreary day, not great for flying anyway. Besides, they had completed all the test flights. They were just waiting on the performance charts from Kelly Johnson. The airplane was being taken care of and whatever needed doing today could be done from the comfort of their hotel suite. He was confident they would meet their planned departure date.

G.P. also knew Amelia needed to get some rest. They had a very busy nine days ahead of them to complete all the remaining details, not to mention the many challenges Amelia would face over the next several weeks.

"Okay, thanks," G.P. said, as he finished his conversation and hung up the phone.

"Who was that?" Amelia asked, looking up from the map spread out on her lap, her feet curled underneath her.

G.P. had walked over to the dining room table and poured himself another cup of coffee before he made his way to Amelia.

"That was Harry. He's heading back to the Union Air Terminal," G.P. replied as he sat at the end of the sofa, throwing his arm over the back.

"What on earth for?"

"He said he wanted to make sure all the maps were there and in the correct sequence." G.P. reflected for a moment, then continued. "I know he's a dear friend of yours, Amelia, but I'm concerned."

"About what?"

"Remember three weeks ago, when we left Cleveland for Burbank?"

"Of course," Amelia said.

"Harry was still practising his navigation skills, as you know. He passed you up a note saying our position was over southern Kansas when in fact we were actually over northern Oklahoma. He didn't even have us in the right state!" G.P.'s voice slowly increased in volume and anxiety.

"G.P., relax. We were only a few miles south of the Kansas border. Harry wasn't off by much," Amelia assured.

"A few miles off out in the middle of the Pacific could mean the difference between life and death, Amelia," G.P. countered. "Howland Island is a very tiny island, thousands of miles from anywhere, with no elevation or trees and practically impossible to spot from the air. He's a sea captain, Amelia, not an aviation navigator."

"If you remember, we were also having trouble synchronizing the propellers. The right propeller's pitch was frozen and stuck in cruise position. I couldn't get full power out of that engine. It may have affected Harry's calculations, because he didn't know I was having a problem with airspeed," Amelia tried to defend her dear friend by redirecting blame.

"I'm still not convinced he can do this."

"G.P., Harry is one of the few sea captains to have trained under sail. He told me he apprenticed on a four-masted American barque, which required the ultimate understanding of winds and seas. The same skills required for aircraft navigation. His years at sea have also made him an expert radio operator. And to top it off, he has his own airplane and has been flying for years," Amelia finished confidently. She wanted Harry with her. She trusted him completely. Besides, they had made a promise to each other almost nine years ago.

A knock came at the door. "Come in, it's open," G.P. hollered across the living room.

Paul Mantz entered the suite, making his way to the chair. It didn't take long for him to recognize the look of agitation on G.P.'s face. "What's up?" Paul asked.

"We were discussing Harry's ability, or lack thereof, to be the navigator on this flight," G.P. spat. "Do you have any doubts, Paul?"

"Well, navigating a ship is a little different from navigating an airplane," Paul hedged.

"We know that," Amelia said coldly.

"Well, there's one way to find out." Paul made sure he had their attention.

"We could take Harry out over the sea, before sunrise, to test his ability to get us back to our point of origin using celestial navigation. Joe could test the radios at the same time," Paul suggested. "Kill two birds with one stone."

"Amelia, would you agree? If Harry has any problems with this exercise, we will need to rethink this," G.P. pressed.

"Okay, let's do it," Amelia conceded. "Paul, can you make the arrangements for early Wednesday morning? If everything goes as planned, which I expect it will, we'll take the plane to Oakland later that afternoon."

"I'm on it," Paul said as he showed himself out of their suite.

18

A KNOCK CAME at the door of Harry's room. Daric cautiously pulled open the door, only to find his anxious sister standing on the other side of the threshold.

"We need to talk," Dani said while pushing herself past Daric into the room.

Dani was wearing a pair of Amelia's navy trousers, belted at the waist, a pale blue blouse, and a pair of black leather dress boots, with two-inch heels. She completed her ensemble with a navy blue silk scarf tucked under her collar. Daric stared at his sister as she made her way into the room; he had to admit she looked elegant, yet practical. For cool early mornings, Amelia had also provided her with a stylish black leather bomber jacket that looked so soft it screamed out to be touched.

"Come on in, won't you?" Daric said sarcastically.

Daric had on a crisp white shirt with a narrow smoke-black neck tie, covered with a V-neck charcoal-grey wool vest and black trousers, all supplied by Harry. G.P. had provided his black shoes and socks and had also purchased a new grey tweed Newsboy cap to finish Daric's new 1930s look.

"Well, it's not as if I could text, tweet, Skype or use any other media to reach you, now could I?" Dani snapped back.

Daric closed the door. He followed his sister to the two double beds and perched on the foot of the one opposite Dani. They sat facing each other in what seemed to be a childish stare-down, until he caved. "You wanted to talk, so talk."

"Let me see if I understand what's happened to us, as you see it. Correct me if I'm wrong," Dani began.

"Of course."

"You're trying to tell me that Dad built a time machine . . ." Daric was about to interject, when Dani, holding up her hands, stifled him and quickly corrected herself, ". . . bands."

Daric grinned shyly in acknowledgement, encouraging Dani to continue.

"And then you said we put the bands on in Dad's lab and bam, we magically appear here and that here is somewhere between late 1936 and early 1937," Dani finished.

"Yup, that's what I said, but without the 'bam'." Daric tried to lighten the mood; his sister was very edgy.

"But, now I know we're in 1937; March 1937 to be exact. A few days before Amelia attempts her world flight," Daric said, suddenly serious.

"How did you figure that?" Dani was stunned by Daric's computation.

"We both know Amelia hasn't left on her world flight yet. Her first attempt at her world flight started on March 17, 1937. Her second attempt was made on May 20 of that same year," Daric continued with his deduction. "So, today's date is sometime before March 17. But, I haven't been able to narrow it down."

"Today is actually Monday, March 8th," Dani announced.

"How on earth did you come up with that?"

"I caught the date on the front page of yesterday's newspaper I saw on the counter at the terminal," Dani admitted. "But why here and why this time period?" she wondered.

"I don't know," Daric replied thoughtfully.

"And what actually caused us to travel in time? You put the travel band on your wrist first and nothing happened to you."

"I don't know!" Daric barked. He had just as many questions that needed answering and he was just as frustrated and scared, but he sure as hell didn't want to let his sister know. So he reverted to one of his old techniques—striking out.

"You're the genius in the family. Everything always came so easily for you. Why don't you have the answers?" Daric snapped.

"You know very well I have hypermnesia. That gives me a huge advantage," Dani countered. "But that doesn't mean I have all the answers."

"Yeah, it must be nice to be able to recall anything that has ever entered that brain of yours. It must have made it a real breeze for majoring in History, Literature, and Physics. Did I forget any? Oh yeah, how many languages can you speak?"

"Well, considering our present predicament, we should both be grateful. At least I can provide us with some guidance about whatever time period we end up in; to some degree anyway," Dani replied smugly and with a little satisfaction.

"Oh my God, you don't think we're going to time travel again, do you?" Daric cried out, hoping it didn't sound as pathetic to Dani as it sounded to him.

"I don't know, simply because I don't know what caused us to be here in the first place. I think when we figure that out, we should be able to control how and when we travel," Dani reasoned.

"Dani, how are we going to get home?" Daric asked bleakly.

"I don't know, but you can be sure Dad will know," Dani said sympathetically.

"He doesn't even know we're gone or where we are, or when for that matter." Daric was moving beyond frightened. "We need to figure something out; we have to get home."

Dani sat beside her brother, gently grabbing his hands. "Daric, you know Dad will do everything he can to get us home. I think it's just a matter of time, that's all."

Daric reflected for a minute. He knew his sister was right. Their dad would go to the ends of the earth to bring them home. As Dani said, it was probably just a matter of time.

Dani could feel Daric calming somewhat. She knew they both needed to accept their situation and that they both had to deal with it as best they could under the circumstances.

"Maybe you're right," Daric said.

"We have to make the best of our current situation, until Dad can get us home," Dani said reassuringly. "Until then, we just have to be very careful in how we interact with events as they unfold in this time period. We don't want to change history, in any way. We don't know what the repercussions could be."

"But wait, what about Amelia? We can't let her go on her world flight," Daric exclaimed.

"We can't interfere, Daric," Dani emphasized. "We have to let history play out as it did. And we both know how that ends."

"How do we know that our being here hasn't already altered history?" Daric asked defiantly.

"We don't."

19

QUINN FINISHED EXPLAINING the situation to Sandra, who was staring blindly past him, off into oblivion. It was a lot of unbelievable information Quinn had just dropped on her. He knew he couldn't bring his children home tonight. He also knew he needed more time to finish his work. And possibly some help, too. He couldn't accomplish anything more tonight. The kids were fine according to their travel band readouts. Their heart rates were a little elevated, but that was to be expected, under the circumstances. His main concern now was Sandra.

"Sandra, please, you're exhausted. There's nothing more I can do here tonight. Let's go back to the house," Quinn pleaded.

"But . . ." Sandra stammered, pulling herself back from her wanderings and then cutting her objection short. She knew Quinn was right. She reluctantly gave in. Besides, she was emotionally exhausted.

"Come on, Bear," Quinn said to the melancholy dog. She had made her way back to where Dani and Daric had vanished; she seemed to be protecting that spot, anxiously awaiting their return.

"Bear, Dani and Daric aren't coming home tonight." Quinn didn't realize how much that statement had caught in his throat and had stabbed at his heart; not until he spoke it out loud. Clearing his throat, he continued, "Come on, girl, let's go."

Bear looked at Quinn as he helped Sandra to her feet. Then Bear looked at the spot in front of her, contemplating what she should do.

"Come on, Bear, let's get you some dinner," Sandra encouraged. The reference to food made the decision easy for Bear. She got to her feet and led the way out of the lab.

"Dinner," Sandra murmured. "It's ruined by now. But I guess that's fine, because it seems I've lost my appetite." Then something invaded her thoughts. "I bet the kids are hungry. They've had nothing to eat since lunch. I hope they're okay."

Quinn placed his arm around Sandra's shoulder as they walked across the vast lawn, dotted with a wide variety of trees with buds ready to burst open on the naked branches of winter. In the distance, they heard the haunting call of a loon, echoing across the calm evening water. Sandra wrapped her arm around Quinn's waist, leaning her head on his shoulder.

"We'll get them back," Quinn tried to assure her. It was a declaration he wasn't one-hundred percent sure of at the moment, but he didn't want to upset his wife further.

"I know," Sandra murmured. The emotional tension of the day had drained whatever energy she had left. She sniffled and continued. "What if . . ." She stopped her train of thought from going down that track. "It's just that . . . they're only children . . ."

"Sandra, let's give them some credit," Quinn cut her off. He didn't want to know where her thoughts were leading her. "They're not children anymore. They're young adults. And they're both intelligent. You know Dani can talk herself out of any situation and Daric . . ."

Quinn had to stop and think for a moment. Sandra looked up at him, waiting for him to continue.

"And Daric can take care of himself," he said with conviction, and then added, "as long as he thinks before he acts."

Reaching the house, Quinn opened the side door and ushered

Sandra into the family room, helping her to the soft plush sofa. Quinn walked behind the bar, took down two glasses and poured a generous amount of scotch into each. He added a couple of ice cubes. Returning to the sofa, he handed Sandra her glass and sat down beside her.

"Quinn, I think we should have stayed at the lab. What if something happens?" Sandra asked uneasily.

"Sandra, we went over this before we left. We know from their travel bands they are in Los Angeles in 1937 and we know that they're both safe. Hermes will monitor the travel band signals twenty-four hours a day. If anything comes up, he'll call me on my comm." Quinn lifted his wrist to reveal an elaborate watch that could have come straight out of a James Bond movie. The comm was a direct link to his lab. It could project a miniaturized version of Hermes' hologram and allowed for interactive dialogue and analysis. He could also call up Hermes to get updates on data computations while they ran on his sophisticated computer system. He didn't have to be in the lab to do his work. All he had to do was instruct Hermes and Hermes would execute the request. This gave Quinn the ability to be in two places at once.

"I should go clean up the kitchen," Sandra muttered, as she dragged herself to her feet.

"I'll get it," Quinn said, as he popped up. "Why don't you head upstairs? I'll be right there."

"Okay."

Quinn entered the kitchen and removed the pots from the stove. He strained the spaghetti and threw it in the trash. Placing the pot containing the sauce in the sink, he filled it with hot water. No amount of cleaning would help; the pot looked ruined.

Quinn rejoined Sandra, who was slowly making her way up the stairs and into the bedroom. A king-sized bed sat on an Oriental rug that covered the polished hardwood floors. There was a fieldstone fireplace on the wall at the foot of the bed, with a television mounted above a small oak mantle. A rocking chair, draped with an afghan, sat in the corner. One wall was covered with floor-to-ceiling windows overlooking the pristine yard and the moonlight-bathed lake beyond. To one side of the fireplace, French doors led out onto a forty-foot-long wooden balcony. At one end, there were two sun lounges. At the other, there were four high-backed cushioned chairs around an oblong tempered glass-top table. The ensuite bathroom also had French doors that opened out onto the same balcony. The large shower stall and the bathroom floor were stone-grey marble, with matching vanity countertops. A Jacuzzi tub was on a raised marble platform beside a large window that overlooked the lake.

Sandra flopped onto the bed face down. Quinn turned on the gas fireplace to take the slight spring dampness out of the air. After helping Sandra change, he joined her under the covers. Quinn snuggled in behind her, wrapping his arms around her. Both were lost in their own thoughts. Sandra was thinking about what her children must be going through, how scared they must be. Quinn was scrambling to figure out how he would get them back because he hadn't been able to solve that piece of the puzzle yet.

Bear had followed them upstairs and curled up in front of the French doors, looking outside, across the yard toward Quinn's lab. Even though the lab was obscured by trees, her focus didn't waver. She showed no interest in her usual bedtime place on the small foam bed in front of the fireplace.

Bear looked up at Quinn with her sad brown eyes and he knew she was missing Dani and Daric, too. Quinn couldn't help but feel sorry for her, because she didn't know what was going on, just that they were gone.

Sandra looked out the window at the new moon in the cloudless sky, its illumination streaking across the mirror-like stillness of the water. She had only one thought on her mind: her children. She hoped somewhere out there they could hear her silent prayer: *Be safe; take care of each other. I need you home. I don't know what I'd ever do without you.*

Tuesday, March 9, 1937

20

HARRY AND DARIC left early in the morning for the airport. Harry was going to introduce Daric to Bo McKneely, Amelia's mechanic. The others were going to follow a couple of hours later. Pidge was flying home today, and they were taking her to the Union Air Terminal for her 10:00 A.M. flight to Boston.

The Cadillac pulled out of the hotel front entrance onto Olive Avenue. Millie and Pidge were in the back seat, regaling each other over their childhood antics. Dani was sitting quietly in the front, with G.P. behind the wheel.

"Do you remember that collection we kept out in the tool shed?" Pidge asked gleefully.

"Are you referring to the collection of worms, moths, katydids and tree toads or the collection of rats we had hunted and kept in a tin?" Amelia asked, recalling the tomboyish antics she used to drag her sister into when they were children.

At the stop sign, G.P. looked both ways before pulling out to make a left onto San Fernando Road. Out of nowhere, a dark blue Chevy half-ton pickup truck turned right onto San Fernando Road at the same time, careening off the passenger side of the Cadillac. The car was propelled into the oncoming traffic. Amelia and Pidge were tossed around in the expansive back seat; a startled scream erupted from Pidge. G.P. struggled to regain control of the car, steering it scant inches away from a head-on collision with a transport truck, before driving it, nose-first, into the roadside drainage ditch.

Dani took a quick glance out her window, catching a glimpse of the blue pickup as it raced away down the road, the driver apparently oblivious to the accident he had just caused.

"Is everyone okay?" G.P. asked, turning to check on the two in the back seat.

"Yeah, fine, just a bump on my head," Amelia replied. "Pidge?"

"Fine, just a little shaken, is all."

"It almost seemed like that guy, driving the pickup, intentionally tried to ram us. But that's crazy, right?" Dani asked warily.

G.P. gave Dani a perplexed glance, the same thought had occurred to him, too. He smiled uneasily. "Let me see if I can get us out of this ditch. After all, we have a flight to catch."

* * *

The driver of the dark blue 1934 Chevy pickup looked in his rearview mirror and slammed his fist against the steering wheel. He had failed. He would have to try something else. He just hoped the young woman in the front seat hadn't gotten a good look at him.

21

"I WISH I could be here to see you off, but I have to get home; responsibilities, you know," Pidge said sadly.

"I know," Millie said, grabbing her sister's hands. "It was great you could get away at all. I've missed you something fierce. I'm just so sorry that it's been so hectic over this past week while you were here. With all the details to sort out for this flight, it seemed like we didn't get much time to ourselves."

"Millie, get G.P. to wire me when you are a few days from completing your world flight. I want to be here to welcome you home," Pidge said.

"Oh, Pidge, you don't have to do that." Millie didn't want Pidge to spend that kind of money, with the times being so tough. "You know how tight-fisted Albert can be."

"Nonsense, I want to, end of discussion," Pidge persisted. "I'll deal with my husband. And you be careful, you hear me. Don't be reckless or take any unnecessary risks. I want my big sister back home, safe and sound. Promise?"

"I promise," Millie said reassuringly. "There's absolutely nothing to worry about. I've got the best airplane, latest in radio equipment and an exceptional navigator on board."

They hugged quickly. "Give Amy and David a kiss for me. Tell them their aunt will visit as soon I get back, okay? And give my best to Albert, too," she added reluctantly. She wasn't fond of Albert. She always felt he had too tight a rein on Pidge.

"I will." Pidge gave her sister one final hug and climbed the stairs to board her flight to Boston and then home to her waiting family.

22

THE EXTERIOR OF the United Air Services hangar was constructed of wooden planking. The interior skeleton was all steel beams and girders. Just below the roof line, a band of three-foot-high windows encircled the hangar, providing natural lighting to the dull grey interior. For additional lighting on overcast days like today, a suspended string of metal light fixtures ran down the middle of the hangar from one end to the other. Two large sliding barn-like doors, hanging from metal tracks, defined the two stalls for the company's aircraft. Amelia's airplane was in the right-hand stall.

Harry and Daric approached the lone figure in the hangar, bent over a tool chest. "Hi, Bo," Harry said cheerfully. Not waiting for a response, Harry started the introductions.

"Daric, this is Bo McKneely, Amelia's mechanic. He's been with her for almost a year now. Before that, he was an overhaul mechanic with Pratt & Whitney for six years, so he's perfect for this job."

Ruckins "Bo" McKneely was a quiet, good-natured man with wavy brown hair and smiling light blue eyes. He was barrel-chested and stood roughly five-foot-eight. He was wearing ash-grey coveralls, with his name "Bo" stitched in black letters over the right breast pocket.

"Bo, this is Daric Delaney, our newest team member. He says he's an expert with engines." Harry's attention was redirected to Daric. "Didn't you tell Amelia you used to take apart a Pratt & Whitney engine you had in your garage at home?" he prodded, hoping to highlight Daric's abilities and to soften Bo's stubborn posture.

"Yes, I did, but it doesn't compare to these," Daric asserted, pointing at the engines hanging off the Electra's wing.

"Bo, you now have an extra pair of hands. Can you get him a pair of coveralls?" Harry instructed, giving up on Bo's cold attitude toward Daric. "Don't want to get grease on those new clothes."

"Sure thing," Bo mumbled, on his way to complete the request, never acknowledging Daric. "Be right back."

"Never mind him, Daric, he'll come around. Just give him some time," Harry offered, sort of apologizing for Bo's lack of manners. "I'll come back to get you when we're about to call it a day and head back to the hotel."

"Yeah, sure thing. Thanks, Harry," Daric muttered, his eyes never wavering from the Electra.

Harry could only smile at his young companion's evident excitement. It was almost contagious. He made his way across the apron toward to the Union Air Terminal and another day of crunching numbers and arranging maps for what seemed the hundredth time. Amelia had often said, 'Preparation is rightly two-thirds of any venture.' Harry wanted to make sure he overlooked nothing and was prepared to review every detail daily just to be sure.

Daric was ecstatic. He was actually going to work on Amelia Earhart's airplane. He had to pinch himself to make sure he wasn't dreaming. Sure, he had an aircraft engine he dabbled with at home, but right here, right now, this engine was legendary.

In the back right corner, where Bo had disappeared, was a partitioned-off storage room with an attached restroom. Along the back wall was an array of tools, benches, vises, trolleys, etc., all the equipment for every eventuality when it came to servicing airplanes. In the far left corner, there were two steel drums with pumps, for fueling the aircraft.

Bo returned with an old pair of coveralls he tossed at Daric. "Here you go, kid. So you're an expert with engines, are ya?"

"I've had some experience, yes," Daric replied modestly.

"Well, kid, you've never seen one of these before." He motioned to the engine. "This is the Pratt & Whitney R . . ."

"R-1340 Wasp, the first reciprocating engine built by Pratt & Whitney. It has a single-row, nine-cylinder air-cooled radial design and displaces 1,344 cubic inches," Daric finished.

"Now, how on earth could you possibly know that?" Bo was blown away by the young man's knowledge of this new engine.

"My dad used to work for Lockheed in the design department. He had access to all the new stuff," Daric quickly supplied, hoping Bo wouldn't ask for any further details.

"Well, then, Daric, you *do* seem to know your engines," Bo reluctantly acknowledged. "So let's get started. We have a lot to cover today."

Daric didn't miss the fact that this was the first time Bo had used his actual name.

Kelly Johnson had entered the hangar and approached the two men beside the Electra. "Hi, Bo, Daric."

"You guys have met?" Bo asked, bemused.

"Yes, yesterday. Is Daric lending you a hand?" Kelly inquired, grinning at Bo, knowing the stubborn mechanic could be overly possessive when it came to his engines.

"We're just starting. What brings you here today? Not a good one for a flight, even if the airplane were ready," Bo stated. "Paul wanted us to check everything over again and to gas her up for an early morning flight tomorrow."

"I just needed to check on a couple of things before I finish with my calculations. Mind if I climb aboard for a few minutes?" Kelly motioned to the cockpit.

"Go right ahead, we're working down here for now, checking the landing gear," Bo supplied as he and Daric made their way under the fuselage.

"Now, there is a true genius, when it comes to airplanes." Bo's admiration for Kelly was evident in his voice.

"Why do you say that?" Daric probed.

"Kelly had been conducting wind tunnel tests on the prototype of the twin-engine Lockheed Electra 10 model, when he was still in university. He discovered that the aircraft didn't have acceptable directional stability. Unfortunately, no one would listen to him," Bo said regretfully. "He didn't stop there, though," he added.

"What did he do?"

"When Kelly graduated, he joined Lockheed's staff as a tool designer. Eventually, he was able to convince their chief engineer that the Lockheed Electra 10 model was unstable. So the chief engineer sent Kelly back to the university to conduct more tests. Kelly made several changes to the wind tunnel model, including adding an 'H' tail, to address the stability problem. Lockheed finally agreed with Kelly's suggestions and made the changes to the Electra," Bo finished with pride.

"Really?" was all Daric could say.

"Yup, they later promoted him to aeronautical engineer," Bo added. "And what you see before you now is Kelly's design."

23

"DANI, WE HAVE a thousand details that need to be worked out. I think this is where you can help us," Amelia suggested, after seeing Pidge off on her flight back to Boston.

"Sure, what do you need?" Dani asked eagerly.

"Each country we fly into has its own set of rules and regulations governing aircraft licencing, landing rights, overfly rights, passports, visas, vaccinations, insurance, airports, charts and maps, weather, fuel, maintenance, communications, hotels, and last but not least, money," Amelia recited, counting off on her fingers the list by memory.

Dani stood there looking at Amelia, speechless.

Amelia could only smile at Dani's reaction to the task at hand. "Relax, we have most of this already documented. We only need to finish the last few legs of the flight, from South America back to Miami. From there we know how to get back to Oakland. A list of the countries where we'll be landing is on the desk in the office. Do you think you can handle that?"

"Sure, no problem, just point me to the terminal," Dani replied confidently. She'd have this done in no time.

"Uh, Dani, it's right over there. You remember, where we had breakfast the other day," Amelia said, uncertain of her new team member's mental acuity.

Dani couldn't believe her blunder. Computers didn't exist in this era; what was she thinking? She would have to do this job the hard way.

"Come on, I'll get you set up," Amelia offered as she and Dani made their way over to the Union Air Terminal, where all the charts, maps and directories were located.

To break the silence on the walk, Dani asked, "What got you interested in flying?"

Amelia smiled as she recalled that one particular day, so many years ago. She had told no one this story before. "When I was seven years old, my Uncle Albert helped me build a ramp fashioned after a roller coaster I had seen in St. Louis, but of course not as high. Anyway, we secured it to the roof of the tool shed out back. When the grownups were in the house, Pidge helped me carry a wooden crate onto the shed roof."

"You didn't?" Dani interjected.

"Yup, I did. I climbed into that box and down the ramp I went. The landing wasn't all that great. I banged up my lip and tore my dress, but it was exhilarating. I told Pidge at the time it was like flying."

"So I guess that was essentially your first real flight," Dani joked.

"I think that's what started it all, yes," Amelia said reflectively. "Then in 1918, I was just twenty-one-years-old, and I was in Toronto at the Canadian National Exhibition airshow with a friend. A flying demonstration was being performed by a World War I flying ace. He must have spotted me and my friend in the clearing. I'm sure he said to himself, 'Watch me make them scamper'. Anyway, he came diving at us, but we stood our ground as the aircraft came close."

Amelia paused to reflect. "I didn't understand it at the time, but I believe that little red airplane said something to me as it swished by. Then a couple years later in Long Beach, I got my first ride. By the time I had got two or three hundred feet off the ground, I knew I had to fly. And I've never looked back."

Amelia opened the terminal's door and ushered Dani in, following close behind.

"You can use the spare desk in the office. There you'll find a list of phone numbers for the airports we'll be using and a list of the details we need. Make the calls and record the information we need, okay?" Amelia said.

"Got it," Dani said, making her way to the office to complete her assigned task. How could she be so stupid? Adjusting to the differences in time periods could be a real challenge. What would normally have taken her an hour to complete might take days.

24

"OKAY, DARIC, LET'S call it a day and go grab a cup of coffee," Bo said, as he eagerly extracted himself from his confining coveralls. They had accomplished more than Bo had thought he'd be able to get done when the day had started. He had to admit, Daric knew his stuff and was a tremendous help. His enthusiasm and genuine interest were commendable. They had actually covered the entire airplane, from top to bottom and from stem to stern or, in this case, from nose to tail.

"Sounds great," Daric agreed.

"You can hang the coveralls in the storage room and I'll meet you outside," Bo volunteered. "The others will be calling it a day soon, too. Save Harry the trip over here to get you."

"Okay." Daric made his way to the back of the hangar. He opened the storage room door only to find someone lurking in the darkness.

"You startled me," Daric said nervously, reaching to turn on the light. He hadn't been expecting to find anyone here. He also thought he had met all the mechanics over the course of the day, but he didn't recall this man.

"What were you doing in the dark?" Daric asked, curiosity getting the better of him. He was picking up an unusual odor in the air. It reminded him of some kind of tobacco, but with a more pungent smell.

The stranger thought quickly; he had to come up with a reasonable explanation—now. This kid didn't look like he would be easily fooled.

"I was looking for a fluorescent marker for the runway," the stranger said. "It's always easier to find it in the dark, because it glows."

"Makes sense," Daric agreed. "My name is Daric, by the way. I'm working with Bo. I don't think I met you today with the other staff."

"Name's Rick Barak Case," the stranger offered, as he extended his hand to Daric, who took it hesitantly, staring closely at the man standing in front of him.

Rick Barak Case stood six feet tall, had a good build, was clean shaven, and displayed a receding hairline. He was thin-lipped with a pointed jaw, broad nose and wide-set cold brown eyes.

"What are you staring at?" Case asked uneasily, looking for a quick exit. He would now have to change his plans.

"Uh . . . you . . . uh look exactly like someone I know and the name's almost the same, too," Daric stammered hesitantly.

"Well, I'm not him, kid; so get over it," Case snapped as he pushed past Daric and briskly walked away.

Daric hung up the coveralls, snatched his hat from a hook, and followed after Case. There was something about this guy that just didn't seem right to him.

Case paused just outside the hangar's back door, casually striking a wooden match with his thumbnail and lighting a cigarette. He carefully scanned the area to make sure no one was watching. He had to yank hard on the door handle of the dented driver's door to get it open.

Daric hung back just enough so as not to be seen. He watched Case climb into the old blue Chevy pickup truck, slam the door and speed away. He couldn't get over the uncanny resemblance to his dad's best friend or the fact that Case had left without the fluorescent marker.

25

THE WAKE-UP CALL came much too early: it was 2:00 A.M. As requested by G.P., Paul had made arrangements for an early morning flight, so they could test Harry's navigational skills. And as long as they were at it, Joe was going along, so they could run another test of the radio equipment.

At 3:35 A.M., Harry, G.P. and Joe, with Paul at the controls, taxied the Electra from the front of the United Air Services hangar onto the apron, then onto the adjoining runway. Once airborne, they headed north-westward toward San Francisco Bay. Then the plan was to head west out over the sea, well out of sight of land, and to have Harry navigate them back to the airport in Burbank using celestial navigation only.

During the flight, Joe checked all the radios, using the night-time frequency of 3105 kilocycles. "Signal's weak and we're only four-hundred miles out of Burbank," Joe informed the others. "I'm switching over to 6210 kilocycles, even though it's not quite daylight."

Harry checked his watch; it was about 5:50 A.M. "Paul, I have us over San Francisco. I need you to turn to the west on a heading of 257 degrees." Paul responded by banking the plane left, heading out to sea.

Behind them, a solid bank of clouds covered the coast. A faint glow was the first indication of the approaching sunrise. At 6:10 A.M., Harry instructed Paul to turn on a southeasterly heading, taking them back to Burbank.

The sun slowly rose above the horizon, making the stars invisible in the daylight. Harry looked across the horizon, but could see nothing but the tops of stratocumulus clouds. He couldn't see the ocean below and therefore couldn't take a drift sight. He ruled out using a smoke bomb, which would provide wind speed information, because the cloud layer would obscure it.

Harry also knew the sun would soon be high enough for him to take an accurate observation. Using the twenty-six-day-old moon in the southern sky, about forty-five degrees to the west of the sun, he could get a celestial fix that would be accurate within fifteen miles. About one-hundred-fifty miles from Burbank, Harry took the sun and moon shots.

During the flight back to Burbank, Harry had missed the airport by over twenty miles. They were all thinking the same thing: if Burbank had been a small island in the middle of the Pacific, they would have missed it completely. Harry knew they were right; but, unlike his colleagues, he also understood that such imprecision was the reality of aerial celestial navigation. He had done nothing wrong!

Paul taxied the Electra up to the hangar for refueling. It was now 8:25 A.M. Once the engines were off and conversation could be comfortably heard, G.P. started. "Harry, I'm concerned about your navigation skills. This test proved to me that you could completely miss Howland Island."

"G.P., I understand your concern, but I won't apologize for my performance. Under the circumstances, I did exactly what was required. It's just the way celestial navigation works. There will always be a possible ten percent dead-reckoning error," Harry explained. "I've had nearly twenty years of experience as a navigator and I've been flying for over seven as a pilot. I know what I'm doing."

G.P. and Paul had exchanged glances, knowing that this wasn't good enough. The tension was so thick in the airplane it felt like the cramped space was shrinking, cutting off the air inside the plane.

"I think this test simply confirms that we need to install a radio direction-finder," Joe suggested, hoping to break some tension.

"I agree," G.P. said coldly as he exited the airplane. "Make it happen."

26

G.P. ENTERED THE office where Dani was working on collecting the final details for Amelia's world flight. She looked up upon hearing him enter and retrieved a piece of paper from the corner of the desk.

"G.P., you have a message here from Bill Miller. He said that he's at the Oakland office and that you'd know what that means."

William "Bill" Miller was with the Bureau of Air Commerce and was responsible for laying out future air routes between Australia and some colonized islands in the middle of the Pacific.

"Thank you, Dani." G.P. couldn't contain the smile that played across his lips. *What an attractive young woman,* he thought. He took the message and picked up the telephone to return Bill's call. It rang three times before a voice on the other end said, "Hello."

"Good morning, Bill."

"G.P., how was the flight this morning? Did everything go all right?"

G.P. had expressed his concern to Bill earlier about Harry's navigational skills and that they were going to run a navigation test flight this morning.

"Wasn't done as well as I would have liked," G.P. replied coldly. "We were off the mark by more than twenty miles."

"That could be a real problem when flying over the Pacific, or the Atlantic for that matter, when you only have dead-reckoning and the stars to rely on as your guide."

"Tell me about it. At least the exercise confirmed something for us this morning."

"What's that?" Bill asked, intrigued.

"I ordered a radio direction-finder to be installed. That should help, but I'm still not convinced Harry's our man for this job."

Bill, knowing how concerned G.P. was with Amelia's safety, thought for a moment and then provided some news he thought G.P. might find useful.

"Look, G.P. I just heard from a friend at Pan American Airways that the chief navigator for their Clippers has resigned. His name is Fred Noonan; he's forty-three-years-old and has been with them for seven years. He's considered one of the best aerial navigators in the world. I could set up an interview for you. He lives out here in Oakland."

"Okay, go ahead, Bill. Amelia and I should be there sometime this afternoon. The rest will be along later. They're coming by car," G.P. said, feeling somewhat hopeful as a result of this news. "What about the Guard ships?"

"The Coast Guard cutter *Shoshone* has already left Honolulu and is on its way to Howland Island with thirty-one drums of aviation gasoline and two barrels of lubricating oil. And the Navy tug *Ontario* will be leaving American Samoa as soon as it takes on supplies and gets refueled," Bill said confidently.

"I contacted Pan American Airways. They're prepared to cooperate fully with Amelia's flight from Oakland to Honolulu. I've also been able to acquire temporary office space from them here in the Oakland Airport administration building, where the weather bureau, telegraph companies, and Department of Commerce offices are located," Bill finished.

"Great. See you in a couple of hours." G.P. hung up the phone and was about to leave the office when he remembered he had to make arrangements for Daric and Dani to get to Oakland.

"Dani, we'll be flying the Electra to Oakland this afternoon. Since there is room for only four in the airplane, Harry, Paul and his fiancée, Terry Minor, will be taking my car. You and Daric can follow them in Amelia's car. We'll meet you at the Oakland Airport Inn tomorrow," G.P. said matter-of-factly.

"Okay, see you later," Dani replied, turning back to her task at hand as G.P. left the office.

27

AFTER LUNCH AT the hotel, Amelia and G.P. returned to the airport to finish loading the equipment and to make the final preparations to fly the Electra to Oakland. Bo and Joe met them at the hangar. After stowing the luggage, supplies, and all the spare parts, they took off for Oakland.

Since it had been such an early morning for G.P., he napped during the flight, despite the noise from the engines. Joe made a point of checking the radios. He continued to be troubled by the fact that they had lost the signal during their morning test.

The flight from Burbank to Oakland was smooth and uneventful. At the Oakland airport, a long siren blast resonated through the still air, warning all at the field that a plane was about to land. The Electra majestically appeared through a very thin layer of cirrus clouds just east of the airport and made one circuit of the field prior to landing.

After making a perfect two-point landing, Amelia made a sharp turn to exit the runway and taxied on the apron over to the Navy Hangar. Bill Miller was waiting to greet them. Beside him was the commanding officer of the U.S. Naval Reserve aviation base.

William "Bill" T. Miller was a rather heavy-set man, exaggerated by his short height of five-foot-six. He was in his early fifties, had thinning brown hair and was wearing a doubled-breasted three-piece black suit. He looked more like a banker than a businessman.

After Amelia shut down the engines, the commanding officer instructed his men to secure the Electra in the Navy hangar. After loading their luggage into Bill's car, they headed toward the hotel. As he drove out of the airport, Bill pointed, "Amelia, look at the street sign." As they passed it, Amelia smiled as she read: Amelia Earhart Road.

"They renamed the road after your flight from Hawaii to Oakland two years ago," Bill explained with pride.

After the short trip from the airport, they arrived at the front entrance of the Oakland Airport Inn. They checked in and awaited the arrival of the others.

28

"COME ON, DANI, everyone's ready to go," Daric urged from the office doorway, eager to get on the road.

"Just give me a second. I'll be right there," Dani replied, while gathering up some papers from the desk. Daric had already made his way back outside to tell the others they were ready for the road trip to Oakland.

"Ouch, what happened to the Caddy?" Daric asked when he saw the dented and scratched passenger side of G.P.'s car. He had seen only the driver's side when it had left the hotel in the morning.

"G.P. said a blue pickup truck sideswiped them yesterday on their way to the airport. Lucky no one was hurt," Harry said. "The jerk didn't even stop; just drove away as if nothing had happened."

Harry, Paul, and Terry Minor were in G.P.'s Cadillac. Daric climbed behind the wheel of Amelia's car. They were all waiting outside the Union Air Terminal for Dani to exit the building.

"Whoa," Dani uttered in total awe. She was staring at a beautiful pale yellow 1936 Cord 810 Sportsman convertible coupe: pure automobile royalty in its time. The front-wheel-drive Cord had a 2-barrel Lycoming 288 CI V-8 engine under its "coffin-nose" hood with wrap-around louvers mounted on a 125-inch wheelbase. The regal design featured chromed bumpers and wheel covers and a plush tan leather interior with needle gauges on an engine-turned bezel and an electric pre-select shifter on the steering column.

"No kidding," was Daric's reply. "Get in. I can't wait to get this baby on the road and open her up."

"Just mind the speed limit, okay. We can't afford to get a ticket. There would be too many questions we wouldn't be able to answer," Dani said, opening the suicide door and sliding into the car, pulling it closed behind her. "Hey, where's the seat belt?"

"They haven't been invented yet," Daric stated, putting the car in gear and pulling out of the airport behind the Cadillac.

"What's wrong with your finger?" Daric's tone showed concern, which surprised her.

"It's nothing. I was making a bunch of phone calls. You know, they don't have buttons on their telephones," Dani said sadly, as she looked at the bandage wrapped around her sore index finger. "The phones are rotary dial. After all the calls I had to make, I got a blister on my dialing finger. It's no big deal."

"And what have you got there?" Daric asked, referring to the pages Dani was sorting through on her lap, while trying to keep them from blowing out of the car, with its convertible top down.

"I need to organize my notes for Amelia for the last few stages of her flight," Dani replied, not taking her eyes off what she was doing. "I had to write everything out long-hand. The office had a typewriter, an old Smith Corona, but its keys were too stiff to use. It's as if it hadn't been used in years, which is probably the case."

After driving for a few hours, Dani, out of shear frustration, had given up on organizing her notes and had put them away. Now that she was no longer focussed on her work, Daric finally felt he could broach a subject that had been on his mind for a while now.

"Dani, don't you think it's kind of odd that Dad hasn't brought us back home yet?"

"Daric, you have to realize that time doesn't travel at the same speed. It's sort of like a river; the current will travel quickly, like raging rapids in some places, but it can also be tranquil, in other parts," Dani supplied from her abundant knowledge.

"So, what are you saying?" Daric needed clarification.

"While we have been in this time period for four days, it may be only a matter of a couple of minutes or hours at home," Dani said encouragingly.

"Well, there is one thing I'm certain of, and that is that we must never take these bands off. When Dad tries to bring us back home, we have to be ready. And these bands are the key," Daric asserted.

They sat in silence again, uncertain about what was around the next corner and about when they would get back home. The thought that neither of them wanted to utter aloud was: what if they never got back home?

29

DARIC LEANED ON the horn to signal the Cadillac in front of him that he was pulling off the road. He had been looking for a gas station for the last hour as the Cord 810 got lower and lower on fuel. He drove the car up to the only gas pump at the station and turned off the engine. He noticed Paul had received his signal, as the Cadillac up ahead pulled a U-turn and headed back to the gas station, stopping on the other side of the pump.

The trip so far had been uneventful. The roads were almost deserted. There were a few cars travelling in the opposite direction. The only vehicle going their way was about a quarter of a mile behind them; Daric sometimes caught a glimpse of it on the road's long straightaways.

Daric had exited the car and was reaching for the hose, when he heard, "Hey, what do ya think yer doin'?"

Daric turned to a man wearing dark blue coveralls and a cap with an *Ethyl* patch above the brim. He was wiping his grease-covered meaty hands on a dirty slate-grey rag that had been another color years ago.

"I was getting some gas," Daric replied innocently to the angry gas station attendant.

"That's my job pal, so step back," he snarled.

Paul had gotten out of the Cadillac and told the flustered attendant, "Fill 'em both up."

Paul turned to Daric, noticing how confused he looked. "Come on, let's get some cold drinks." They made their way over to a fire-engine red *Coca-Cola* cooler against the station's front wall. Paul lifted the lid and pulled out five cold bottles of *Coca-Cola*. Popping the tops, he took a long slug from one of the small bottles. "Man I was thirsty." Paul sighed after he had swallowed.

Harry was leaning against the car exchanging small talk with the attendant. The girls were making their way back to the cars from the restroom and eagerly accepted the cold drinks from Daric and Paul.

The station attendant had fuelled the Cord 810, checked the oil, cleaned the windshield and headlights and was now fueling the Cadillac. When he saw Daric returning to his car, he thrust out his hand and demanded, "That'll be $1.40."

Daric could only stare blankly at the attendant. *Did he just say $1.40? That can't be*, Daric thought.

"That's okay, I'm paying for both. We're travelling together," Paul told the attendant.

Daric did some quick math while Paul waited for the attendant to finish filling the Caddy. The gas came to ten cents per gallon—amazing. What a difference a few years could make.

Paul paid the attendant for the gas and the cold drinks. Both cars were back on the road fifteen minutes after pulling off to continue their trip to Oakland. It would be several hours before they arrived at their destination and Daric knew that the next time they needed to gas up, he'd stay in the car. He now knew what "full-service" meant.

But one thing was gnawing at Daric; something he couldn't quite figure out. While they were getting gas, the car that had been a quarter of a mile behind them hadn't passed the gas station.

30

G.P. MADE PRIOR arrangements for Amelia to meet the press after an early morning flight. She pulled herself out of the cockpit and gracefully walked down the sun-glistened wing of the Electra to face the eager crowd of reporters. G.P. gently helped her down.

"Miss Earhart? How was your flight?" one young reporter yelled, anxious to be the first to direct a question in what, he was sure, would be a long string of questions to the beautiful aviatrix.

"We practised some blind flying this morning, and all went as planned," Amelia said, smiling warmly at the young man, who appeared to blush slightly in the early morning's rose-tinted sunlight. "Everything is set to go," she continued, "except for a couple small adjustments. I really don't want to put any unnecessary time on the engines before the world flight."

"Miss Earhart, when are you planning to start your world flight?" another reporter asked.

"We will just study the weather and wait to see if conditions are favorable on Sunday. Then, if they are, away we'll go." Amelia couldn't hide how anxious she was to get started on this new and exciting adventure.

"Are you scared?" the first young reporter asked, clearly

concerned for her safety.

"No, not scared, just thrilled," she replied.

"Mr. Putman, are you worried for your wife's safety, considering the dangers of the flight she'll be undertaking?" another reporter enquired, picking up on the previous line of questioning.

"I'm not worried," he said with confidence. "Amelia is an accomplished aviator. She knows what she's doing. I would like to go along," he conceded. "But on a flight like this, when it comes to a question of one-hundred-eighty-five pounds of husband or one-hundred-eighty-five pounds of gasoline, the gasoline wins."

31

LATER THAT AFTERNOON, G.P. and Amelia met Harry, Paul and Dani in G.P.'s temporary office, at the Oakland Airport administrative building, for a final review of all the flight details.

"G.P., before you get started, I've set up an interview with Fred Noonan for tomorrow morning," Bill said, as G.P. walked into his office.

"Great, Bill, thanks. Amelia and I will be here early tomorrow morning."

For the next two hours, G.P. sat listening to the group check and double check all the arrangements that had been made for the world flight; it was overwhelming.

"Here are the details for the end of the world flight you asked me to get, Amelia," Dani said eagerly. "I've covered the trip from the Parnamirio Airport in Natal, Brazil to Fortaleza, Brazil, then to the Zandery Airport in Paramaribo, Dutch Guiana, and on to Caripito, Venezuela. From there, to San Juan, Puerto Rico and finally to Miami. You said you had the Miami-to-Oakland leg covered, but I included that, too," Dani finished.

Amelia smiled at Dani after she had finished her report. She had known Dani would do a great job, and she had done it in short order, too.

G.P. hadn't realized how many details there were. Now that he knew, he was starting to seriously wonder whether Amelia would be able to handle all of this, in addition to flying the airplane. He knew she wasn't sleeping well, and this would definitely seem to be the reason why, in his mind, anyway. There was just too much for her to think about. He needed to find a way to reduce her load.

After the meeting, G.P. asked Paul to remain behind after the others had left the office. "Paul, I'm concerned about Amelia's workload. After sitting in here and listening for the past couple of hours, I'm completely overwhelmed. And I'm not the one having to fly an airplane, with the whole world watching," he said apprehensively.

"Would you consider flying with Amelia, on the first leg, from here to Honolulu, to take some of the responsibilities off her?" G.P. asked. Before Paul could say no, G.P. quickly continued, "You could oversee any servicing the plane might need in Honolulu before the next leg to Howland Island; that would give Amelia a chance to rest." G.P. stood up, walked over and looked out the window for a moment before continuing. "You know, she hasn't been sleeping very well."

Paul could see by G.P.'s uncharacteristic slumped posture that he was worried, so he tried to reassure him. "G.P., Amelia's flown this route before, mind you from the other direction. She will be fine, she knows what . . ."

G.P. spun around to face Paul. "True, but this is only the first leg of three for the Pacific crossing, all to be completed in a matter of days. And not only does Amelia need to attend to all the details of the flight, she also has to attend press conferences and she has to write her daily articles for the *Tribune*."

G.P. drew in a slow breath, then continued. "Paul, I'm concerned. It's the first leg of a long flight and I just want to make sure everything goes as planned." G.P. didn't want to beg, but he knew he had to lighten Amelia's load, somehow and having an extra pilot on board would be a tremendous help.

"Okay, I'll do it. But on one condition," Paul said.

"Name it."

"You send my fiancée ahead to meet me in Honolulu," Paul said. Terry and Paul were planning to take a small trip once Amelia left on her world flight. He thought Honolulu would make a wonderful trip and a great honeymoon destination if he could talk Terry into getting married while they were vacationing in paradise.

"Done." G.P. quickly shook hands with Paul to seal the deal. He was relieved to have got a little extra help for Amelia and Harry on the first leg of their flight.

"G.P., since we're sending Terry ahead, why don't we also send Dani and Daric," Paul suggested as an afterthought. "Dani could keep Terry company on the crossing. When we get to Honolulu, Dani could help with any last-minute details for the Howland and New Guinea legs. Daric would be there to give me a hand overseeing any repairs to the airplane. He knows that airplane just about as well as Bo."

"That's a lot of extra money we just can't spare right now," G.P. was embarrassed to admit.

"Look, you know yourself that Amelia wanted Bo to accompany her on the world flight, but he couldn't because his father is quite ill. At least this way, she'll have someone who has been working with Bo, and who according to him, is a real natural around engines," Paul pressed.

"Before you say no," Paul jumped in, "let me look into the various options for passage to Honolulu. I might be able to get all three of them on a cheaper fare. I'm sure they won't mind," Paul added, hoping to convince G.P.

"All right, I can't argue with that line of thinking. It may help put Amelia's mind at ease knowing her second mechanic will meet her plane in Honolulu. Go ahead and book their passage. I'll let Daric and Dani know they just got a free cruise to Hawaii," G.P. said.

Paul was turning to leave G.P.'s office and make the necessary arrangements when he heard G.P. say, "Thanks, Paul."

"Don't mention it," Paul said. He knew how much was at stake here.

* * *

Later that afternoon, they received a telegram via Lockheed. It was from Kelly Johnson and, as he had promised, it set out his recommendations for optimum power and key flight procedures. He also reminded them to check the spark plugs before they left on their flight. The message concluded by stressing that it was critical for them to stay within 2,000 feet of the recommended altitude.

32

AS PREVIOUSLY ARRANGED, G.P. and Paul met with Fred Noonan to ask him whether he would assist with the navigation, but only as far as Howland Island. They both believed this task was far too challenging for Harry to handle. Fred agreed to help.

After the interview, with Amelia and Harry joining the group, they drove in the pouring rain to Alameda to finalize arrangements with Pan American Airways and the Coast Guard.

Pan American had informed them they had a survey flight to New Zealand that was departing for Honolulu shortly before Amelia's planned departure. Because the Electra was a faster aircraft, it would easily overtake the survey flight. That meant they would have to use altitude to provide enough separation to avoid a possible mid-air collision.

Harry met with the Coast Guard to outline the communication plan for the trip to Howland Island. They would work out the plan for the leg to New Guinea from Howland later.

The skies had started to clear, and the sun was desperately trying to make an appearance by the time they got back to Bill Miller's office at the Oakland Airport. Paul immediately sent a message to Kelly Johnson, asking him to recalculate the optimum performance charts. They needed to fly 4,000 feet higher than his previously recommended altitude. Paul asked him to include the new power-setting and fuel-burn charts for a cruising altitude of 8,000 feet.

G.P. introduced Fred Noonan to the rest of the team and explained his role: to assist with the navigation as far as Howland Island.

Fred Noonan was taller than Harry and Paul, at just over six feet. He was very slim with dark auburn hair, blue eyes and a ruddy complexion. There was a protrusion on his forehead just over his right eye . . . a souvenir from a bar fight in his younger days.

"I'd like to get a chance to check out the navigation equipment on board before we start for Honolulu," Fred conveyed, after the introductions had been concluded.

"The meteorologist said the weather was supposed to be clear tomorrow, for a short period, anyway. Why not go early in the morning?" Bill proposed.

"Let's meet at the hangar at 10:00 A.M. tomorrow. We can test the compass and radio equipment while we're at it," Amelia added.

"Great, that's settled," G.P. said. "Harry, can you meet with the press and tell them Fred will be joining the flight as far as Howland Island to assist with navigation? And don't forget to finish the communication plan. The Coast Guard needs to get that information out to their ships."

Almost as an afterthought, Paul added, "Oh, I got Terry, Daric and Dani on the S.S. Malolo, departing at 4:00 P.M. tomorrow for Honolulu, arriving on March 17th."

Harry met with the press to announce Fred Noonan's role and indulged the reporters by answering a few questions regarding the upcoming flight. He relayed that all traffic and radio bearings would be via Pan American stations and that they would use both voice and Morse code. He finished by telling them they would fly over the ocean in the morning for a final check of the radios and compass.

"Captain Manning, are you nervous about the flight?" a reporter asked.

"No, not nervous, just eager to get started," Harry replied.

After the press conference, Harry went back into the office and spent the next hour finishing the communication plan and sending the message to the Coast Guard.

33

CASE HAD TO think of something fast. He had overheard the press conference and knew, if the weather held, the world flight could take off as early as Sunday. In an enclosed wooden telephone booth at a nearby diner, Case placed a long distance call to his employer.

"Hello?" There was static on the line.

"Admiral Yama . . ."

"Do not use my name, you fool!" Case's employer chastised. "I take it you have not accomplished your mission; that is why you are calling. So, what have you to report?"

"I tried to push their car into a head-on collision, which would have injured or killed everyone in the car, but the driver swerved at the last minute and avoided the crash," Case started his report.

"Then, I tried to get access to the airplane in the hangar in Burbank, disguised as a mechanic, but I was discovered by some kid," Case continued, knowing excuses would not be well received. "That kid could be a real problem, actually."

"Trying is not good enough! There is a lot at stake here. The Japanese Imperial Navy is en route as we speak. Over the next several days, the armada will be in the direct path of 'THAT' flight. We cannot take the chance that they will spot the fleet. You need to take care of 'your' problems."

"I understand, Admir . . . sorry. I understand and I will get it done. You can count on me," Case tried to reassure his employer. He knew the price of failure and he had no desire to pay it.

"You are being paid a substantial amount of money to make this happen. I do not expect to be hearing from you again and wish only to read in the newspapers that you have completed your mission." The phone line went dead.

"Well, that was pleasant," Case said aloud to himself. He hung up the receiver and exited the telephone booth. He left the diner and stepped into the bright afternoon sunlight.

Case had to stop the flight; Amelia Earhart couldn't be allowed to reach Howland Island. Which meant he had only two opportunities to stop her: here at Oakland or in Honolulu. He needed to act quickly. They were planning to start the world flight the day after tomorrow. He had to get to the airplane tomorrow after their morning flight. In case his efforts here failed, he would book passage to Honolulu, for one last attempt. After that, it would be too late and he could say goodbye to his fortune and, more importantly, his life. He was determined not to let that happen!

34

MORNING DAWNED BRIGHT and clear. It was going to be a busy day. They had the morning flight and, weather permitting, the world flight would start the next afternoon. But right now, the forecasts for the next few days were not promising. They also had to get three members of their team onto a ship bound for Honolulu.

G.P. and Amelia left the hotel in Amelia's Cord 810. They were headed for the Oakland Airport administration building, and on their way enjoyed the balmy breeze in the convertible. They needed to make the final arrangements for weather forecasts for Honolulu and Howland Island.

"Good morning," Bill Miller greeted as they arrived at his office. "I just sent a message to the *Shoshone* for the weather forecast from Australia and New Guinea."

"Great. Thanks, Bill," Amelia acknowledged. "Have you seen my flight crew yet?"

"Yeah, they just left for the Navy hangar. I understand you have a flight this morning."

"Just to check a couple of things and to give Fred a look at the navigation equipment on board," Amelia answered casually.

"I'll arrange a press conference for you when you get back.

We need to announce that Paul will be joining the flight, as far as Honolulu," G.P. said.

Amelia headed for the door. "I'll be back in a couple of hours," Amelia said to G.P., as she left the office and headed for the Navy hangar.

The Electra had been pushed out of the hangar and was fueled and ready to go by the time Amelia arrived. She noticed that Bo McKneely and Daric were both there, talking with her flight crew.

"Good morning, you two. I didn't expect to see you here this morning." Amelia was pleased, though, that they were.

"Anything to do with that aircraft concerns me," Bo asserted firmly. "Until it leaves here, that is. I, rather we, just wanted to make sure that everything went as planned this morning and that if anything needed attending to, we'd be here to make it right." Bo was committed to making the Electra the envy of aviation lore.

"Great," Amelia acknowledged. "Daric, can I see you for a moment, in private?" Amelia ducked around a corner in the hangar, with Daric close on her heels.

"Here," Amelia said, as she handed Daric a small package. She wasn't one for sentiment and she wanted to get this over with quickly. "Open it."

Daric stripped the paper away to reveal a beautiful red *Victorinox Swiss Army* knife. He looked up at Amelia, puzzled.

"It's to replace the pocket knife you lost back in Burbank and to say thank you for all your hard work with the Electra," Amelia explained.

"I can't accept this," Daric protested, extending his hand to give the knife back.

"Nonsense. I picked it up after my solo crossing of the Atlantic in 1932. We toured around Europe after the flight and that's where I came across this knife. They said it would be a 'companion for life'. Well, I've had it for years now and have never used it. I can't even remember why I bought it."

"Thank you," Daric said shyly.

Amelia flashed Daric a gracious smile and then walked back to the others who were all waiting patiently.

"Okay, let's get this show on the road. This fine weather isn't supposed to last long today," Amelia said, while pulling herself up onto the left wing and making her way to the cockpit.

Once airborne, around 10:30 A.M., the Electra soared over the Golden Gate Bridge, heading out to sea. The bridge would not open to traffic for almost another two months and would go down in history as the most beautiful and most photographed bridge in the world.

Fred shot the sun with Harry's octant, a device used for determining one's location based on the position of the sun and the horizon. Although Fred found the octant somewhat awkward to use, compared to celestial navigation he usually used, he said nothing.

Harry called the Pan American Airways station in Alameda. They acknowledged receiving his signal loud and clear. Unfortunately, their reply was received loud and clear too—so loud that Harry had to lift the earphones off his ears.

After returning to the Oakland Airport, the Electra was pushed back into the Navy hangar, where Bo and Daric secured the airplane. It would stay in the hangar until the start of the world flight. Outside the hangar, a flood of reporters waited for Amelia, who graciously addressed them.

"Paul Mantz, our technical advisor, will be coming with us, only as far as Honolulu."

"Miss Earhart, can you afford the extra weight?"

"Yes, we are able to add the additional crew member, because our fuel consumption rate is better than we previously thought. Instead of starting with a full tank of 1,151 gallons of fuel, we will need only nine-hundred gallons, which means we will save 1,500 pounds."

"Weather permitting," Amelia continued, "we will leave tomorrow afternoon sometime between 2:00 P.M. and 4:30 P.M."

"Miss Earhart, why do you want to make this flight?" yelled one reporter.

"I want to do it, because I want to do it," Amelia replied sassily.

Taking on a more serious tone, she added, "Please know that I am aware of the hazards. Women must try to do things as men have tried. When they fail, their failure must be but a challenge to others. I want to stir the interest of women in aviation. Additionally, we will test some of the latest scientific aids to aerial navigation."

After the press conference, Bill Miller's secretary handed Amelia a message from Kelly Johnson. It was the new power settings they had requested. Comparing the two different power charts, she understood why Kelly was so adamant they stay within 2,000 feet of the recommended altitude. The fuel consumption rates at 4,000 feet compared to 8,000 feet would result in burning an extra twelve gallons of fuel.

35

"DAMN, I FORGOT my hat back at the hangar," Daric berated himself.

"You'd forget your head, if it wasn't attached," Dani muttered sarcastically.

Paul was waiting in the Cadillac, with Terry, to take them to San Francisco Pier 35, for their 4:00 P.M. departure to Honolulu.

"I'll be right back." Daric took off, running across the asphalt toward the Navy hangar, before his sister could argue further.

"We're going to miss the boat," she shouted after her brother. With those words echoing in her ears, she muttered, "I can't believe I just said that."

Daric approached the hangar door where a solider was standing guard. Recognizing the young man, the soldier unlocked and opened the door to allow him access. "I just need to grab my hat. I'll just be a minute," Daric said.

Out of the corner of his eye, Daric caught a glimpse of a figure darting through the shadows in the back of the hangar, then fleeing out the back door.

"Hey," Daric yelled. "Wait! What are you doing in here?"

Daric ran after the figure, but by the time he had crossed the hangar and reached the back door, there was no sign of the intruder, just an empty field beyond.

"What's all the ruckus?" The soldier at the front door had entered the hangar to see what was going on.

"Did you let anyone else in here?" Daric asked, clearly concerned.

"Just you. Place's been locked up tight as a drum since you left here earlier today," the soldier assured him. He made his way to the back of the hangar where Daric stood scanning the area outside, still hoping to catch a glimpse of the intruder.

"Been given direct orders not to let nobody in this here hangar, if they ain't on this here list," the soldier drawled, referring to the short list on his clipboard.

"I just saw someone run out this door," said Daric. "By the time I got here, he was gone."

"That there door is always locked. Never been used; only there for emergencies, you know, like another way out of here," the soldier said as he bent over to examine the lock.

"Hey, this here lock's been busted. I better contact maintenance to fix it, right quick," the soldier said firmly.

Daric was picking up a faint odor. He could swear he had come across it before, but couldn't quite put his finger on where or when. "Do you smell anything strange?"

"This here honker can't smell anything, not with my allergies," the soldier replied, pointing to his rather large puffy red nose.

"It's probably nothing," Daric said skeptically. He grabbed his hat and was heading back toward the front door. "Can you make sure that lock gets fixed, today?"

"Sure thing," the soldier replied.

"Thanks." Daric left the Navy hangar and made his way back to the airport office, where his sister was bound to be furious for his untimely delay.

"It's about time. What took you so long?" Daric was right. Dani was upset.

"I caught someone in the hangar," Daric said.

"Who?" Dani asked abruptly.

"Well, I didn't actually catch him. There was someone around the plane when I got there, but he ran out the back door. I didn't even get a good look at him. And he had to break the lock on the door to get into the hangar."

"What was he doing around the airplane?"

"I don't know, but I know I don't like it. Something just doesn't feel right. Strange thing, though; he was wearing Navy fatigues. So why would he need to run away when he saw me?"

"Well, not much we can do about it now. Come on. Paul and Terry are waiting in the car. We have to get to the Pier." Dani ushered Daric over to the waiting car.

36

THE S.S. MALOLO, Hawaiian for "flying fish" was as long as two city blocks and was the widest ship afloat at eighty-three feet. She was also known as one of the world's fastest passenger ships with her top speed at twenty-one knots. Her superstructure was all white, with two masts and two tall yellow funnels, whose tops were ringed in black. Just below the black, each funnel was emblazoned with a blue "M", the traditional logo of the Matson Lines. She was considered the most luxurious liner to have been built in the United States.

The late afternoon sun shining on the ship's gleaming white hull was in stark contrast to the dark waters in whose arms it was being cradled. The pier was a bustle of freight, cargo, passengers and well-wishers. Paul had parked the car and was carrying Terry's luggage to the boarding ramp. Dani and Daric were a few paces ahead of them.

Before Daric boarded, he felt he needed to tell Paul about the intruder.

"Paul, there was someone in the hangar when I went back to get my hat. When he saw me, he ran out the back door which has always been locked. I don't know who he was or what he was doing there, but I thought you should know."

"It was probably just one of the maintenance guys," Paul offered.

"Then, why did he run when he saw me, and why was the lock on the back door broken?" Daric countered.

"Don't worry about it, Daric, everything will be fine. Come on, now, you need to get on board and I need to say goodbye to Terry," Paul reassured. He was getting a little impatient since he wanted to spend these last few minutes with his fiancée in relative privacy.

"I just have a strange feeling, that's all." Then, Daric suddenly realized he had told no one about Burbank.

"And there was this guy in the United Air Services hangar, too. I found him in a storage room with the lights off. He gave me an explanation I thought made sense at the time, but now I'm not so sure," Daric persisted.

"Look, I'll mention it to Bo. He'll keep a close eye on the Electra. And I'll even ask the base commander to put an extra detail on the hangar. Okay?" Paul asked pointedly.

"I guess," Daric conceded; he knew he couldn't do anything more. "See you in Honolulu, Paul. Have a safe flight."

Daric walked away, meeting up with his sister at the base of the boarding ramp. They were waiting for Terry to join them before they boarded.

"It's a good thing security isn't anything like it is today . . . I mean back home or we'd never get aboard," Dani whispered.

"Never get aboard?" Terry had overheard the last part of the conversation. Terry Minor was a little slip of a thing; at five-foot-two, she would barely tip one-hundred pounds on the scale, even soaking wet. She had flaming-red shoulder-length hair and sea-green eyes.

"I said if we don't hurry, we'll never get aboard," Dani replied as they ascended the ramp, thankful she was a quick thinker.

37

HAVING STOWED THEIR luggage in their adjoining cabins, Dani, Daric and Terry made their way back up on deck for the casting-off ceremony.

Terry quickly spotted Paul in the mass of people lining the pier, all there to wish their friends and family a safe voyage. Paul was standing just to the left of the boarding ramp's base. Terry frantically waved and blew him kisses.

Dani was fascinated by the ritual of ship departures; even to this day, it was still a huge deal. Her eyes were scanning the entire pier, trying to take it all in: the impeccably dressed men; the glamorously dressed women; the deckhands, manning the ropes that secured the ship to the pier; the ship's crew in dress-whites, preparing to swing the boarding ramp alongside the ship. The activity stopped abruptly, as a man made a dash for the ship, yelling something Dani couldn't hear. The crew re-secured the ramp, and one of the ship's officers checked the man's boarding pass before allowing him access to the ramp.

Dani stared at the man for what seemed to be minutes but was, in fact, only seconds, as he dashed up the ramp and disappeared into the bowels of the ship. Then it hit her and a gasp escaped her lips.

"What?" Daric asked when he heard Dani gasp. He had been gazing at the "Mare's Tails" in the evening sky, recognizing the telltale signs that the weather, over the next few days, would not be favourable.

"You're not going to believe me if I tell you," Dani replied. There had been a lot going on and she must have been mistaken. Her eyes must have been playing tricks on her. Or the fading light might have been affecting her vision.

"Try me. I'd believe anything right now," Daric grumbled.

"Okay, but I warned you," Dani started, taking a deep breath before continuing. "I thought I just saw Uncle Richard run up the boarding ramp."

Daric spun around and grabbed his sister's arms. "What did you say?" he demanded.

"Ouch, take it easy. What's gotten into you? You've been out of sorts ever since we left the airport," Dani scolded. Something was bothering Daric; she could clearly see that now.

Before Daric could answer or pursue his inquiry, the ship's horn thundered, announcing their departure and preventing further conversation. Amidst the deafening noise, the ship pulled away from the pier and pointed out to sea.

"Come on," Daric yelled to be heard above the noise, as he dragged his sister through the crowd packed on the Promenade Deck.

Sunday, March 14, 1937

38

AFTER LEAVING THE hotel early in the morning, G.P. and Amelia drove through a light drizzle to the Oakland Airport administration building to get the latest weather forecast from Bill Miller. It was plain to see from the color of the sky that the weather did not look favourable.

"Sorry to have to tell you this, folks, but, the *Shoshone* is reporting brisk headwinds for 1,500 miles en route to Honolulu and crosswinds from the north the rest of the way," Bill Miller reported glumly.

"That's not good," G.P. said.

"No, it's not," Amelia concurred.

"On a more positive note, I also received a message from the Coast Guard in Honolulu. They said they have completed all three runways on Howland Island," Bill said.

"That's fantastic. It gives us more options for landing, depending on speed and wind direction," Amelia said. "Bill, could you send a cable, on my behalf, thanking the Coast Guard and the *Shoshone* for their generous cooperation?"

"I'll get right on it." Bill left for the communications office to get Amelia's cable out.

"We'll have to tell the press outside we're delaying the flight until tomorrow," G.P. said disappointedly.

"I'll go speak to them," Amelia offered, leaving the office.

Amelia met with the press outside the administration building. She informed them of the delay and apologized for causing them to come all the way out here and not get the story they wanted: the start of her world flight.

"Miss Earhart, are you disappointed with the delay?" a reporter asked.

Amelia thought seriously for a moment before answering. "I'm anxious to get started, but I'm too old a hand at this game to be impatient over necessary delays."

After answering a few more questions, Amelia met G.P. and returned to the hotel. There was nothing they could do now but wait to see what tomorrow brought.

Back at the hotel, Amelia rested while G.P. made a few telephone calls.

I hope the strong winds don't make too rough a crossing for Dani, Daric and Terry, Amelia thought.

39

THE SEAS HAD been rough all night and today wasn't much better. Poor Terry had spent the entire trip, so far, in her cabin, seasick. Even though it was the widest ship on the seas, modern-day stabilizers were still a thing of the future. What made it even worse was that Paul had booked them on one of the cheapest fares, E-Deck, in Tourist Class; as a result, they didn't have private bathrooms.

The *S.S. Malolo* accommodated four-hundred-fifty-seven First Class and one-hundred-sixty-three Tourist Class passengers in ultimate style and comfort. While not a large ship, she was spacious. Public rooms in both classes were elegant; their walls were lined with fine timbers complemented by subdued colors and luxurious furnishings. *The S.S. Malolo* was one of the first liners to have an indoor swimming pool, which had become a popular feature of the ship. The liner also offered hula classes on deck, open-air buffets, and a carefree Polynesian lifestyle.

Dani and Terry shared a cabin; Daric's was right next door. Furnishings in the rooms were simple but adequate: two twin beds, a dressing table with a mirror, and a padded wooden chair. The only source of natural light was a small porthole.

The ship had an automatic ventilation system. The system

had powerful air blowers that drew in and distributed fresh air throughout all public rooms and staterooms below. All the air in the ship was replaced every three minutes.

Dani and Daric felt badly for Terry. They didn't like to see her seasick and confined to her cabin; it was no way to enjoy the trip to Honolulu. At the same time, however, they recognized that Terry's condition made it easier for them to talk privately. And Daric wanted to talk. He had a burning desire to find out whether the man he had met in the hangar and the man Dani had seen boarding the ship were one and the same person. He firmly believed they were.

While Terry tried to get some rest, Dani and Daric got together in Daric's cabin next door. It was Daric who spoke first. "If this were back home, we'd never get access to the passenger list on a ship. Here, they provide it freely to every passenger," Daric observed as he scanned the list for one name in particular.

"The thinking was that if you knew who was on the voyage with you, it would encourage social interaction and create a family-like environment," Dani volunteered.

"You're just a fountain of information, aren't you?" Daric muttered absent-mindedly.

"Here he is!" Daric cried excitedly. "Rick Barak Case. That's him. That's the same name he gave me in Burbank. It has to be the same guy."

"We've been on board for over a day and I haven't seen him anywhere," Daric continued. "Have you seen him since we left San Francisco?"

"No, but he may be in First Class. You know how they hate us lower-class passengers mingling with the upper crust. But we could try wandering around the Promenade Deck and some of the common areas over the next few days to see if we can spot him," Dani suggested.

"I need to get some answers," Daric said stubbornly. "Like when he left Burbank, and when he got to Oakland, and whether that was him in the Navy hangar and, if it was, why?"

"Let's take this one step at a time. If he's that shifty, he could be dangerous," Dani cautioned.

"If he's up to something, and it affects Amelia, we have to find out . . . and soon. We don't know how long we'll be in this time period. Dad could pull us home at any moment, without warning," Daric said resolutely.

"Wait, you said he's a smoker, didn't you?" Dani had just got a great idea. "So, let's go check out the Smoking Room."

40

THE MORNING'S ROUTINE was the same as it had been yesterday. G.P. and Amelia left the hotel early for Bill Miller's office to get the latest weather report. This morning, however, the reporters had caught them outside their hotel.

"Is today the day, Miss Earhart?" one reporter asked.

"We're ready to go," G.P. interjected. "All that remains to be done is to arrange for some lunch and fill the Thermos bottles."

"Pilots often say it's better to be on the ground wishing you could be flying, than in the air, flying but wishing you were on the ground," Amelia said jauntily. "We're heading to the airport now to check on the latest weather report. That will tell us whether we'll be going today."

When G.P. and Amelia arrived at Bill Miller's office, Harry and Paul were already there.

"I talked with Pan American Airways this morning," Bill said. "They said the weather has changed little since yesterday. Their regular Hawaii Clipper flight had to return to Alameda due to strong headwinds."

"If their regular flight was recalled, that would mean the Sikorsky Clipper will be grounded, too," G.P. rationalized.

"Which also means Pan American Airways will now have two

Clippers heading to Hawaii, both having to leave before us, when we're finally able to get going," Amelia complained.

"So, I guess we sit tight for another day and try again tomorrow," Paul concluded.

"I hate these delays," Harry mumbled.

The others, while not vocalizing their disappointment, had to agree with Harry.

41

THE SMOKING ROOM was a traditional-style lounge, but with a British feel. The walls were clad in beautiful timber; the wall at the far end was adorned with an elegant fireplace with a clock poised on the mantle above. The room featured a central domed ceiling with a timber feature and grand pillars dividing the room into sections. The furnishings were more casual than those in the First-Class lounge; sofas and lounge chairs with light-colored-floral-patterned upholstery, tables with checkered tablecloths, and quaint timber chairs. Light fixtures hung along all the walls, complemented by lights along the ceiling's perimeter.

Case was sitting by himself, partially obscured by one of the palms scattered throughout the Smoking Room. He had no desire to socialize with his fellow passengers. He just wanted to remain inconspicuous and get to Honolulu to finish his assignment. He pulled a cigarette from its pack and, snapping his thumbnail across the head of a wooden match, ignited the match before proceeding to light the cigarette. He took a deep drag. He exhaled slowly, luxuriating in the intoxication of his smoke.

Dani and Daric got into the Fore express elevator at E-Deck. They were going up to A-Deck, which was devoted exclusively to public rooms. It boasted a succession of grand galleries leading from the Library through the Lounge and the Smoking Room to the Veranda Café. Arriving at A-Deck, Dani and Daric exited the elevator and made their way aft, through the galleries toward the Smoking Room.

"How are we going to approach him without spooking him first, if we see him at all, that is?" Daric asked uncertainly. Now that he was this close to possibly confronting the man who kept popping up unexpectedly, Daric wasn't at all sure what to do.

"Let's just wait and see if he's here. He may not even remember you," Dani offered.

Case could see the two young people heading his way. He immediately recognized them. One had been in the Cadillac that he'd tried to run off the road. The other was the pest that kept turning up in the hangars.

Daric held the door open for his sister as they entered the haze-filled room.

Case couldn't afford to be seen by them. He snuffed out his cigarette in the ashtray and hastily departed through the door at the other end of the lounge.

"Dani, that's him," Daric whispered.

"Let's go." Dani started toward the back of the Smoking Room, passing the spot where Case had been enjoying his cigarette.

"There's that odor again," Daric said. "I smell that every time he's around. Must be the brand he's smoking. If nothing else, it proves to me that it's been the same guy in the two places I've run into him previously. But I still don't know what he's up to."

"Well, he sure must have recognized you, cause he just high-tailed it outta here and disappeared down the back stairs. We'll never catch him now." Dani sighed.

"We still have a couple of days. Let's keep looking. He may turn up again," Daric offered.

"Okay. Let's go back and check on Terry," Dani proposed as they left the room the way they had entered. "I think she's feeling better. She said she might even join us for dinner tonight."

Case had been hiding in the aft stairwell, waiting for them to leave. *That was too close,* he thought.

I'd better stay out of sight for the rest of the voyage. I don't want to run into them again, he concluded. He made his way down to the deck below and disappeared into his stateroom.

42

AS HE STARED out the cabin's porthole, Daric was determined to find Case before the ship docked in Honolulu the next evening. After that, Case would leave the ship and would be impossible to find, like trying to find a diamond in a bucket of ice cubes. As long as he was onboard the S.S. *Malolo*, Case was trapped, and Daric strongly believed it was only a matter of time before their paths would cross again.

Dani had left the cabin a few minutes earlier with Terry. She was going to show Terry the ship, since Terry had spent most of the voyage, so far, in her cabin; she had been out for only a couple of hours last night for dinner.

Daric had told his sister he was going to go up to the Promenade Deck to enjoy the fresh tropical breezes and to take in a few rays of sun. In fact, he had no intention of going there. He had quite a different plan in mind, one he had kept to himself. He was sure Dani would have objected strongly if she had known about it

Daric opened his cabin door and checked the hallway to make sure Dani and Terry were gone. He knew they had been planning to head toward the bow to take the Fore elevator to A-Deck. He made his way toward the stern where, instead of taking the elevator, he took the stairs. His plan was to stop at every deck to check the halls. He would eventually make his way up to A-Deck and the Smoking Room, where they had first found Case. This time Daric would be blocking the back exit.

Daric had checked all the decks and, so far, he had found nothing. He thought it quite strange that he hadn't seen or passed anyone else using the stairs. He guessed that everyone was enjoying the express elevators: they certainly made getting around the ship much easier and faster.

As Daric rounded the last corner to the final flight of stairs to A-Deck, he smelt something. It was a faint odor . . . and it registered just a fraction of a second too late.

43

WHEN G.P. AND Amelia arrived at Bill Miller's office in the morning, it was under rain-laden cloud-filled skies.

"The meteorologist is predicting that the rain showers will lessen and that the weather en route to Honolulu will become more favorable over the next twenty-four hours," Bill told them. Harry was already in Bill's office, when G.P. and Amelia arrived.

"I also just got off the telephone with Pan American Airways and they informed me they were delaying their two Clipper flights for another day. They hope to reschedule both flights for tomorrow afternoon," Bill explained.

Paul came into the office and caught the tail end of Bill's message.

"I was just out inspecting the runways, and another day would allow them to dry out some more. If the weather forecast is correct, and the rain stops, it would allow us to take off without any problems," Paul said confidently.

"Okay. Let's say we reschedule for tomorrow. We want to land in Honolulu just after dawn. With no headwind, our flight time should be about sixteen hours," Harry said. "If we leave here at 5:00 P.M., we would be in Honolulu at 9:00 A.M. Taking into account the two-and-a-half-hour time difference, that would make it 6:30

A.M. Honolulu time, just after sunrise."

"So, let's plan on leaving here around 5:00 P.M.," Amelia said. "We'll need to touch base with Pan American to make sure their flights have departed before 4:30 P.M. at the latest."

"I'm on it," Bill said eagerly.

Everyone could feel the excitement in the room. The adventure was about to begin, finally. And the weather was, at last, going to cooperate for them.

"Bill, can you also contact the Coast Guard and ask them to notify the team that with the improving weather conditions, we will be making our departure from Oakland on March 17th?" Amelia asked.

Back at the Oakland Airport Inn, Amelia held a press conference.

"The weather conditions are predicted to steadily improve over the next twenty-four hours and also en route to Honolulu. We are delaying our departure until tomorrow afternoon at 5:00 P.M. This delay will also give the runway extra time to dry out and, we believe, it will then be able to handle our heavy takeoff load."

44

THAT DAMN KID, Case thought. He had heard someone coming up the stairs and had spotted Daric two flights below; he realized he wouldn't get past the kid this time. And he couldn't retreat to A-Deck, where, a few minutes before, he had seen the kid's sister with a friend. They had been heading toward the Smoking Room, forcing him to head down the back stairs, as he had done the last time. He never dreamt he'd get caught in a squeeze. Now, he was out of options.

Timing was everything. Case couldn't risk being seen. He looked up the last few stairs to the A-Deck entrance; no one was there. *Here goes.* He committed himself; there was no turning back now.

Case reached under his jacket and pulled out his M1911 single-action, semi-automatic, 45-caliber handgun. Flipping his grip to the barrel, he swung his arm out around the blind corner, with deadly force.

The gun butt caught Daric on the side of the head, flipping him backwards and tumbling down the flight of stairs he had just ascended. He came to rest, motionless, in a heap on the B-Deck landing.

Case made his way down to see whether his attack had

produced the results he had hoped for. *That would be one problem taken care of,* he thought. As he bent down to check Daric's pulse, he heard voices coming down the stairs from A-Deck. He quickly abandoned his efforts and fled down two flights and exited onto D-Deck. He could hear someone shouting for help as the sound echoed down the stairwell.

Case sped up his pace toward the Fore elevator, but not too quickly; he didn't want to draw any attention to himself. He took the elevator back up to B-Deck and back to the security of his stateroom.

Case would have to catch some ship gossip later to discover the kid's condition. Thank God he would be able to get off this confining ship tomorrow.

45

DANI AND TERRY had returned to their cabin over an hour ago. They had expected to catch up with Daric on the Promenade Deck, but he had been nowhere to be found. So, they had returned to E-Deck to check his cabin. They had knocked on his door. There was no answer.

"It's almost time for dinner and Daric never misses a good meal," Dani grumbled. "And he still has to get cleaned up and changed before we can go to the dining room." A gentle knock came at the door. "It's about time. We're going to be late for dinner," she finished, as she pulled open the door. Standing there was the ship's third mate.

"Miss Dani Delaney?" he asked softly.

"Yes," Dani replied, hesitantly to the young man in uniform at her doorway.

"There's been an accident, miss. Will you come with me?"

"Accident? What kind of accident?" Dani asked nervously.

"Would you please follow me, miss? The doctor will give you the details."

"It's Daric, isn't it? What happened to him?" Dani asked frantically. "Tell me."

"Miss, please. I don't have any information for you," the third mate pleaded. He hated this part of his job: dealing with hysterical women.

"Fine. Let's go," Dani said firmly. "Terry, why don't you go ahead with dinner? I don't know how long I'm going to be."

"Are you kidding? How could I possibly think about eating at a time like this? I'm coming with you," she stated decisively.

"I'm sorry, miss," the third mate said to Terry holding up his hand. "I was sent to bring Miss Delaney and only Miss Delaney to the infirmary," he stated with finality. "Please follow me," he said to Dani as he walked down the long hallway.

"Terry, I'll let you know what's going on as soon as I can," Dani called over her shoulder as she hurried to keep pace with the third mate, who was determined to finish this assignment as quickly as possible.

The third mate wound his way through the bowels of the ship. Since he refused to utter another word, Dani eventually stopped asking him questions. She resigned herself to the fact that she would have to wait and get the answers from the doctor. It seemed to be taking forever to get to the infirmary, but she knew she was just anxious and that it had actually been only a few minutes.

Dani just hoped it wasn't anything serious. Her brother had a tendency of getting into trouble, always reacting before thinking things through. It had gotten him into more trouble growing up than she cared to recall right now.

Dani hadn't been to this deck on her previous explorations of the ship. The infirmary was in the bow section of F-Deck. The third mate opened the door and ushered Dani in. Once she had entered, he closed the door behind her and left to fulfil his more important duties. She was alone in a small outer room which doubled as a reception area and as the doctor's office.

The doctor must have heard the door close. He appeared from behind a small divider curtain. "Miss Delaney?" he asked.

"Yes," Dani stuttered. "Is my brother here? Is he all right?"

"I hate to have to tell you this, but there's been an accident," the doctor started kindly.

"Where is he?" she demanded frantically. "I want to see him, now!"

"Miss Delaney, please, keep your voice down," the doctor said firmly but softly. "He's resting quietly, now. Come. Sit. I'll tell you what I know." The doctor gently took Dani's arm and helped her into one of the few chairs in the outer room. She had calmed somewhat after hearing that Daric was resting, her worst fears abated.

"Miss Delaney . . .," the doctor started again.

"Dani, please," she offered.

"Dani, it would appear that your brother fell down a flight of stairs, hit his head, and lost consciousness. He has a rather nasty lump on the right side of his head, near his temple. If he had struck his head an inch lower, the blow would have killed him. He's suffered some bruising from the fall, but nothing appears broken. But he does have a concussion."

"Can I see him?" Dani asked, relieved.

"Sure," the doctor said. "Come with me."

Dani followed the doctor behind the divider curtain. Daric was lying on a small metal gurney. His body was draped in a soft white blanket.

"Once he wakes up again, I'll reassess his condition. If there's nothing broken, he should be able to return to his cabin, provided someone stays with him. He'll have to be awakened every two hours because of his concussion to make sure he returns to normal consciousness," the doctor said sternly.

"I'll take care of him, Doctor," Dani assured him, looking tenderly at her motionless brother. "Wait . . . what do you mean, 'when he wakes up *again*'?" Dani asked.

"We had to wait until he regained consciousness to find out who he was. He wasn't carrying any identification," the doctor stated bluntly. "That was the only way we were able to know whom he was travelling with. Once we had determined that, we contacted you."

"How long has he been here?" Dani wondered.

"He was found in the stairwell at 1:45 P.M.," the doctor replied, checking the wall clock. "He's been here for four hours."

"I noticed his bracelet, with the medical symbol on it. Is he in the medical profession?" the doctor inquired.

"Actually, the symbol is a caduceus, the staff of the Greek god Hermes and not the rod of Asclepius." Dani knew the US Army Medical Corps had chosen the caduceus as their medical symbol, but in fact it was the staff with a single intertwined snake that was the true medical symbol. "And, no, he's not in the medical profession." Dani revealed hers. "The bracelets were gifts from our parents."

"I guess that would also explain the 'H'," the doctor mused.

Present Day

46

"PROFESSOR?" A VOICE whispered in the dark. "Professor?"

Quinn was jolted from a restless sleep. "What is it? What happened?" he asked tiredly as he reached for the lamp on the bedside table.

"Quinn, what is it?" Sandra mumbled, still half asleep.

"Things have changed, Professor. You told me to report any changes in vital signs," the voice continued.

"Hermes, report!" Quinn demanded, snapping fully awake instantly.

"Oh my God, the kids," Sandra cried. "Are they all right?"

Quinn activated the hologram on his comm and Hermes appeared.

"Awroooo," Bear yowled as she sprang from her prone position, scanning the bedroom for the intruder.

Both Quinn and Sandra were now sitting up in bed, staring intently at the three-dimensional image of Hermes. They were waiting anxiously for his report.

"Professor, I first noticed a sudden and significant decrease in Daric's respiratory rate. I didn't think it was anything at the time. But shortly thereafter, I received signals from Dani's band. They indicated a sudden spike in heart rate and an increase in her blood pressure."

Having located the intruder, Bear approached cautiously and stuck her nose close to Hermes. The image wavered and distorted, startling Bear and resulting in another vocal protest.

"Bear, it's just me, Hermes. It's all right, girl, go back to bed," he said in a gentle assuring voice.

"Analyse," Quinn instructed.

"I speculate that Daric lost consciousness; I cannot tell why since I lack sufficient data. The sudden change in Dani's vital signs could be attributed to her reaction to that event," Hermes supplied.

"Oh my God," Sandra murmured.

Bear could not detect any strange scent and, from her family's reaction to the intruder, she realized her family wasn't in any danger. She returned to her spot in front of the French doors to continue her watch for Dani and Daric's return. She curled up in a ball, placing her head on top of her front paws and stared out into the darkness of the night.

"Speculate," Quinn ordered.

"I hypothesize that Daric fell and hit his head or that someone hit him, resulting in his loss of consciousness and causing the sudden drop in his respiratory rate. I further hypothesize that the injury did not result in any significant blood loss since there was no change in his blood pressure. I therefore conclude that there was no subdural hemorrhage, and that there was a concussive traumatic brain injury," Hermes said flatly.

"Based on the aforementioned, I assert confidently that the change in Dani's vital signs was an emotional reaction to learning of Daric's injury. Such a reaction would be the logical human female response to trauma," Hermes finished.

"And now?" Quinn asked.

Hermes paused momentarily before responding. "All vital signs have returned to normal. Whatever the problem was, it is no longer an issue."

"Sandra?" Quinn asked, looking at Sandra, who was just staring blankly at Hermes.

"Oh, yeah. Uh, it sounds plausible. I mean, from what the vital signs read and from what Hermes said, it makes sense," Sandra said dazedly. "I wish we knew for certain."

"At least, they're all right," Quinn said softly.

47

THE NEW DAY looked no different from the previous few days. The weather was overcast and, more importantly, it was still raining, with no apparent breaks in the cloud cover. It did not look promising for the start of the 27,000-mile world flight. And Amelia and her team were already two days behind schedule.

A little disappointed with the way the day was starting, G.P. and Amelia made their daily trek out to the Oakland Airport administration building and Bill Miller's office to get the latest weather report.

Bill saw them coming down the hall and rushed out to meet them. "I know, I know, it doesn't look good, right now. But the weather bureau assures me that this weather system is rapidly moving out. It's already moved past the San Francisco Bay Area. They said, by late afternoon, it will have cleared completely," Bill said confidently.

"What about Pan American Airways? Where do they stand?" G.P. asked while they walked into Bill's office. Harry and Paul were already there as usual.

"Pan American has scheduled their regular Hawaiian Clipper for departure from Alameda at 3:00 P.M. and the Sikorsky Clipper to leave at 4:00 P.M.," Bill said.

"Well ahead of our departure time, that's good," Amelia said. "So, if Pan American is flying today, so are we. Let's go check out the runway and see what kind of shape it's in. We have a heavy load it will have to bear if we want to get airborne."

Paul and Amelia left Bill Miller's office and walked the length of the runway. They had placed white flags along the runway which ran from northeast to southwest. The wind was forecast to be blowing out of the southwest today. The Electra would start its takeoff on the concrete apron and run southwesterly down the length of the regular paved runway. If due to its heavy load, the airplane wasn't airborne before the paved runway ended, it would continue along the gravelled runway that had been added to the end of the paved section in 1927 to accommodate the Dole flights to Hawaii. That would give them a total of 4,300 feet of runway, but Paul thought they would need only 3,500 feet.

"The concrete runway is fine, just some small puddles. But the gravel runway has some rather large lakes," Amelia observed.

"When this drizzle stops like it's supposed to, the sun and the wind will help to dry out the gravel enough for us to take off later this afternoon," Paul assured her.

Returning to Bill Miller's office after their inspection, Paul and Amelia ran into a group of reporters. Before anyone could fire off a question, Amelia addressed them.

"We are definitely going today," Amelia said to the cheers of the press, who had been coming to the airport for days just to hear this news and to be here to capture history in the making. "The weather looks fine over the Pacific."

"I've been waiting for four days to start this world flight," Amelia continued. She was finding it difficult to contain the excited grin stretching across her delicate features.

"Are you going to beat your old record for this crossing, Miss Earhart?" a reporter asked.

"I don't want to push the engines on the crossing to Hawaii, so I will not be attempting to break any speed records. With our heavy fuel load, I'd be happy to maintain a speed of one-hundred-fifty miles per hour. I'd rather have the engines in good shape for the flight over India. See you all later today." Amelia concluded her press address. She turned and made her way with Paul back to Bill Miller's office.

Bill reported that he had received the noon ship positions and weather reports. The reports stated the flight would encounter crosswinds on the first three-hundred miles, with a tailwind of approximately fifteen miles per hour on the remainder of the flight. Amelia would have to take these factors into consideration since the tailwind would increase their ground speed.

When G.P., Amelia, Paul and Harry left the airport for the hotel to collect their belongings and to pick up Fred, hundreds of spectators were already streaming into the airport to watch Amelia take off. Police officers had been assigned to direct the steady flow of traffic and to keep the crowds away from the runway.

"This is going to be a circus," Harry muttered.

48

TERRY AND DANI had been taking turns watching Daric sleep. Terry had taken the first shift while Dani had slept fitfully in the other bed. Every two hours, she had reached over and gently nudged Daric until he had awakened. He had stayed awake for only a few minutes before returning to the land of slumber.

Now it was Dani's turn to watch her brother. It had been a long night, but Daric was gradually staying awake for longer periods. Dani checked the clock in the cabin. It was 6:00 A.M. and time to wake her brother again.

"Daric," Dani whispered while gently shaking his shoulder. "Daric."

"What time is it?" he mumbled groggily.

"It's six in the morning. How do you feel?"

"I've got one hell of a headache, but, besides that, not too bad."

"The doctor said you'd have a nasty one. He gave me some pills he said you could have in the morning. Let me get you some water." Dani rose from her chair to get the pitcher from the dressing table.

"Not a great way to start off our birthday," he mumbled quietly.

"What?"

"Today is March 17th; the year may not be right, but the day is. So, happy birthday, sis," Daric said, a smile etched across his handsome face. He had pulled himself up to a sitting position to take the water and pills from Dani.

"Happy birthday to you, too, bro." Dani leaned over and gave Daric a peck on the cheek.

Daric looked across at the other bed and saw Terry's prone and rumpled form. "Has she been here all night?" he asked, fretfully.

"Yeah. We took shifts. She wanted the first one which was most of the night," Dani supplied quietly.

Daric grasped Dani's hand and pulled her closer, so he could keep his voice low. He didn't want Terry to overhear what he was going to say. "What did they tell you happened?"

"They said you had an accident, that you fell down the stairs and hit your head."

"It was no accident. I was attacked."

"What?" Dani exclaimed.

"I was walking up the aft stairs, stopping at each deck, looking for Case." Daric quickly held up his hand to stop his sister's predicable protest. "I know, but I did it anyway. As I was saying, I was about to climb the last set of stairs to A-Deck when I caught that odor again. Next thing I know, I'm lying on a bed in the infirmary."

"You don't think . . ." Dani started.

"I don't have to think . . . I know! It was Case. He hit me," Daric persisted.

"But why? Why would he attack you?" Dani wasn't convinced.

"He must have some reason. Maybe he's trying to stop me, from what I'm not sure."

"The doctor said if that hit on your head had been an inch lower, it would have killed you. Daric, I don't like this. If it was Case, he's dangerous; we need to stay clear of him," she pleaded, knowing full well Daric wasn't going to drop this.

49

IT WAS JUST after 3:00 P.M. when G.P., Amelia and Fred returned to the airport. The Navy men had helped Bo McKneely push the Electra out of the hangar onto the apron and were helping with the plane's fueling. Paul was already in the cockpit supervising the procedure.

G.P. and Amelia dropped Fred at the hangar and continued on to Bill Miller's office for the latest update from Pan American Airways. Bill told them that the Hawaii Clipper had left Alameda at 3:13 P.M. and the Sikorsky was still on schedule to leave at 4:00 P.M.

"Well, it looks like we're all set to go," Amelia said excitedly.

"Not without the pilot," G.P. teased. "Come on, let's get you out to your plane."

G.P. drove Amelia to the Electra, past the hundreds of spectators lining the runway. It was a quiet ride inside the car, both lost in their own thoughts. G.P. pulled the car over in front of the hangar. He turned to Amelia and reached over to gently fold her hands into his.

"Come back to me," G.P. whispered tenderly.

"Always." Amelia leaned over and gave him a peck on the cheek, then let herself out of the car. G.P. slowly extracted himself and walked around the car toward the plane, a few paces behind Amelia.

As Amelia walked toward the airplane, she spotted a little girl wearing a pale blue dress with matching ribbons tied in her pigtails. She walked over and noticed the little girl was clutching a tattered copy of her autobiography titled *The Fun of It*.

"Hey there," Amelia said, bending down.

The little girl was dumbstruck. Here was her idol standing, or rather crouching, in front of her and she was actually addressing *her*, out of all the people who had come out here to see Amelia take off. The crowd went silent, waiting for the child to respond, but she only stood there, wide-eyed, open-mouthed, and staring into the blue eyes of her hero.

Finally the girl leaned in closer to Amelia, who responded in kind, to hear the little voice whisper, "I'm going to fly like you some day."

Amelia was delighted. She hugged the girl who giggled with glee. Amelia stood up and reached for a pen in her jacket pocket. She gently pried the little girl's prized possession from her arms, opened the cover and started to write. She paused briefly and asked, "What's your name?"

"Helen; Helen Hammond."

Amelia finished writing in the book and returned it to Helen. She gently squeezed Helen's shoulder, then turned and made her way down the apron toward the Electra.

Helen watched for a few moments as her hero walked away, seemingly swallowed up by the crowd of spectators and reporters. Only then did she look down at the book in her hands. She carefully opened the cover and read the inscription:

You haven't seen a tree until you've seen its shadow from the sky.
Remember to have fun, Helen.
Your friend, Amelia.

Helen looked up, staring in the direction where Amelia had disappeared. A tiny tear trickling down her soft cheeks glistened in the late afternoon sunlight.

By the time Amelia reached the airplane, Harry and Fred were already in the rear cabin compartment. Paul was in the cockpit's co-pilot seat. Everyone was waiting for her.

The rain had finally stopped. For the first time in over four days, the sun had finally broken through the clouds.

This is it, Amelia thought, as she performed the final walk-about of her aircraft: the pre-flight inspection. She knew Paul, as her co-pilot, would have meticulously completed the inspection for her, but she wanted to be thorough. Besides, it was an ingrained habit.

The sunlight reflected off the all-metal, silver skin of the Electra. The leading edge of the wings was painted a deep red, with a matching swatch across the middle of the twin tail fins and rudder. This tail configuration would later become a Lockheed trademark.

Etched in bold black letters across the upper part of the right wing and the undercarriage of the left wing was the plane's registration number: NR16020. Amelia ran her hand along the trailing-edge of the wing flaps. It was almost as if it were a lover's caress.

The engines had the low-drag NACA engine cowlings and had two-bladed controllable-pitch propellers. Amelia checked to make sure that there were no obstructions and that the pitot tubes were clear. The pitot tubes operated a system of pressure-sensitive instruments, including the aircraft's airspeed, altitude, and vertical speed indicators.

After checking the landing gear, which was a conventional tail-dragger arrangement, Amelia made her way back to the rear cabin door. G.P. was waiting patiently there for her. She gave him a quick hug and said shyly, "See ya," as she entered the airplane.

Fred was sitting at the navigator's table, across from the cabin door. He had a shamrock pinned on his jacket to commemorate Saint Patrick's Day and his Irish heritage. Harry was sitting against the opposite wall, strapped in and ready to go.

Amelia made her way along the top of the fuselage tanks to the cockpit. She carefully swung herself around and came off the top of the tanks into the left pilot's seat.

"The 4:00 P.M. weather report says the wind is out of the southwest at fourteen miles an hour and the current temperature is forty-eight degrees Fahrenheit," Paul said, relating the latest conditions. "We'll have more than enough room for takeoff with that headwind."

Amelia settled into the pilot's seat. While she checked the instruments to ensure they were properly set, Paul continued with his briefing.

"I oversaw the fueling of the Electra. We have nine-hundred-forty-seven gallons on board. And Bill just reported that the Sikorsky Clipper took off at 4:21 P.M.," Paul concluded. "So, that means we are cleared to go, whenever you're ready."

"I guess we're all set, then," Amelia said confidently. "Let's do it."

Paul yelled out his open window, "Clear!" And they started the engines.

The crowd of over three-thousand, who had come to witness history and had been gathering since early morning, erupted into an ecstatic cheer. Amelia grinned and tossed them a wave out her window, acknowledging their enthusiasm and encouragement.

Amelia received the all-clear signal. "Here we go," she yelled, struggling to be heard over the roar of the engines. Fred and Harry both gave her a thumbs-up, which she returned.

Amelia gradually advanced the throttles just enough to get the Electra moving. She slowly taxied the Electra along the apron over to the northeast corner of the field. When the airplane came to the end of the marked runway, she lined up facing southwest, keeping the flags to her left. Paul and Amelia ran the final check on the engines, propellers, controls, trim tabs, gas selector and flaps. Paul reset the directional gyro compass to match the wet compass. They were finally ready to go.

Paul advanced the throttles evenly as Amelia released the brakes. The plane began rolling down the runway, accelerating as it went. The engines roared louder and louder as they continued to beat in perfect unison.

The plane's wheels plowed through the numerous puddles that dotted the runway, the spray streaking across the fuselage. The Electra gracefully slipped the surly bonds of Earth and was finally airborne. As the plane slowly gained altitude, the landing gear was retracted backwards into the engine nacelles. The Electra was designed so that, after retraction, the bottoms of the wheels remain exposed in case a wheels-up emergency landing was necessary.

G.P. beamed with pride, as he stood and watched Amelia's perfect takeoff in such wet and muddy conditions. He looked down at his stopwatch. It had taken exactly twenty-five seconds from when the plane started moving down the runway until it had got off the ground. Looking at the runway flag markers, he also realized it had used only 1,897 feet of runway.

Back at Bill Miller's office, G.P. sent a message to the Coast Guard in San Francisco. It read:

'MISS EARHART OFFICIAL TAKEOFF FROM OAKLAND AIRPORT FOR HONOLULU IS FOUR THIRTY SEVEN AND A HALF P.M. PACIFIC TIME'.

50

AMELIA STARTED A gradual right turn over the bay toward San Francisco. Once she leveled the wings, she checked the engine instruments. The plane was climbing sluggishly, and she wanted to make sure Paul had set the power correctly. Once they cleared the towers of the west span of the San Francisco Bay Bridge, Amelia gently banked the airplane to the left. Heading westward, they flew over the Golden Gate Bridge, whose burnt-orange color glistened in late afternoon sunlight. Then she headed toward the expansive blue of the Pacific Ocean.

As they were heading out to sea, Amelia took a moment to reflect. It was finally here; the adventure had begun. It had taken over a year to plan and was the costliest adventure she had ever attempted. Over the next few days and weeks, there would be challenges she would have to face and overcome. She was determined to take them on, one by one. She knew it was a once-in-a-lifetime opportunity, and she was ready for it.

It wasn't long before they had caught up to the Sikorsky Clipper, silhouetted against a towering bank of sun-flecked cumulus clouds. The Electra, with its greater speed, gradually overtook the Clipper at 5:40 P.M. Soon it was just a speck in the sky behind them. Amelia reflected for a moment and pulled out her notebook to record her thoughts. *It was the first time I had ever seen another plane at sea. Unusual as such an occurrence is today, before long it doubtless will be as commonplace as passing transports on our continental highways.*

Harry got on the radio to Pan American Airways in Alameda and reported, "All's well." He received a reply by Morse code. It was 6:04 P.M. He scribbled the message on a piece of paper and passed it up to the cockpit using an improvised bamboo fishing pole. His note read: *winds out of the northwest at thirty-five miles an hour, squalls in the area, visibility ten miles.* They were two-hundred-fifty miles out of San Francisco.

Shortly after Harry had passed Pan American's information to Amelia, the right engine began to cough and run rough due to ice forming in the carburetor. Paul adjusted both mixture controls to "rich". At the same time, he opened the carburetor heat valves, which directed heated air into the carburetor. The heat would melt the ice and prevent any further accumulation. Gradually, the engines stabilized.

Amelia was thankful that they had left when they had since it had provided them with a few hours of daylight. With the sky now darkening, she climbed above the cloud layer to 8,000 feet. Paul adjusted the mixture controls and set the engines to climb power.

When the plane reached 8,000 feet, Amelia leveled off and waited until the airspeed indicators were showing one-hundred-thirty miles an hour. At this altitude, the air was less dense, resulting in a true airspeed of approximately one-hundred-fifty miles an hour.

51

THE RAILINGS ALONG the starboard side of the Promenade Deck were lined three deep with passengers as the S.S. *Malolo* sailed into the Honolulu harbor, past the Aloha Tower, which stood as a sentinel across the pier. The sun was slowly sinking into the turquoise sea, as the ship pulled into Pier 8. Hula dancers, musicians and what appeared to be most of the local residents crowded the pier, all on hand to welcome the new visitors to their beautiful island.

Dani and Daric hadn't seen Rick Barak Case since watching him make a hasty exit from the Smoking Room three days ago. He had simply vanished, which suited Dani just fine. She wanted nothing to do with him. Daric, however, had a very different view. He wanted to know what Case was up to and he wouldn't mind getting in a little payback, either.

As Dani and Daric disembarked with Terry, their hosts met them: Chris and Mona Holmes. "Welcome to Honolulu," Mona said, as she placed a lei over each head and a kiss on their cheeks.

Chris and Mona Holmes couldn't have been more opposite. He was tall, with a slender build and sun-baked skin; she was short and rotund with an alabaster complexion.

"Thank you for having us," Terry said, as she accepted the

second lei from Chris.

"We just received a telegram from G.P. saying Amelia left Oakland at 4:37 P.M. this afternoon and they are expected to land here just after dawn tomorrow," Chris said excitedly.

"I would have thought they'd have been here already," Daric responded, sounding a bit puzzled.

"Bad weather caused a delay in the flight. Pan American was grounded, too. They couldn't get away until today," Chris said.

"Well, it's going to be a short night and a very early morning; so, let's get back to the house and get you all settled," Mona offered.

With the visitors following close behind, Chris and Mona made their way to their car: a deep burgundy 1936 Packard Super Eight 1404 convertible. It looked like a car Al Capone would drive. The car was designed as a whole; the body, hood, fenders and running boards were all integrated into a smoothly executed design. It was regarded as one of the most attractive bodies of the era. The Super Eight had a sloped grille with chrome vertical bars that gave the vehicle a unique look. The grille, not only attractive, served as thermostatically controlled shutters that could be opened or closed based on engine heat. A Delco-Remy ignition system fired the eight-cylinder engine under the hood, providing one-hundred-fifty horsepower.

Daric could only stare in awe at the exquisite automobile in front of him. "What a beauty," he murmured.

"Come on," Dani said, pulling him out of his stupor.

They drove to Waikiki, where the estate of Christian R. Holmes, heir to the Fleischmann Yeast fortune, was situated on Kalakaua Avenue at Queen Surf. The estate sat on three acres of majestic beachfront property. A mountain range loomed close behind the estate, creating a stunning backdrop. A unique lava rock wall surrounded the property on three sides with an iron-gated entranceway. It was hard to see through all the foliage and the wall along the perimeter. The estate featured a large main house, a separate guesthouse, orchards, a caretaker's house, a secluded, semi-private beach, and a man-made tidal pool framed by a stone wall which was once a turtle pond.

Chris pulled the Packard up to the front door where they were greeted by the housekeeping staff. "John, can you show Daric and Dani to the guesthouse?" Chris instructed.

"After you've had a chance to freshen up, come back to the house and we'll have dinner, before we call it an early night," Mona offered. "Come on, Terry, I'll show you to your room."

John escorted Daric and Dani to the guesthouse which was located in the southwest corner of the property overlooking the ocean. It quickly became clear that John wasn't much of a conversationalist. The resulting silence suited Daric just fine since he was still nursing a doozy of a headache. It also suited Dani, who was too busy taking in her surroundings and enjoying the tranquility of the moment.

As he watched John walking beside him, Daric couldn't help being reminded of the character Lurch from the Addams Family: tall, stone-faced, square-jawed, quiet, and very daunting. John was also the Holmeses' personal chauffeur, bodyguard, and staff manager.

On arriving at the guesthouse, John opened the front door, walked through and deposited the luggage in the two bedrooms. He returned to the living room area to instruct the Holmeses' guests.

"There's fresh pineapple juice in the refrigerator; please help yourself. Mrs. Holmes will be serving dinner in the main dining room. Enter the house through the front door and turn left at the first room you come to that is the main dining room. Dinner will be served promptly at 8:30. Please be on time," John said as he showed himself out the door to continue with his other duties.

The guesthouse, like the main house, was a Spanish colonial revival-style design. It featured stucco walls, a low-pitched, clay tile roof, and an oceanfront lanai. It had a large main room with a high ceiling. Its two guest bedrooms and two full bathrooms would accommodate four guests. The main room contained a small kitchen which was elevated from the rest of the room.

"Let's do like the man said. We don't want to be late for dinner. Besides, I want to call it an early night. I want to be at the airport before dawn to meet Amelia's plane. I need to tell Paul about our friend Rick Barak Case," Daric said determinedly.

52

DURING THE NIGHT, Fred took continuous star sightings to fix their position. Meanwhile, up front in the confines of a noisy cockpit, Amelia was continually checking the flight and engine instruments, diligently switching the complicated fuel tank system, and meticulously keeping the plane in trim. The Sperry autopilot, which was basically flying the airplane, also needed her constant attention, as the rudder gyro seemed to drift off the desired heading faster than it should.

Although most of her time and energy was devoted to the many details associated with flying the airplane, Amelia found a few moments during the flight to scribble some thoughts in her notebook. It would be a challenge, she thought, to decipher her notes later, because the mild turbulence was making a mockery of her penmanship; nonetheless she persevered.

Even though I have three other people with me on this flight, at times it feels as though I am alone, dancing among the clouds with only my thoughts to keep me company. I have never felt so free and liberated as I do when I am flying. The only limitations I have up here are those that I place upon myself.

At midnight, Harry sent their position over the radio and

reported, "All's well". This time Pan American in Alameda didn't hear him, but for the first time Pan American on Oahu heard the garbled message. Harry quickly scribbled a note and passed the message forward to Amelia in the cockpit. It noted that they were ahead of their dead-reckoned time and were now making one-hundred-eighty miles an hour.

Amelia had still been writing in her notebook when she received Harry's message. She thought for a moment and then wrote: *I truly hope Harry knows what he's talking about.* Putting her notes away for the moment, she referred to Kelly Johnson's power and fuel-burning charts.

It was sometime after 2:00 A.M. when Amelia applied power to climb to their final cruise altitude of 10,000 feet in accordance with the Kelly's charts. His power and fuel-burn calculations were working well so far. It took only a few minutes to level off after the climb, set the trim and adjust the mixture.

The engines coughed again from carburetor icing. Paul enriched the mixture and turned on the carburetor heat. It only took a few moments before the engines settled again.

When Paul finished adjusting the mixture, he and Amelia heard a sound resulting from the propellers turning out of unison. She quickly adjusted the propeller controls to bring the pulsating sound to a stop. But the right propeller didn't respond. She tried to adjust the left propeller and bring it into synchronization with the right one. The sound stopped, but now both propellers were running at 1,600 rpm.

Amelia looked at Paul. They understood the gravity of the situation. If the left engine failed with the right propeller stuck at its current rpm setting, the right engine alone would not provide enough power to get them to Honolulu. They could be in big trouble.

At 2:07 A.M. PST, Fred plotted his next celestial fix on his chart. After making some measurements and calculations, he consulted with Harry, who concurred with Fred's calculations. Harry made his way forward on top of the plywood covered the fuselage fuel tanks.

"Amelia," Harry shouted, "we're still ahead of our dead-reckoned flight time. We have to slow down or we'll arrive in Honolulu before daylight."

"I've never run into the problem of flying too fast before. The tailwind must be stronger than we thought," Amelia yelled.

With the right propeller stuck, Amelia wanted to get to her destination as quickly as possible, but she knew that trying to land the airplane in its current condition before sunrise would only compound the problem. So, she adjusted her airspeed, making sure she wasn't going so slowly that there could be a danger of stalling the airplane.

After flying for roughly eleven hours, Paul informed Amelia, "I need to stretch." He climbed out of his seat and up onto the fuel tanks. He crawled back into the cabin to work the cramped muscles in his legs and to confer with Harry and Fred.

Now that Paul had mentioned it, Amelia realized she was feeling a little stiff, too, and decided a change in position would help. She eased herself out of her seat and slid over into the right-hand seat. After checking the flight and engine instruments again, she settled back to enjoy this short time in the cockpit alone. It reminded her of her previous crossing in 1935.

But all too soon, Paul had made his way up front again. With his seat taken, he twisted his body around and wriggled into the seat Amelia had recently vacated. "It's a lot easier getting out of the cockpit than it is getting back in," he grunted. "I feel like a contortionist."

About an hour later, Fred, using the bamboo fishing pole, passed another message forward to the cockpit. It read: *Sunrise at 6:08 A.M. HST; estimated arrival at 5:45 A.M. HST. There will be enough light for us to land.* Amelia waved her hand to acknowledge Fred's message as she rechecked her heading and airspeed.

Harry was on the radio calling Pan American again for another bearing when the generator ammeter suddenly went into a negative reading. "Now what?" he muttered.

The generator was out. They still had the airplane's battery and the backup battery to keep the electrical equipment operating, hopefully, for the rest of the flight, providing they didn't put too much demand on the batteries.

Paul was still in the pilot's seat at 5:10 A.M. HST when he lowered the nose of the airplane to start their descent. Amelia was busy handling the mixtures and the throttles and adjusting the power during the descent.

Amelia could see the dark outline of the mountainous island off to the right through the smattering of clouds. It was 5:40 A.M. HST when Diamond Head made an appearance through the morning mist, exactly where and when Fred expected, which was comforting.

Paul added some power with the throttles. Waikiki Beach was easily seen in the early morning twilight. At 5:47 A.M., they passed Honolulu and continued north-westwards over Pearl Harbor toward Wheeler Field.

Paul switched on the landing lights, immediately putting a heavy drain on the airplane's battery. The electric motors for the landing gear and flaps would increase that load tremendously. Paul realized that, if they had to go around for another approach at the landing, they might not have enough power left in the battery to retract the landing gear or flaps. He knew he had only one shot at the landing. He was determined to make it a good one.

They were at an altitude of only five-hundred feet when Paul dipped the airplane across Wheeler Field from the southeast. He put the plane into a steep bank to make a tight circle of the field.

"Don't! Don't!" Amelia yelled.

"Damn," he muttered. He quickly reduced the bank angle of the airplane to proceed with a normal flight pattern to complete the landing.

How stupid can I be? Paul thought. He had forgotten that the right propeller was stuck at 1,600 rpm. If he ever needed full power from the right engine during his approach, he could not get it. His stunt-pilot flair for an exciting approach could have cost them dearly.

Amelia checked to make sure the gas selector was turned to the proper tank for landing and that the mixtures were rich. She put the landing gear down on the downwind leg of their approach. She would have also set the propellers to a lower pitch for landing if she could have, but she couldn't. They were going to be coming in fast.

Amelia put the wing flaps part way down when they approached the base leg turn. After flying for a few minutes on base leg, Paul turned to the final approach path. Amelia put on full flaps for the landing.

Paul knew his airspeed was too high as he crossed the edge of the field and put the plane down. The plane bounced back into the air because of the extra speed and the roughness of the landing field. *Not a pretty landing*, Paul thought, in front of all these spectators.

When the plane had settled on the runway and the ground speed had reduced, Paul turned the airplane around and followed the Army crew along the apron to the 75th Service Squadron hangar. Normally, he would have stopped the airplane outside the hangar, but, knowing it required servicing, he decided to taxi it into the hangar before shutting down the engines.

The flight time was officially recorded as fifteen hours, forty-seven-and-a-half minutes from the time the Electra took off in Oakland until its wheels touched down in Honolulu. They had broken the old speed record to Honolulu by more than an hour.

53

WHEELER FIELD WAS dotted with spectators, reporters, photographers, radio announcers and Army personnel. All were gathered there to witness a historic event: Amelia's landing on the first leg of her world flight.

Paul and Amelia worked their way out of the cockpit and down the wing of the airplane. Paul stopped to offer Amelia a hand as she jumped down from the wing's trailing edge. Fred and Harry had already disembarked through the rear cabin door.

Terry ran across the apron, through the hangar doors and leaped into Paul's waiting arms. Behind her were Daric and Dani, followed closely by Chris and Mona Holmes, all offering their congratulations. The Holmeses, following an old Hawaiian tradition, placed leis around the necks of the new arrivals.

After the photographers finished taking their pictures, Amelia addressed the press. "The flight from Oakland was fairly uneventful, and the plane performed perfectly."

"How does it compare to your flight in 1935 from here to Oakland?" one reporter asked.

"The night seemed longer," she replied, resulting in laughter from the gathered crowd.

"When do you leave again, Miss Earhart?"

"We hope to make a daylight landing at Howland Island, which means we would leave either later today or tomorrow morning. Mr. Paul Mantz will remain behind in Hawaii. Mr. Fred Noonan will continue with the flight as far as Howland Island, and Captain Harry Manning will go as far as Darwin, Australia. From there, I'll continue the world flight on my own," Amelia concluded as she thanked them all for coming and then excused herself.

Colonel John C. McDonnell, the commander of Wheeler Field, introduced himself and offered his assistance. "Miss Earhart, is there any maintenance or servicing your aircraft requires?"

"Thank you, Commander. Actually, there is. Paul, could you handle the details with the commander?" Amelia asked.

"Sure thing," Paul replied, as he shook hands with the commander.

"Come on, you guys. Let's get you something to eat, and I'm sure you could all use some rest," Chris Holmes said, as he and Mona ushered Amelia, Fred and Harry to their car. Dani decided to join them, in case she could be of some assistance to Amelia.

"Sounds wonderful, I'm famished. I've had only an orange and one sandwich since leaving Oakland," Amelia said.

The Holmeses had made arrangements for John to return with the car and pick up the others within the hour. Daric wanted to stay behind to hear what needed attending to regarding the Electra. He also hoped to get an opportunity to talk to Paul alone. But, when he glanced over at Paul, as he spoke with the commander, he realized that getting him alone could be a challenge. Terry seemed to be permanently glued to his side.

"For the last six or seven hours coming into Honolulu, we weren't able to change the pitch of the right propeller. It probably needs greasing," Paul suggested as he addressed the commander.

"That explains the hot landing," Daric reasoned.

"Yeah," Paul confirmed and continued with his list of mechanical problems. "Then, the generator didn't show a positive charge during the last part of the flight. I'm sure you'll find that the problem is the generator control box. You can replace the box from our spare parts kit."

The commander was making a list as Paul continued with his servicing requirements. Daric was also taking notes as he listened to the items Paul wanted addressed. He wanted to make sure they handled everything before Amelia took off on the next leg of her world flight. Getting good mechanical service for the Electra at some of the more remote locations along the flight route could prove to be quite difficult, so he wanted to ensure everything was one-hundred percent before the airplane left Honolulu.

"Can you also replace all the spark plugs in both engines with brand-new ones? And one last thing that shouldn't be too much of a chore to fix: the instrument light on the pilot's panel needs to be dimmed. It's too bright when flying at night," Paul finished.

"We'll get right on it. I'll personally supervise the work," the commander assured him as he turned and began yelling orders to his crew, who had been waiting patiently in the hangar for his instructions.

Looking down at his list, Daric couldn't help but wonder. He knew the Electra would have been thoroughly inspected before it left Oakland. Bo would have seen to that. Some items Paul asked for were minor in nature or just routine, but what about the problems with the propeller pitch control and the generator? He knew either one of these, individually, could have severely jeopardized the flight.

54

CASE HAD BEEN watching everything that had happened at Wheeler Field that morning. He had been sufficiently disguised to blend with the press to hear how the flight had gone. He had been just outside the hangar door when Paul talked to the commander about servicing the Electra.

The Holmeses' car was just pulling up to the front of the hangar to pick up Paul, Terry and Daric. Case was within earshot, tucked behind some fuel drums.

"Paul, I'll stay behind and work with the commander to make sure everything on this list gets addressed," Daric said firmly.

"You sure?" Paul asked half-heartedly. If he hadn't been so tired from the long flight, he would have preferred to stay as well. But he was comforted that someone he knew and trusted was watching over the Electra.

"I'm sure," Daric said confidently. He knew he had missed his chance to talk to Paul alone. That would have to wait. But at least he could keep an eye on the Electra and keep a look out for Case, in the event he made another appearance. If Daric pegged him right, he would.

"All right," Paul said. "I'll be back in a couple of hours to check on the progress. I'll bring back some lunch for you."

"Thanks," Daric replied. Turning, he walked past the fuel drums into the hangar to watch the Electra being serviced.

"Damn," Case muttered as he extricated himself from his hiding place. It wasn't surprising to him that Daric had remained behind. He knew this would be his last chance, and no kid would get in his way, not this time.

Case looked around his immediate surroundings, hoping to find a solution to how he would complete his task. An Army supply truck pulled up and parked alongside another hangar about one-hundred yards away. The sole occupant left the vehicle and then opened the small hangar door and disappeared inside.

Case casually made his way to the hangar. He was still dressed like a reporter and, although most of them had already left to file their stories, he didn't appear to be out of place. He leaned in close to the door which had been left ajar, to listen for any conversation that would indicate someone else was in the hangar. When he heard nothing, he took a chance and quietly entered.

Case saw no one at first, in the dim interior. Then he saw the soldier coming out of a supply room, carrying a box.

The soldier, having spotted what he recognized was a reporter, said, "Hey, you're not supposed to be in here."

Case answered somewhat meekly as he walked toward the soldier, quickly closing the distance. "Sorry, I was looking for a restroom. I thought there might be one in here."

"There isn't, but there is one . . ."

The soldier never finished his sentence. Case had reached up, placed both hands firmly on each side of his head and, with a sharp twist, snapped his neck. The soldier didn't even see Case's hands move.

Case dragged the body to the supply room. It was fortunate that the soldier was the same height and approximate build as Case. The uniform was a little baggy around the waist, but it would have to do. He closed the door, locked it, picked up the box and left the hangar. He knew they would eventually discover the body, but he now had the means and the time to complete his task, undetected.

55

SHORTLY AFTER ARRIVING at the Holmeses' estate, Amelia walked into the study to place a call to G.P. in Oakland. She outlined the few minor problems they had had with the Electra and assured G.P. that they were being handled. She also told him how impressed she had been with Fred's navigation.

"Fred knew exactly where we were at every moment and how we were progressing," Amelia raved. "He even developed a special procedure that lets him calculate a celestial fix in only six minutes. It would normally take Harry thirty minutes to do the same thing."

"I even had to reduce our airspeed over the last few hours because we would have arrived before sunrise. And we still broke the old record by over an hour." Amelia had a hard time keeping the excitement out of her voice.

"I wish Fred was going with us." Amelia sighed.

"Ask him," G.P. said

"Okay, I will." Amelia perked up.

"Look, Amelia, it's all over the wire that Paul landed the Electra in Honolulu," G.P. said. "Remember when you were flying a while ago with Bo, some people said it wasn't you doing the flying, it was Bo."

"But that wasn't the case," Amelia protested.

"I know that, but they don't," G.P. said calmly. "I think it would be better if you were the only one in the cockpit for all the takeoffs and landings."

"I understand," Amelia said. "I'll make sure they see only me from now on."

"Good. Now, I think you should get some rest, if you're planning on leaving later tonight."

"I'm going right now. I am a little tired. And I'll talk to Fred about continuing on with the flight, at least as far as Australia," she said.

56

AFTER A FEW hours and feeling somewhat refreshed, Amelia went out onto the lanai. She found Mona and Chris and most of her team already there. Paul and Terry were dancing to some beautiful, gently flowing Hawaiian music.

"Good afternoon," Amelia greeted her hosts.

"Fred and I came down about a half-hour ago," Harry said. They had had been talking to Mona and Chris.

"There's some fresh pineapple juice on the table, dear. Help yourself," Mona offered.

"Thank you, sounds wonderful." Amelia poured herself a glass and found a lounge. Lying back in the plush lounge on the lanai in the sun, sipping fresh pineapple juice, she thought, *This is the life.*

When the music stopped, Paul made his way to the table to top up Terry's glass and to add some ice to his own.

"Paul, has the work on the plane been completed?" Amelia asked.

"No one's called yet," Paul replied as he handed Terry her glass. "I was just going to Wheeler Field to check on the plane and to get the latest weather forecast."

"Can you call back here and let me know if we'll be able to take off later today or if we must wait until tomorrow?"

"Sure thing. If you'll excuse me, I have to stop by the kitchen on my way out. I promised to take lunch back for Daric. Poor guy must be half-starved by now." With that, Paul disappeared into the house.

"Where's Paul going?" Dani asked, coming up from the guest house to join the group on the lanai.

"He's going to check on the airplane and to feed Daric," Amelia replied lazily.

"That's no small task," Dani quipped, as she found herself a chair.

"Amelia, just before you came out, I finished making the final arrangements for the radio transmissions for the Howland Island and New Guinea legs," Harry stated. "I also called the Fleet Air Base to check on the weather and winds at Howland Island. With that information, Fred and I were able to calculate that the flight time to Howland Island would be about eleven-and-a-half hours."

"With the two-hour time difference, that means we could make an all-daylight flight to Howland Island, if we left early tomorrow morning. We wouldn't have to leave later tonight," Amelia concluded.

"That would give us more time to catch our breath," Fred said, stretched out in another lounge.

"Let's wait to hear what Paul has to say when he calls, before we decide." Amelia didn't want to decide until she had all the facts.

57

THE CAR TURNED into Wheeler Field and pulled up outside the 75ᵗʰ Service Squadron hangar shortly after 2 P.M. Daric saw Paul getting out of the back of the car and walked over to greet him. Paul noticed they had pushed the Electra out of the hangar. The commander must have expected that Paul would want to check the engines.

"Did you remember my lunch? I'm starving," Daric asked, looking anxiously into the car.

Paul reached in and pulled a brown paper bag off the back seat and handed it to Daric. "Here, hope you like bologna. How's the work going?" Paul asked, referring to the Electra.

Tearing away the paper and taking a huge bite out of his sandwich, Daric filled Paul in on the servicing of the airplane, around a mouthful of food.

"They found the right propeller hub was nearly dry. They had to pump in a lot of lubricant. They figured the propeller had left Oakland that way. I told them 'no way'. You know, as well as I do, that Bo wouldn't have let that happen. So they checked the propeller for leaks and found no signs of leaking lubricant anywhere on the propeller hub or blades." Daric took another bite from his quickly disappearing lunch.

"The problem with the generator was a blown current limiter fuse. Someone set the maximum current at sixty to seventy amps. It was too much amperage for the generator, and the extra load caused the fuse to blow. They reset it to the correct maximum current of forty-five amps. They also recommended Amelia try to limit the number of electrical devices she uses at any one time."

"On that last transmission, Harry had to hold the transmitter key down longer than normal for Pan American to get a better radio bearing. That could have caused the problem," Paul speculated. "I'll mention it to Amelia. Anything else?"

"They also cleaned and re-capped the electrodes of the spark plugs. For the last item on the list, they painted the instrument bulb in the cockpit white to reduce the glare on the pilot's instrument panel." Daric finished his report to Paul and his sandwich at the same time.

"Great. I think I'd like to run-up the engines to make sure they've fixed the pitch problem. Care to join me?"

"Are you kidding?" Daric exclaimed excitedly. *I can't believe it,* he thought. *I'm going to sit in the cockpit of Amelia Earhart's Electra.*

Paul closed the rear cabin door and walked up the wing to enter the cockpit. He didn't want to crawl over those tanks again. Once they were both settled in their seats, Paul primed the engines with fuel. Looking out the window, he yelled a warning to the service crew who were patiently waiting to be dismissed. "Clear right," as he started the right engine. After the engine roared to life, he repeated the same procedure for the left engine.

Paul ran-up both engines and tested the propellers' pitch controls for a few minutes. Daric felt a slight rhythmic vibration in the aircraft's frame; it appeared to be accompanied by a dull thrumming sound he wasn't familiar with.

"Damn," Paul grumbled, as he shut down both engines. He and Daric extracted themselves from the cockpit and walked to the officer in charge. The commander had stepped out of the hangar just half an hour before Paul had returned.

"Get me the commander," Paul instructed the officer.

Paul turned to Daric. "Can you call Amelia and tell her there's no way she'll be leaving before dark today? The right propeller is still frozen solid. It wouldn't budge at all. She might want to consider a morning takeoff. Also tell her the weather forecast was reporting tail winds again."

"Got it," Daric acknowledged, as he headed into the hangar to make the call.

"What can I do for you, Mr. Mantz?" the commander asked.

"The right propeller is still frozen," Paul informed him.

"Damn, I thought we had found the problem," the commander said, embarrassed. "We'll push the plane back into the hangar and remove the right propeller to see what the problem is."

The commander waved to his men and instructed them on the procedures. Paul didn't want to remove the propeller because he knew they would have to test fly the airplane before the world flight could continue. The result would be another delay.

The right propeller had been removed and partially disassembled by the time Daric returned from placing his call to Amelia. "That can't be good," he said, when he saw the parts laid out on the table.

"What did Amelia have to say?" Paul asked.

"She was disappointed, but understood," Daric reported.

"Mr. Mantz?" The commander was drawing Paul's attention to the parts.

"Call me Paul, please."

"Okay, Paul. The propeller is badly galled and the blades are frozen solid in the hub," the commander explained.

"If you believe the Electra left Oakland without sufficient lubricant or maybe even with the wrong lubricant for the right propeller, it's likely the left propeller could also be questionable," Paul speculated. "Since we'll have to perform a test flight before Amelia can leave for Howland Island, I think we should remove the left one and inspect it, too."

The commander quickly gave the order to his men to remove

the left propeller.

"May I suggest that we take them both to our Hawaiian Air Depot at Luke Field for a complete overhaul? We have better facilities there and I have a crew of men standing by," the commander offered.

"Let's do it. I'll call you later to see how you're making out." Paul shook the commander's hand and, with that, he and Daric left the hangar and made their way toward the car.

The commander watched them drive off the field before he turned his attention to the huge task at hand. He spotted a soldier standing in the back of the hangar.

"You, Corporal," he yelled at the soldier.

"Yes, sir," he replied smartly, as he approached the commander and snapped to attention.

Looking at his name badge, the commander gave him his orders. "Corporal Griffin, we're taking the propellers over to Luke Field for a complete overhaul. I want you to stand guard at this hangar and let no one near that airplane until we get back. Got it?"

"Yes, sir," Griffin replied smartly.

"Let's go, men." The commander instructed his maintenance crew to load the propellers onto the back of the flat-bed truck. Once everything had been secured, the maintenance crew, and the commander piled into several vehicles and left Wheeler Field.

"Don't worry, Commander, I won't let anyone near that airplane, but me." Case couldn't believe his luck. He had been at the right place at the right time. And, speaking of time, he knew he didn't have much of it to get his work done. He couldn't tamper with the engines as he had done in Oakland. He would have to think of something else to stop Amelia's world flight.

58

AMELIA WAS SITTING out on the lanai in the late afternoon sun, sipping on another cold glass of pure liquid gold: the pineapple juice which she just couldn't seem to get enough of. She put her glass down and picked up her pen and her notebook.

I felt I owed an apology to the people who rose early to greet us when we landed at Wheeler Field. Perhaps I should have been more considerate and tried to arrange the arrival at a later hour. But that was difficult because it was so desirable to time the departure from Oakland in daylight. Having visited these lovely islands before, I was accustomed to the very special hospitality of Hawaii, but I did not expect so many of its friendly people to go without breakfast that they might welcome us. And speaking of breakfast, a bright particular memory of the immediate aftermath of our arrival were the so-fresh scrambled eggs miraculously awaiting us at the home of Chris and Mona Holmes.

"Here you are, lounging in the lap of luxury while I've been slaving over your airplane," Paul said, collapsing into the chair across from Amelia.

"That's what I pay you the big bucks for," Amelia quipped as she put her notes away. "Besides, you had Daric helping you; so stop complaining and tell me what's happening with the Electra."

"We removed both propellers and sent them to Luke Field for a complete overhaul. The commander said they had facilities over there and men trained for such emergencies."

"Are we going to be able to leave in the morning?" Amelia asked eagerly.

"I'm not sure the propellers will be ready in time. I'll call Luke Field in a couple of hours to check on their progress. I should be able to give you a better answer then."

Paul had just finished filling Amelia in about the other repairs to the airplane when Fred, Harry, Terry, Daric, Dani and the Holmes all came out onto the lanai. Terry walked over to Paul and sat on the edge of his chair, throwing her arm over his shoulder. "What a beautiful afternoon," Terry said dreamily, leaning in to place a gentle kiss on Paul's cheek.

"Get a room, you two," Harry grumbled.

"We have one, thank you," Terry replied in all seriousness, missing Harry's implication. He just shrugged and sadly shook his head.

"You're right, and it's going to be a beautiful evening, too. I have a great idea. Why don't we have dinner out here on the lanai?" Mona proposed excitedly. Before she received a reply from any of her guests, she started planning the evening. "I'll get the kitchen to make Lau Lau which is salt butterfish, pork and chicken wrapped in layers of taro leaves and ti leaves, and then it's steamed for three to four hours. And I'll have them prepare a tropical salad with pineapple vinaigrette. Oh, this will be so much fun."

With that, Mona ran off into the house to get dinner started. "I guess that's settled, then." Chris grinned.

"Actually, I think I'll go lie down for a couple of hours," Paul said around a gaping yawn. "I haven't slept in the last twenty-six hours and I'm beat. I'll see you at dinner." Paul pushed himself wearily to his feet. With Terry holding his arm, he left the lanai and entered the house.

59

IT WAS A perfect evening in paradise. A balmy breeze blew in from the Pacific Ocean. The distant sound of gentle waves rolling onto the shore was barely audible. The sky was clear of clouds and dotted with a million glistening lights. The moonlight seemed to create an illuminated path directly to the Holmeses' Waikiki beach-front estate, as if extending a celestial invitation to join the party.

"That was fantastic," Daric muttered, as he finished the last morsel from his previously heaping plate. "All that was missing were the Hawaiian shirts."

"Yes, it was delicious, thank you, Mrs. Holmes," Dani added.

"Mona, please, and you are more than welcome. With just Chris and me here, we seldom take the time to actually sit and enjoy a meal together. We always seem to be too busy. It's a real pleasure to be able to enjoy our repast with such good company and being outdoors makes it even better."

"I totally agree," Chris added. "And I think we should make a point of doing this more often, even if it is only the two of us. We deserve it. This might just give us a temporary reprieve from our busy schedules and a delightful alternative venue to bask in."

"Mr. Mantz, you have a phone call," a member of the house staff announced. "It's from Luke Field."

"It will be the commander with an update on the propellers. If you'll excuse me," Paul said as he got up. He followed the staff member into the house and picked up the receiver. The commander began to fill Paul in with their progress so far.

"Paul, we took the right propeller completely apart. We had to use hot kerosene to disassemble it. If we don't come across any surprises, we should have both propellers back at Wheeler Field by two in the morning. We'll get them back on the Electra in time for a test flight at first light."

"That's great, Commander, thank you. I know Amelia is eager to continue with her flight. I'll see you first thing in the morning."

While Paul was in the house, he placed a couple calls. The first call was to Standard Oil, asking them to make sure they were at Wheeler Field by seven o'clock. He would test fly the plane and, if everything checked out, they would fill the plane with eight-hundred-twenty-five gallons of fuel and would be ready to leave for Howland Island by eight or nine. He placed his second call to Wheeler Field to inform them of the early morning test flight and the possible departure that morning.

Paul hung up the phone and walked back out onto the lanai. Everyone was waiting for his news.

"Because they had to disassemble both propellers, I'll need to test fly the Electra tomorrow morning before you can leave for Howland Island. I've made the necessary arrangements and, if everything checks out okay, you can leave around eight o'clock, nine at the latest. It's going to be tight, but I believe you can get to Howland Island before it gets dark."

"Well, since we'll be getting an early start tomorrow, I suggest we all call it a night," Harry said, as he thanked his hosts and left for his room.

Friday, March 19, 1937

60

THE SMALL ARMY convoy pulled into Wheeler Field around 2:00 A.M. with a truckload of tired soldiers and one grumpy commander. They pulled up to the 75th Service Squadron hangar.

The commander got out of his jeep, immediately noticing the closed hangar doors and the dark interior. "Where's that corporal I left to guard this hangar," he yelled at no one in particular.

The men were getting out of their vehicles to start the gruelling task of removing the cumbersome propellers from the trucks and, then, spending the next several hours putting them back on the airplane.

"You and you," the commander yelled, as he singled out two individuals. "Go find me Corporal Griffin. He better have one damn good excuse for leaving his post. Even if he does, it's not going to be good enough for me! Now go."

The two soldiers scurried off to fulfill their task, thankful they weren't in Griffin's boots.

"Okay, men, get these things unloaded and remounted on that airplane, pronto." *I need some sleep,* he thought, *but I could use a tall shot of whiskey right now, too.*

"Come on, come on, we don't have all night."

* * *

Case had caught the lights from the trucks as they pulled into Wheeler Field and knew the troops had finished their work at Luke Field. He'd done as much as he could tonight; he hoped it was enough. He had a few other tricks up his sleeve he could try tomorrow if the opportunity presented itself. But for now, it was time to make himself scarce and ditch the uniform.

"Thanks Corporal Griffin, you've been a great help," he murmured to himself, as he threw the uniform in the dumpster out back.

61

THE ALARM WENT off at 4:30 A.M., rudely awakening Amelia from a pleasant dream. Through the partially opened window, she heard rain falling outside. She dressed quickly and headed for the kitchen and a much-needed cup of coffee.

"Good Morning, Amelia. Did you sleep well?" Mona asked cheerily, from the dining room, as she reached for a glass. She poured pineapple juice for Amelia.

"Actually, yes, I did, thank you," she said, entering the dining room and taking the glass from Mona. She took a long drink of the golden nectar.

"It's been raining most of the night. I'm sorry to say, it doesn't look like a very good day for flying," Mona remarked sadly.

Paul had just arrived in the dining room and helped himself to a cup of coffee. "I'm going to head over to Wheeler Field. I'll check the condition of the runway. If the grass is too soggy from all this rain, we might want to consider using Luke Field. They have a concrete runway which will handle the heavily loaded airplane."

"I'll go with you," Daric offered eagerly. He and Dani had made their way into the main house and just caught the end of Paul's comments.

"We have to test fly the airplane this morning," Paul continued.

"If everything checks out, I'll land over at Luke Field. I can have the fuel tanks filled there, but it will probably be too late to take off for Howland this morning, anyway." With that, Paul and Daric left.

Harry and Fred came into the dining room, just missing Paul and Daric's departure.

"What's up?" Harry asked around a yawn.

"Why don't you two grab a cup of coffee and I'll fill you in," Amelia said.

Amelia told them about the runway situation and added, "Paul will call after the test flight this morning. That will tell us whether we're heading for Howland Island tonight or not, but this morning's departure isn't happening."

"Then, I'm going back to bed," Fred said, as he did an about-face and left the dining room.

Amelia poured herself another glass of pineapple juice, opened her notebook and wrote: *If one has to wait, in all the world there is no pleasanter place to do the waiting than in Honolulu. Again, as before on my 1935 Pacific solo, I was ensconced in the lovely Waikiki beach home of Mr. and Mrs. Chris Holmes. Six hours of sleep there, topped off by luxurious sunbathing on the lanai, whence one may regard the tropic scene through the rippling fronds of coconut palms, banished all traces of fatigue. Meals appeared wherever and whenever one awoke while the quantities of pineapple juice I consumed between times were fabulous.*

62

THE RAIN HAD finally stopped, but a damp mist still hung in the air. It was about six o'clock by the time Paul and Daric arrived at Wheeler Field and pulled up outside the 75th Service Squadron hangar. The commander was there to greet them.

"Commander, you look terrible," Paul said, knowing he was the cause of the commander's current state of dishevelment.

"It's been a long night, but we got the job done," he grumbled.

After the commander filled them in on the work that had been done during the night, they inspected the grass runway. The grass was too soft from all the recent rain. And, on top of that, a new construction project at the field had created trenches, which bisected the runway they intended to use.

"I think with the heavy fuel load and the shape of this runway, we should use Luke Field for the takeoff for Howland Island," Paul concluded. "I'll call Amelia and let her know."

* * *

"Amelia, the field is too soft to use, so I'll fly the Electra over to Luke Field after the test flight and see if it would be the better option," Paul advised.

"What about leaving tonight?" asked Amelia.

"I still have to make new arrangements for fueling the Electra at Luke Field and get clearance to use their runway. But, let's first see how the test flight goes, okay? I don't want to rush things." Paul wanted to be thorough. Shortening his test flight, just so they could leave later today, could prove costly later on.

"I'll let Fred and Harry know what's happening," Amelia said drearily, her mood matching the current weather outside.

* * *

By the time Paul returned from his telephone call, the Electra had been pushed out of the hangar and the Standard Oil truck had pulled up alongside. He instructed them to pump the fuel into the left main tank, which he would use for the test flight.

"Everything okay?" Daric asked

"Fine, but I could tell Amelia's disappointed she won't be leaving this morning." Turning his attention to the commander, he continued. "If the test flight checks out okay, I'll land at Luke Field, so I can inspect the condition of their runway. If I'm satisfied, I will not be flying back here." Paul extended his hand. "So here's hoping and, with that, I'll say thank you for all your hard work. Now, my friend, it's time for you to get some rest," Paul said graciously.

"First, let me make a call to the operations officer over at Luke Field to tell them to expect you and that you'll most likely be using their runway to take off for Howland Island," the commander said. "Good luck."

Paul walked back to the car, leaning down to talk to the driver through the open window. "John, if we're not back here in an hour, we'll be at Luke Field. Drive over and pick us up there," Paul instructed.

When the fueling was finished, Paul performed his pre-flight inspection. He took ten minutes to run-up the engines before he was satisfied that everything was okay. Then, he shut them down and came out of the cockpit. He walked around the airplane, checking the engine nacelles and landing gear for any signs of oil leaks. There were none. But the right oleo strut, which is an oil-and-air-filled shock absorber on the landing gear, caught his sharp eye. Whereas the right strut was extended four inches, the left one extended only two inches. Paul called a mechanic over and instructed him to let some air out of the right oleo air valve until it extended the same as the left one.

"Okay, Daric, let's go," Paul said.

"Yes," Daric exclaimed excitedly, while pumping his fist. *It was one thing to sit in the cockpit; it's another to actually go flying in Amelia Earhart's Electra,* he thought.

Daric and Paul made their way up the wing and into the cockpit. After starting the engines, Paul taxied to the far end of Wheeler Field for takeoff. Paul applied full power and the relatively light plane seemed to pop off the runway and spring into the air, a drastic difference from the heavily burdened airplane that had left Oakland. Once the Electra reached one-thousand feet, he retracted the landing gear and reduced the airspeed.

Pearl Harbor was just ahead. Luke Field was on Ford Island, which was in the middle of Pearl Harbor. The field was shared equally between the Army Air Corps and the Navy Fleet Air Base. Paul pointed to the left to show Daric Diamond Head, off in the distance. Daric could also see the Aloha Tower and a cruise ship at the pier. He wondered whether it was the *S.S. Malolo* they had come across on.

When they flew over Waikiki Beach, Daric strained to spot anyone at the Holmeses' estate, but the trees obstructed a clear view of the grounds.

63

AMELIA WAS SITTING under a palm tree in the shade, enjoying the warmth and the light breeze drifting in off the ocean. The day had improved considerably since early morning and all evidence of the previous rain showers had vanished. She decided to get out and enjoy the day, because, she realized, over the next couple of weeks she'd find little time to do just that.

A faint sound off in the distance caught her attention. She'd know that sound anywhere. Looking up from her notebook, she saw the glistening silhouette of the Electra as it made its way over to Luke Field. She watched for a few minutes, mesmerized by the sight, before returning to her notes.

A reporter in Oakland had asked me if I was attempting to break any records. I told him that I didn't want to push the engines on the crossing to Hawaii. As it turned out, I did break the old record, and I wasn't even trying. The element of speed is far from upper-most in such a flight as this. It can't be. Quite truly, I'm in no hurry. It was disappointing yesterday that repairs to the airplane prevented us from carrying on. But doubtless similar delays will occur later. My ambition is no time mark. There is no 'record' to shoot at. That will come for others later. We'll see globe-girding flights whose brevity will take your breath away. As for this present venture, I just want to progress as safely and sanely as day-to-day conditions make possible, give myself and the Electra the experience of seeing what we can of this very interesting world at its waistline, and, with good fortune, get back with plane and pilot all 'in one piece'.

Dani spotted Amelia sitting on the lawn by the ocean and walked down to join her. She sat beside her, resting her back against the trunk of a palm tree. She tilted her head back, closed her eyes and took in a long deep breath of sea air. Amelia had been writing and, not wanting to disturb her thought process or the tranquility of the moment, Dani waited for Amelia to start the conversation.

For a few peaceful moments, they both sat there in silence, overlooking the gentle swells on the ocean beyond.

"It's a very big ocean—so much water," Amelia said with a little sigh which promptly dissipated into a reassuring chuckle.

"Would you ever consider giving up your world flight?" Dani asked softly. Dani knew she couldn't ask or say too much, but she wanted to know what Amelia thought.

"Please don't be concerned, Dani," Amelia said endearingly. "It just seems that I must try this flight. I've weighed it all carefully. With it behind me, life will be fuller and richer. I can be content."

Amelia paused before continuing. "The more one does and sees and feels, the more one is able to do and the more genuine may be one's appreciation of fundamental things like home, and love, and understanding companionship."

"It's such a dangerous adventure."

"Adventure is worthwhile in itself," Amelia responded excitedly. "After the pleasant accident of being the first woman to cross the Atlantic by air, I was launched into a life full of interest. Aviation offered such fun as crossing the continent in planes large and small, trying the whirling rotors of an autogyro, making record flights. With these activities came opportunities to know women everywhere who shared my conviction that there is so much women can do in the modern world and should be permitted to do irrespective of their sex. Probably my greatest satisfaction was to indicate by example, now and then, that women can sometimes do things themselves, if given the chance."

Amelia hesitantly pulled her gaze from the calming effect of the ocean and looked directly at Dani. "I don't want to be another wave on the ocean. I want my life to have some meaning, some purpose. And when I believe I have fulfilled that purpose, and it's time for me to go, I'd like best to go in my plane. Quickly."

Dani reflected for a moment. *If she only knew the impact her life had or the role, she could have played as a crusader for women's rights. She could have been a modern-day version of Joan of Arc. She was at least twenty years ahead of her time in promoting women's rights. It's a shame the movement didn't make full use of her legend and her example. But I have no doubt that Amelia will eventually find the contentment she so desperately craves.* Dani glanced over at Amelia, *It's as if, somehow, Amelia already knew she would,* Dani thought.

Wanting to lighten the mood, Dani said, "Since you're staying, at least until after dinner, Mona is arranging a genuine Hawaiian luau, in your honour. She's got the kitchen staff running in circles."

"She started talking about a Kalua Pua'a, which I understand means pig, and then she went on about grilled mahi mahi which is some kind of fish, and, of course, Poi. She said she had so much fun last night eating outside, she really wanted to do it again tonight, but have the more traditional luau," Dani finished, with a cheery grin.

"Well, let's go see if we can help, shall we? Or at least try to save the kitchen staff." Amelia chuckled as she got to her feet. She extended a hand to pull Dani to her feet and, then, the two of them walked arm in arm back up to the house and what they both knew was going to be an interesting evening.

64

PAUL HAD TAKEN Daric on a complete tour of the island of Oahu, all the while methodically checking the engine and flight instruments, listening intently for the beat of the propellers turning in unison.

Now that he was satisfied with the performance of the airplane, Paul started to circle back over Pearl Harbor toward Ford Island. He couldn't help but get caught up in Daric's excitement; it was almost contagious. Daric had been grinning ever since taking off from Wheeler Field. So now Paul wanted to give his enthusiastic passenger a small thrill.

"Have you ever flown an airplane before, Daric?" Paul yelled to be heard over the engine noise. He was sure he knew the answer, but wanted to see Daric's reaction.

"Sure. I have over 350 hours logged. But I've never flown anything like this," Daric replied, not daring to assume what was coming next, for fear of jinxing it.

"You have control," Paul said, as he turned control of the Electra over to Daric.

Daric took the yolk and applied gentle pressure to the rudder pedals as he flew the Electra on a heading back toward Ford Island. *Time travel may not be such a bad thing after all,* he thought, cherishing this once-in-a-life-time experience.

After Paul landed the Electra at Luke Field, he followed the Army guide truck, taxiing the airplane to the front of the final assembly hangar on the Army side of Luke Field before shutting down the engines.

Paul and Daric clambered out of the cockpit and walked down the wing to be greeted by Lieutenant Arnold.

"The propellers have never worked better. You did a fantastic job overhauling them," Paul exclaimed ardently, after the introductions had been completed.

"That's great," Lieutenant Arnold replied.

"Do you think you could have someone check the Sperry autopilot?" Paul asked. "The rudder control kept drifting off course when we were flying here from Oakland."

"I'll have an instrument mechanic check it for you. Is there anything else we can do?"

Paul was walking around the airplane, followed closely by Daric. Both were looking for any potential problems, and it wasn't long before Paul noticed the right landing gear oleo strut was again out of sync with the left one.

"Hey, it's been leaking," Daric noted upon closer inspection.

"Could you have someone replace the right valve core and pump the strut up to match the left one?" Paul asked the lieutenant.

"I'll get someone right on it."

"As far as fueling goes, I'd like the tanks filled directly from the Standard Oil Company truck, through a chamois-lined funnel to ensure we remove all contaminants that might be in the gas," Paul directed. "Just wanting to be thorough," he added. He didn't want to come across as insulting, by implying there might be an inferior grade of fuel at the facility.

"Understandable. If I was making this world flight, I'd want to use every precaution to ensure nothing could go wrong," the lieutenant agreed.

"Thank you."

65

AMELIA HAD BEEN looking all over the house for Fred when she finally found him sleeping in a lounge out on the lanai. She had never thought to look there first because Fred hadn't seemed to be the outdoor enthusiast-type of guy. She figured he'd have been slumped in a comfortable padded chair inside the house, out of the reach of any pesky biting insects and creepy crawly creatures.

Amelia quietly pulled a chair up beside the lounge. Although she hated to wake the peacefully slumbering man, she had business that needed attending to. She reached over and gently shook Fred's shoulder. He woke instantly and would have bolted upright if he hadn't had a few too many glasses of spiked pineapple juice.

Amelia noticed the reddened eyes and the unfocused glare, but chalked it up to Fred being rudely awakened and, therefore, dismissed it.

"Fred, I spoke to G.P. and we would like you to continue the flight after Howland Island to Australia," Amelia said.

"You already have a navigator."

"I know, but you can compute a celestial fix faster and I've seen for myself how accurate you are. You had us heading directly at Diamond Head at the precise time you said we would. It was very impressive."

"What about Harry?" Fred asked cautiously. He was trying desperately to concentrate on the conversation when all he wanted to do was drift back into oblivion.

"I'll talk to him. He'll be co-navigator and radio operator. I'm sure everything will be fine."

"All right, but wouldn't it be cheaper and faster, for me anyway, to go all the way rather than getting off in Australia and having to make my way back home from there?" Fred reasoned.

"Miss Earhart, there's a telephone call for you in the kitchen," the serving staff interrupted.

"I'll be right there," Amelia replied. "Fred, I'll have to check with G.P. before I can make a final decision, but I'm sure it will be okay."

Leaning back in his lounge and closing his eyes, Fred muttered, "Let me know soon, because I'll have to send a wire to my fiancée to tell her I'll be a little late coming home."

Amelia shook her head woefully, thinking about Fred sleeping away this beautiful day when, in only a few hours, he could find himself wedged into the cramped rear cabin of the Electra for hours on end, with no opportunity to breathe in fresh air or to stretch out tired muscles.

Not her, Amelia thought. She was going to soak in as much sunlight and fresh air as she could. Being stuck in the airplane for hours with two men, that plane's atmosphere was going to be ripe before too long. She cringed just thinking about it as she made her way into the house to take the phone call.

66

THE COMMANDER OF Wheeler Field had returned to his office around 10:00 A.M., after grabbing a couple hours of sleep. It had been a long night, but he had a few things he had to deal with before he could call it a day.

* * *

Case was again dressed to pass as a reporter, thinking he could blend in with the others who would be here to catch Amelia's morning departure. He instinctively knew from the morning's weather that Earhart wouldn't be leaving any time soon, so he was in no hurry to get to the field. When he finally arrived at the 75th Service Squadron hangar, it was empty. "Shit, this isn't good," Case muttered. "What happened to the Electra?"

* * *

A knock came at the commander's door, which immediately opened. "Commander, you have a call from a Sergeant McGregor," his aide said.

"Who?" he barked. *I don't have time for this crap,* he thought.

All he wanted to do was finish up here and go back home, put his feet up and enjoy a tall shot of whiskey.

"He said to tell you, that last night, you told him to find Corporal Griffin," the aid answered awkwardly.

"Fine, I'll take it in here." The commander dismissed his aide, who swiftly transferred the call into the office.

The phone barely finished its first ring when it was snatched from its cradle. "Speak," the commander bellowed.

"Sir, we found Corporal Griffin," replied the sergeant, his voice trembling slightly.

"Well, bring him here, Sergeant."

"He's dead, sir."

"What?"

"We found him in the supply room in D Hangar, sir."

"I'll be right there." The commander shot out of his chair, driving it back against the wall. The door banged against the wall as he left his office.

"Send two MPs over to D Hangar, immediately," he ordered his aide as he stormed out of the building.

* * *

Case heard a door slam and caught a glimpse of the commander heading toward the hangar right next to the 75th Service Squadron hangar. He was quickly joined by two MPs, who struggled to match the commander's determined gait.

Case knew he was running out of time. He had to find out what had happened to the Electra and get off this field before all hell broke loose.

Case was making his way back to his car when he ran into a fellow reporter who was also heading for the parking lot.

"Hey!" Case yelled from a safe distance, not wanting to get too close. The fewer people who could identify him, the better. "Where's Earhart's plane? Did she leave already?"

"No, just moved locations," the reporter grumbled. "You'd

think they'd have the common decency to tell a fella, save him the time of coming all the way out here, just to find out he's at the wrong field. Damned inconsiderate, if you ask me."

"Where did they go?" Case asked impatiently, opening his car door.

"Luke Field. Apparently it has a better runway," the reporter said distractedly, as he dug into his deep, baggy pockets in search of his car keys. "At least now, they're leaving tonight and not later this morning, so it gives us time to catch the ferry over to Ford Island. Hey, do you want to . . ."

The reporter looked over and realized he was talking to no one. Case had already left Wheeler Field. "Well, that was rude. What is it with people today?" he muttered.

* * *

The commander had lost no time in getting to D Hangar. He entered, spotting a small group gathered outside the supply room.

"Show me," the commander ordered.

Sergeant McGregor opened the supply room door and stood aside to let the commander enter. There in a heap on the floor was a man. His dog tags were the only means of identification as he was without his uniform. The commander bent down to examine the dog tags and, then, looked closely at the man's pasty, stone-cold face.

"That's not Griffin," the commander shouted. "That's not the man I left in charge outside the squadron hangar last night. And where's his uniform?"

"Sir, we believe someone killed Griffin and took his uniform, for what we're not sure," the Sergeant supplied.

"Lock down the field, NOW! And get me some answers!"

67

"AMELIA, IT'S PAUL. I have good news and bad news. Which would you like first?" he asked from the other end of the phone line.

"Quit playing around and just give it to me," Amelia scolded. She was in no mood for playing games. She somehow knew they would not be leaving for Howland Island today and that was painful to swallow.

"Okay," Paul said timidly, never having been on the receiving end of a slight from Amelia and not liking it much either. "The Electra performed beautifully during the test flight this morning. I don't think the engines have ever run so smoothly."

"So, what's the problem?"

"Before the flight, I noticed the right oleo strut was out of sync with the left one. We fixed it before the flight, or so I thought. When we landed at Luke Field, it was out of sync again. That's when Daric noticed it was leaking, so we're having the valve replaced." Paul tried to relay the information with as much positive spin as possible, but he knew what was coming next would not sit well.

"Can we still leave tonight?" Amelia asked bluntly.

"No. It took us over forty minutes to deliver fifteen gallons of fuel to the Electra's tanks," Paul blurted out and, then, waited for the explosion.

"What? That's ridiculous."

"We were siphoning the fuel through a chamois filter to remove any contaminants, which, by the way, we found. The truck driver said there was nothing wrong with his fuel. So, I called the Standard Oil Company and asked them to send a representative to Luke Field," Paul tried to explain.

"When he finally got here, he was adamant that there was nothing wrong with their fuel. Then I asked the rep to pump some gasoline directly from the truck through the chamois, and it showed a deposit of sediment. He claimed the chamois we used was already dirty, and it wasn't his fuel. Daric got a brand new chamois from inside the airplane and we tried the fuel test again. We got the same result," Paul continued.

"The rep from Standard Oil was totally baffled. He couldn't understand how his fuel could have become contaminated. I asked that the airplane be fueled with Air Corps gasoline. We had to wait to get permission from the Luke Field operations officer, Lieutenant Arnold, before we could proceed," Paul said defensively.

"What next?" Amelia mumbled irritably. She had bitten Paul's head off and through no fault of his own. He had made a brilliant decision to use a filter for the gas and, if he hadn't, the flight would have been badly compromised. Not to mention the potential of crashing somewhere over the Pacific.

"While we were waiting, I got the latest weather report. Amelia, I think it would be better if you arrived at Howland Island late tomorrow instead of at dawn," Paul advised hesitantly. "You could make it an all-daylight flight if you leave tomorrow morning."

"All right," Amelia reluctantly agreed.

"Look, Daric and I will stay here until all the fuel strainers are cleaned, the fueling is completed, and the plane is locked away in the hangar for the night. Lieutenant Arnold also offered to place a guard on the hangar overnight, which I accepted," Paul said in an empathetic tone.

"Great, thanks, Paul," Amelia said sincerely. "I'm sorry I

snapped. I'm just frustrated with all the delays. It's as if someone is trying to tell me this world flight isn't such a good idea," Amelia quipped light-heartedly.

"Nonsense," Paul encouraged.

"Look, Mona has a big luau planned for tonight. So don't be too long in getting back here. We wouldn't want to disappoint her, now would we?"

"We'll be along shortly," Paul said as he ended the call.

* * *

Case had stolen a small motor boat to cross the harbor. In the future, Ford Island would be forever remembered as the main site of the Pearl Harbor attacks that occurred on December 7, 1941. The air fleet was stationed there and battleship row surrounded the island, making it a prime target.

Case avoided the docks and chose to pull the boat up on the gravel shore, hidden from sight amongst some small sage brush. He made his way across the field and paused to catch his breath only when he reached the back of the closest hangar, which, coincidentally, happened to be the final assembly hangar on the Army side of Luke Field.

68

AFTER THEY HAD tucked away the Electra for the night, Paul and Daric left Luke Field. It was shortly after 4:00 P.M. when they were finally on the road, heading back to the Holmeses' estate on Waikiki beach for the much-anticipated luau. At the corner of Fort and King Streets, Paul saw an interesting gift shop and had an idea.

"John, can you pull over here for a minute?" Paul instructed. "Come on, Daric. You said last night that all we were missing were the Hawaiian shirts. Since we're having a proper luau tonight, it would be only fitting to go in traditional style." He grinned.

Next to the Benson Smith Drug Store, a popular meeting place for the town's socialites, was the Leilani Gift Shop. Chimes rang out as Paul and Daric entered the shop's front door.

"Aloha," a buxom woman greeted cheerfully. She was wearing one of the many floral-patterned dresses that the shop sold.

"Aloha," Paul said, returning the greeting. "We're looking for some men's shirts and ladies' dresses."

"We have a nice selection of individual and matching sets," she said. "Mila, come and help out."

From behind a curtained door emerged a beautiful Hawaiian princess, or so Daric thought. She was breathtaking: a slender, well-defined delicate frame, with long black hair that seemed to dance and shimmer in the afternoon light. Her native complexion was flawless and her eyes darted shyly away when she realized she was the centre of some appreciative attention from a handsome young man.

Mila walked to Paul. She knew she was less likely to embarrass herself in front of him than with the more attractive younger man with unwavering eyes that followed her every movement. "How may I help you?" she asked demurely. Her voice was like a siren's song to Daric.

Paul seemed to be oblivious to the woman's captivating beauty. "We're looking for some shirts and dresses. For myself in particular, I would like to see a matching set."

"Follow me, please."

Mila showed Paul a rack of matching Hawaiian outfits. Once he started riffling through the items in front of him, he called over his shoulder. "Daric, get Mila to show you the women's dresses and pick something out for Amelia and Dani."

"This way, please," Mila said softly. Then it hit her. "Did he say Amelia?"

"Yes, he did," Daric whispered, leaning closer to watch as a reserved girl transformed into a captivated young woman in front of his very eyes.

"You know her? What's she like? When is she leaving Honolulu? Are you going with her? Do you fly, too?"

"Easy, easy," Daric said trying to calm her down. "As for your questions, the answers would be, yes, delightful, tomorrow, no and sometimes." Daric hoped he had answered them in the correct order.

"I'm sorry," Mila said wistfully, quickly turning her face away. "This way, please," she said quietly, as she walked toward a rack of brightly colored clothing.

"These are the dresses we have. What sizes are you looking for?" Mila couldn't meet Daric's eyes.

"Let's see, they should both be about the same size," Daric smiled, the corners of his blue eyes crinkling in mirth.

"Mila, where are the men's shirts?" Paul yelled from the back of the shop.

"To your left," Mila replied. "I'll be right there."

"No need, I found them," Paul said. "Besides, I think Daric could use your help." He could see Daric was captivated by the young lady.

"I think this should fit Amelia." Mila held up a beautiful plumeria floral-patterned black dress.

"Great, now I'll need one for . . ."

"Dani, I know," Mila snorted. If Daric didn't know better, he could have sworn there was a hint of jealousy in Mila's tone.

"Yes, but I think I'd like to get a matching set, too," Daric said, baiting Mila to test his theory.

"This way," Mila grumbled, as she led him to the back of the shop, where Paul had first started his shopping.

Daric couldn't continue his charade any longer. It was having such a disagreeable effect on Mila and he so wanted to see the light in her eyes again.

"Since we're twins, it might be kind of fun to relive part of our childhood, when our mom used to dress us alike," Daric supplied.

Mila's disposition changed immediately. He was right; she was interested in him.

"I think this would look great with your coloring." Mila held up a plumeria hibiscus-patterned navy aloha shirt.

Daric couldn't help noticing how close she was standing; her aroma was even more intoxicating. He looked down into the depths of her brown eyes. It seemed as if time had simply stood still, both lost in each other's gaze.

Mila was the first to break the spell; she stepped back, a rosy tinge to her cheeks. "We also have the matching aloha dress, too," she whispered.

"Great, I'll take them both."

"Come on, Daric, let's go. We don't want to be late for the luau," Paul called from the cashier's desk.

"Mama, this dress is for Amelia," Mila said, when she placed

Daric's items on the counter to be rung into the till.

"In that case, it's on the house."

Daric and Paul took their bags of clothing and were heading for the door. "Give me a sec," Daric said, turning back toward Mila.

"Would you be my guest at Amelia's takeoff tomorrow morning? It will be early and I do mean real early. You'll have to be there just before daylight. It's at Luke Field," Daric added.

"I'd love to." Mila grinned shyly.

"If I get the opportunity and she's not too busy, I'll introduce you to Amelia," Daric added.

There was that excited smile he wanted to see as much of as possible. "See you tomorrow, then."

69

"I'VE BEEN AROUND the Electra almost twenty-four/seven since it arrived in Honolulu and I have yet to see Case," Daric told his sister as they were getting ready for the evening's luau.

"Maybe you scared him off," Dani mumbled. She wasn't really paying him much attention. She was turning in front of the full-length mirror on the back of the bathroom door, admiring her reflection. Dani was thrilled with the dress he had picked out for her and was impressed that it actually fit. The attention to detail was astounding, right down to the genuine coconut buttons; furthermore, the dress's color brought out the blue in her eyes.

"Yeah, right," Daric muttered.

"It just seems to me that, with all the issues we've had with the Electra, it can't be simply equipment problems. I think someone's been tampering with the plane," he concluded.

"Have you talked to Paul about your suspicions?"

"No, not yet," he replied, somewhat embarrassed.

"What are you waiting for? You were so determined to talk to him before we left Oakland . . . that was six days ago," Dani chided her brother.

"I know. I guess I got busy. Besides, the Electra has been under close guard since it landed here. Someone's been with it constantly.

I don't know how Case could have gotten access to the airplane without someone noticing," Daric reasoned. "Maybe it's not such a big issue now as it was back on the mainland."

"Listen to you," Dani chuckled, as she joined Daric in the living room.

"What?"

"You sound like a native: 'mainland'."

"And except for the color of your hair, you look like one. You look stunning," Daric said admiringly.

"Well, you don't look too shabby yourself. Care to escort a lady to a Hawaiian luau?"

"It would be my pleasure."

70

DANI AND DARIC HAD no trouble finding the party. They needed only to follow the planted tiki torches that formed an illuminated path from the main house down to the beach.

When Daric and Dani reached the luau, everyone else was already there, all decked out in Hawaiian tapestry. Heads turned when the two of them came into the circle of light radiating from the fire pit.

"I must say, you two look very handsome," Chris said approvingly.

"Whoever came up with the idea of getting the Hawaiian wear, thank you. I think everyone looks very festive for our luau," Mona remarked delightedly.

Paul and Terry were wearing a matching set like Dani and Daric, but with a red background covered in palm fronds and hibiscus flowers. Harry's was a brown shirt with cream palm fronds and Fred's was black with calla lilies. Amelia had on a beautifully elegant black plumeria floral dress. And, finally, Chris and Mona Holmes wore their Hawaiian finest, not some inexpensive tourist souvenir.

"Come, grab a seat by the fire. We were just getting started." As the gracious host, Chris stood and offered Dani his place.

The stars shone brightly in the eastern sky, but would soon be masked by a front rolling in from the west, signifying foul weather was imminent. But the weather for the luau, right now, was perfect.

The food was exceptional and abundant and the drinks were cool and refreshing. After dining, Paul and Terry headed down the beach, hand-in-hand, enjoying the splendors that paradise so willingly offered.

Harry noticed Fred leaving his seat by the fire to help himself to another drink. He knew it was now or never, for he had something he wanted to say to him. Harry quickly downed the rest of his drink to help him gain some courage and to give him an excuse to leave the fire, too.

Harry walked up behind Fred, startling him, which in itself gave him a weird sense of pleasure. "So, Amelia tells me you're flying with us as far as Australia," Harry mumbled matter-of-factly.

"Not only flying with you, but as the plane's chief navigator," Fred sneered, rubbing it in Harry's face.

"As far as I'm concerned, you're just extra baggage we don't need. If we needed to take on another person, I'd prefer it be Paul; at least he can fly the airplane," Harry shot back.

"Amelia doesn't need any help flying, but from where I stand, she sure needs help with navigating," Fred said antagonistically.

"Why, you arrogant piece of . . ."

71

"EXCUSE ME, MR. Holmes. This is Colonel John C. McDonnell, commander of Wheeler Field. He said it was urgent that he speak with Miss Earhart and Mr. Mantz," John said smartly after escorting the commander down to the beach and interrupting an unpleasant confrontation at the makeshift bar.

"I'm sorry, sir. I told the commander you don't like to be disturbed in the evenings, but the commander insisted," John offered as an excuse for the interruption.

"Thank you, John," Chris said, rising to greet the commander.

"Please come and sit." Chris directed the commander to a vacant chair by the fire. "Paul is down the beach a ways. Daric, can you go and tell him the commander is here to see him?"

"Right away." Daric sprang to his feet, throwing sand in the air as he raced down the beach. He didn't want to miss anything the commander had come here to say.

"So, what brings you all the way out here, Commander?" Amelia asked.

"I'd rather wait for Mr. Mantz to return, if you don't mind?"

"Not at all," Amelia replied.

"Commander, may I offer you something to drink?" Mona asked, always being the gracious hostess.

"Juice would be fine, thank you."

"Commander, while you're here, I'd like to thank you and your men for all their hard work and the long hours they've spent on the Electra. Paul says the engines have never run so well," Amelia said appreciatively.

"You're welcome, Miss Earhart."

"Amelia, please." The commander nodded in response.

By the time Mona had handed the commander his drink, Daric had returned with Paul and Terry in tow.

The commander stood and shook hands with Paul.

"Commander, what brings you out here? I would have thought you'd be tucked into a soft bed by now, considering you didn't sleep at all last night."

"Nor tonight, it would seem," the commander groaned.

"Why?" Amelia interrupted.

"I wanted to bring you this news in person, because right now I'm still not sure what it all means," the commander started.

"Go on," Paul urged.

"This afternoon, we discovered a body. Corporal Griffin was murdered, his neck snapped," the commander said grimly.

"Oh my word," Mona shrieked, momentarily interrupting the commander.

"When his body was discovered, his uniform was missing. He was found in a supply room in D Hangar, which is the hangar right beside the 75th Service Squadron's hangar, where Miss Earhart's airplane was stowed." The commander paused for a moment before continuing.

"When we took the propellers over to Luke Field for overhauling yesterday afternoon, I left a corporal in charge of guarding the hangar containing Miss Earhart's airplane. The corporal's name was Griffin."

"What are you getting at?" Chris was beyond curious.

"According to the coroner's report, Corporal Griffin would have been dead for almost four hours when I gave him his orders, so it couldn't have been him I left in charge."

72

IT ONLY TOOK a few seconds before Daric had put the pieces together. "It was Case!"

"Who?" Paul, Amelia and the commander all said in unison.

"You can't be sure," Dani jumped in.

"Think about it," Daric blurted excitedly. "I saw him in the storage room in the United Air Services hangar back in Burbank. That's where he passed himself off as a mechanic and actually told me his name was Rick Barak Case. I thought something was off at the time, so I hung back to see what he was up to. I watched him climb into an old blue Chevy pickup truck and drive away."

"What's so 'off' about that?" Paul asked.

"As I said, I found him in the storage room, in total darkness. He said he was there to get some fluorescent markers, but he left empty-handed," Daric replied brusquely before continuing.

"Then, there was the intruder in the Navy hangar in Oakland. When he saw me, he ran out the back door. The guard said he had let no one into the hangar. And, then, we found the lock on the back door had been broken. Even though I didn't get a good look at his face, what I thought strange was, why did a man in Navy fatigues run away when he saw me? For all I knew, he could have been working there."

"Why didn't you tell us about this earlier?" Paul snapped.

"If you recall, I tried to, before we sailed to Hawaii, but you didn't want to listen," Daric said coldly.

"And what about the ship?" Dani added.

"What about the ship?" Amelia asked anxiously.

"Daric had an accident," Terry interjected innocently.

"It was no accident; I was attacked," Daric countered.

"Daric was struck on the head. The doctor said he was lucky," Dani supplied.

"How can you be sure it's the same man?" the commander questioned.

"Easy. What did Corporal Griffin look like, not the real one, but the one you left in charge of the airplane?" Daric asked, already sure of what the commander would say.

"It was dark, but I'd say he was a little shorter than me, say around six feet. He had a pointed jaw and a rather broad-looking nose; not an attractive combination as I recall. I'm not sure of the color of his eyes. As I said, it was dark," the commander summarized.

"Uncle Richard," Daric and Dani chimed together. "That's him!"

"Uncle Richard?" the commander asked quizzically.

"Well, not actually our uncle, but when we first saw him, we both thought he was the spitting image of our uncle," Daric explained.

"I first caught a glimpse of him on the boarding ramp in San Francisco," Dani added. "And, then, we saw him running out of the Smoking Room, when he saw us coming."

"And every time I get anywhere near him, there's that strange odor from the brand of cigarettes he smokes. It was there in Burbank, in Oakland and on the ship. It has to be the same guy," Daric concluded.

"But why? Why would he be following you and why on earth would he attack you?" Paul asked suspiciously.

"Wait, a minute. Did you say old blue pickup?" Dani asked abruptly.

"Yeah, a Chevy pickup, pretty beat up, too. It was parked behind the hangar in Burbank. Case drove off in it."

"Oh my God, that was Case, too!" Dani exclaimed.

"Who too?" the commander asked.

"The one who tried to push us into oncoming traffic," Amelia growled, as she realized where Dani was going. "We were taking my sister to the airport, when this jerk rammed us. We could have all been killed."

"But that still doesn't tell us why. Or why he killed Corporal Griffin," Paul persisted.

"Since he's been following us from Burbank to Oakland to Honolulu and I've spotted him around the airports, I think it's safe to say it all has to do with Amelia's world flight," Daric surmised.

"The world flight? Do you think someone is trying to stop me?" Amelia asked.

"It would explain all the problems we've been having with the Electra: the propellers, the autopilot, the generator, the oleo struts, the fuel, just to name a few. Any one of them could have jeopardized the flight. We all know Bo wouldn't have let the Electra leave Oakland if he had been aware of these problems," Daric stated unequivocally.

"It appears to be a logical explanation, but we still don't know why," Paul stated.

"And we may never know, but one thing is for sure." The commander's tone was glacial. "That plane and Miss Earhart will be closely guarded until she leaves Honolulu. That I promise you."

"Lieutenant Arnold has the Electra locked in the assembly hangar at Luke Field and he has also placed a guard there, too," Paul said.

"I'll call Arnold and give him a description of this guy Case and tell him what's happening. It doesn't hurt to have everyone on their toes for the next twelve to twenty-four hours. If you'll excuse me; good evening." With that, the commander turned and made his way back up the illuminated path to the house and his waiting car.

"I hate to be a party pooper, but, I think, under the circumstances, we should all call it a night," Chris said unhappily.

73

IT WAS RAINING lightly at 3:30 A.M. when Chris Holmes and John drove Amelia and her crew, in two cars, to Pearl Harbor. It had poured all night, so Wheeler Field would be a mess. Amelia was thankful Paul had moved the airplane to Luke Field the day before.

The dark, wet streets of Honolulu were deserted at this early hour on a Saturday morning. There wasn't much conversation in the one car, especially from Harry or Fred; they were both nursing nasty hangovers from the previous night's imbibing.

It was just after 4:00 A.M. when the two cars pulled into the parking lot at the ferryboat pier. Daric sprang from the car and ran over to the lone silhouette huddled under an umbrella.

"You made it," Daric babbled elatedly.

"Wouldn't miss it for the world," Mila replied excitedly. "But ferry service over to Ford Island doesn't start until 6:15 A.M."

"Lieutenant Arnold arranged transportation for us for this morning. Come on." Daric grabbed Mila's hand and rushed her over to where the others were boarding a private charter for the island.

"Mila, good morning," Paul said cordially.

"Good morning," she replied shyly.

"Everyone, this is Mila, my guest this morning. Careful getting into the boat," Daric said, helping her down and getting her seated.

"May I introduce Miss Amelia Earhart? Amelia, this is Mila. We met yesterday, when we were shopping for clothes for the luau," Daric said cheerfully.

"Good morning, Mila. Not a very hospitable morning to be out and about this early, is it?" Amelia bantered.

"It's an honour to meet you, Miss Earhart," Mila said, overwhelmed to be sitting right next to a legend, someone she'd looked up to for years.

"Amelia, please. I'm glad you could join us."

"Mila, this is my sister Dani," Daric offered.

"Pleased to meet you," Mila said, noticing the family resemblance instantly.

"So, you're the one that's captured my brother's heart," Dani teased and quickly received a punch in the upper arm for her efforts. "Ouch!"

Once the introductions were finished and everyone was secure in their seats, the boat headed across the dark, calm harbour. It didn't take long before they were moored at the Fleet Air Base dock on Ford Island.

Harry and Fred went to the weather station to get the latest weather reports while the others headed over to the hangar.

"Good morning," Lieutenant Arnold said pleasantly, despite the weather and the unfortunate circumstances at Wheeler Field. "I want to assure you that no one got near the Electra after you left yesterday and that I personally supervised the extraction from the hangar this morning."

"My goodness, you and your men haven't had a moment's rest since my arrival," Amelia declared.

"They all volunteered, ma'am," the lieutenant offered, to ease her anxiety.

"Thank you, Lieutenant," Amelia said graciously.

Paul and Daric were meticulously inspecting the outer surfaces of the airplane, with flashlights in hand. They checked the control surfaces for security, freedom of movement, and damage. Special attention was given to the landing gear and tires. The entire plane was checked closely for oil or fuel leaks. They made sure all access panels and scrubber covers were tightly secured. Shining his light into the pitot tube, Paul found no obstructions. Finally, he pushed his foot against the wheel chocks to make sure they were secure, which they were.

"There's a tailwind of fifteen miles an hour. Do you still want to be able to come back to Honolulu after flying for eight hours?" Fred asked Amelia. She simply nodded to indicate that she wanted the option.

"Then, we must account for eighteen hours flying time: eight outbound and ten back, with that tailwind," Fred continued, having quickly made the calculations.

"Put on an additional seventy-five gallons of fuel," Harry instructed. "We'll still be four-hundred-fifty pounds lighter than we were when we left Oakland."

It didn't take long to add the extra fuel. Once it had been completed, Paul reported, "Amelia, the pre-flight examination is done and everything checks out. I'm ready to run-up the engines, now."

Amelia nodded in response and took cover under the roof of the nearby hangar, taking Mila, Terry and Dani with her.

"Come on, Daric, one last time, eh," Paul said, as the two clambered up the wing and into the cockpit. When they were ready, Paul yelled, "Clear right," as he turned over the right engine. After the right engine had started, he repeated the procedure for the left engine. He let them run for five minutes to get warm before setting them at a higher power setting to ensure the engines ran properly. Once satisfied, he shut them down and left the cockpit. Daric followed. The light rain had finally stopped.

Amelia had walked out from under the shelter of the hangar to meet Paul. "Everything looks great," Paul assured her. "We're just going to do one last check around the nacelles and landing gear for any leaks. Then, you're good to go."

"Thanks, Paul, for everything." Amelia hugged him briefly; she wasn't normally one for public displays of affection.

"Good luck and be safe."

After Paul and Daric had walked around the airplane and satisfied themselves that all was in order, Paul gave Amelia the 'thumbs-up'. He then walked off to join Terry. The two of them would stay in Hawaii. Terry had agreed to marry Paul there in paradise and they would have their honeymoon there, too.

Amelia turned to Dani and Daric. She had met them only nine days ago, but, already, felt a strange kinship to both. She couldn't quite explain it, but it was there. Now, it was time to say goodbye.

"I'm so glad you guys decided to stay on in Hawaii. It's really beautiful here, and the weather is usually perfect," Amelia said cheerfully.

"The Holmeses were very gracious to extend their invitation for us to remain in their guest house, until we can get established here." Dani said, trying hard to keep the melancholy out of her voice.

"There isn't anything for us back on the mainland, so we might as well live in paradise, if given the choice, eh?" Daric tried to joke, but failed miserably.

Dani and Daric both knew what was about to happen. They just wished they could save their friend the trauma and heartache of having to endure it. But both realized they dared not do anything to prevent history from taking its course.

"Why the long faces?" Amelia couldn't understand their glum mood.

"Just be careful, okay? And don't take any unnecessary risks," Dani pleaded.

Dani hugged Amelia, then quickly joined Chris and Lieutenant Arnold, who were standing a safe distance away from the airplane.

Daric gave Amelia an embrace and quietly whispered in her ear, "Whatever you do, keep your life raft. Trust me." He turned and walked to stand beside Mila and his sister.

Amelia was extremely puzzled by their moods, and especially

Daric's last comment that made little sense to her. Why would she give up her life raft? That was simply crazy, considering the amount of water she was about to fly over.

Amelia shrugged, realizing she had no time for distractions right now. She was about to set out on the second leg of her world flight. Nothing would spoil her excitement.

As Amelia walked over to the airplane, she hoped one day she would meet up with Daric and Dani again, just to make sure they were all right. She decided right then and there she would call the Holmes for an update when she finished her world flight; the decision immediately put her mind at ease. Now, off to the business at hand!

74

AMELIA EASED HERSELF through the overhead hatch and into the pilot's seat. She looked out the windshield and realized there wasn't enough natural light yet. Checking her watch, she decided to wait another ten minutes. The extra time would also give the runway a chance to dry up a bit from the earlier rain.

While Amelia was waiting, newspaper reporters and photographers continued to gather along the length of the runway, all hoping to be the first to record history in the making. There was sufficient light for the spectators to see her takeoff, but she wasn't sure there would be enough for the photographers to get good clear shots.

When the time was right, Amelia yelled out the window to tell Fred and Harry to get on-board. They entered through the rear cabin door, securing it and themselves. Soon after, they signaled Amelia they were set to go.

"Clear right," Amelia yelled out the cockpit window. When she received the all clear sign, she started the right engine and, then, repeated the process to start the left engine. When both were running perfectly, she signaled for the wheel chocks to be removed.

Amelia taxied the airplane to the northeast end of the runway. She swung the Electra around and lined it up slightly to the right of the centre line of the runway. She turned to check on Fred and Harry; they were both ready.

A light wind was coming out of the southwest, barely enough to move the windsock on top of the hangar. The sky was now broken and visibility was good. Amelia made one last check of the engines' gauges and reset the directional gyros to match the compass reading.

Everything was ready. Amelia, with her feet firmly planted on the brakes, closed her eyes for just a moment, took one deep breath, and then opened them. While her left hand gripped the control yoke, her right advanced the throttles to half power. Keeping her right hand on both throttles, she released the brakes as she applied full power.

As the airplane slowly gathered speed, Amelia applied back pressure on the control yoke to keep the tail wheel firmly on the ground. She applied more pressure to the left rudder since the plane was drifting toward the right.

One of the mechanics, who had worked on the propellers earlier, had positioned himself at about the midway point along the runway to watch Miss Earhart's takeoff. As he watched and listened to the approaching airplane, he thought the left engine was turning over a little faster than the right and it was pushing the plane off to the right, closer to where he was standing.

"I can't watch," Dani whispered, as she buried her face in Daric's shoulder.

"You know she'll be all right," Daric whispered, not wanting Mila, who was standing on the other side of him, to hear their conversation.

"We don't know that. Our being here may have altered things," Dani murmured.

The airplane accelerated down the runway, Amelia applied elevator and aileron forces as needed. With her feet on the left and right rudder pedals, she worked them to keep the airplane travelling down the centre of the runway.

As the tail wheel lifted off the runway, Amelia thought, *In another ten seconds, we'll be up and on our way.* Then she noticed the plane was drifting farther to the right. She applied more pressure to the left rudder pedal, pushing it all the way to its stop, but the plane continued to stray off course.

Amelia realized if she didn't do something quickly, the airplane would run off the right side of the runway before she could get it into the air. So she did the only thing she could. She eased back on the left engine's throttle to reduce some of its power and help the rudders bring the plane back on course.

The mechanic who had been watching the takeoff saw the wing tip wobble. He assumed the aircraft had run over some rough patch on the runway. Then he sensed the right engine surge and take a quick hold; the airplane changed course from turning to the right to turning sharply to the left while its speed continued to increase. He braced for what he knew was coming: Amelia's airplane was in the initial stages of a ground loop.

Amelia felt the sensation of the right wing dropping and thought the right tire had blown or the oleo strut had collapsed.

"Brace yourself!" she yelled.

Amelia glanced at the left engine's manifold pressure gauge; it showed the reduced power setting. Looking out the cockpit window, she realized the plane was in a sweeping left turn.

The right wing was tilted down, almost touching the runway; pulling the left wheel off the ground. The entire weight of the airplane was now on the right wheel, causing the right landing gear to collapse. The left gear collapsed soon after. The plane immediately skidded into a left hand slide on its belly. Sparks flew all around the undercarriage as it scraped along the tarmac.

75

"LET'S GO," DARIC yelled as he raced toward the nearest car, which happened to be the lieutenant's. Chris, Paul and Dani were right on his heels. Lieutenant Arnold was close behind, yelling orders to his men on the way. "Get the fire truck out there, now!"

The five scrambled into the car, the lieutenant behind the wheel. They raced along the runway toward the airplane. The fire truck was right behind them; with 900 gallons of fuel on board the plane, everyone was praying for the inevitable not to happen. Meanwhile, the plane was continuing to career down the runway. By the time it finally stopped, it had travelled over 1,200 feet from its starting point, which it was now facing.

Amelia calmly shut down the engines, turned off the master switches, and popped open the overhead hatch. From her vantage point, she saw the fire truck right behind her and she watched it pull up on the left side of the airplane. The firemen quickly rolled out the truck's hose and pointed it at the fuselage. Everyone's prayers had been answered: there was no fire.

Chris and Daric leaped from the car before it had come to a complete stop and ran to the Electra. They arrived just as Amelia was exiting the cockpit and making her way along the left wing. Chris helped her down.

Amelia asked, "What happened?"

"Are you all right?" Daric asked anxiously.

"I'm fine. Where are Fred and Harry?"

Lieutenant Arnold had opened the rear cabin door. He found Harry just inside the door and Fred at the navigator's table, carefully folding up his charts.

"They're fine, Miss Earhart," the lieutenant reported.

"I'll put a guard detail on the plane and get them to start draining the fuel tanks." The lieutenant quickly gave the necessary orders.

"I don't understand what happened," Amelia said, totally at a loss for how things could have gone so wrong so quickly.

"We'll figure it out," Paul assured her.

"I'll check the plane to determine the extent of damage," Paul said decisively. "Why don't you guys check the runway? Check the tire marks to see if you can figure out what happened." Paul immediately started to inspect the airplane's damage.

Amelia, Dani, Fred and Lieutenant Arnold walked back down the runway, stopping at intervals to examine the tire marks on the tarmac.

"I just don't understand," Amelia muttered.

"Right here, look, the right track looks wider than the left," Fred observed. It was the only anomaly they found on the runway.

The group headed back toward the lieutenant's car; everyone lost in their own thoughts, trying to make sense of what had happened.

When they reached the car, Harry was already there, nursing a bruised elbow in the back seat. No one showed any interest in getting into the car; they all seemed restless as they started to analyse what had occurred, based on their recollections of the events.

"The plane functioned perfectly at the start," Amelia recalled. "As it gained speed, the right wing dropped down and the plane seemed to pull to the right. I eased off the left engine, and the plane started a long persistent left turn and ended up where it is now. It was all over instantly. The first thing I thought of was the right oleo strut or the right tire letting go. The way the plane pulled, it was probably a flat tire."

"This is a piece of G.D. bad luck," Fred mumbled.

"Yes, it is a little bit disappointing," Amelia admitted sadly.

"Well," Fred said, "when you're ready to fly again, I'll be ready to go along."

Harry had been sitting quietly in the back of the car, never entering the conversation.

They returned to the airplane for a closer inspection. The press was there and began firing questions from all sides.

"You ran through bunches of grass, didn't you?" one reporter claimed.

"The runway was perfect. The grass had nothing to do with it. I am sure it was a result of a structural failure," Amelia answered firmly.

"Of course, now you will give up the trip?" asked a reporter who sported a pointy jaw and broad nose.

"I think not. This is merely a setback, nothing else."

Amelia made her way over to Paul and Daric. "What's the damage?"

"I won't kid you, Amelia, it looks pretty bad," said Paul. "The right wing is damaged, and the right engine and nacelle are being held to the wing by only two bolts. The right oil tank burst and spilled oil on the runway. The fuel filler neck was torn open and spilled gas. It was a miracle there was no fire."

Amelia looked crestfallen as she lowered her head.

"Before I can assess the total damage, I'll need to do a further check," Paul said heavily. "Lieutenant, is there somewhere we can store our equipment from the plane?"

"I'll have everything removed and put into the tool room of the hangar where it will be kept under lock and key."

"Come on, there's not much we can do here now. Let's go back to the house," Chris suggested. He could see how upset Amelia was.

"Daric and I will stay here to make sure everything is taken care of. I'll also send a telegram to G.P. to let him know what happened, before he hears it from the media," Paul offered.

76

G.P. AND BILL Miller were waiting patiently in Bill's office at the Oakland administration building. The unbearable silence was shattered by the telephone ringing on Bill's desk. G.P. snatched up the receiver, giving Bill an apologetic look as he did so. He needed to take this call: he had to take this call.

"Hello," G.P. said anxiously.

"Have you got the news?"

"No," G.P. replied.

"Sorry . . . plane crashed taking off. Burst into flames . . ."

"Here, you take this," G.P. said, as he calmly handed the receiver over to Bill Miller. "I'll step outside . . . call me when you find out . . ." G.P. walked out of the office.

In the chilly early morning fog, G.P. paced back and forth outside the administration building for only a few moments. He knew Amelia was an excellent aviator, but, in his heart, he feared the worst. He crumpled to his knees and buried his face in his hands.

After what seemed like an eternity to G.P., but was actually only a few minutes, Bill ran out of the building. He met a messenger and intercepted a telegram addressed to G.P. He debated whether to read it and had decided to do so; he didn't think G.P. would mind. After he read it, he went in search of G.P.

Bill found G.P. slumped in a heap on the ground. He opened the message and reread it, this time out loud.

"*AMELIA IN CRACK-UP WHILE ATTEMPTING TAKEOFF, TIRE BLEW OUT, ONE WHEEL OFF, OIL DRIPPING ON RUN-WAY. NO ONE HURT. AMELIA CALM, COLLECTED.*"

"G.P., the message is from Paul . . . it's all right . . . there wasn't any fire . . . they're all safe," Bill said softly. He wanted to make sure that what he was saying was getting through to a distraught G.P.

77

IT WAS 7:00 A.M. when Amelia and her group returned to the Holmeses' estate, after dropping Mila off at her mother's shop. When Amelia entered the main house, Mona told her Paul was on the telephone and directed her to the study to take the call.

"The airplane isn't damaged as badly as I first thought," Paul started optimistically. "But I think we should have it shipped back to Burbank for the repair work to be completed."

"How are the engines?"

"All four propeller blades were curled, which is a good thing. It means there wasn't any sudden stoppage, which would have resulted in major damage to the internal parts of the engines," Paul replied confidently.

"How long do you think it will take to get the Electra ready for shipping? And how long do you think it will take for the repairs?" Amelia asked enthusiastically.

"I should think the plane could be ready for shipping in a couple of days. As far as the repairs go, my best estimate would be two to three months."

"Okay. Let me call G.P. to run this by him and, then, I'll get right back to you." Amelia was about to hang up the telephone when Paul stopped her.

"Before you hang up, I just want to say one thing first," Paul started.

"Okay," she said reluctantly.

"I heard a saying once. It said a pilot's life is hours of boredom, punctuated by moments of sheer terror. How you handle those moments defines how good a pilot you really are. And you, my friend, handled yourself admirably," Paul said proudly.

"Thank you, Paul," Amelia said shyly, as she ended the call.

78

"HOW ARE YOU?" G.P.'s tone conveyed true concern. He had been anxiously awaiting a telephone call from Amelia. He had to hear her voice; hear from her personally that she was okay. The telegram just didn't do it for him.

"I'm fine. We're all fine. Only our spirits are bruised," Amelia assured him. "But my bird is wounded."

"Look, if you want to call this off, I'm fine with that," G.P. said, secretly hoping she would call the world flight off and come home to him.

"No, I want to keep going, but I'm afraid we don't have the money to make the repairs to be able to continue." Amelia's tone told G.P. everything he needed to know.

"Don't you worry about the money. I'll start right away raising the funds," G.P. assured her. He knew she was determined to see this through, no matter the cost.

"That would be wonderful," Amelia gushed. She was more than pleased that G.P. believed she could do this. "About the crash, should I issue a statement to the press?"

"No, I'll do it. I have more outlets here. Why don't you work on your article for the *Tribune* and get it filed?"

"Okay." Amelia paused for a moment, not hanging up. There

was something else she had to say, but she was finding it extremely hard to express.

"What is it?" G.P. sensed there was more.

"I'm sorry, for the crash. I don't know what went wrong," she finally got out, around the lump in her throat. She didn't want to disappoint him and she didn't want to disappoint herself either.

"As long as you're not hurt, the crash doesn't matter. Come home as soon as you can and we'll get ready to start again," G.P. said and, then, ended the call.

79

AMELIA RETURNED TO the lanai after her call with G.P. The others had already gathered and were enjoying a light morning snack, compliments of Mona.

"I just got off the phone with G.P. He wants us home as soon as possible," Amelia said. "Chris, how soon do you think we can get passage back to the States for Fred, Harry and myself?"

"Let me go see what I can do," Chris said and then left.

A few minutes later, Chris returned to the lanai. "I have you all booked on the *S.S. Malolo*, which sails at noon today. You'll be back in Los Angeles, early on the 25th. Tickets will be waiting at the pier for you."

"Great. Let me call Paul and tell him what's happening." Amelia left to place her call.

* * *

"Paul, we're leaving today on the *S.S. Malolo* for Los Angeles. When will the Electra be ready for shipping?" Amelia asked anxiously.

"You'll have to sign some paperwork and releases first, but it can be ready for shipping in two days," Paul assured her.

"The Army Air Corps will finish crating the airplane and

equipment for shipping. I've made arrangements with Young Brothers, a local shipping company, to move the airplane from Luke Field by barge, for shipment on the next transport to Los Angeles. It will be loaded on the *S.S. Lurline* leaving here on Monday, the 22nd," Paul conveyed.

"One other thing," Paul added. "Daric wants to sail back with the Electra. I think he's still a little spooked about this Case character."

"I can't say I blame him, after all that's happened," Amelia muttered.

"Daric also told me he had talked to one of the mechanics who had worked on the engines. This guy told Daric he had distinctly heard the left engine running faster than the right. That would explain the plane drifting to the right as it accelerated down the runway," Paul added. "I want Lockheed to check the airplane specifically for any tampering before they start the repairs. I want to get some answers before you start the world flight again. We don't want a repeat of what just happened."

"So you, too, think there was a problem with the airplane?" Amelia asked.

"Yes, I do."

"Then, I wouldn't mind Daric staying with the airplane, just to keep an eye on it. When you finish with the shipping arrangements for the Electra, can you arrange for two passenger tickets, too? Dani will most likely want to go with him," Amelia stated.

"Consider it done. Have a safe trip back to the mainland. I'll be in touch when Terry and I get back to Burbank in a couple of weeks," said Paul, as he finished the call.

While Amelia was still in the house, she phoned G.P. "Hi, it's me. We're sailing today at noon on the *S.S. Malolo* and should be back in Los Angeles early Thursday morning."

"That was quick," G.P. responded excitedly.

"Paul has made all the arrangements to ship the Electra to Los Angeles. He wants the repairs done at the Lockheed factory in Burbank, which I agreed to. It will be leaving here on Monday."

"Great," G.P. said.

"How's the press on the mainland handling the crash?" Amelia asked, even though she was somewhat reluctant to hear the answer.

"Everyone understands what could happen if a tire blows going seventy miles an hour in a car. They're all treating it sympathetically. They don't blame you."

"But I don't think it was a blown tire. I'm not really sure what went wrong," Amelia confessed.

"Whatever the cause, I've already started contacting sponsors to get financial help to repair the Electra. I'm going to head back to Los Angeles and should be home tomorrow, if you need to reach me. And I'll be there to meet your ship. I'm happy you're coming home," G.P. said and, then, hung up.

As Amelia replaced the telephone in its cradle, Chris came into the study. "It's time to go."

Amelia, Fred and Harry carried very little luggage, as they had packed lightly for the world flight. They were always packed and ready to leave at a moment's notice.

They made their way back out to the lanai, to say their goodbyes. Amelia walked up to Dani and gently grasped both of her hands, cradling them in hers.

"Dani, Daric wants to sail back to the mainland with the airplane. I asked Paul to make all the arrangements for both of you. I assumed you would want to travel with him," Amelia stated. "The Electra will be ready for shipping on Monday. Chris and Mona said you can stay here until then."

"Thank you, Amelia, for everything. The car will be crowded, so I'll wait here with Terry for Daric and Paul to return. I'll see you in a few days," Dani said. However, she wasn't so sure she would ever see Amelia again, because she could be going home, herself, at any time.

Amelia bid goodbye to Terry and, then, left with Fred and Harry.

"We'll be back soon and, then, I'll get us some lunch," Mona said to Terry and Dani as she followed Chris to the car.

80

THE TELEPHONE RANG only once before it was picked up. "Hello."

"Admiral . . . sorry, I forgot; no names. I called to let you know the mission was a success. The world flight has been stopped," Case reported proudly. "They're leaving for the mainland today."

"From what I am hearing, it has not been stopped, only delayed. She plans to continue," the admiral spat.

"I did what you told me to do. I fulfilled my contract and expect to be paid now, as agreed," Case demanded.

"Your contract will be fulfilled when I say it is," the admiral snapped back. "What is happening with the airplane?"

"It's being shipped back to Los Angeles on Monday," Case said dejectedly.

"Stay with the airplane. Call me when you know what the repair timeline will be and how they are progressing," the admiral ordered.

"You told me to stop the flight from Hawaii to Howland Island. I did that. Now I want my money," Case tried again.

"You fool! This is not about your money."

"It is to me," Case muttered.

"This is just the start of something big: something bigger than you could possibly imagine. And we cannot afford to have anyone watching our activities in the Pacific over the next few months. That is what your contract is all about. Now, just get on with it," the admiral snapped and slammed down the receiver.

The admiral stood, turned, and looked out his office window at the beautiful cherry blossoms. He had worked hard to become an expert on naval aviation. He was determined to prove to the emperor that they needed aircraft carriers to be the dominant force in Japan's navy and that included all modern weaponry and fighter planes to operate from them. He continually came up against opposition; those who clung firmly to the belief in the supremacy of battleships—a weapon he considered similar to a samurai sword—a powerful weapon from the past, one that belonged in the annals of history books.

This undertaking was not sanctioned by the Imperial Supreme War Council; he was doing this on his own. What was about to transpire over the next few months was going to eventually affect the entire world. He wasn't about to have one insignificant stooge ruin it.

He spun around, grabbed the telephone, dialed a number from memory, and waited for the other end to answer. When the receiver was picked up the admiral uttered only two words, "Finish it," and disconnected the call.

81

WHEN AMELIA'S PARTY arrived at the wharf, band music was playing and lending to the festive mood at Pier 11. Passengers were starting to board and friends were bidding them farewell.

Chris had parked the car and gone to the passenger ticketing office to pick up the tickets. While he was gone, Mona had gone to buy some leis for her departing guests, in accordance with tradition.

When Chris returned, the group gently pushed their way through the crowds on the pier, working their way toward the ship with what little luggage they carried.

They made their way up the boarding ramp and were escorted by the purser to their cabins. Once they had stowed their luggage, they all gathered in Amelia's stateroom.

"Well, my friends, I guess this is goodbye," Amelia said.

"No, it's aloha," Mona corrected, as she gave Amelia a big hug and put a lei over her head. She moved away to continue the tradition with Fred and Harry.

"Besides, it's not goodbye. You'll be stopping by here again when you resume your world flight," Chris said optimistically.

"So true, my friend. Until then, aloha," Amelia said, hugging Chris.

All too soon, a blast from the ship's horn signalled it was time for all who weren't sailing for the mainland to leave the ship. "Thank you, again, for our wonderful accommodations and the meals were, as usual, exquisite," Amelia said.

"And everything will be waiting for your return. Be safe," Mona said. She and Chris left the stateroom and went back to the pier. As they watched the *S.S. Malolo* pull away from the dock, they waved at their friends, who lined the railings, all eager to get home and try again.

82

"WHERE DO YOU want to go?" Mila asked Daric shyly. Yesterday when they dropped Mila at the shop, she and Daric had agreed to spend today together.

"I don't know. You decide. I've never been to Hawaii before." Daric smiled charmingly.

"Really? Someone like you?" Mila truly thought Daric was pulling her leg. She reached down and clasped his hand and walked down Fort Street.

"Really. And what do you mean, 'someone like me'?"

"Oh, I don't know. You seem like someone who gets around." Mila immediately realized how that sounded once she said it out loud. "I'm sorry. I didn't mean it like that. What I was trying to say is that you seem well educated and worldly, I guess. Not someone that lives a sheltered life like me," Mila mumbled sadly.

"If you could do anything you wanted, what would it be?" Daric wanted to know what inspired this young beauty.

"I'd like to do something like Miss Earhart. Something that most women wouldn't dare dream of doing, even what most men wouldn't dream of doing." Mila's eyes were alight with her imagined future of possibilities.

"Like what?"

"I don't know. I haven't given it much thought. I just know I want to make a name for myself, like Miss Earhart. I want to make a difference. I do know I don't want to run the gift shop, but that's all my mom sees in my future. She's grooming me to take over from her someday, soon, too, I think. She doesn't get around as well as she used to and she gets tired real easy."

"My mother has always said you could do anything you put your mind to. I truly believe that. So don't give up on your dreams. Find something you're really passionate about and go for it whole-heartedly," Daric encouraged.

"And what is it you're passionate about?"

"You," he whispered, as he leaned in to steal a kiss. A shadow caught the corner of his eye as he pulled away from Mila's warm and inviting lips. He wasn't sure what he had seen, but decided he would be more attentive to his surroundings.

Mila and Daric walked down Fort Street to the Aloha Market and spent the afternoon walking amongst the stalls, hand-in-hand, enjoying each other's company. As the sun started to set, it reminded Daric that he had to get back to the Holmeses' estate. He and Dani were leaving for California in the morning.

Daric walked Mila back to the gift shop and stood outside. He held her hands and looked deeply into her warm brown eyes.

"I've really enjoyed today," he said sincerely.

"Me too," Mila agreed.

Daric leaned in close and whispered, "Don't look too quickly, but casually turn your head around and look at the guy with the long brown coat." She did as she was asked. "Do you know him?"

"No. Why?" Mila asked nervously as she turned back to face Daric.

"It's probably nothing, but he's been watching us all day. I thought maybe your mom had sent him to make sure I behaved," he said jokingly, trying to lessen Mila's apparent concern. The guy looked like a native Hawaiian to Daric; he certainly didn't look like Case.

"I don't think she would do that," Mila said hesitantly.

"As I said, it's probably nothing." Daric leaned in and kissed Mila, who returned his affection willingly. "I'm so glad I got to know you, Mila."

"Me too."

"I have to go."

"I know," she said sadly. "I'll be down at the pier to say goodbye tomorrow."

"You mean aloha," Daric teased as he pecked her on the cheek and left her standing in front of the store. She watched him walk away. As she turned and climbed the two steps to enter the shop, she took one last look down the street to where the stranger had been. He was gone.

83

AS PROMISED, STANDING there on the wharf and looking like a Hawaiian princess, was Mila. Daric got out of the Holmeses' car and ran over to her. He grabbed her around her narrow waist, swept her off her feet, and twirled her in the air amidst a stream of giggles that spilled from her lips.

"Put me down, silly. You're causing a scene," Mila scoffed half-heartedly.

"So what?" Daric shouted, still twirling Mila. "I don't care if we cause a scene. I'm thrilled you came down to see me off and I want everyone here to know it."

"Put the poor girl down, before you make her dizzy," Dani cautioned as she walked up. "Hi, Mila."

"Hi, Dani." Mila laughed as she finally found there was ground under her feet again.

"Here, I got these for you," Mila said, as she placed a lei over Daric's head and another over Dani's.

"Thank you," Dani said.

"Give me a minute," Daric said as he ran to Terry and Paul.

"Keep a good eye on that plane for us, okay?" Paul directed as they shook hands.

"You bet," Daric replied. "We'll see you in a couple of weeks, when you get back to the mainland."

Daric turned to Chris and Mona, just as Dani walked over. "Thank you both so much for your generous hospitality," Dani started.

"Yeah," Daric added.

"You're both more than welcome," Mona replied, embracing first Dani and then Daric.

"And the invitation is still open anytime you want to come back to Hawaii," Chris said, as he shook Daric's hand and bent to embrace Dani.

"Thank you, we might just take you up on that," Daric replied, looking over his shoulder and smiling at Mila.

A blast from the ship's horn ended all further conversation until its sound stopped resonating.

"Okay, you two, get going," Chris insisted.

Dani and Daric finished their goodbyes, made their way up the boarding ramp and found a place along the Promenade's railing. It didn't take them long to single out their friends among the crowd on the wharf. They all waved as the ship slowly pulled away from the pier.

"What's Chris doing?" Dani asked.

"Waving. Why?"

"It doesn't look like a natural goodbye wave to me."

While Chris was waving to Dani and Daric, as the ship pulled away, he saw a man standing at the railing of one of the First Class balconies. Something about the man was familiar. Chris strained and looked at him more carefully. Then it hit him. He knew the man. He had to warn Daric and Dani about him somehow.

As the ship left Honolulu harbor, Dani pulled her lei from around her neck. "This is a tradition," she said as she indicated to Daric to follow her example. "You toss your lei into the sea. Legend has it, that, if the lei floats back toward the island, it means you will return one day," Dani explained.

"One . . . two . . . three . . ."

Daric and Dani threw their leis into the sea and watched with anticipation. The ship's wake washed over the leis; they seemed to just hang there, neither going ashore nor drifting out to sea: as if they were suspended in time.

84

THE FIRST FULL day onboard the *S.S. Lurline* was relatively relaxing. She was one of Matson's White Ships and a sister ship to the *S.S. Malolo*, but she carried fewer passengers.

Daric had gone up on deck several times, since leaving Honolulu, to check on the Electra and the fourteen boxes and crates loaded on the Aft Deck. Every visit was the same: he would check to make sure that the fuselage was as he had previously left it and that all the crates and boxes were still properly sealed. While he was on deck, he would scan the area to see whether he could spot anything out of the ordinary. There was never anything amiss.

Dani and Daric were just finishing dinner in the Main Dining Room. The tables all had white linen tablecloths and centerpieces with fresh-cut flowers. Daric wiped his mouth on the white linen napkin and placed it on his empty plate. "I'm going out on deck to check on the plane again. I won't be long," he told Dani, as he excused himself from the table and left the dining room.

Dani finished her dessert and coffee and decided she would go out on deck, too. It was such a beautiful evening, and the air was still tropically warm. She knew it wouldn't be in another day or two when they would be getting closer to Los Angeles.

Dani strolled around the Promenade Deck. She spotted a few other guests heading back inside. On the forward deck, she found a couple on one of the lounges, huddled under a blue-and-white-striped blanket, enjoying the fresh evening air. She smiled and carried on toward the aft section of the ship. If she was lucky, she might find Daric still checking over his precious cargo on the open deck below.

As Dani approached the aft part of the Promenade Deck, she thought she could hear faint voices below. When she peered over the railing, her heart jumped into her throat.

Oh my God! Think! Do something quick! her mind screamed.

85

DARIC WAS JUST finishing his inspection of the last two crates stored at the back of the deck's cargo area. When he looked up, he was staring into the barrel of a gun. Holding the gun was Rick Barak Case.

"So good of you to make my next task so easy," Case sneered, as Daric slowly stood up.

"And what task might that be?" Daric grunted, trying desperately to muster some bravado.

"Getting rid of some loose ends, of course."

"Why are you doing this? What did I ever do to you?"

"You stuck your nose where it didn't belong, one too many times."

"But why are you trying to stop Amelia's flight? What could it possibly have to do with you?" Daric was trying to stall as long as he could, hoping someone would catch what was happening and swoop in to rescue him at the last minute, just like he had seen in so many old movies.

"I couldn't give a damn about some dumb broad trying to prove she's man enough to fly a stupid plane around the world. It'll never happen, anyway. As for why I'm doing this, it's for the money, of course, and lots of it," Case proclaimed.

"So, is killing me part of the deal?"

"Hell, no. As I said, I'm just tying up some loose ends."

"Look, I won't say anything. I promise." He sounded pretty lame, even to his ears.

"Yeah, right. Now, back up just a tad, would ya, back against the rail like a good kid."

Daric took a few slow steps backwards, looking for anything within reach he could use against Case. Movement from above caught his attention. It was Dani. He slowly shook his head no, but he was sure she hadn't seen his signal, since she had already disappeared from the railing.

86

IT SEEMED TO take forever to find the stairs, but, once she did, Dani raced down them, two at a time, flying down the three flights to where Daric was being held at gunpoint. She didn't need to be a genius to know what fate had in store for Daric.

Dani knew Daric had seen her. She hoped he would know enough to stall as long as possible. Her plan was to sneak up on Case and, then, run at him, grab his gun hand and knock him down. Daric could grab the gun and then they would escort Case to the ship's brig. She hoped ships in this era still had brigs.

When Dani reached the Aft Deck, she was out of breath. Knowing she couldn't sneak up on Case while she was gasping for air, she took a few moments to settle her breathing and her nerves. She could still hear the faint conversation.

As Dani crept along the bulkhead, hidden among the shadows, a movement to her left made her freeze in mid-stride. A man had emerged from the exact spot where she was heading. His attention was focused on the two people at the stern of the ship; he didn't even notice Dani concealed in the shadows.

The man stealthily moved toward Daric and Case. As he slowly and silently closed the distance, he reached under his long dark coat and pulled out a gun.

What happened next was a complete blur. Dani hurled herself from her hiding place and screamed for all she was worth, "NO!"

She crashed into the man in the coat, just as his gun went off. The crash knocked the man to the deck, but Dani kept her balance and never missed a stride as she raced toward her brother.

Dani's scream distracted Case, who turned to see what the commotion was. The shot that had been aimed for the back of his head grazed his forehead instead. When Dani plowed into him, he felt as if a high-speed locomotive had hit him; then, his world turned upside down.

87

"DANI!" DARIC SCREAMED as he lunged in desperation after his sister. He watched in horror as Dani's momentum and Case's dazed off-balance state propelled them both over the stern rail.

Daric looked over the rail into the churning black sea below. He hoped to find his sister, all the while knowing a fall from this height would have killed her. But he kept looking and hoping, anyway.

"Help me," a panting voice pleaded.

Daric looked harder. He finally spotted Dani; she had a precarious grip on a broken rail. In the same instant, he saw Case hanging from another rail, swinging his body like a pendulum; at just the right moment, he let go and landed on one of the first class balconies.

"Dani, grab my hand," Daric yelled, as he hung over the railing, trying desperately to reach his sister.

Dani reached up with one hand and grabbed Daric's, but she couldn't get a secure enough hold. Daric wrapped his legs around the railing and reached further over. "Grab my wrist. I need a better grip to pull you up," stretching his other arm lower for Dani to get a better hold.

"The bands, they'll touch. We don't know what'll happen," Dani cautioned.

"Well, we know what will happen if you don't. Now grab my wrist," Daric insisted.

Dani reached with her other hand and grabbed Daric's wrist. The travel bands touched and, instantly, everything went black.

The man in the long coat who had been trying to locate Case, watched in disbelief as the two vanished. He figured the shadows and the moonlight were playing tricks on him. They must have fallen overboard that's all. Now, he had some unfinished business to attend to.

88

"PROFESSOR?" HERMES WHISPERED. He didn't want to wake Sandra.

"Awroooo," Bear yowled at that strange voice, stirring the occupants of the bedroom.

"Again, Hermes? What is it this time?" Quinn mumbled, still half asleep. It seemed like just a couple of hours ago that Hermes had interrupted their sleep the first time. Quinn rolled over, opened one eye and confirmed that it was exactly three hours ago.

"Professor, they're on the move," Hermes announced.

"What?" Quinn bolted upright, quickly activating the comm; Hermes appeared, instantly. "Where?"

"I first realized they were no longer in California when the coordinates had them a significant distance to the west of that location," Hermes said.

"Quinn, what is it? Who are you talking to?" Sandra mumbled, pulling herself up into a sitting position. "Oh," she said, seeing Hermes's 3D image in their bedroom again.

"Sorry, Dr. Delaney, I was hoping I wouldn't wake you," Hermes apologized. "But apparently Bear made that unachievable."

Bear had cautiously made her way to where Hermes image was projected and sniffed.

"Is it the kids?"

"Yes."

"Then wake me," she ordered. "I have to know what's happening."

"Go on," Quinn pressed.

"When they first appeared on my screen, I had them at 34.2006°N by 118.3586°W. Then, they were stationary for a while at 21.3069°N, 157.8583°W. Because their vital signs didn't change significantly, I didn't want to disturb you."

"And now?" Quinn asked, anxiously.

Bear realized it was the same guy who had visited earlier and decided he wasn't worth expending any more energy on. She returned to her spot by the French doors and soon fell back to sleep.

"Well, it seems they moved from Burbank, California to Honolulu, Hawaii. They spent some time there and were moving slowly on an easterly heading. When they reached 24.7035°N, 155.8793°W, they were suddenly at 51° 30' 30" N, 0° 4' 25" W. I can only deduce that the travel bands were activated, taking them from the middle of the Pacific Ocean to London, England.

"When?" Quinn asked.

"Just moments ago, Professor," Hermes said proudly, on top of the situation.

"No, not when it happened. When in time are they?" Quinn demanded.

"Oh, my simple mistake, Professor. The chronometer indicates they are in 1888."

"What!" Sandra cried out.

Bear sprang wide awake at Sandra's shriek.

Part III

At One Time or Another

89

IT WAS COLD. It was damp. It was dark. It was smelly. These were the first sensations that registered in Dani's perplexed mind.

"Daric?" Dani whispered, anxiously waiting for the curtain of blackness to lift, but it only regressed to variant shades of grey. Their first jump through time, it took a few minutes for their new surrounding to come into focus. This was different: it must be dusk.

"What's that awful smell?" Daric moaned, sitting on the hard damp surface.

"You mean what smells like dead fish, sour milk, rotten cabbage and horse manure?" If Daric's first thought was to complain, then Dani knew he was all right, even though she couldn't clearly see him under the veil of darkness.

"That would be it," Daric agreed. "Are you okay?" He searched for Dani's hand, just to reassure himself that she was, in fact, all right.

"I'm fine. You?"

"I'm good." He looked at their surroundings, as best he could, through the haze blanking the area. He finally spotted a silhouette off in the distance. Although its shape differed slightly from what he remembered, two distinct features were very familiar. "Well, I'll be," he muttered.

"What?"

"It would seem that we've arrived in London, England," Daric said confidently.

"How can you be so sure?"

"Look off to your right and tell me what you see."

Through the late evening sky Dani saw the outline of a structure. Even though it was still under construction and wouldn't be finished for a few more years, the two massive square piers sunk into the river bed were unmistakably the foundations of the Tower Bridge. Dani looked across the peninsula, created by the meandering Thames River, and found another familiar shape off in the distance. It was Big Ben, and it was right where she thought it would be.

"So, I guess the next question is: why here? why London?" Dani pondered aloud.

"And in what time period?" Daric added.

"I wish this was home," Dani said unhappily. "I'm wondering if we'll ever get back."

Daric had never heard his sister sound so despondent before. It's wasn't like her to abandon hope so easily. Dani always looked at the glass as being half-full. Something wasn't right. He had no idea when they'd get home, but he knew their dad would stop at nothing until they were.

"Dani, remember you said time travels at different speeds? For all we know, it could be a matter of only hours since our disappearance," Daric said encouragingly.

"Or it could be a matter of months or even years. How are we supposed to know?"

"I refuse to believe that and so should you. Dad's a genius. He'll figure this out. We just have to be patient . . . and try to fit in here as best we can, until that happens."

"And try not to alter history, as we know it," Dani muttered.

"As for right now, I don't know about you, but I'd like to get as far away from the river and its horrid stench as possible. Then, we can figure out the current date and try to blend into whatever time period this is," Daric suggested.

"Agreed, but let's stay in the shadows for now, until we can figure this out. We don't want to draw any unwanted attention our way."

90

QUINN HAD TOSSED and turned most of the night. His feeling of guilt for his children's predicament was weighing heavily on his troubled mind.

After Hermes had interrupted them for a second time that night, and realizing sleep was eluding him, Quinn decided he might as well get up and go back to the lab. The sooner he got started, the sooner Dani and Daric would be safely back home. The only problem was he wasn't quite sure where to start.

With a flashlight in hand, Quinn walked across the dew-covered lawn, between the scattered pine trees and out toward the gazebo. Bear accompanied him, eagerly wagging her tail, while chasing the bouncing flashlight beam out in front.

The lake was like a mirror in the still of the early morning. Quinn could see the faint crimson-orange glow on the eastern horizon, a prelude to the rising sun. The weather forecast promised another beautiful spring day that he knew he would see little of.

Quinn could hear a faint call of a lone loon echoing around the corner of the peninsula. A nest had been built into the rocky shoreline there. He smiled when he thought of Sandra's overprotectiveness of the nest and of the pair of loons. She had posted signs warning boaters not to cause too much wake, which could disturb or possibly destroy the nest. There were only a few mating pairs in the area and she hoped their numbers would increase over the next few years.

Sandra always loved the call of the loon, especially at dusk. She said the haunting sound, echoing across the lake, took her to another world, a mystical one where she could lie in the gentle embrace of tranquillity and escape the pressures of her hectic day.

Quinn reached the gazebo and punched in his entry code. He followed Bear inside and quickly made his way to the rear panel. Flipping up the cover plate, he inserted his USB key to gain access to the lab's lower level. Nothing happened. The access panel light remained red.

"That's strange," Quinn muttered. He removed the key, inserted it a second time, and got the same results.

Quinn tapped his wrist comm and within a millisecond Hermes responded, "Yes, Professor."

Bear heard that strange voice again. She looked around for the intruder, but found nothing.

"Hermes, the access door won't open. Override the code and let me in. Then, I want you to run a diagnostic to find out why it wouldn't accept my key," Quinn instructed.

"On it, Professor," Hermes replied, just as the access panel light flashed green. A faint click immediately followed. Part of the floor and the adjacent wall pulled apart, exposing the hidden staircase. Bear vanished through the opening in search of the phantom intruder.

Quinn descended and moved directly to his command center.

91

RICHARD BARAK CASE couldn't stop that horrific sound that he heard yesterday from resonating in his head. It had haunted his every waking moment. He knew there was only one thing he could do about it. He had to go back to the Delaney estate and find the cause of Quinn's anguished wail.

Richard got into his car, a titanium-silver Abruzzi, one of only eighty-one ever built. It looked like a modern version of the *Batmobile*. The Abruzzi, however, was more than a technological masterpiece; it was a new chapter in automotive production, linked to the world's most demanding car race: Le Mans.

The hand-built Abruzzi *Spirit of Le Mans* was a unique, front-engine, rear-transaxle and rear-radiator super sports car that delivered six-hundred-plus horsepower. The advanced design and aerodynamics offered astounding down-force for road handling.

Its performance wasn't the only feature that set the Abruzzi apart from other exotic cars. Its ground-breaking environmental design and construction of its body system offered advantages that no other automobile body system on the planet could match. The multi-layer composite system was lighter than and just as strong as carbon fiber; in addition, however, it was also dent-resistant, shatter-proof and recyclable. These advancements opened up a brand new era of automotive design.

Richard had to admit he liked his expensive toys which included a fleet of exotic cars, a flotilla of luxury yachts in a range of shapes and sizes, and a couple of private jets. As a narcissistic billionaire, he enjoyed flaunting his wealth in front of others less fortunate.

Richard headed for the Delaneys', normally a forty-five minute drive from his house, but he was in a hurry and easily reduced his travel time by fifteen minutes. He pulled off the highway and followed the long, winding, tree-canopied dirt road. He turned into the driveway and parked beside Daric's silver Panoz AIV Roadster. The Roadster's presence meant that Daric must be home from university.

Richard admired Daric's car, but it wasn't practical for him. It did, however, make him wish he was twenty years younger and a little more free-spirited to be comfortable behind the wheel. The Aluminum-Intensive Vehicle (AIV) Roadster was designed purely for fun. The three-hundred-five horsepower, quad-cam aluminum Ford SVT V-8 engine could go from zero to sixty in under five seconds.

Richard got out of the Abruzzi. He scanned the yard, paying particular attention to the peninsula, as he made his way to the front door and rang the doorbell. He waited only a few moments before the door swung open.

"Richard, what a pleasant surprise. What are you doing here?" Sandra asked nervously, but politely. This was the last thing she needed right now: company.

"You mentioned a few weeks ago when I saw you in town, that Dani and Daric would be home during their spring break. So, I wanted to pop by to say hi. I haven't seen them since Thanksgiving. I hope this isn't an inconvenient time," Richard said, with a dashing smile. Frankly, he didn't really care whether it was inconvenient. He needed to know what had Quinn so rattled, and his visit with Dani and Daric was the perfect excuse. Besides, he always enjoyed being in Sandra's company. *Quinn was so lucky,* he thought enviously. She was almost his once.

"Uh . . . um . . . well, Richard, you just missed them. They aren't here right now," Sandra sputtered nervously. "I wish you had called first before coming out all this way. It would have saved you the trip and the time."

Sandra hated to lie; it went against the very fiber of her being. But she quickly reassured herself that it wasn't really a lie; it just wasn't the whole truth because Dani and Daric weren't actually home at the moment.

"Oh, I thought they would be. I noticed Daric's car in the drive-way. Will they be back soon? I could come in and wait a while," Richard suggested, as he prepared to enter the house.

"I don't know when they'll be back, Richard," Sandra blurted, quickly stepping through the doorway, effectively blocking Richard's advance. "I'd hate for you to ruin such a beautiful day waiting around here. Why don't I call you when they return and we'll set a time for you to come back for a visit? You could join us for a family dinner."

"That sounds great, Sandra. Thanks. I'd like to catch up with them, find out how their classes are going," Richard replied agreeably. But he wasn't finished yet.

Sandra looked physically relieved by Richard's response. But, before she could usher him to his car, he added, "Now that I think about it, you're right. I'd hate to waste my trip out here. So, why don't I see how Quinn's doing? Is he around? I haven't seen or heard from him since he went on leave from the university."

92

"RICHARD, I REALLY don't think that's such a good idea," Sandra insisted, panic hovering on the edge of her voice.

"Why not?" Richard asked stubbornly.

"Well," she started, "it's just not a good time." She couldn't come up with a plausible reason at the moment.

"Nonsense. If Quinn knew I was here, he'd want to see me. I won't stay long," Richard assured her. Without waiting for Sandra's objection, he pressed further. "Is he out there?" Richard asked, pointing at the gazebo in the distance.

Sandra nodded, defeated. Knowing Richard's insistent determination and her inability to come up with a good excuse, she accepted that this was a battle she just couldn't win.

"Great." Richard smiled triumphantly, then turned and started his trek to the peninsula, hoping to finally get some answers.

Richard thought how strangely Sandra was behaving. He looked back over his shoulder once, then resumed his journey. He had never seen her so nervous or flustered. She was always so confident, polished and professional. As Head of Emergency Services at Mount Albert Hospital, nothing ever fazed Sandra. Something was definitely out of sync here.

Sandra watched Richard walk away. "Damn," she muttered. She

turned and entered the house, making her way to the kitchen. She had to warn Quinn.

She pressed the intercom button. "Quinn?"

"Yes, Sandra, what is it? I'm kind of busy right now." Quinn tried very hard to keep the annoyance out of his voice.

"Well, you're about to become busier. You have company coming," she said, equally annoyed.

"What?" Quinn panicked. "I can't have company out here, not now."

"It's Richard, and you know how insistent he can be," Sandra stated. "Quinn, I couldn't talk him out of it. I'm sorry."

"I know, honey. It's all right. Thanks for the heads-up," Quinn said, signing off. "Hermes, it's cover-up time. We have an uninvited guest arriving in a few minutes," Quinn grumbled.

"As you wish, Professor," Hermes replied, already having begun the transformation of the upper level into a working laboratory, starting with remotely activating the console, projector and three-dimensional screen.

There's that strange voice again. Bear looked around and again saw nothing. Determined to find its source, she began sniffing out every nook and cranny.

"Wait, Professor . . . it's Dani. Her body temperature is alarmingly high."

"How high?" Quinn asked anxiously.

"It has just reached one-hundred-two degrees."

"Damn," Quinn uttered. He was helpless to do anything for his daughter and he was nowhere near being able to bring his children home. He could only pray that Daric could take care of her.

"Hermes, let me know immediately if anything changes," Quinn directed.

Monday, August 27, 1888

93

"MOM?" DANI MURMURED softly.

"No, it's me."

"Dad?"

"No, Dani. It's Daric," he replied, worried. Dani had been getting worse by the hour.

Earlier, Dani had found a few dirty pages from a discarded newspaper, *The Star*. The stained and crumpled pages showed a date of Thursday, August 23, 1888.

As soon as they had seen the date, Dani and Daric realized their attire wasn't appropriate for the time period. Dani's evening dress, which she had been wearing on their last night aboard the cruise ship, was especially inappropriate.

Partly because their attire wasn't in keeping for the period, they'd been hiding in the shadows for four days, now. It had been raining almost steadily since their arrival and the evenings were unseasonably cold. They hadn't seen even a ray of sunlight. And they weren't sure they ever would through the soot and fog that continued to blanket the region.

Daric had slept by day while Dani had kept watch. Daric, in his business suit, was able to mingle in the crowds without drawing attention to himself. As a result, he had ventured out at night, moving between the shadows of the lampposts as he hunted throughout the neighborhoods hoping to find some food and clothing. One night, he had almost been caught trying to steal fruit from a street vendor, but he had slipped away, empty handed, unfortunately. Another night, however, he had found some dirty rags in one backyard he had hoped no one would miss. He had doubted they would considering their state. Dani and Daric could at least throw them around each other for a little extra warmth at night.

"Is it dinner time yet? I'm hungry." Dani sounded like a small, pathetic child, reminding Daric of the story of Oliver Twist. Her voice was so weak.

Boy, I could go for a bacon double cheeseburger with a side order of fries, right now, Daric thought.

"No, Dani, we've already eaten dinner, remember?" Daric lied, hoping to take her mind off her empty stomach. They hadn't eaten a thing for four days. Their last meal had been the dinner they had had on the cruise ship before arriving here.

"Oh." Dani sighed sadly. She was struggling to sit up, but Daric gently eased her back down.

"Hey, why don't you wait here and rest? I'll go get you a snack," Daric said encouragingly, trying to keep his worry from creeping into his voice.

"Okay." Dani put her head back down on the pile of filthy rags she was using for a pillow. She soon drifted off to sleep again.

Daric gently spread his jacket over her. He reached down and placed his wrist against her forehead. "Not good," he muttered.

Daric quickly disappeared into the night, determined to have some success this time. He was sure, with a little food in her, Dani would be able to fight off this bug.

94

AS DARIC PROWLED the streets, he thought back to an earlier conversation he had had with Dani.

"My knife, it's gone!" Daric stated with astonishment.

"Well, maybe it's because Amelia hasn't been born yet; therefore, she couldn't possibly have given it to you. Or, it could be that the Swiss Army knife hasn't been invented yet. You pick," Dani quipped.

"You're too funny. Amelia gave you that dress. Why hasn't it vanished?" Daric retorted.

"The only thing I can figure is that fabric has been around for thousands of years; therefore, it existed in this time period, even if styles have changed somewhat over time," Dani rationalized.

Daric was missing the quick wit of his sister. He had hoped he could have pawned his knife so they could buy some supplies. He had even tried to get a bit of work over the past few days, but he had received only distrustful glares. Now, he was forced to resort to stealing, again. This time, he had to succeed.

Dani had complained a few days ago about being cold. She had said she didn't think she'd ever feel dry and warm again. Yesterday, she suggested they use their travel bands to get out of this 'hell-hole', as she put it. *That should have been my first clue that something was wrong,* Daric thought in retrospect. He had told her they should stick it out because there were no guarantees that where they ended up next would be any better than this dismal place.

Daric turned the corner on to Brick Lane. He was paying close attention to his route this time. He got lost once before in this labyrinth of dingy courts, dark alleyways, and narrow streets. Everything looked the same. Every street looked like the next, including a public house found on almost every corner.

Daric had a recurring sense of claustrophobia here, with multi-storey warehouses and common lodging houses blocking out any fragment of the sun's rays that tried so desperately to cut through the smog-laden air. There were no trees, no green lawns, only soot-covered brick buildings encroaching on cobblestone streets encrusted with dirt and horse manure.

Daric walked past the Frying Pan pub. He peered through the grime-covered windows. He could tell by the shadows milling about inside that the place was busy.

Daric crept around the side of the building and turned down Thrawl Street where he spotted an alleyway that cut behind the pub. As he approached the fence surrounding the yard, he found a loose fence board. It didn't take him long to wrestle it free. He wriggled between the boards and entered the quiet, unlit yard behind the pub.

Daric cautiously made his way toward the sound he knew would lead him directly to the pub's back door. He felt his way around the area, stopping abruptly when his hands came upon a wooden crate beside the steps to the back door. "Bingo," he muttered. He gently lifted the lid and felt around for something he hoped they could use. But before he could retrieve the goods, the back door opened and there stood a man the size of *Paul Bunyan.*

"Well, what do we have here? Another gutter-wolf?" The man's voice thundered, as his arm shot out and seized Daric by the collar.

"Inspector, if you'd please," the man hollered into the pub.

Daric realized if he got arrested, his sister would be alone, out on the streets, and defenseless in her current condition.

95

A SHADOWY FIGURE cautiously approached the huddled mass he had spotted at the back of the darkened alley. When he got close enough, he realized it was a woman. He gently nudged her foot with the toe of his shoe. There was no reaction.

He inched closer. He bent down and touched her cheek. It was warm; unusually warm, he thought. At first, he believed she might be dead. "There's a lot of that going on around here these days," he chortled.

Then something caught his eye. He reached for the woman's left arm, which was peering out from under a coat.

"Well, aren't you a pretty little bobble," he murmured.

"You'll make me a tidy little sum, you will," he snickered. He took a glance back up the alley. He was still alone, but he might not be for long. He needed to act quickly. "Now, come to Papa." He gently picked up the slender wrist and turned the bracelet, looking for a clasp to unhook it.

After fumbling for several minutes, he still had not figured out how to remove the bracelet. He was getting very nervous. He knew it was dumb luck that no one had seen him yet. Then, suddenly, an idea came to mind.

"If I can't get you off one way, my precious bobble, there's always another way," he croaked delightedly. He reached under his long trench coat and drew out an eight-inch knife.

A soft moan emanated from the motionless figure, curled in a tight ball, lying on the damp ground.

"But first, I can't have you waking up and screaming while I do this, now can I?" He cackled malevolently again, reaching under his coat a second time.

96

"WHAT IS IT, William?" the inspector replied from inside the pub.

William Farrow, the owner of the Frying Pan pub, was known to his friends as the 'gentle giant'. But cross him or try to damage his property and you'd be facing a Minotaur, the monster chronicled as half man and half bull in Greek mythology.

The inspector appeared in the doorway and looked down at what William had detained.

Panic suddenly seized Daric, crushing the very breath within him. Even with the dim light that escaped the pub's interior, Daric knew he had to get away. He intensified his struggle with William's vise-like grip, desperate to break free.

"Steady on, lad," William said, hanging on tightly and giving Daric a firm shake to settle him down.

Daric felt like a marionette on the ends of a puppeteer's strings, as William tossed him about so easily, using only one of his trunk-like arms.

"Take it easy; this big ox isn't going to hurt you," the inspector tried to assure Daric. He couldn't understand why the young man had intensified his fight to break free when he had stepped into the doorway.

Daric settled a bit, looking up skeptically at the inspector.

"Let him go, William. He won't run away . . . will you?" The inspector's voice warned that Daric should concede.

Daric shook his head, seeing no other viable options at the moment. He was instantly released. He reached for the front of his shirt and pulled it away from his throat. He gulped down a deep breath.

"William, go back inside and tend to your customers. I've got this," the inspector said.

William stared at the inspector; he didn't like the fact he was being summarily dismissed. "I want my pound of flesh," the giant boomed.

"You'll get what's coming to you, William. Now, go back inside," the inspector insisted.

The giant bent down. Daric cringed; waiting for the blow he thought was coming.

William burst out laughing at Daric's reaction. He reached into the crate and extracted a small canvas sack. After securing the lid, he stood erect and glared directly at the inspector, as if giving him a warning. William then turned and headed back into the pub, leaving Daric staring up into an all too familiar face.

"I am Detective Inspector Case, from H Division of the Metropolitan Police. What's your name?"

"Daric Delaney, sir." Daric couldn't believe his eyes. He was staring at another Uncle Richard, a younger version, but unmistakably 'Uncle Richard'. How was that possible?

Inspector Case wore a dark blue sack coat and trousers with a matching waistcoat, complete with a gold pocket watch and watch fob over a stark white shirt. He stood six-foot tall and had a good build, a neatly trimmed Franz Joseph beard and short brown hair. He was thin-lipped with a pointed jaw, broad nose and wide-set brown eyes. He appeared to be in his late twenties or early thirties. He held a pint of beer in one hand and his bowler hat in the other.

Inspector Case could tell by Daric's accent that he was an immigrant, but not one of the many poor Russian, Polish and German Jews coming from Central and Eastern Europe to seek shelter here in the East End. He could also tell that Daric wasn't one of those hardened criminals he was so used to encountering. Besides, this one didn't have the skills for it.

The East End of London encompassed the London docks and the rundown areas of Spitalfields, Bethnal Green and Whitechapel. It was bordered to the south by the River Thames, to the west by the city of London, to the north by Hackney and Shoreditch, and to the east by the River Lea. The East End had become a popular area for refugees because the main road through the area was a major artery for entering or leaving the city. In addition, the ground here was relatively level and easy to build upon.

"Now, Daric, why don't you tell me what you were doing back here?" Inspector Case asked calmly.

97

DARIC RECITED TO the inspector the story that he and Dani had concocted: how they came to be here, in London.

"My sister and I . . . Oh, my God, my sister! Please, I have to go to her. She's really sick!" Daric pleaded. "I've been gone too long. Please, I have to go. I promise I won't try to steal again. Just don't arrest me. Please! She won't survive on these streets without me!"

Daric's pleas tugged at Inspector Case's heart. It was only nine months ago when he had lost his own sister, Beatrice, to the streets of this city. Being raised in a 'privileged' family, the Case children had everything they could ever want. But Beatrice wasn't content to play the role of a dutiful daughter and there was no way she would ever be a subservient housewife. She ran away from home in protest of the established norms that society demanded of her and she was swallowed up by the hungry city. The inspector spent weeks scouring the streets for his younger sister until he finally found her lifeless body under Hammersmith Bridge. He didn't want the same fate to fall to Daric's sister, not if he could help it.

Inspector Case could see, even in the dim light from the doorway, how distraught Daric was and how he truly cared for the well-being of his sister. It didn't matter to him where he conducted his interrogation, just as long as he got some answers.

"Okay, relax, Daric. Let's go to her. You lead the way." The inspector barely got the words out before he had to take off after Daric.

Daric ran through the backyard, pushed aside the broken fence board, and squeezed his way through. Inspector Case was right on his heels as they ran through the streets, darting around people, carts and carriages, on their way to Dani.

"Hey, wait up!" the inspector shouted, struggling to match Daric's pace and to keep him in sight.

Police Constable Barrett was walking his beat when he spotted a man running toward him with Inspector Case in hot pursuit.

Police Constable Thomas Barrett, 226H, was from H Division. He had been with the Metropolitan Police for nine years. Barrett was five-foot-seven and weighed approximately one-hundred-eighty-five pounds. He wore the standard police uniform and carried the standard equipment. The uniform consisted of dark blue pants, a custodian helmet with a shiny Brunswick star, and a dark blue, button-down tunic. The tunic came with a high collar to protect the wearer from being garrotted. It also featured white bars on its sleeves to distinguish the police officer from naval or maritime personnel. As for the standard equipment, it included a truncheon, handcuffs, a bull's-eye lantern, and a silver whistle secured to the tunic by a silver chain.

The bull's-eye lantern was a dangerous and unwieldy device. It had a steel cylinder that was ten inches high and was topped with a chimney shaped like two pleated dunce caps. Also on its top was a metal handle for carrying the lantern; two more handles on the back of the lantern could be used to attach the lantern to a belt. On one side of the cylinder was a magnifying lens, three inches in diameter and made of thick, convex glass; a small oil pan and wick in the cylinder provided the lantern's light. The light was weak compared to today's flashlights, but a police officer could nevertheless use the lantern to help see into dark areas. He could also use it as a signaling device to attract the attention a fellow police officer.

Revolvers were issued to only a select few who, in the opinion of a senior officer, could be trusted to use them safely and with discretion.

Police Constable Barrett ducked around a corner, waiting for the fleeing man to approach. He placed his lantern on the ground because in short order he would need both hands. He heard the running footsteps getting closer. He gauged his timing and, when the moment was just right, he sprang from his hiding place and tackled the man to the ground.

"I've got him, Inspector," Barrett yelled proudly.

"Get off me!" Daric yelled, tossing the smaller constable aside.

"It's all right, Barrett, he's with me. We're in rather a hurry." The inspector paused for a moment to catch his breath while Daric scrambled to his feet and took off.

"I'll explain later." The inspector panted before running, again, after Daric.

"Right you are, Inspector," Barrett replied, doubting that the inspector had heard him or even cared, for that matter. *And here, all I was trying to do was help.*

98

THE THIEF PULLED out a thick wooden stick from under his coat. He took a quick look over his shoulder. *Good, no one there,* he thought.

"This will only take a minute and you won't feel a thing. At least, I don't think you will," he snickered. Raising his arm to strike the blow . . .

"Get away from her!" Daric shrieked. He turned the corner into the alleyway and saw a figure crouched over Dani. His pace accelerated, rapidly closing the distance between himself and the startled thief.

Realizing he had lost his opportunity to claim his prize, the thief darted off and was immediately swallowed by the shadows. His hasty retreat wasn't because he was afraid of the young man; he knew he could handle him with no problem. It was the inspector a few paces behind Daric that made him nervous. He couldn't afford to get caught again. He knew this inspector all too well; moreover, the inspector knew him, too. He'd been previously warned: there would be no second chance.

Daric rushed to Dani's side. She wasn't moving. Noticing Dani's exposed arm, he realized instantly what the thief had been after. He was relieved to see the thief hadn't stolen her travel band. *That was close, too damn close.*

"Is she all right?" Inspector Case asked, bending down beside Daric, still panting from their race through the East End. *Odd,* the inspector thought; *Daric wasn't even breathing hard.*

Inspector Case saw an eight-inch knife next to Dani's body. He picked it up, wrapped the blade in his handkerchief and gently secured it in his inside coat pocket.

"He didn't hurt her, if that's what you mean. But I need to get her some help; she's burning up," Daric said urgently.

"Pick her up and follow me," Inspector Case instructed. "I know just what to do," he added, as he led the way out of the alley and onto the narrow street.

Daric picked Dani up gently; she didn't stir. He cradled her in his arms while he followed the inspector. They soon came across Police Constable Barrett again, walking his beat.

So that's what all the hurry was about, Barrett thought, noticing the motionless form cradled in the young man's arms.

99

INSPECTOR CASE HEADED directly to the London Hospital, just a short distance away. He wasn't going there to admit Dani. In all honesty, he didn't care for hospitals; he viewed them as places where people went to die. He was there to find his wife, who worked at the hospital. She would know exactly what to do.

"Wait here," Case said to Daric. He turned and ran up the back steps of the hospital and disappeared inside.

Daric sat on one of the steps, still cradling his sister in his arms.

"Dani, can you hear me?" he whispered apprehensively.

"Awwwww," was the weak response.

"We're going to get you some help; just hang in there. Everything will be okay, I promise," Daric said, hopefully. He had no idea what the inspector was up to.

Several minutes later a carriage pulled up and stopped by the steps. The door opened. Case popped his head out and said, "Get in."

Without hesitation, Daric stood, still carrying Dani, and walked to the open carriage door.

"Here, give her to me," Case said, leaning out of the carriage. He gently took Dani and pulled her inside. Daric climbed in and settled himself on a bench before taking Dani back. Sitting directly across from him was an attractive young woman.

"Daric, this is my wife, Mary. She's a teaching nurse at the London Hospital," Case said with pride and affection.

"This is a hospital? We need to take Dani inside," Daric urged. He was puzzled.

"Relax, Daric. Mary will know what to do for your sister. Besides, hospitals are for the poor," Case stated frankly.

"Driver, in haste, if you would," Case instructed the carriage driver. The carriage lurched forward, gaining speed as it went.

"What happened?" Mary asked quietly, reaching forward to feel Dani's forehead.

Mary was a beautiful woman. She was five-five with soft auburn hair. She appeared to be in her early to mid-twenties. Mary had warm hazel eyes, and she was wearing her nurse's uniform.

"We've been out on the streets for four days, with nothing to eat and only the clothes on our backs," Daric stated. Then he remembered; he had to stick to their fabricated story. If someone asked, when Dani and Daric were not together, their stories had to match.

Daric recalled when Dani and he had first talked about their 'story'. He had suggested they use their original orphan storyline. Dani had disagreed. She had argued that, while the orphan story worked for 1937, it would not work for 1888. She had pointed out that, in the 1880s, most people their age would have been married with kids, not living with their parents. As a result, the two of them had come up with a more plausible story.

"We came here three months ago, after our parents were killed in an accident," Daric said sadly.

"How tragic! I'm so sorry," Mary said sympathetically, and then looked at her husband.

"Thank you," Daric acknowledged. "Our only living relative was our grandmother, who lived here in England, Stratford, actually. So, we came to stay with her until we got established here. Four days ago, her house caught fire and burnt to the ground. Everything we owned went up in flames. Our grandmother died in the fire."

"That's terrible," Mary exclaimed. "What did you do?"

Case was a little surprised to realize he was developing a soft spot for this young man. He wanted to do something to help him and his sister. He figured anyone who appreciated his family as this young man did deserved a break.

"We've been on the streets looking for work and a place to live since the fire, but we've had no luck. Then, yesterday morning, Dani started to complain about being cold. She's been getting worse ever since. I was trying to get some food, thinking it might help her. That's when you caught me," Daric said, finishing his story. He looked caringly down at his sister, still sleeping in his arms.

"Please, Inspector Case, help my sister. I'll do anything to repay you," Daric pleaded.

"Call me Rich," Case said, with a warm smile, looking at Mary who had so easily read his mind. She returned his smile knowingly. Rich took a glance out the window and said, "We're here."

Rich opened the carriage door and got out. He helped Mary down and then turned to Daric, "Give her to me," he said.

Daric gently placed Dani in Rich's arms. As soon as he had exited the carriage, he retook possession of his sister and followed Rich up the steps and through the front door of Case's terraced home.

100

MARY STOOD IN the grand foyer of her home shouting orders, to whom Daric didn't know, because he couldn't see anyone.

"Martha, draw a warm bath and prepare the spare bedroom on the first floor as a sickroom," the order echoed.

The kitchen door swung open and one hulk-of-a-woman burst into the foyer and surprisingly sprinted up the stairs, as swiftly as a cheetah, considering her size.

"And I need you to set up the nursemaid's room for our other guest," Mary added.

"Right away, Missus." Martha's reply came from above.

Martha Debo was the Cases's housekeeper. She was of German descent. Hers was a somewhat masculine physique. She wore the typical servant's uniform: a white apron tied over a simple-print housedress, a white cap and sensible flat-healed black shoes.

"Elsie, I need you to prepare a mustard plaster and take it up to the spare bedroom on the first floor."

A small head darted out from behind the same door through which Martha had emerged moments before. "Straight away, Missus," the gentle voice said. The head disappeared just as quickly as it had appeared.

Then Mary turned to Daric who was still holding a sleeping

Dani in his arms. "Follow me," she said. She headed up the staircase to the right of the entrance way. They proceeded down the hall. They passed two bedrooms; Martha was making the bed in the second one. Shortly they came to the bathroom at the end of the hall; water was filling a large bathtub.

The bathroom floor was covered with a light-color linoleum and the walls were painted eggshell white. The bathtub, sink and lavatory were made of porcelain and were all decorated with a mazarine blue and gold morning glory design.

Martha followed Daric into the bathroom. "I'll take her from here," she instructed, leaving no room for argument.

Daric looked puzzled, not sure what to do.

"It's all right, Daric. She's in good hands," Mary encouraged. "Why don't you go downstairs and join Rich in the drawing room. I'll send for you when we're finished."

Martha stepped forward and took Dani in her arms as if she were just a babe. "Go on with ya, now," Martha urged, shutting the bathroom door behind him.

Daric stood there dumbfounded, staring at the closed door for a minute. He then turned and made his way back along the hall and down the stairs.

101

DARIC FOUND RICH in what must have been the drawing room. He was standing beside the fireplace, his arm leaning against the mantel, while he drew on his pipe.

"I was told to wait here," Daric uttered timidly.

"Come, let me pour you a brandy while we sit and wait," Rich said amiably. He placed the bowl of his pipe in the ashtray on the mantel and walked over to a sideboard that contained a variety of decanters. Pulling the top from one, he poured its amber liquid into two glasses, stopped the decanter and handed Daric his drink.

"Come and sit a spell," Rich said, as he sank into a large wing-back chair.

"I'm filthy. I'd better stay standing," Daric stated, embarrassed by his shabby appearance.

"My apologies," Rich said, pulling himself from his comfortable chair. "Let's get you cleaned up a bit, shall we? The bathroom is being used at the moment, but the scullery has a large sink you can use to wash up. I'll go fetch some supplies. Be right back," Rich said, then hurried off.

While Daric waited for Rich to return, he enjoyed his drink and systematically took in his surroundings.

The room's most striking feature was its fireplace. Located in the center of the wall opposite the entrance, it was set off by an ornately carved marble surround. A simple, embroidered cover lay on the overmantel. On the center of the cover was a beautiful wooden pendulum clock with four carved wooden feet; the entire clock was hand painted and trimmed with gold leaf. Golden candlesticks were positioned on either side of the clock, along with Rich's decorative tobacco jar and amber glass ashtray. Above the overmantel was a gold-framed mirror. A partly empty coal scuttle sat on one side of the hearth; on the other stood a finely embroidered fire screen.

Daric's gaze travelled away from the fireplace, along the walls which were painted a restful olive green. Family portraits hung at various locations around the room. Wall-bracketed gas lights cast a warm glow that gave the room a decidedly homey feel. A large oriental rug lay on the highly polished wooden floor.

Daric turned his attention to the room's only window. It was a large bay window, dressed with white curtains with delicate lace edging. In front was a deep red velvet curtain with gold fringe, tie-backs and a valance. In front of the bay window was an oval table, covered in white lace. On top was a crystal vase with fresh-cut flowers: blue cornflowers, white lisianthus and red carnations. Beside the vase was an argand table lamp with Baccarat crystal prisms.

Daric recognized the Queen Anne style furniture that filled the room: curved shapes, cushioned seats, cabriole legs and pad feet. In the room's center, to the right of the fireplace were two oxblood leather wing back arm chairs. Between the chairs was a mahogany drop-leaf table; across from them was a sofa, upholstered in hunter-green brocade. Four upright chairs were positioned elsewhere around the room. Two large mahogany sideboards lined the walls on either side of the entrance into the room.

Daric noticed large folding doors at the end of the room he believed divided it from the dining room. Just as his curiosity was calling him to open those doors, he heard someone approaching.

"All set," Rich said upon his return to the drawing room. "I noticed you and I are about the same size, so I brought you some clean clothes, if that's okay."

"I don't want to be any trouble," Daric replied politely, taking the items from Rich.

"Nonsense. Follow me," he said, ushering Daric through the swinging kitchen door.

102

THE KITCHEN WAS small, Daric thought, compared to today's standards. But it appeared functional and was impeccably clean.

Elsie looked up from her worktable when she heard someone enter.

"Daric is going to use the sink in the scullery to clean up," Rich informed Elsie. She smiled pleasantly and quickly resumed her task.

Elsie White was an elderly woman of slight build. These were unusual characteristics for the domestic service profession of a cook, considering the heavy sacks of flour and grain and the pounds of meat she had to lift and move around. But looks could be deceiving; she was a spry, efficient worker who could definitely hold her own in the kitchen. She was five-foot-two with sparkling silver hair and soft hazel eyes. She wore the same uniform as Martha: a simple housedress, apron and cap.

"It's through that door." Rich pointed toward the right door at the back of the kitchen. "Join me in the drawing room when you're finished."

"Thanks," Daric said.

"Elsie, can you prepare a snack for Daric? I don't think he'll last until dinner." Rich chuckled when he heard Daric's stomach grumble, probably brought about by the wonderful aroma emanating from the stove.

"As soon as I run this upstairs," and Elsie was off like a flash. Daric thought she moved rather quickly for a woman of her advanced years.

The kitchen range was set against the left wall; a pot was simmering on the surface. Daric had to admit it smelled inviting. There was something wonderful roasting in the closed oven, as its fragrance permeated the room, too.

Pots and pans were stacked to the left of the kitchen range; to the right was a variety of wash basins. The floor was covered with lightly patterned linoleum, and the walls were painted a dove-grey. In the center of the room, there was a square wooden table, where Elsie had been working, with two wooden chairs.

At the back of the room were two doors. The one on the left led to the pantry. This small room was used for washing and storing china and glassware. It was equipped with a small counter, a small wood-lined sink with running water and cupboards containing several shelves laden with china and glassware.

The door on the right, the door to which Rich had pointed, led into a long hallway known as the scullery.

The hallway area nearest the kitchen had a counter with a sink and running water, along one wall; it was used to carry out food preparation activities, such as scaling fish and washing and trimming vegetables, and to keep the ensuing mess out of the kitchen. Farther along the hallway was the larder which housed fresh food. Then came the storeroom closet for dried goods and cleaning equipment. And last, but not least, there was a small washroom or, as Londoners would say, a lavatory or water closet, in the back corner.

Daric stopped at the large sink. Placing the items Rich had given him on the counter, he noted Rich had generously left various toiletries, besides the clothes. He turned the tap and watched the sink fill with warm water. He would refill the sink four more times before he was satisfied he had rid himself of his stubbly whiskers and all the dirt and grime of the past four days.

At last, Daric put on the clean clothes. How good they felt and they fit him pretty well, too. He folded his filthy clothes and left them piled neatly on the floor.

By the time Daric was ready to leave the scullery, Elsie had returned to the kitchen. She was preparing a plate of cheese and biscuits.

Upon hearing the door behind her open, Elsie turned and dropped the knife she was holding. She was getting her first glimpse of the clean-shaven, well-groomed young man. "Well, I'll be. Were you under all that dirt this whole time?" she asked gaily.

Daric was wearing a white shirt with brown pinstripes, a brown tweed vest and trousers, and a chocolate-brown tie. He had even polished his black shoes.

"I feel much better now," Daric stated whole-heartedly.

He smiled at Elsie and she swooned. *If I were only forty years younger,* she thought.

"You are a handsome devil, I'll give you that. Come on, I'll take this into the drawing room for you," Elsie said, leading the way.

103

MARY LAID A blanket on the cold linoleum floor. "Set her down here, Martha," Mary instructed.

Martha knelt and gently placed Dani on the blanket. Then she turned the running water off and checked the temperature of the bath. "Perfect," she said. She returned to Mary's side, knelt down and helped with the removal of Dani's dirty clothing.

"What's that?" Martha asked. They had removed Dani's dress and were staring at her sports bra.

"I don't know," Mary replied. "We'll have to ask her later."

After several attempts to remove the bracelet from Dani's wrist, they decided a little water wouldn't hurt her jewellery.

Now that Dani was fully undressed, Martha picked her up gently placed her in the tub. When Dani felt the warm water against her skin, a moan escaped her lips and her eyes fluttered open for a moment.

"It's all right, dear. You're safe here," Mary assured her. "We'll take care of you."

"Daric?" came a raspy whisper.

"He's fine. He's here, too," Mary said. "I'll bring him to you after we get you settled."

Dani simply nodded her head in reply. It seemed to take too

much effort to even speak.

After Mary and Martha had washed the street filth from Dani, they were amazed at what lay beneath all of that dirt.

"Whoa, she's a real beauty, she is," Martha proclaimed.

"Yes, she is," Mary agreed readily. "Now, let's get her dressed and into bed."

Having towelled her off, Martha pulled a nightgown over Dani's head and settled it. After a very weak protest from Dani, Martha picked her up and carried her into the bedroom. Mary had pulled the bedcovers back so Martha could lie her down.

The bedroom had been prepared as a sickroom, meaning most of the furnishings had been removed. Only the essentials for taking care of the sick were left. There was the bed, with no bed curtains or valances. A chest of drawers held towels, blankets, a change of bed linens and clean nightclothes. And lastly, there was a wash-stand, one straight-back wooden chair, and two tables.

On the table nearer the bed, Elsie had placed a glass of water, a small jar of vegetable shortening, and a hand towel.

On the second table, the larger of the two, Elsie had put a small porcelain bowl containing one tablespoon of dry mustard and four tablespoons of flour. Beside the bowl was a mason jar, contain-ing the same measured ingredients. The table also held a wooden spoon, a pitcher of hot water, and four folded cloths.

Mary poured the hot water into the small porcelain bowl. She stirred the contents waiting, for just the right consistency. When she was satisfied, she opened one cloth and scooped the mixture out of the bowl onto the cloth, spreading it with the back of the wooden spoon. Next, she covered the mixture with a second cloth, creating a poultice.

Carefully picking up the poultice, Mary returned to the side of the bed. Martha had already opened the front of Dani's nightgown and had covered her chest with vegetable shortening. Mary placed the mustard plaster on Dani's chest. She refastened the nightgown and pulled the blankets up under Dani's chin.

"Martha, can you check in a couple of minutes, to make sure

the poultice isn't causing a rash on her skin? If it is, remove it and come and get me. We'll have to try something else. If it's okay, leave it on until it gets cool, then remove it," Mary instructed. "I should be back by then and we'll fix another one to put on her back."

"Yes, Missus," Martha said, pulling the chair up next to the bed and taking watch over her charge.

104

AS MARY MADE her way downstairs, the hairs on the back of her neck rose and her face flushed. She walked across the foyer and entered the drawing room. Her suspicions were confirmed.

"Put that damn thing out!" she scolded Rich. "We have a sick woman in this house."

Rich quickly snuffed out his pipe. "Sorry, dear, I wasn't thinking."

"Apparently not," Mary retorted.

"How's Dani?" Daric asked anxiously, as he popped out of his chair.

Mary turned to address Daric and couldn't help but admire the handsome young man standing in front of her. "She's much cleaner now, too," Mary said charmingly.

She teasingly extended her hand to Daric. "I don't believe we've met," she said playfully. "My name is Mary."

Sensing that Dani was in no immediate danger by Mary's levity, Daric decided to play along. He clasped Mary's hand delicately, turned it over, and gently kissed the back of it. "I'm very pleased to meet you, Mary. My name is Daric," he said, flashing her one of his charming smiles.

They both laughed, but, on a more serious note, Mary said,

"Dani is resting comfortably. Martha's watching her. I'm treating her with a mustard plaster. We use them at the hospital all the time to relieve symptoms of many respiratory ailments, including bronchitis. I'm hoping we can arrest this before it goes that far."

Mary was still wearing her nurse's uniform: an ankle-length deep-blue chambray dress with a white collar and cuffs. Attached to her dress by a gold bead at each breast and tied in the back was a white-on-white striped apron. Her detachable black armband signified she was a teaching nurse. Her brunette hair had been pulled up into a bun and was topped with a starched buckram cap.

Rich picked up his empty glass and made his way over for a refill.

"I'll have one of those, while you're at it," Mary said, collapsing onto the sofa. She pulled the pins from her hair and removed her cap.

"We'll do everything we can to get her fever to break. Once that happens, she'll be well on the road to recovery," Mary said reassuringly.

"I can't thank you enough for all that you're doing, for both of us," Daric stated.

"Think nothing of it," Rich jumped into the conversation. He handed Mary her drink. She took a delicate sip of the amber nectar. "Mmmm, just what the doctor ordered," she said.

"I'm afraid we couldn't find the clasp to remove Dani's bracelet before her bath," Mary said regretfully.

"That's all right," Daric replied. He was thankful that Dani was still wearing her travel band because one never knew when their dad would summon them home.

"Daric, if you were so desperate for money, why didn't you pawn your bracelets instead of resorting to stealing?" Rich asked. He had noticed Daric's bracelet earlier and was waiting to bring up the question.

Daric pulled up his sleeve and looked at his own bracelet. "These bracelets were the last gifts our parents gave us. We just couldn't bring ourselves to part with them. You understand, don't you?" Daric asked hopefully.

Mary noticed the plate on the table between the two chairs. "I see Elsie has prepared a snack. That's good. It could be a while before we're able to sit down to dinner."

Mary got up and snagged a piece of cheese. "I'll go ask Elsie to make a big batch of chicken soup. It's always good for what ails you and we'll have plenty of ingredients after tonight's dinner. When Dani's feeling a little better, we'll try to get some soup into her."

Mary finished her drink and was about to head for the kitchen when she remembered . . . "Oh, I almost forgot. Dani woke up for a moment and asked about you. I told her you were here, and that you were both safe."

"Thank you," Daric replied appreciatively.

105

IT PROVED TO be a long and tiring evening. After Mary had applied Dani's second poultice, Daric and the Cases finally sat down to dinner. Daric was somewhat embarrassed by the quantity of food he consumed. But it was at the encouragement of Mary that he did so. She knew he hadn't eaten in four days and she wanted to make sure he didn't go to bed hungry. There was no fear of that happening; in fact, he wanted to loosen his belt because he was sure he would pop a button or two.

Upon retiring for the evening, Mary took Daric to see Dani. She wanted to reassure him that she was being well cared for. Mary informed him she and her staff would monitor Dani throughout the night, alternating shifts. This wasn't only to keep an eye of her condition, but, should Dani awaken, Mary didn't want her to be alone, especially in a strange place. Daric offered to take a shift, but Mary insisted he get a good night's sleep. Even his handsome face was showing signs of exhaustion.

Having brushed aside his objection, Mary escorted Daric to his room and bade him goodnight. She returned to her bedroom to find Rich preparing for bed.

"All settled in?" Rich asked, folding his pants over the mahogany clothes valet stand.

"Rich, I want to help Daric and Dani. I feel so badly for them," Mary admitted.

"So do I," Rich agreed. "What do you have in mind?"

"We have plenty of room here. Why don't they stay here until they can get back on their feet?" Mary proposed. "Besides, Dani's in no condition to be pounding the streets looking for work."

"Are you sure you want them to stay here?" Rich asked. He was rather surprised at Mary's suggestion. It had been just the two of them for over five years now. They had grown accustomed to their own routines and Rich knew how particular Mary could be.

"Yes, I'm sure. Besides, it'll be nice to have some company for a while. And they're about our age or just a bit younger. We'll have so much in common," Mary said excitedly.

"I suppose it would be okay," Rich said, finding himself warming to the idea.

"Look, in the morning I'll go to the hospital and tell them I'm going to take the rest of the week off. That way I can take care of Dani. When she's feeling better and, if she's interested, I'm sure I could get her some work at the hospital. They're always looking for nurses and the qualifications are minimal. All she needs to know is how to read and write. And as Florence Nightingale often says, 'Every woman makes a good nurse. The most important values are compassion, sympathy and the desire to serve'," Mary said proudly, reflecting on her training at the Nightingale School for Nurses and her graduation not that long ago.

"Good. And when you get back, I'll take Daric to Headquarters with me. After I've updated the superintendent about the Tabran case, I'll drop Daric off at the Frying Pan pub," Rich said, mentally running through his agenda for tomorrow.

"The Frying Pan pub?"

"Oh, Daric was trying to steal from the owner. That's where we first met," Rich explained. "The owner, as he put it, 'wants his pound of flesh'. So, I figured Daric could work there for a few days to satisfy the owner. I could pick him up after my shift."

"Then it's settled," Mary said happily.

106

DARIC HAD ONE of his best night's sleep in a long time. He felt refreshed and revitalized. He made use of the items that had been laid out on the washstand for him. Once dressed, he headed downstairs to check on Dani.

When Daric entered the bedroom, he saw Martha sitting beside the bed, right where she had been when he had left the night before.

"You haven't . . ."

"No, just got here," Martha interrupted. "The Missus just left. I was to tell you to join the Master in the dining room for breakfast. He'll tell you what you need to know," Martha finished brusquely.

By her stern look, Daric knew better than to argue. He could see his sister was in good hands, so he left the room and headed downstairs.

The dining room, similar to the drawing room, had Queen Anne style furniture. The large rectangular mahogany table had five chairs placed on either side. Suspended directly over the middle of the table was a gaselier, with hanging Baccarat crystal prisms, similar to the ones on the table lamp in the drawing room. On the wooden floor was another Oriental carpet. The walls were painted the same color as the drawing room: olive green. A tapestry hung on the back wall, depicting a scene from the Old Testament where a king, probably Solomon, was worshipping the Golden Idol; a smaller image of Solomon entertaining the Queen of Sheba was shown below. There were two matching chairs on either side of the sideboard directly beneath the tapestry.

A warm glow radiated from the fireplace. On each side, positioned against the wall, was a semi-circular mahogany table known as hunt tables. When gentlemen returned from the hunt, the outer curved section was put in front of the fire. The hunters could then place their drinks on the table, while they warmed their feet, without the table getting burned. Hence the name: hunt table.

On the left side of the overmantel was a pendulum clock under a glass dome; to the right was a vase containing fresh-cut flowers. Directly above the fireplace hung a large family portrait. Daric knew immediately that it was one of Rich's ancestors.

There were other portraits hung throughout the room, interspersed with serene landscapes. Two English oak sideboards with inlaid mahogany were against the wall opposite the fireplace, framing the entrance to the dining room.

"Good morning. Sleep well?" Rich asked when he saw Daric approach.

"Very well, thank you."

"Come, sit." Rich folded the morning edition of the newspaper and placed it beside his plate. He picked up a small silver bell and gave it a shake.

Almost immediately, Elsie appeared with a fresh pot of coffee. She lifted Daric's cup and began to pour.

"Mary and I prefer coffee in the morning. If you'd rather have tea . . ."

"No, this is great, thank you," Daric replied, taking in the spread of food laid out on the table before him.

"Help yourself, you must be starving," Rich teased.

On the table, there were a number of dishes containing broiled bacon, bloaters, which were cured herring, cold chicken from last night's dinner, toast and several jars of homemade jams and jellies.

Daric picked up his plate and served himself.

Daric pointed to the portrait above the fireplace and asked, "Is that your father?"

Rich turned and glanced at the portrait he'd seen a thousand times before and every time it never left him feeling any affection at all for the man.

"Yes. And as per tradition, the first male child of the family gets the same name: Richard Barak Case. It's been passed down through generations. I couldn't begin to guess what number I am," Rich said coldly.

Daric tried to hide his cringe behind his next mouthful of food, while Rich, oblivious to Daric's reaction, returned to his cup of coffee and quickly changed the subject. "Mary left early this morning for the hospital. She's taking the week off, so she can take care of Dani."

"I can look after Dani. Please, I don't want Mary to take time off and lose her income," Daric said imploringly.

"Daric, Mary and I are very comfortable when it comes to our finances. We both come from families of wealth and standing," Rich started to explain. "Actually, neither of us ever needs to work. We do it because we both want to give something back to this community. Not just by throwing money at charities, but by rolling up our sleeves and pitching in. It makes us feel like we're doing something of consequence. We can actually see the results of our efforts. Besides, it keeps us both rather busy."

"We don't want to be a burden," Daric said. "You've already done more than enough."

"Nonsense," Rich said firmly. "Mary and I discussed it last night. We have lots of room and we want to help you and Dani. We'd like both of you to stay here until you can find suitable jobs and can get yourselves settled."

"We couldn't . . ."

"Yes, you can . . . end of discussion," Rich announced.

"That's very kind of you. We'll pay you back, I promise," Daric asserted.

"No need. Now, when Mary gets back, you and I are going to the station. I have to touch base with the superintendent. Then, I'm going to drop you off at the Frying Pan pub. I'm going to offer your services to the owner as payment for your attempted crime." Before Rich could explain further, he noticed the worried look on Daric's face.

"It'll be for only a day or two. Who knows, the big ox might even hire you," Rich said jokingly. "I'll pick you up at the end of my shift. Okay?"

"Okay, and, thank you."

"Oh . . . and Mary is going to kill me for not telling you this first off. Dani's fever broke early this morning, while Mary was sitting with her. She woke briefly, drank some water and, of course, asked about you."

"That's great news." Daric's relief was evident.

"Mary said Dani should be able to receive visitors, namely you, when we return later tonight. But for now, her orders were that Dani should rest," Rich said as he finished delivering his instruction from Mary.

107

AFTER MARY RETURNED, Rich and Daric took the hansom cab to H Division Headquarters. Daric had never been in one before and found that the ride wasn't as jarring as he had imagined it would be. Its large wheels and padded leather seats allowed for a modicum of comfort.

"Wait here. We'll be only a minute," Rich said to the cabbie, through a trapdoor in the roof. "Come on," he said to Daric, as he exited the cab. He climbed the stairs and entered the building, with Daric close behind.

"Do you work here?" Daric asked.

"No, this is Headquarters. I prefer to keep the superintendent at arm's length," Rich replied in a hushed tone. "I work out of the Commercial Street station."

H Division Headquarters was situated at Arbour Square and was the office of Superintendent Thomas Arnold, whom Rich was here to visit. "Grab a seat, Daric. I won't be long," Rich said, as they passed by a row of wooden benches.

Daric made himself comfortable. While he waited for Rich, he checked out the place. He wanted to see what police work in the 1880s was like compared to police work in the twenty-first century. The first thing that jumped out at him was the lack of electronics.

Damn, that must make the job rather difficult, he thought.

The floors were wooden planking and the brick walls were painted pale yellow. All the furniture was made of wood: the large leather-inlaid desks, the straight-back chairs, and numerous filing cabinets. Where there had been a vacant spot on the wall, it was now occupied with shelving heaped with mounds of papers. Easel-style chalk boards on casters, which could be wheeled about the open office area, exhibited someone's indecipherable writing. There were only a few enclosed offices that were partitioned off with a ʻcombination of wood and glass panels. Some offices had their blinds drawn. Lighting was provided by wall-bracketed gas fixtures and what little natural light leached through the soot-covered windows.

"Hey, how's the little lady?" Daric looked up into a constable's friendly face.

"She's doing much better, thank you. Constable Barrett, isn't it?" Daric replied.

"Yeah, that's right. Is Inspector Case here, too?"

"He's speaking with the superintendent, I believe," Daric replied, hoping he had got the title correct.

"Oh, then, I'll catch him later. See ya," Barrett said, as he continued on his way.

A few minutes later, Rich reappeared. "Okay, let's go."

Daric got up and followed Rich out of the building. He was a little uncomfortable being hauled around with no say in the matter. Daric had always been his own man; he was accustomed to making his own decisions, albeit not always smart ones. He enjoyed his independence; indeed, he craved it. But now, he was in unfamiliar territory and Dani would tell him to just go along with it. So he did.

108

SHORTLY AFTER LEAVING H Division Headquarters, the cab pulled up in front of the Frying Pan pub. Rich asked the driver to wait once more and he and Daric disappeared into the pub.

"Come to tell me what you did with my gutter-wolf, Inspector? I told you I want my pound of flesh," William Farrow grunted angrily, lumbering out from behind the wooden bar.

"He's right here, William, so take it easy," Rich said curtly.

William looked at the young man standing next to the inspector. He was dressed like a respectable businessman, in his 'ditto suit': a sack coat, with matching waistcoat and trousers.

"That ain't him," William snorted.

"Mr. Farrow, I'm here to apologize for my actions last night," Daric said. "I was desperate. I had to help my sister. No one would hire me, so I resorted to stealing. Please forgive me."

William just stared slack-jawed at this well-spoken lad. He was nothing like the trash he had picked out of his back yard last night.

"Daric is going to repay his debt to you, William, by working for you for free. Anything you need doing, just tell him and he'll see that it gets done," Rich stated bluntly.

William slowly nodded his head in agreement, still staring at Daric, unconvinced that he was the same delinquent he had caught barely twenty-four hours ago.

"I'll pick you up at the end of my shift, Daric," Rich said then left.

"Thank you for giving me a second chance," Daric said to a cynical William.

"Don't thank me. I'd have had your arse in jail, as quick as you could spit," William snapped.

"There's an apron behind the bar. Go put it on. We wouldn't want to ruin your new clothes, now would we?" That tough exterior was softening just a touch, Daric believed, and he was determined to win over this big lug.

109

"YOU'LL BE STAYING right where you are, miss, until the Missus says otherwise," Martha said. Her voice was stern and would brook no argument. She gently, but firmly, pushed Dani's shoulders back down onto the bed.

"But I feel fine. I just want to stretch my legs," Dani replied, trying to be convincing, but failing miserably. Being in an unfamiliar place was making her anxious, and she had no idea where Daric was or whether he was all right. The uncertainty was making her restless, but, in her weakened state, she was finding it difficult to be insistent.

"I'll take it from here, Martha," Mary said, entering the bedroom. "Why don't you go down and grab something to eat. It'll be a while before lunch."

"Aye, Missus," Martha said, leaving the room.

Mary sat on the recently vacated chair and reached over to feel Dani's forehead.

"Much better," Mary said encouragingly. "You had us worried there for a bit."

Dani looked into Mary's concerned face and tried to remember if they had met before.

"You may not remember me, Dani. Martha and I have been

taking care of you since your brother brought you here last night. My name is Mary Case. I'm afraid you weren't quite with it when you first arrived, fever and all. How are you feeling, now?"

"Weak as a newborn kitten, I hate to admit," Dani acknowledged, although reluctantly.

"That's to be expected. And having had nothing to eat for several days isn't helping you, either. Do you think you could handle a little soup?" Mary asked hopefully. A returning appetite was always a good sign.

"That would be wonderful, thank you," Dani replied.

"Great. You just relax here. I'll go fetch you some soup. Something in your stomach will help you get your strength back. Later, you may feel like something with a bit more substance, but let's take it one step at a time."

"Is my brother here? I'd like to see him," Dani said. She wanted to see for herself that he was okay.

"He went with my husband, Rich, to pay back some debt or other; I'm not sure I got the whole story. Anyway, they'll be back by dinner time. Just relax and get some rest. I'll be back shortly with that soup."

While Dani waited for Mary's return, she heard the noises of the early morning coming from the street below. The various costermongers or hawkers were pitching their wares: "eels, three pounds a shilling"; "salmon alive, six pence a pound"; "five-pound crab cheap"; "penny-a-bunch a turnips". Now that she thought about it, she was rather hungry.

110

"OKAY, MR. FARROW, I've swept the floors and wiped down all the tables and chairs. I've washed the windows and I've even fixed the hinge on the front door. I've washed and dried the dishes and taken out the trash," Daric said, as he listed his accomplishments for the day.

Rich had quietly entered the pub and heard what Daric's day had been like. He was impressed by Daric's hard work and the fact that he didn't seem to mind the tasks he had had to perform. Rich even believed the place looked better than he'd ever seen it before.

"You can bring up a case of beer from the basement and, then, you can . . ." William Farrow was cut short giving his orders to Daric.

"That'll have to wait until tomorrow, William. Let's call it a day," Rich said. Before he could protest, Rich continued, "Hang up your apron, Daric. Let's go. The cab's waiting."

Daric ran behind the bar and hung his apron on a peg. He snatched up his coat and hat, then skirted around the corner of the bar. He turned and bid Mr. Farrow goodnight, then hastily exited the pub before William could utter a protest.

Daric climbed into the cab and sat beside Rich. He was thankful to finally get off his feet. A grateful sigh escaped his lips as he let his head rest against the padded back of the cab's seat.

"Rough day?" Rich asked, laughing good naturedly.

"You have no idea," Daric replied. "But I think Mr. Farrow is finally getting used to me."

"Don't get too comfortable there. This is only temporary. You're much too intelligent to be wasting away in a pub." Rich had other plans for Daric.

Daric looked quizzically at Rich, wondering what he had in store for him. But the first thing on his agenda was to check on his sister.

111

"YOU LOOK MUCH better than you did yesterday, or even this morning for that matter," Daric said, entering Dani's bedroom and taking a seat.

"You don't look so bad yourself," Dani replied, checking out her brother's new attire and admiring his handsome appearance in his three-piece suit.

"Rich and I are about the same size, so he let me borrow some of his clothes," Daric said, looking down at his fine suit.

"Someone mention my name?" Rich asked, as he rounded the corner and entered the bedroom. "Just came to see how our other house guest was doing."

As soon as Dani got one look at Rich, panic seized her. She frantically tried to crawl away from the approaching figure. Daric knew what was going through his sister's mind. He reached over, grabbed Dani's hand and gave it a firm squeeze to get her attention.

Speaking calmly, Daric said, "Dani, this is Rich, our host. If it weren't for him, I'd be in jail, and God only knows what would have become of you." Daric tried to get across to Dani that she was safe and in good hands.

Dani relaxed as soon as she realizing that Daric didn't feel alarmed or threatened. When her heart rate had calmed down, she said, "I'm sorry, you startled me for a moment."

It hadn't escaped Rich's notice that Dani had had the same reaction to his presence as Daric had had the night before.

"How are you feeling, my dear?" Rich asked softly, putting the incident aside for the moment.

"Much better, thank you," Dani replied, having regained her composure. "And thank you for taking us in. I don't know how we'll ever repay you."

"Nonsense. I'm rather looking forward to it," Rich replied. "Mary said I wasn't to stay too long. Don't want to tire you out. Daric, I'll meet you in the drawing room when you're finished here." With that, Rich left.

"Oh my God, you've got to be kidding me!" Dani whispered, when she was sure Rich was out of hearing range.

"I know. I had the same reaction when I met him last night. But, Dani, he's nothing like the last one we encountered," Daric said reassuringly. "And he's a lot younger, too."

"But two 'Uncle Richards', how is that possible?"

"I don't know . . . and with two completely opposite personalities," Daric informed her.

"Rich is an inspector with the Metropolitan Police and Mary is a teaching nurse at the London Hospital," Daric continued. "They've asked us to share their home with them until we get ourselves settled. I told them our grandmother story, the one we had agreed on, and it worked."

"Mary filled me in this afternoon. I think we're very fortunate to have found them," Dani sighed.

"More like they found us, or rather Rich did," Daric said light-heartedly.

"Either way, we would still be out on the street if it weren't for their generosity," Dani said.

"I was really worried about you. I've never seen you that sick before," Daric said, conveying a sense of both anxiety and relief.

"Thanks for looking out for me," Dani said softly.

"You'd do the same, if our places were reversed," Daric said.

"But first things first. You need to start by getting better. And since Mary is the doctor, or in this case, the nurse, I'll let you get some rest." Daric leaned over and gave Dani a peck on the forehead. "Get some rest. I'll pop in to see you in the morning."

"Good night."

112

AFTER CHECKING ON his sister, Daric made his way downstairs to the dining room, automatically drawn to the aroma. Rich and Mary were both at the table enjoying breakfast. Rich was reading the morning paper and passing on something he thought would interest Mary.

"It says here that Prince Albert Victor has left for the Danby Lodge in Grosmont, Yorkshire."

"Good morning," Daric said, after Rich had finished.

"Good morning," the Cases said in unison.

"I just checked in on Dani. She seems much better today," Daric said cheerfully.

"Yes, she does. I stopped in to see her this morning, too. If she feels up to some fresh air, we may take a walk in the park this afternoon. It looks like it's going to be a beautiful day," Mary said.

"And you, my friend, will be going back to the Frying Pan pub, I'm afraid. One day will not satisfy that big ox," Rich said sadly. "But hopefully not for too much longer."

"I don't mind, honestly," Daric said. "There sure are some interesting people who come into that place. And at early hours, too. Mr. Farrow said he rarely closes the pub's doors. It seems as though he stays open as long as he has a paying customer."

"Most of the early folks would be shift workers and unfortu-nates," Rich said matter-of-factly, while he continued to scan the paper.

"Unfortunates?" Daric asked, unfamiliar with the term.

"That's how the press, the public and the police refer to prosti-tutes," Rich said.

"Not the professional ones. But the women who, without a man to support them and with limited or no means of supporting themselves or their children, are forced to rent out their bodies for a few coins. All to get enough for food and a bed for the night," Mary further explained.

"It's really pathetic, that, in today's society, girls aren't edu-cated the same as boys. If they were, they could be self-sufficient, too," Mary said sadly. "But girls are taught at home, on important things, like how to run a household. They're not taught any practi-cal skills, where they can earn a decent wage."

"Now, you sound like your friend, Clara," Rich teased.

"Well, Clara's right. Even if a woman can find work making coats in a sweat shop, she's forced to work six twelve-hour days for a measly twenty-five cents a week." As Mary progressed on this topic, her passion increased and so did her volume. "And if she's really lucky, she might find work gluing matchboxes together. That would be a fourteen-hour day, seven days a week, for seventy-five cents a week. And whatever little she earns would go to greedy slumlords."

Mary took a breath, slumped her shoulders and apologized for her outburst. "I'm sorry. But it infuriates me that not enough is being done, or not being done fast enough, to address this problem. It's been only in recent years that universities have started to award women degrees on the same terms as men. But getting people to break from old entrenched traditions, to provide women with a decent education, is an almost impossible task."

Mary's comments had made an impression on Daric. He had not known the number, the variety or the seriousness of the challenges facing women every day. Now that he knew, he felt an empathy he had not felt the previous day for the women at the pub. He hoped he would better appreciate the women he would almost certainly be serving there later today. Maybe there would be something he could do to help.

113

"PROFESSOR?"

Bear growled, scanning the entire place and was frustrated she had located no intruder. She decided further effort wasn't required and stayed curled up on the floor next to Quinn.

"Yes, Hermes," Quinn replied.

Hermes materialized directly in front of Bear, who leaped back protesting fiercely, "Arwooo." Having voiced her displeasure, Bear cautiously approached the stranger. "Hi, Bear," Hermes said amiably. He enjoyed interacting with Bear, it made him feel like the human he aspired to be.

"Professor, you asked me to inform you when there were changes in Dani's vital signs."

"What is it?" Quinn asked anxiously.

"I'm pleased to inform you that Dani's vital signs have returned to normal," Hermes said.

Quinn paused for a moment and bowed his head in utter relief. He hated being completely useless when it came to taking care of his children. He had always been there for them. He had been there to pick them up when they fell off their bicycles on their first attempts without training wheels. And he had been there when Daric had fallen out of a tree he had climbed to escape the unwanted advances of an eight-year-old little girl. Unfortunately, the tree he had chosen to climb had not been a wise choice. His ascent had become a very rapid descent, resulting in two broken limbs. One was the tree branch Daric had crawled out on; the other was Daric's left arm. Quinn had taken Daric to the hospital. He had also been on the receiving end of Sandra's wrath for not cutting the tree down months before.

"Um, Professor?" Hermes could see Quinn was lost in thought. "We have company." Hermes announced, moments before he vanished.

114

RICHARD QUIETLY APPROACHED the gazebo. He did not want to alert Quinn to his presence. He wanted to see whether he could find out what Quinn was working on before announcing himself. As he had discovered on his earlier clandestine visit, the windows would reveal none of their inner secrets.

Richard had the access code to open the front door, but using it would be extremely difficult to explain to Quinn. He wisely chose to knock instead. He rapped firmly on the door several times, while hollering, "Hey, Quinn, open up. It's Richard."

Richard heard Bear howl. It was a matter of only seconds before Quinn pulled open the front door. "Richard, what a pleasant surprise. What are you doing out here?" Quinn asked, curious.

Richard pushed past Quinn to enter the lab before Quinn could protest. "I stopped by to see Dani and Daric, but Sandra said they're not home. So, I decided to come out and see how you're doing," Richard explained while scanning the interior. Richard noticed nothing glaringly different from his last visit, except the computer console was on and a presentation about what looked like quantum mechanics was projected on the screen at the back of the room.

Bear stood between Quinn and Richard, the hairs on her back standing erect, running in a line from her neck to the base of her curled tail. "Grrrrrrrr."

Richard looked down at the dog and immediately ignored her. "I could have sworn I heard you talking to someone," Richard said.

"It's okay, Bear." Quinn comforted the unhappy family member. "You probably overheard me talking to my computer. It uses voice-recognition software."

"Oh. So tell me, what are you working on, Buddy?" Richard asked directly, never one for beating around the bush.

"Nothing much, really, just reviewing old lectures, you know, to make sure they're up to date," Quinn tried to bluff.

"Why on earth would you waste your time updating some old lectures, especially when you're on sabbatical?"

"You know how it is. One minute you're overwhelmed with work, the next you're at a loss for something to do," Quinn lied.

"Well, that's funny. Sandra said it wasn't a good time for me to visit. I wonder why she would have said that," Richard stated sarcastically.

"You know Sandra; she's so wrapped up in her own work, she thinks everyone's as busy as she is." Again, Quinn was fabricating a story he hoped would satisfy Richard's incessant curiosity. But unfortunately . . .

"Enough, Quinn. Something's going on here. Both you and Sandra are acting weird and I should know. So spill it, what's going on?" Richard insisted. "And I'm not leaving here until I get a satisfactory answer."

115

"HOW CAN YOU possibly move with all this stuff on?" Dani asked. She couldn't get comfortable with all the layers of material associated with women's clothing of this era. The dress Mary offered her to wear had a long train, a crinoline and a bustle, plus a long jacket, a choker necklace and a bonnet.

"You get used to it, I guess," Mary replied, not having really given it much consideration until now. It was just how women dressed.

"Can't I wear my own dress?"

"I'm afraid not. Martha wasn't able to salvage it. It was badly stained, and it was torn in several places. I'm sorry, but it was beyond repair," Mary said.

"She did, however, save these," Mary said, handing Dani her undergarments.

"Oh, thanks," Dani said shyly.

"Can I ask: what are they?"

"This is my sports bra," Dani said holding up the item. "And this is my underwear. The material is designed to move with you, not constrict you."

"What kind of sports do you play?" Mary asked. She could tell, by Dani's physique, that she was an athlete.

Dani thought quickly. The sports she enjoyed and, in most cases excelled in at home would not be appropriate for this time period. "I play golf and tennis," she said confidently.

"I play tennis, too," Mary said excitedly. "Maybe we could play a game when you're feeling better."

"That would be fun," Dani encouraged.

"But first, we will have to find you something to wear. You can't go out wearing just those," Mary said, referring to Dani's under-garments. "And I'm afraid I have nothing that will fit you," Mary said sadly.

Dani plopped back down on the edge of the bed, deflated. She wanted to please Mary, but she just couldn't get comfortable in that dress, no matter how hard she tried.

"Hey, I have an idea. Wait right here," Mary said, as she darted out of the room.

Ten minutes later, Mary reappeared with a bundle under her arm. "These should do the trick," Mary said, while laying out several items of clothing on the bed. There, before Dani's eyes appeared a woman's riding habit. There was a matching jacket and skirt, without the volume of material and without a bustle. There was a high-collared shirt and a top hat with a veil.

Dani considered her options. "The jacket and skirt look as though they ought to work nicely," Dani offered. "But maybe I could manage without the hat and veil," she added, as a grin inched across her face. She turned to Mary and gave her an appreciative hug.

"My neighbour is more your height than I am. But we'll have to pick you up some additional clothes, later. You can't live in those forever."

"Thank you. This will be great." Dani dressed quickly so they could get out and enjoy the beautiful, sun-filled day.

116

AFTER HAVING DRESSED, Dani had gone downstairs and had had her first substantial meal in days. Even though the fare was only scrambled eggs and toast, she had devoured it with delight.

With breakfast behind her, Dani had joined Mary to go for a walk. As soon as they had stepped through the front door, they had been embraced by a truly beautiful day. Dani had paused to soak in the fresh air and to take in her surroundings before she and Mary had set off.

The Cases's terraced house, at 265 Old Ford Road, sat across the street from the west end of the beautiful Victoria Park. Behind the house was Duckett's Canal, which the locals referred to as simply Duckett's. The canal provided a shortcut between the River Thames and the River Lea, a major tributary of the Thames.

Victoria Park had been opened to the public in 1845 and encompassed two-hundred-eighteen acres of parkland. It had been and still was considered to be the finest park in the East End.

"Do you want to sit a spell?" Mary asked, after they had been walking for half an hour. She didn't want Dani to overexert herself. And the timing was perfect; they were just coming up to a good spot to rest.

"Maybe, just for a few minutes," Dani said, hating to admit that she could use a break. "This is an interesting spot," Dani remarked, as she entered and sat down on an old bench just off the path they had been following.

"This is one of two pedestrian alcoves in the park. They're surviving pieces of the old London Bridge that was demolished in the 1830s. One alcove is here; the other is at the east end of the park. You can see the bridge insignia here," Mary said, pointing to a section on the inside the alcove.

After a few quiet minutes of enjoying their surroundings, Dani turned to Mary and said sincerely, "I want to thank you again for letting us stay with you until we can get ourselves settled here in London."

"It's nothing, really. Besides, you're in no condition to be roaming the streets right now looking for work," Mary replied warmly.

"You have a very beautiful home and in an ideal location, too," Dani said. She couldn't get over the sharp contrast between the dark damp alleyways where she and Daric had been hiding and the luscious greenery and fresh air in abundance here.

"We immediately fell in love with this house and the neighbourhood. We felt it was a perfect location for raising a family. Sadly, I haven't been able to get pregnant," Mary admitted despondently. "Rich is so disappointed. He's an only child, and it's up to him to make sure his family name continues on to the next generation."

Dani reached over and gently took Mary's hand in hers. She looked deeply into Mary's sorrowful hazel eyes. "Please, don't despair, Mary. I have a feeling that you will have the family you're dreaming of. And you and Rich will be wonderful parents."

"I hope you're right."

Dani knew she was right. After seeing Rich and the picture hanging in the dining room, she knew Rich had to be a direct ancestor of Uncle Richard.

After a short rest, Dani and Mary continued on their walk. Before long, they came upon a beautiful structure, a drinking fountain. It was fifty-eight feet high with steps leading up to slender pointed arches on columns of red granite. Four cherubs seated on dolphins poured water from jugs. Between them were taps for water and bronze cups engraved with the words: *Temperance is a bridle of gold.*

"That's beautiful," Dani remarked, admiring the structure.

"This drinking fountain was erected in 1862 by Baroness Burdett-Coutts, the wealthiest woman in England and a dear friend of my parents," Mary said admiringly. "There were over 10,000 people in attendance for the opening ceremonies. I'd love for you to meet her. But her philanthropic work keeps her busy."

"What kind of work?" Dani asked, intrigued.

"Well, let's see, there's so much. She sponsors scholarships and endowments and has funded the building of several schools. But two of her more influential efforts were the establishment of the National Society for the Prevention of Cruelty to Children and her close involvement with the Royal Society for the Prevention of Cruelty to Animals," Mary recounted.

"But my personal favorite is one of her earliest philanthropic acts. Along with Charles Dickens, she co-founded the Urania Cottage in Lime Grove. It's a home that helps young women who have turned to prostitution get off the streets and return them to a better life."

"Why would they turn to prostitution in the first place?" Dani asked, finding it difficult to believe women could get to such a state of desperation. She thought there had to be better alternatives.

"These women don't choose prostitution as a profession. It's usually because of circumstances beyond their control they resort to it."

"I don't understand."

"From an early age, girls are sheltered by their fathers. They're not allowed to go to school. They're taught everything they need to know at home. They're taught what their role and responsibilities will be when they're grown up," Mary stated coldly.

"A woman's primary role is to be the comfort-giver, to ensure the smooth running of the home, for the benefit of the man who finances it. Ignorance is considered a desirable state and knowledge is considered burdensome. The only thing a woman needs to know is how to listen attentively. Once a woman is of age, she's married off to a provider, her husband. It's only when something happens to her husband that she finds she's with no means to support herself or her children."

"That's terrible. Everyone should be entitled to a decent education, to learn to make decisions for themselves, and to be able to support themselves!" Dani fumed.

"I'm so glad you agree." Mary smiled at Dani's genuine outrage for the current situation. *A kindred spirit,* Mary thought.

"I'm sorry, Mary. Please forgive my outburst. It just makes me angry."

"You should have heard me spout off this morning on this very subject. I think I surprised your brother," Mary said.

"No, he's used to it. My mother and I are very outspoken," Dani said and quickly realized her slip. "I mean, she was." And then Dani quietly hung her head.

Mary reached over and placed her arm around Dani's shoulders, trying to offer some comfort and knowing only time would lessen the pain.

Dani felt a tad guilty for her deception. She really liked Mary and hated the fact she had to lie to her, but there was no other way.

117

DARIC'S SHIFT AT the Frying Pan pub was turning out to be longer than expected. Police Constable Barrett had arrived a few hours ago and had told Daric that the inspector would be late picking him up. Something had come up that needed his attention before he could head home for the evening. The inspector had thoughtfully sent Barrett with some cash; he had also given the constable an hour off his shift so he could have dinner with Daric.

Mr. Farrow was taking full advantage of Daric's extra hours, assigning him chores that had not been performed in years, perhaps decades. His duties, however, were not preventing Daric from observing a few of the more interesting patrons during his late evening shift.

One of those patrons was a lady who appeared to be in her early forties. She was about five-foot-two and fairly plump. She had a rather plain face, brown eyes and greying dark brown hair that peeked out from under a black straw bonnet trimmed in black velvet. She was wearing a brown ulster or heavy woollen overcoat fastened with big brass buttons. Underneath were a brown linsey frock or medium length jacket and two grey woollen petticoats. On her feet was a pair of men's sidespring boots that had been cut for a better fit.

Daric had served her several times during the day, afternoon and, now, evening. She would disappear, usually in the company of a man, and reappear alone a little while later. And each time she sat at the same table and ordered a large glass of gin, throwing down the three pence she had just earned.

"Here you go, Polly," Daric said, while placing the tall glass on the table and picking up the coin. Polly smiled in return. That's when Daric first noticed she was missing some front teeth. Polly snatched up her glass and took a drink, quickly concealing her unsightly smile from the handsome young man.

Daric went to another table where two women were quietly carrying on a conversation. The first woman appeared to be in her late thirties. She wore a forest-green skirt, a dark brown petticoat, a long black jacket, a black bonnet and side-spring boots—all old.

The other woman, who appeared to be a bit younger, sat on the opposite side of the small wooden table. She looked out of place here. She didn't look like she was from this neighbourhood, not like the other patrons Daric had seen. Her complexion was fresh. Her brown hair was clean and pulled up into a neat bun. Her clothes were well pressed and looked as if they had been tailored-made. Daric had to admit, she was a very attractive woman.

"Can I get you ladies another drink?" Daric asked.

The finely dressed woman replied, "I'll have another glass of wine. Ruth?"

"I'm afraid I ain't got no money, Clara," Ruth, said in a hushed tone.

"That's all right. It's my treat," Clara said. Turning her attention back to Daric, she said, "Ruth with have the same, thank you."

"Coming right up." Daric left the table to fill the order and just glimpsed Polly walking out the door, with her arm around another man.

"The work is only seasonal. I don't get paid when there's no work. So I have to go looking elsewhere," Ruth was explaining to Clara when Daric returned with their drinks.

"And because we're only women, the boss says he don't have to pay us the same as a man. When I asked why, he threatened to fire me," Ruth said.

"'That's not right," Daric muttered under his breath, while he was walking away.

"What did you say?" Clara asked indignantly.

"Sorry. I just said that it's not right: a woman not being paid properly for the work she's doing," Daric replied, turning back around to face the younger woman's wrath. *If looks could kill,* Daric thought, gazing into the enraged, but still beautiful, young face.

"And you're right, it isn't. But that's what's happening!" Clara said curtly.

Daric was about to reply when the crash of a door being thrown open door captured his attention.

118

"DARIC, QUICK, I need your help!" Rich yelled, as he stuck his head in the pub's doorway and quickly disappeared again.

Daric dropped his apron, grabbed his coat and raced out the door, hopping into the waiting cab. "What is it?"

"There's a fire down at the docks. It looks big. I spotted it on my way here. We need to go help out," Rich replied. The eerie glow from the leaping flames could be seen dancing against the black sky for miles around.

* * *

It had taken hours, but the fire was finally under control. A large crowd had gathered to watch the warehouse of Messrs Dible and Co., Engineers, light up the night sky. Not only had the fire gutted the building, it had damaged the rigging of a sailing vessel, the *Connovia*, which was under repair there.

A good fire was a real draw for the poor people of the East End, because there wasn't much by way of entertainment or not much that they could afford. Emily Holland was one of those people, watching as flames pierced through the blackened sky. But she was not alone.

Not far away, hidden in the shadows, was a silent observer. But he wasn't there to watch the fire like the others, who had gathered during the early hours of the morning. He was there to watch Emily.

Once the flames had died down, Emily realized the best of the night's entertainment was over. She walked up Osborn Street, headed for her lodging house at 18 Thrawl Street. She didn't notice she had a stalker, quietly slipping among the shadows of the dimly lit streets.

At the corner of Whitechapel and Osborn, Emily saw a familiar figure staggering past a grocer's shop.

"Polly, where are you going?" Emily asked, worried about her friend's obvious inebriated condition.

"Nothing like a good fire for some free entertainment," Polly slurred.

"It's over. You missed it."

Polly slumped against the wall. She wasn't sure whether she was supporting it, or whether it was supporting her.

"Polly, why don't you come back to the lodging house with me?" Emily said.

"Nonsense. It's too early to call it a night," Polly slurred, just as the bells of St. Mary's Church tolled 2:30 A.M. "Besides, I don't have my doss money. I had it twice already, but I went to the Frying Pan instead. But with my jolly bonnet, it won't take me long to get my money. And I'd rather stay at the White House, where I can share my bed with a man."

Emily was familiar with the common lodging house on the corner of Flower and Dean Street, which in her opinion, operated more like a brothel. And it was quite evident by Polly's current condition that her rent money for her bed tonight was spent on booze.

With that, Polly set out for the Frying Pan pub in search of another client. Or so she thought, but she was going in the wrong direction. Instead of turning around and going back the way she had come, she turned left onto Whitechapel Road. Little did she know, in her drunken state, that she wasn't taking that trek alone. The stranger, who had been following Emily, believed Polly would be more interesting.

119

CHARLES CROSS, A carter, was making his way to work along Buck's Row, which ran east-west from Brady Street to Baker's Row. The north side was lined by dark daunting warehouses, with blackened windows, and on the south side by a row of terraced houses. He noticed only one light on in a second-storey window.

The darkness of the early morning and the diffused street lighting played tricks in the shadows and with Cross's imagination. As he approached the walled-off Board School at the west end of Buck's Row, he noticed what he thought was a discarded tarpaulin. Thinking he could use the tarp at work, he crossed the street to retrieve the bundle.

As Cross got closer to the bundle on the ground, he realized it wasn't a tarpaulin. Even with only the speck of light cast from a distant lamppost, he could see it was a woman. But before he could get closer, he heard footsteps approaching from behind, causing him to halt. He turned to find another man coming down the street from the direction he himself had just come.

"Come and look over here; there's a woman lying on the pavement," Cross cried out.

Robert Paul was also a carter and, like Cross, he was on his way to work. Making deliveries for a living meant extremely early hours. They never knew whom or what they'd come across with the breaking of a new dawn. It wasn't uncommon to find drunks lying on the streets, those who couldn't make it home last night or those who had no homes to go to. Paul preferred to mind his own business, but this time decided to check it out.

The woman was lying on her back, with her hands down at her sides. Her bonnet was on the ground by her right side. Her legs were slightly apart and her skirts were raised above her hips. It was too dark to see anything clearly.

Cross reached down and touched the woman's hand. It was cold. "I believe she's dead."

Paul checked to see if she was breathing, but as he brushed against her breast, he thought he saw a slight movement. "I think she's breathing, but very little, if she is."

Paul reached down and straightened her skirts, preserve her modesty. He was certain the poor dear was a victim of an assault or had been raped. "Help me prop her up," he said.

"I'm not touching her," Cross squawked. "Besides, I'm going to be late for work."

"So am I," Paul agreed. "We'll tell the first bobby we come across. Come on, let's go."

The two men left, leaving the woman where they had found her. Lurking in the shadows was another man who had witnessed the entire exchange. After the two carters had turned the corner, he emerged from the shadows, turned behind the school and disappeared down the alleyway known as Wood's Buildings.

120

"INSPECTOR, INSPECTOR!" A voice bellowed over the banging on the front door.

"Will you stop all that caterwauling! It's enough to wake the dead, even at this ungodly hour," Elsie scolded loudly, as she unlocked and pulled open the front door to confront the offender. Being the cook, she, rather than the housekeeper, was expected to open the door in the morning, since it was the time of day when carters delivered the goods the cook had ordered the previous day.

"Forgive my outburst, Sergeant; I didn't know it was you," Elsie apologized, while she stepped aside to let the sergeant enter.

"Think nothing of it, Elsie. But, I need to speak to the Inspector, at once."

Detective Sergeant Frank Borto had been with the Metropolitan Police, H Division, for his entire thirty-five-year career. He wasn't a very ambitious man. Many of his coworkers thought it had to do with his size. After all, he did not project the ideal image of law enforcement. He was five-foot-eight and tipped the scales at two-hundred-seventy-five pounds. He had a receding hairline and what was left of his hair was a salt-and-pepper color, as was his Van Dyke style beard.

"The inspector just got in, not more than a half hour ago," Elsie said coldly. She admired and respected her employer, a sentiment that was rare for domestic service staff. But the Cases had always treated her fairly. In return, she felt almost motherly toward them and, like a mother, she could be very stubborn and overly protective when it came to looking after her employers.

"Please, Elsie, it's an emergency," the sergeant insisted.

"What is it, Frank?" Rich grumbled, descending the stairs. He had just finished cleaning up after the fire and was looking forward to climbing into a nice warm bed beside his wife.

"There's been a murder at Buck's Row, Inspector," Frank reported excitedly.

"So, why bother me? That's in Bethnal Green; that's J Division; that's Spratling's jurisdiction."

"Aye, but the body was reported by two carters to Constable Mizen and he's one of yours," Frank stated bluntly.

"Damn; all right. Give me a minute to change." Rich started up the stairs where he was intercepted by Daric.

"I couldn't help but overhear. Could you use another hand?" Daric offered.

"Thanks, but why don't you get some sleep. It's been a long night. I've got this."

"Rich, I'd really like to help. Look, I've had some experience with police work." Daric didn't want to say his involvement was on the opposite side of the law when he was wrongly accused of reckless driving. It was his car, but he wasn't behind the wheel. "It's the least I can do and I promise I won't get in the way."

"All right. Guess it can't hurt. But I think you should put on my old uniform. That way you can provide some assistance without getting booted out of the area for being a gawker. Spratling can be a real pain, sometimes." Rich paused only for a moment. "Hell, most of the time, actually."

121

AFTER RICH HAD completed the brief introductions, he, Daric and Frank climbed into the police wagon. While they travelled en route to the crime scene, Frank filled them in on the murder details. "This is what we know so far. Constable Neil was first on the scene. He used his lantern to get a better look at the body. That's when he noticed blood oozing from the woman's throat. He then signaled Constable Thain, who was walking north along Brady Street. When Thain arrived, Neil sent him to fetch Dr. Llewellyn at his surgery at 152 Whitechapel Road."

Whitechapel. Daric thought. *Why does that sound so familiar?*

"While Constable Neil waited for the doctor to arrive, Constable Mizen appeared on scene. He was making his rounds when two carters stopped him at the corner of Hanbury and Old Montague Streets. They said they had found a woman's body on Buck's Row at . . ." Frank paused and looked at his notes again. "At 3:40 A.M. They told him she was either drunk or dead. Mizen headed there immediately."

"When Constable Mizen arrived at the murder scene, Neil told him to go to J Division for an ambulance and to get reinforcements, while Neil searched the area. Mizen left the scene," Frank reported.

"Inspector Spratling will not like our involvement, but it can't be helped," Rich groaned. "Continue, Frank."

* * *

When the police wagon pulled up to the crime scene, Rich noticed a large crowd had already gathered. He jumped down from the wagon and walked directly over to Spratling to get a progress report. "What the hell are you doing here, Case? This is my jurisdiction," Spratling barked.

"It would appear that my station is involved, too; so you'll just have to share," Rich said dryly.

Inspector John Spratling had joined the Metropolitan Police in 1870. He was a keen-eyed man, or so his subordinates believed, with ivory grey hair and beard.

Spratling grumbled something Rich didn't quite catch; however, Spratling was not happy with the situation. Even though Spratling had moved up through the ranks quickly, he was only half the inspector that Rich was and everyone knew it, especially Spratling. Rich had bested him on a number of occasions, which, of course, only intensified Spratling's burning resentment: like gasoline tossed on a flame. This animosity did not bode well for a productive working relationship.

Spratling spotted a fresh recruit studying the ground where the blood had already been washed away. *Fool,* he thought. "You, come here!" he snapped.

Daric walked to Spratling. "Who are you?" the inspector growled

Daric had to think quickly. He didn't want the inspector to make any connection between him and Rich. He replied, "Constable Cartwright, Inspector."

"Well, Cartwright, make yourself useful. Go search the neighbourhood and don't forget to check the walls, the yards, and the adjoining railway."

"Aye, sir," Daric replied, and made a hasty exit.

Rich had been within earshot of the exchange and was impressed at how quickly Daric could think on his feet. *Good lad.*

122

HAVING SUFFERED SPRATLING'S ill temperament for the past hour, Rich, Daric and Frank headed to the mortuary to view the body and its belongings for any clues.

When they entered the Whitechapel Workhouse Mortuary, a private 'dead house' for workhouse inmates, they saw Dr. Llewellyn hunched over the body.

Dr. Rees Ralph Llewellyn was a rather large man standing six-feet tall. His black hair was slicked back with perfumed macassar oil, and he was sporting a handlebar mustache and goatee.

"Where are her clothes?" Rich asked, walking up to the body laid out on a raised wooden table.

"I'm afraid, Inspector, that the two buffoons who work here removed them, before I started my examination. They tossed them into a pile in the yard, along with all the other discarded clothing from the workhouse," Llewellyn stated brusquely, without looking up from his work.

Frank and Daric had followed Rich over to the examination table. On viewing the body, Daric let out a gasp.

"I know, hard to swallow, isn't it?" Frank teased. He recalled his first experience with a corpse; 'he had tossed his cookies', as a fellow officer had put it.

"No, that's Polly," Daric blurted out.

"You know her?" Rich asked astounded.

"Yes. She was at the Frying Pan pub last night," Daric explained. He felt terrible for Polly. She had seemed like a nice lady. As Rich had said, an unfortunate trying to survive as best she could. And now this: what a shame.

"Do you know her last name?" Rich asked hopefully. "Half the battle is trying to determine who the victim is."

"No; I know her only as Polly," Daric said sadly. He excused himself and walked out the back door.

"Poor lad, can't stomach the sight, I reckon," Frank said.

"Doctor, can you tell me what you've found?" Rich asked, ignoring Frank's comment.

* * *

Daric hadn't left the room because of the body. He had left because the doctor had said Polly's clothes were out in the back yard and Daric wanted to do a little investigating on his own. He knew what Polly had been wearing the night before and realized it would be relatively easy for him to identify which clothes were hers. Daric also recognized they might hold a clue that could help with the investigation. In addition, he knew there were no guarantees about how long the clothes would be accessible before they were either destroyed or recycled for use by another inmate.

123

AFTER GATHERING FROM Dr. Llewellyn as much information as was currently available, Rich showed Dr. Llewellyn a knife. It was the one he had picked up a few nights ago, the one that had been lying beside Dani's motionless body.

"Doctor, could a knife like this one be similar to the murder weapon?"

Dr. Llewellyn took the knife from the inspector and examined its shape, hilt, length, and sharpness. "I'd say most certainly."

"Thanks, Doctor."

Rich, Frank and Daric left the morgue and returned to the crime scene. They wanted to perform one final search of the area before the day's traffic obliterated any evidence that might still remain.

While Frank and Daric examined the ground where the body had been found, Rich looked at all the surrounding windows. He noticed that all the curtains were drawn shut. He reached into his front trouser pocket and extracted a few coins. Looking up at the windows of the terraced houses, he tossed the coins into the air. Gravity pulled them back to the damp cobblestone street. Within seconds, several window curtains were thrown open. The occupants anxiously scanned for the treasures that produced that oh so familiar sound. As soon as they caught sight of the inspector, they quickly retreated into the sanctuary of their homes.

"It astounds me," Rich muttered.

"What?" Frank asked, standing up from his search of the gutter.

"It astounds me that these people can hear a few coins dropping, but no one heard anything during Polly's murder." Rich sighed in disbelief.

Frank pulled out his notebook and scanned it until he found what he was looking for. "It says here that Constable Neil talked to Mr. Walter Purkiss, the manager of Essex Wharf, right over there," Frank said pointing to a third-storey bedroom window of Mr. Purkiss. "Purkiss said he heard nothing unusual. Even his wife, who had been pacing up and down in their bedroom, heard nothing. And Mrs. Emma Green," Frank said, pointing across the street, "who lives right next to where the body was found and who professes to be a light sleeper, said she didn't wake up until the police arrived early this morning."

A man was standing at the far end of the Board School. He was wearing a long coat, hat and was carrying a bag. And he was staring in their direction. The fact that he wasn't continuing on his way caught the inspector's attention.

"Excuse me, sir, could I have a moment?" the inspector shouted as he made his way quickly–but not too quickly–down the street; he didn't want to frighten or alarm the stranger.

"What can I do for you, Inspector?" the stranger asked. He was roughly five-foot-six. He had a mustache the color of maple sugar and a muscular build and was about twenty-seven years old, give or take. He wore a dark colored Inverness coat and a deerstalker hat similar to that worn by Sherlock Holmes. In his right hand he carried a Gladstone bag; in the left, the latest edition of *The Star* newspaper.

"Do you live around here?" Rich began his inquiry.

"No, I live over on Fashion Street," the stranger replied cordially.

"What are you doing in this neighborhood?" Rich questioned, suspicious.

"I'm just returning home after visiting my mother at the

hospital. I took the Wood's Buildings as a shortcut to Old Montague Street." The stranger's answer was calm and coldly efficient.

"Thank you. Sorry to have interrupted your journey," Rich said conversationally.

"Think nothing of it," the stranger replied. He then turned and continued on his way. Rich thought it odd that the man hadn't even asked what all the commotion was all about. Human beings are curious by nature. It would have been the logical reaction to the situation. Rich turned around, hoping to get an answer, but he was staring down an empty street. The man had simply vanished like a ghost.

"Rich," Daric called, bringing the inspector back to the matters at hand.

"Yes, Daric, what is it?" Rich was still thinking about his encounter with the stranger.

"When I was examining the ground where the body was found, I noticed a gutter close by. I presumed that's where all the blood was washed away. But I also notice that the grate hasn't been opened recently."

"So?" Frank said haughtily.

"So, the murderer couldn't have used the sewage tunnels as an escape route. He would have had to walk along the streets, probably right past the police," Daric retorted.

"All right, you two. I know we're all tired, but . . . " Rich was interrupted.

"Rich, Dr. Llewellyn told you he believed the body had been dumped here, and that this wasn't the murder site," Daric pressed on. He was anxious to share what he had discovered.

"That's right. He said there wasn't enough blood here for the number and severity of wounds that Polly sustained."

"It's unfortunate that Mrs. Green's son washed away the evidence before we could see it for ourselves," Frank added.

"Constable Thain told me that his hands were covered in blood after he and Constable Neil placed the body onto the ambulance," Daric continued. *It was really nothing more than a handcart,* Daric thought. "And he also mentioned that Dr. Llewellyn never turned the body over during his initial examination."

"What are you getting at?" Frank groaned, not following Daric's line of thinking, and besides, his feet were sore.

"What I'm saying is this: I believe this *is* the actual murder site."

"How did you come to that conclusion?" Rich asked skeptically.

"At the morgue, I went out back to look at Polly's clothing. I knew what she was wearing the night before, so it was easy to find her clothes. They were literally dripping with blood as if all her blood had soaked into her clothing. This would explain why there was so little blood at the crime scene. It would also explain why there was so much blood on the constables' hands after they picked her up," Daric said confidently.

"Brilliant." Rich beamed.

* * *

The stranger had simply melted into the shadows. He was getting very good at doing so. *That was too close,* he thought. He had returned to the scene, thinking everyone would have already gone. *Luckily, I had a story made up or that bumbling bobby could have been a real problem.* He unrolled his newspaper and reread the headline:

A REVOLTING MURDER.
ANOTHER WOMAN FOUND HORRIBLY MUTILATED IN
WHITECHAPEL. GHASTLY CRIME BY A MANIAC.

Saturday, September 1, 1888

124

"HOW CAN THE inquest have started already? The murder happened only yesterday. We haven't gathered all the evidence yet," Rich bellowed.

Rich and Daric had arrived at the Commercial Street station early that morning; there was a lot to do.

"Sorry, Inspector, but it's what Superintendent Arnold requested," Constable Barrett replied uncomfortably. "He said he wanted the case resolved swiftly."

"We just identified the victim last night!" Rich protested. His fight was with Arnold and Spratling, not with his staff. "Never mind, I'll handle it." He stormed off to his office. Turning, he shouted, "Daric, follow me."

Daric dropped the newspaper he had been reading and followed Rich into his office. "Close the door," Rich ordered, pulling out his chair and plopping down unceremoniously. Daric took the seat in front of the desk and sat patiently, waiting for Rich to gather his thoughts.

The office had a large wooden desk. The surface had inlaid forest-green leather. Two straight-back wooden visitor chairs were in front of the desk. In the left back corner of the office was a large filing cabinet. To the right of the cabinet and covering the majority of the remaining wall was a corkboard. It was covered with roughly scribbled notes, poor quality black and white photographs, and maps. Some were hand-drawn; others were from city files. Daric was looking at Rich's evidence board.

Daric took a closer look, paying attention to one map in particular. There was a date and time etched on the corner: August 7, 1888, 4:45 A.M. There was an 'x' by George Yard Buildings. He recognized some of the street names: Osborn, Old Montague, Whitechapel . . .

Why does that sound so familiar? he wondered.

Turning back to the map after being momentarily distracted, Daric recognized Brick Lane, Thrawl Street . . . *Hey, that's where the Frying Pan pub is located.*

"Daric, I'd like you to keep working at the pub. I want you to keep your eyes and ears open for anything out of place," Rich instructed.

Daric found this request almost laughable if the situation hadn't been so dire. As far as he was concerned, everything was out of place. And out of time, too, for that matter.

"Okay. I'm sure Mr. Farrow will enjoy my free labor," Daric said. "What am I looking for?"

"Look for any unusual behavior. The best way to spot it is to watch the regular patrons. If someone they don't recognize comes into the pub, you should be able to pick it up from their expressions. You'll know by their puzzled or suspicious glares."

"Okay. What else?" Daric asked keenly. He was enjoying this detective stuff. He was also eager to be of some value to Rich. It was the least he could do.

"Try to take note of names and places you hear," Rich said, pulling a small notepad out of the top drawer of the desk and sliding it across the desk.

A knock came at the door. Before Rich could react, it opened and Frank walked in, shaking his brolly. "It's a frog strangler out there," Frank moaned.

"A what?" Daric questioned warily.

"A frog strangler. It's raining so hard that even water-loving frogs have trouble breathing in it."

Daric looked over at Rich, who just shrugged his shoulders.

"Bates said he ran into a bit of trouble this morning," Frank started, as he divested himself of his wet coat.

"What kind of trouble?" Concern was evident in Rich's tone.

"He ran into that Squibby character again. Only this time, he threatened Bates. Told him he would 'do for him' if Bates interfered again. Then Squibby picked up a stone and threw it at Bates. He missed Bates and hit a little girl instead. Bates took off after Squibby, but he got away," Frank said dejectedly.

"We'll find him. Tell the others to keep an eye out for Squibby and make sure you give all of them his description," Rich instructed, getting up and putting on his coat.

"Where are you off to?" Frank asked.

"I'm taking Daric to the Frying Pan pub. He'll be our eyes and ears over there for a while. And then I'm going to pay Superintendent Arnold a visit, to see if I can get the inquest delayed."

"The inquest started already? We just found out who the victim was!" Frank protested.

"If you'd been here earlier," Rich chastised, "you would have heard all about it. Come on, Daric." And with that, Rich and Daric left the office and the station, venturing out into the frog-strangling downpour Frank had recently taken refuge from.

Sunday, September 2, 1888

125

"ARE YOU SURE you're up to this?" Mary asked for the third time that morning.

"Yes, I'm sure, Mary. I feel fine; great actually," Dani replied encouragingly.

"If, you're sure."

"I am."

The carriage stopped in front of the London Hospital. Mary instructed the driver to return at six o'clock for their trip home.

"You're sure?" Mary checked one last time.

"Will you stop, already? Let's go in."

Mary took Dani to the nurses' room and found a uniform for her to wear. It was the same as Mary's: an ankle-length deep-blue chambray dress with white collar and cuffs, a white-on-white striped apron and a starched buckram cap. Mary pulled out a pink arm band and fastened it around Dani's left bicep. "This shows the staff that you are a fresh new nurse," Mary explained. Mary was wearing her black teacher's arm band.

"Great," Dani mumbled, feeling inferior.

"Look at it this way: when they see this band, they won't be asking you to do anything too difficult." Mary's hazel eyes filled with laughter.

"You stick with me and I'll explain everything you need to know. And if you like it here, we might even get you on staff, full-time."

"Lead the way," Dani said eagerly.

* * *

Dani's day at the hospital had been quite the learning experience. She had spent most of her day watching Mary work. She was very impressed with Mary's efficiency. At the same time, the archaic medical practices appalled her.

For example, earlier in the day, Mary had intercepted a request at the front desk for Dr. Treves. She told the receptionist she would deliver the message personally because she knew the doctor was in surgery.

Dani followed Mary to the surgery wing. Having found the right room, Mary knocked on the door. "Come in," called a voice from inside. Mary knew it to be Dr. Treves's. She opened the door and stuck her head in.

"Dr. Treves, Inspector Abberline, from Scotland Yard, is here to see you. I told him you were in surgery."

"Thank you, Mrs. Case. Tell him I'll be out shortly," Dr. Treves replied while cauterizing a blood vessel. Dani was standing directly behind Mary throughout this short exchange and couldn't believe what she was seeing.

A gaselier hung above the operating table in the center of the room. A few other lanterns were scattered about, providing light where needed. The doctor stood on one side of the operating table; an assistant on the other. An attendant was at the foot of the table, pulling on ropes fastened around the patient's ankles. This contraption was to keep the patient as immobile as possible during the operation. Another attendant stood at the head of the table, administering ether, but only when the patient stirred, an occurrence Dani had the misfortune to witness. As for sterilization, it was minimal. Staff wore black aprons and armbands over their everyday street clothes to protect them from any blood splatter. No one wore a face mask. Perhaps, fortunately, the rest of the operating room was blocked from Dani's view.

"I'll let Inspector Abberline know, Doctor." Mary closed the door, but not before Dani heard someone saying, "Machine accidents. You can't reason with them. We're going to see a lot more of them." *Boy has medicine ever come a long way,* Dani thought, as she and Mary headed back to let the inspector know the doctor would be with him shortly.

* * *

As the day progressed, Dani met quite a few nurses. She quickly realized she was one of the youngest if not *the* youngest. She asked Mary whether there was any particular reason why so many of the nurses were older. Mary's response was simple. "Older women have had many of the common diseases and have built up an immunity to them. As a result, they're less vulnerable than younger women would be."

Dani spent the last few hours of the day sitting beside a man, about thirty-eight-years-old, who was lying motionless on an iron bed. An elderly nurse informed her early on that the man was dying and that nothing could be done to prevent his death. In spite of—or maybe because of—this sad prediction, Dani did her best to provide the man with comfort and a little small talk. It wasn't clear, however, that her efforts were yielding any real benefits. She wondered whether there was anything else she could do for the dying man. Her wonderings were interrupted when Dr. Treves, whom Dani had met earlier, stopped by to check on his patient.

Dr. Sir Frederick Treves was a surgeon at the London Hospital. A specialist in abdominal surgery, he performed his first appendectomy on June 29, 1888; soon after he was appointed a Surgeon Extraordinary to Queen Victoria. He was ruggedly handsome, at five-foot-eleven, of average weight, and in his thirty-fifth year. His reddish-brown hair was perfectly coiffed and his handlebar mustache professionally trimmed. He had warm, friendly, sea-green eyes and a gentle, caring, bedside manner.

"How is he?" Dr. Treves whispered, not wanting to disturb his sleeping patient.

"He's been sleeping quite a bit," Dani explained. "When he does wake up, he seems a bit disoriented."

Dr. Treves checked the patient's pupils and, then, his pulse and temperature. Dani hated to see such a young man die for no obvious reason. *If only he were in my time period,* Dani thought, *A nurse practitioner could easily deal with this patient and he'd walk away completely healed.* The senselessness frustrated Dani beyond reason.

"Isn't there anything you can do for him?" Dani asked.

"Dani, the only thing people who are dying require is to be left alone. They need to be allowed to die in peace. As a physician, my role isn't to torment my patient with futile attempts to extend his deteriorating condition; that I could perchance prolong the flutter of his heart for a few more beats. If I, as the physician, cannot improve his condition, then it is my duty to protect my patient from any pain or suffering associated with his illness." With that, Dr. Treves excused himself and continued with his rounds.

Dani was feeling decidedly dejected and discouraged when she heard Mary's cheerful voice calling her. "It's time to go home. You ready?"

"Yeah, I guess so."

As Dani and Mary made their way through the hospital to meet their cab and head back to the Cases's comfortable home, Dani continued to think about the dying man and about everything else she had experienced during the day. She'd learned a lot today; much of it was pretty depressing.

126

DARIC WAITED PATIENTLY for the women to finish their conversation. *Finally*, he thought. The older woman finished her drink, got up from the table and left the pub. The younger woman returned to writing in her notebook. Now was his opportunity.

Daric walked over, took a deep breath and said, "Hi." *That was brilliant.*

The young woman looked up from her notes, checked Daric over and said, "Hi." She then returned to her task.

"Aren't you Clara?" Daric tried again.

"And aren't you that opinionated barkeep?" she asked, her tone glacial.

Daric was taken aback by her cold demeanour, but not discouraged. "Look, I'm sorry about the other day. I didn't mean to make you angry. I was, after all, agreeing with you." He flashed her one of his charming smiles, hoping to soften that frigid exterior.

Clara had to admit, he was a handsome young man. And when he smiled, those deep-blue eyes could pierce any hardened soul. She'd been a little cruel to him during their first encounter. It was probably because she had been pushing herself too hard. Clara smiled shyly in return and extended her hand. "I think we both got off to a bad start. My name's Clara Collet. And you are?"

"Daric Delaney," he replied warmly, while gently shaking the proffered hand.

"Can you join me?"

"Sure, thank you." Daric took the recently vacated seat opposite Clara. He knew Mr. Farrow could give him a hard time, but he deserved a break and he decided now was as good a time as any to take it.

"You're not from around here, are you?" both of them said in unison and immediately broke out laughing at their uncanny timing. "You first," Clara said, after catching her breath.

"No, I'm not from around here. My sister and I arrived here three months ago. We're staying with friends until we can get settled."

"It's your accent that gave you away," Clara said cordially.

"And you?"

"I'm here on an assignment."

"What kind of assignment?"

"I'm gathering information for Charles Booth for his book on the Life and Labour of People. Specifically, I'm investigating women's work in the East End, looking at the types of jobs, working conditions and wages."

"That sounds very impressive. How long have you been at it?" Daric asked. He was genuinely interested in developing the conversation. He was equally interested in the intelligent woman sitting across from him.

"About three weeks."

"And what have you found so far?"

"You know Ruth, the lady I was talking to the other day?" Daric nodded. "Well, her story is like so many others' that I've heard so far. Because of the seasonal nature of the work these women do and the poor wages they receive, many have had to turn to prostitution in order to survive," Clara said, with a touch of hopelessness in her voice. "And I've only begun to gather my statistics."

"What do you hope to accomplish with your research?"

"Well, there has to be some way that women can work and survive on their wages without having to resort to prostitution. There should be a fixed minimum wage," Clara declared.

Daric could see how passionate she was about her work. He sensed she was the type of person who could make a difference.

"Do you remember the London Matchgirls strike in Bow, two months ago?" Clara asked.

"No, not really," Daric hedged, having not been in London at the time. "Tell me."

"On July 2nd, Bryant & May's management fired a worker on some lame excuse that resulted in a strike of approximately four-teen-hundred women and girls. Management quickly offered to rehire the dismissed worker, but the strikers wanted more. They wanted better wages and the elimination of unfair fines that were being deducted directly from their pay. There was also the health issue related to working with white phosphorous. It took a little doing, but working conditions improved, the health concern was addressed and the fines were abolished. In addition, the workers were also given direct access to management for lodging their complaints, which had previously been blocked by the foreman."

"That's great, right?" Daric asked.

"Yes, it is. But it's only one company, and it addresses only four-teen-hundred women. More needs to be done," Clara stated firmly.

The door of the pub swung open and Rich entered, scanning the busy interior in search of Daric. A smile crept across his face as he made his way over to the table. He bent down and placed a chaste kiss on Clara's cheek. "What are you doing in this neck of the woods?"

"You two know each other?" Daric asked, astounded.

"You remember, Daric, I mentioned Clara at dinner the other night."

"You two know each other?" It was Clara's turn to be dumbfounded.

"I told you we were staying with a friend. Meet my friend." Daric laughed.

After sharing a drink and some lively conversation, Daric and Rich dropped Clara off at her home and proceeded to Old Ford Road, where dinner awaited.

127

"DR. LLEWELLYN'S REPORT said he didn't believe the woman has been seized from behind and then had her throat cut. He thinks a hand was placed across her mouth, then the knife was used to cut her throat. He also thinks the killer was left-handed, since the bruising on the victim's face appears to have been caused by a right hand," Rich mumbled around a mouthful of roast beef.

"How logical are those deductions?" Daric questioned.

"What do you mean?" Rich was curious to know Daric's thinking.

"If I were the murderer and executed the crime as Dr. Llewellyn suggests, wouldn't I be covered in blood splatter? After all, it was her carotid artery that was severed," Daric answered.

"I suppose."

"And, don't you think, as a murderer, I'd be concerned with having blood splatter on my face, especially the blood of someone who might have a communicable disease? And wouldn't someone with blood all over the front of him draw attention to himself as he left the scene?"

"Not necessarily," Rich countered. "As the murderer, I could have committed the crime, ducked behind the Board School, got onto Winthorpe Street, and then darted down a few passageways to Whitechapel Road. I could easily have been swallowed up by the crowds, even that early in the morning. And with so many slaughterhouses in the area, nobody would have questioned blood-stained clothes," Rich theorized.

Mary and Dani had been trying to enjoy their dinner, despite the graphic conversation at the table. As the conversation progressed, Mary noticed the increasingly ashen color of Dani's face and grew concerned. Maybe she had pushed her too hard during the day. But that wasn't the reason, Mary realized. Dani was staring directly at Rich, her eyes as wide as saucers.

"Rich, I think you'd better change the topic of conversation," Mary said firmly, tossing her head in Dani's general direction.

"I'm sorry. That was very inappropriate of me," Rich apologized. But his apology had no settling effect on Dani, who had suddenly lost her appetite.

"If you'll excuse me," Dani said quietly. She stood up, placed her napkin beside her plate and left the room.

"Now look what you've done," Mary scolded.

"I said I was sorry," Rich pleaded.

128

MARY WANTED TO jump up from the table and follow Dani, but Daric suggested they give her some space. Besides, he didn't want to spoil Mary's dinner. He assured her that he'd check on Dani after dinner and that he'd report back.

When dinner had concluded, Daric went to see how Dani was doing. He was worried that she might be having a relapse, especially since it wasn't like Dani to be upset by a little blood, real or otherwise. He'd never seen her look as pale as she had at the table and it frightened him.

Daric found Dani in her bedroom. "Hey, are you okay? You didn't look so good at dinner. And you don't look so hot right now."

"Close the door," Dani ordered. She was sitting on the bed, her legs drawn up to her chest, with her arms wrapped around them. She used to sit like that when she was a child. It provided her with comfort and made her feel safe, somehow.

"What is it?" Daric asked anxiously, sitting on the chair beside the bed.

"Did you hear what Rich said?" Dani's voice shook.

"Which part?"

"Come on, Daric, think about it. Where are we?" Dani's frustration was linked to her paranoia.

"London," Daric played along. When his sister got angry, it was best just to go with the flow.

"The East End, to be precise," Dani clarified. "And when are we?"

"Let's see. It's now September 2, 1888," Daric said flatly.

"And there was just a murder, with a knife." Dani was hoping Daric would put two plus two together, but, by the look on his face, she didn't think he was getting it.

"Just tell me, okay?" It was Daric's turn to be frustrated.

"The Autumn of Terror. Does that ring a bell?" Dani tried one last time.

"Should it?"

"The East End of London. Whitechapel to be more specific. The autumn of 1888. There's a murder. There will be several murders." Dani was trying to lead Daric to the answer.

"What are you getting at?" Daric snapped, even more frustrated than before. "Remember, I don't have your exceptionally precise memory."

"Jack the Ripper!" Dani supplied finally.

Daric had that dumbstruck look on his face. "That's why Whitechapel sounded so familiar."

"Was the victim's name, Mary Ann Nichols?"

"No it was Polly."

"Polly was Mary Ann Nichols nickname."

"What?" Daric was taken aback.

"She was believed to be Jack the Ripper's first victim," Dani recalled. "Even though he wouldn't receive that moniker for a few weeks yet."

"What's the name of his next victim? Maybe we can stop him," Daric blurted out.

"Daric, you know we can't interfere," Dani reminded her brother. "We've already talked about this. If we interfere, we don't know what impact our interference could have on history or on what unfolds."

"We don't know how just our even being here may have altered history already. So why not take the chance? If we don't do something, these women will die!" Daric exclaimed.

"Daric, in our time, they're already dead, all of them," Dani said sadly, thinking of Mary and Rich. "We need to let time play out as it did."

Present Day

129

"I'VE BEEN TRYING to complete a project I've been working on for several years now, and I've finally made a significant break-through," Quinn replied, conceding to Richard's persistence to know what had been occupying his time since he went on leave.

"The only problem is my children, somehow, got involved. I have to get them back," Quinn muttered despondently.

"Back?" Richard could see Quinn wasn't himself. He was a mess. He looked as if he hadn't slept in days.

"Never mind. You wouldn't understand. No one would." Quinn shook his head in despair.

"Try me," Richard pressed. "Come on, Quinn. We've worked together for years. You can tell me anything. You know that."

"This may be a little difficult to swallow," Quinn started slowly. Then he added, "You may want to sit down for this."

Richard casually pulled out a chair and got comfortable. "Okay."

"Remember your basic physics classes and Einstein's theories?" Quinn began. Without waiting for Richard to answer, he went on. "Back in 1905, Einstein's special theory of relativity proved that time travel to the future was possible."

"Time travel?" Richard repeated.

"Hear me out, Richard, please?" Quinn pleaded.

"Continue."

"Einstein's special theory of relativity is no longer debated among theoretical physicists today because it has already been proven. But it wasn't until 1949 that Einstein's general theory of relativity proved time travel to the past was possible, too."

"I'm listening," Richard muttered, feigning boredom.

"Within Einstein's general relativity theory, his gravitational field equations showed that space-time can be flat or curved. Simply put, curved space-time tells matter how to move, and matter tells space-time how to curve," Quinn elaborated.

"Go on." Richard was slowly losing patience. He hadn't come here to be lectured by Quinn.

"Curved space-time leads to time travel to the past," Quinn explained.

"But those were just theories, Quinn, nothing more," Richard pointed out.

"Since 1949, Einstein's general relativity theory has passed every experimental test they've subjected it to," Quinn asserted.

"Then, ask yourself this: if it's truly possible to do so, why hasn't someone already built a time machine?"

"The problem with Einstein's theory was it was incomplete," Quinn revealed. "Einstein's general relativity theory wasn't compatible with quantum mechanics—dealing with the behavior of matter and light on the atomic and subatomic scale."

"Are you trying to tell me you've solved this problem?" Richard sat up straight in his chair, now totally intrigued.

"Not only have I solved it." Quinn paused and stared at Richard before delivering the final punch. "I've actually created a time travel device."

"That's not possible!" Richard blurted, looking at him, thunderstruck.

"Think about it," Quinn persisted. "We've observed feats that were thought to be impossible, until they were eventually accomplished; now, for all intents and purposes, they're taken for granted.

Think about the heavier-than-air flying machine. Or how about breaking the sound barrier? And what about flights to the moon? Or the creation of International Space Station? Why couldn't time travel be similar?"

Richard didn't believe what Quinn was telling him. Time travel? It wasn't possible. If this ever got out, Quinn would be the laughingstock of the university, of the entire physics community for that matter. Yet, Richard couldn't completely discount what Quinn had just said. Because, he strongly believed, if time travel could be accomplished, if it really could be done, Quinn would be the man to do it.

Richard had to learn more, not only for Quinn's sake, but for his own.

"You can't be serious?" Richard asked, skeptical.

"I'm dead serious! And I can prove it."

130

"COME ON DANI, you need a break. You've been working really hard this morning and I don't want you to overdo it." Mary was still concerned over what she observed at the dinner table the night before.

"I'd like to introduce you to someone special," Mary said, leading Dani down a long hallway toward the back of the hospital. When they reached the end, Mary opened a door. "Dani, I'd like you to meet . . ."

"The Elephant Man!" Dani blurted. She immediately regretted her outburst, but it was too late. The man had already turned away from the door in shame, a feeling he was all too familiar with.

Dani remembered her parents talking several years before about a widely reported story back in 1987, when the 'King of Pop' had offered the London Hospital $1 million for the Elephant Man's bones. Not knowing what an Elephant Man was and being the inquisitive child she was, Dani had done a little research. She had discovered that Joseph Merrick, a.k.a. the Elephant Man, had begun to develop abnormally at an early age. The cause of his malformed head, curved spine, "lumpy" skin and overgrown right arm and hand had never been definitively explained until recently.

It was originally thought that he was suffering from elephantiasis, a condition that is characterized by a thickening of the skin and underlying tissues and that often leaves the victim seriously disfigured. A more recent study of the evidence concluded that Joseph Merrick suffered from a rare congenital hamartomatous disorder called Proteus syndrome. Dani's research had also revealed that Joseph Merrick had spent his entire life being gawked at by circus-goers and poked and prodded by curious doctors.

Realizing her thoughtlessness, Dani hurried down the two steps into the sunken room. She approached the man and stood directly in front of him. She reached out and gently cradled his left hand in hers.

"Please forgive my outburst. It was very rude of me. I think I was just caught a little by surprise. Please forgive me," Dani pleaded, sincerely.

"Of course," he stuttered, looking down at their entwined hands. He looked back up at Dani's face and could tell she was totally embarrassed by her earlier comment. But what completely fascinated him was the fact that she wasn't repulsed by his appearance. And he was relishing their close proximity. He couldn't remember ever feeling a gentler touch than he was experiencing now. He didn't want it to end. And her fragrance reminded him of the sweet smell of the flowers in the garden just outside his window.

Mary was impressed by the young lady's genuine regret and how quickly she addressed her failing. Mary didn't know whether she would have acted as graciously if she had been in Dani's shoes.

"Dani, this is Joseph Merrick. Joseph, this is Dani Delaney," Mary said, as she finished the introductions she had started earlier.

"Joseph, I am very pleased to meet you," Dani said sweetly, smiling at Joseph.

"Would you like to have a game of draughts?" Joseph asked shyly, reluctant to release Dani's hand.

"I don't know, Joseph; I'm working right now," Dani replied sadly, looking over her shoulder at Mary.

"Go ahead, Dani, you could use a short break. Come back to the common ward when you're done here," Mary encouraged.

"And Joseph, go easy on Dani; give her a chance to win a game or two," Mary scolded good-humouredly, as she left the room so the two could get acquainted.

"I'm afraid I'm not familiar with the game of draughts," Dani admitted.

"I'll teach you; it's easy," Joseph said excitedly. He reluctantly let go of Dani's hand and went over to a set of dresser drawers. He opened the top drawer and pulled out a game board and a box, setting them down on a nearby table. He opened the ten-by-ten inch game board and started setting out the pieces, all the while explaining the game.

"You can have the light pieces, which means you get to go first," Joseph explained. He was as giddy as a child on Christmas day and it reflected in his voice.

"We take turns moving our pieces diagonally on the board to an open square. We can only use the dark squares. You can jump my pieces, which means you capture them and remove them from the board."

"And when I get to the opposite end of the board, you crown my piece," Dani continued.

Joseph stood erect or as erect as his condition would allow. He looked quizzically at Dani. "You have played this."

"Sorry, Joseph, I wasn't familiar with the name of the game. Where I come from, we call it checkers."

131

"CAN'T YOU CONDUCT your research from somewhere else?" Daric asked. He was extremely concerned for Clara's safety.

"Don't be silly. You know I have to talk to the women who work around here," Clara reminded him.

"Can't they go to your house?" Daric had been trying to get Clara to change her mind, but she would have none of it.

"I don't think the streets are safe around here. You know just the other day a body was found on a street not far from here. They believe it to be murder," Daric pleaded.

"And did you know that just last year there were approximately 150,000 people convicted of drunkenness, more than twenty-five-hundred people who committed suicide, and over two-thousand bodies found dead on streets, in parks, and in hovels? Most of them were right here in the East End. So, to answer your question, yes, I know the streets aren't safe," Clara replied, agitated. "But this is where my work is."

A loud bang startled them, almost causing them to jump out of their seats. They turned to face the source of the commotion. "Beer and make it quick," the man bellowed. A second, smaller man ordered the same, walking up to the bar.

"Hang onto your hat, Lusk. I'll get to you in a minute," William growled back.

George Lusk was a local builder and contractor and a member of the Metropolitan Board of Works. He was a stalky six-foot-two and looked to be close to fifty-years-old. He was wearing a calf-length frock coat and a high Derby hat. He also carried an intricately carved walking stick. Lusk didn't use it to aid his steps, but carried it more like a baseball bat. His handlebar mustache and cold penetrating eyes only intensified his no-nonsense aura.

The smaller man accompanying him was Frederick "Fred" Best, a journalist for *The Star*, sent to obtain some human interest stories around the Whitechapel murders. He was lucky if he reached five-foot-six and looked to tip the scales at one-hundred-fifty pounds. He had narrow eyes that were deep-set and dark brown.

The two had met earlier that day and, with a few well-chosen words and compelling motivation, Best had lit a fire under Lusk. Best was looking for that sensational story. He pegged Lusk as being very gullible because he was so easily swayed. All Best had to do was tell Lusk that the murderer could easily prey on any of his seven children.

Best had also picked this specific location, the Frying Pan pub, because he knew there would be a large audience at this time of day for Lusk's performance. And, as if on cue . . .

"How many more of our women folk are going to have to lie in the streets dead before the police do something about it?" Lusk bellowed. The pub went deathly quiet.

"I say they're not doing enough to find the culprit responsible for these crimes." That remark stirred up a few affirmative murmurs from some of the male patrons.

"I say we form our own committee of vigilance to protect the women of our neighbourhood and to make the streets safe for all of us." That really stirred up the crowd.

Best stood there, sipping his beer and watching as the crowd got worked up. He wrung his hands with delight. He had picked the perfect partner in crime, so to speak. He chuckled at his own joke.

* * *

Sitting by himself at a table in the back corner was a man wearing an Inverness coat. A deerstalker hat and Gladstone bag sat on the table next to his glass. He was listening intently to the conversation.

132

"HOW DID YOU get that?" Mel Palmer asked her friend when she ran into her on Dorset Street. She was referring to the bruising that was quite evident on her friend's right temple.

Mel Palmer was in her late forties and had a pale face and dark brown hair. She was a domestic servant for a local Jewish resident. And she was a long-time acquaintance of Annie Chapman.

"And that's not all," Annie responded as she opened her dress and revealed more bruising on her chest. "I don't feel so well, either."

Annie Chapman was forty-seven years of age. She was five-foot-tall and rather plump. Her blue eyes were set in an ashen face. Her dark brown hair was short and wavy.

Annie had been living at Crossingham's Lodging House at 35 Dorset Street, where she paid eightpence a night for a double bed. Annie got a paltry income from her crochet work and making and selling artificial flowers. When she needed to make ends meet, she turned to prostitution, like so many others.

As the two women stood together in the street, Annie proceeded to explain what had happened. "This whole mess started two days ago, when I borrowed a bar of soap from one of the other lodgers, a woman by the name of Eliza Cooper. That night, I gave the soap to some man to wash with and never saw it again. But this woman, Eliza, kept asking me to give it back to her. Finally, I'd had enough of her badgering and tossed her a ha'penny and told her to go get a ha'penny of soap."

Then yesterday, I ran into the same bloody woman at the Britannia pub, over there," Annie continued, as she pointed to the eastern corner of Dorset Street. "She was onto me again about that damn bar of soap. I got tired of her ranting and I slapped her across the face and told her, 'Think yourself lucky I don't do more.'"

Annie paused, took a cautious breath and continued. "Then she hauled off and punched me in the right eye and then in the chest, knocking me to the floor. She never said anything. She just turned and stormed out of the pub. She had the nerve to attack me, right there in the pub, in front of all those people, over a lousy piece of soap!"

Mel knew of Eliza. She had a good six inches and fifty pounds over Annie. The short-lived fight had evidently been very one-sided. Mel could tell Annie wasn't herself; she looked like she had got the worse of the exchange with Eliza.

"I may go see my sister," Annie said, changing the subject abruptly. "If I can get a pair of boots from her, I might go hop picking," she mused hopefully, since a bit of hop picking would give her the money she needed for lodging.

133

DARIC HAD FINISHED at the Frying Pan pub for the day. He'd told Rich that he would walk to the station rather than have Rich pick him up. Daric felt he needed to stretch his legs and get a bit of exercise. Besides, it wasn't that far to the station.

As Daric turned the corner onto Commercial Street, a man jumped out in front of him and demanded, "Give me your money!"

"I don't have any," Daric replied calmly. Even if he had, he wasn't about to hand it over to this ruffian.

"Sure you do. You work at the Frying Pan. I've seen you there. Now give it up," he said, giving Daric a shove for emphasis, throwing him back against the wall of a public house.

"I work there to pay off a debt. I don't get paid. So as I told you, I don't have any money." Daric was trying hard not to exacerbate the already tense situation. He was resisting his innate urge to retaliate, as he would normally have done, but he recognized that this was anything but normal.

"Then give me your valuables and make it quick," the man ordered.

"I told you. I don't have anything to give you," Daric said, clearly irritated.

"What about that?" The man was pointing at Daric's bracelet.

"Hand it over, now!"

"Not on your life. Now get out of my way," Daric said, taking a step forward.

The would-be thief didn't budge. He pulled back his arm, made a fist and put all his weight behind the punch he threw Daric's way. Daric dodged right. The thrown punch hit the brick wall right behind Daric's head. There was a guttural eruption that started deep within and grew in volume as the pain intensified. The man spun away, cradling his hand, and writhing in agony. Daric thought now would be an opportune time to continue on his way. "I told you, I have nothing to give you."

* * *

"Hey, Daric, how are you?" Constable Barrett greeted Daric upon entering the station.

"Great, thanks. How about yourself?" Daric asked cordially.

"It's been crazy around here, what with two murders and all," Barrett replied. "How's your sister doing?" Barrett asked as an afterthought, remembering the dash through the streets a few days ago.

"She's much better, thank you. You mentioned two murders. I thought there was only one," Daric responded questioningly.

"We had one about four weeks back. We were still working on it when this one pops up. Even though it's not rightly ours, we've been told by Superintendent Arnold to get them solved, pronto," Barrett grumbled.

After leaving the front reception desk, Daric found Detective Sergeant Frank Borto frantically shuffling through a pile of papers on his desk, several of which had found their way to the floor.

Daric decided to bury the hatchet and offer Frank the proverbial olive branch. "Hey, Frank, how's it going?"

Frank looked up and wasn't overly thrilled with the jovial expression on Daric's face. "I'm as busy as a one-legged arse kicker, what do you think?" he replied gruffly. He then bent down to pick up the mess of papers scattered on the floor. Daric stooped down to lend the poor guy a hand.

"Thanks," Frank stammered, once he had placed the papers back on the desk. He reached into his back trouser pocket and pulled out a silver flask. Spinning the top, he threw back a belt, and then offered the flask to Daric.

"No, thanks."

"Have it your way," Frank scoffed, stopping the flask and putting it back in its customary place.

"Is Inspector Case busy?" Daric inquired.

"Yeah, but go on in; he's expecting you," Frank muttered, continuing to look for something that was determined to evade him.

Daric went to Rich's office. He knocked and entered upon hearing, "Come in."

"Aw, Daric, come, sit. Tell me something that will make my day," Rich encouraged, gesturing to the chair in front of his desk.

"I almost got mugged. Does that make your day?" Daric said flippantly.

"What? Where? Are you all right?" Rich fired off a series of questions in rapid succession.

"Mugged, corner of Commercial and Fashion, by the Queen's Head pub, and, yes, I'm all right," Daric replied in the correct order.

"Can you describe him? Maybe we can track him down."

"It was dark. I think he was about my age, maybe a bit older, muscular build and I thought I saw a tattoo, but don't ask me what it was. I'd know him, if I saw him again," Daric assured Rich.

"Well, I'm glad you're okay. So, what can you tell me about the rest of your day?"

Daric didn't need his notebook because there really wasn't much to report. And what he needed to tell Rich, he could do from memory.

"There were two gentlemen who came into the pub and stirred up the crowd. The loud-mouth was George Lusk, a local builder. The other was a journalist with *The Star*, a Fred Best," Daric reported succinctly.

"I always rely on my first impressions, my gut feeling, and they have yet to steer me wrong," Rich said. "So tell me, what is your gut telling you about these two?"

"I don't like Lusk. I think he's a troublemaker. And I don't trust that little weasel reporter, either. There's just something about him."

Rich erupted into laughter, catching Daric totally off guard.

"What's so funny?"

"Your colorful assessment complemented by your serious expression," Rich explained. "Sorry, I wasn't laughing at you, Daric. But you made my day. Along with the fact that the coroner has adjourned Mary Ann Nichols' inquest until Monday, September 17th. Hopefully, we can dig up some evidence before then. Come on, let's call it a night," Rich said.

Rich and Daric left the office just in time to see Frank jumping out of his chair. It flew backwards, tipped over, and went crashing to the floor. The noise caught the attention of Frank's fellow officers. They all stopped what they were doing to check out the untimely disruption.

Frank was gripping the corner of his desk and vigorously shaking his right leg.

"What's with you," a fellow constable asked.

"Leg cramp," Frank replied, balancing on one leg while continuing to shake the other out to the side. The rest of the officers returned to their duties, shaking their heads at 'good old' Frank's antics.

Rich looked at Daric and whispered, "Have you ever just looked at someone and knew the wheel was turning but the hamster was dead?"

The two men chuckled as they headed home to a delicious, hot meal.

134

AFTER DINNER, THE group retired to the drawing room for a little brandy to aid in the digestion of a wonderful mutton roast that Elsie had prepared. Daric and Rich sat in the two wingback leather chairs while Dani joined Mary on the sofa. The warmth of the fireplace was a welcome contrast to the dampness that lurked outside and was trying to penetrate the walls and invade their space.

Everyone was enjoying their after-dinner drinks and the soft crackle emanating from the fireplace, when the comfortable silence was broken.

"I don't like Clara working in that area. It's not safe," Daric stated emphatically.

"Daric, we've been over this before. It's where she needs to be to complete her work. It's only for a month or two more." Rich shot him a weary glance.

"I agree with Daric," Mary jumped in. "I'm worried about her, all alone in that horrible part of town."

Dani was mentally comparing times and dates to what she knew about this time period. *One or two more months; that would make it November at the latest,* she thought.

"Clara is an intelligent woman, she knows what she's doing, and she knows how to take precautions," Rich assured them.

* * *

After finishing their drinks, they bade each other good night and retired for the evening. Daric followed Dani to her room, understanding her discreet signal to him as the evening wound down.

"Daric, we have to be careful," Dani cautioned.

"I know we do. But I won't stand by and let anything happen to Clara, if I can help it," Daric said adamantly.

"Relax. We know that Clara wasn't one of the Ripper's victims."

"Do we? You don't know what happened to Clara. Neither do I! Maybe she was one of the Ripper's victims," Daric retorted. "Weren't there murders before and after the canonical five? Didn't you say they never identified some bodies and that there were some murders where only pieces of the bodies were found? No one knows for sure how many were victims of Jack the Ripper."

"I understand your concern, but remember, in our time period, all these people are dead, and how they died, at this point, is irrelevant." Dani couldn't believe how cold she sounded until she heard her words out loud.

"It doesn't make it any easier," Daric groaned.

Tuesday, September 4, 1888

135

THE ROUTINE HAD been the same every morning since Mary Ann Nichols' murder. Today was no exception as Rich and Daric arrived early at the station. They would stay for only a few minutes before heading to the Frying Pan pub where they wanted to have a conversation with Clara.

"What on earth?" Rich muttered.

There was Frank, sound asleep, curled up on the floor under his desk, surrounded by a bunch of crumpled and ripped pieces of paper.

It was still relatively early. Not all the station's seventeen staff had arrived yet. *Thank goodness,* Rich thought.

"Detective Sergeant Borto!" Rich bellowed.

Frank sprang awake, hitting his head on the underside of his desk and letting out a yelp.

"Sir," Frank answered dutifully, pulling himself to his feet and standing erect. A soft moan escaped between his pressed lips. His back was killing him.

"Have you been here all night?" Rich asked. Frank wasn't a young man anymore; sleeping under his desk couldn't have been comfortable for him.

"Aye. These interview notes are as useless as a chocolate teapot," Frank snapped back. "I've been trying to make some sense of them, but there's none to be had. There are too many contradictions."

Daric was finding it extremely difficult to keep a smirk from developing. Frank looked ridiculous. What little hair he had, was standing on end. His shirt was pulled out of his trousers on the left side. And his suspenders were halfway down his arms, impeding his flailing hand gestures. *It must be his Italian heritage,* Daric thought.

"What are you laughing at?" Frank snapped at Daric.

"Nothing, Frank." Apparently, Daric had failed miserably at suppressing that determined smile.

"Well, keep at it," Rich said, before wandering into his office. Daric was right on his heels. On his desk was the latest edition of *The Star*. Its headline read:

'LEATHER APRON'
THE ONLY NAME LINKED WITH THE
WHITECHAPEL MURDERS.

The Strange Character who Prowls About Whitechapel After Midnight–Universal Fear Among the Women– Slippered Feet and a Sharp Leather knife.

* * *

An hour later, Rich and Daric arrived at the Frying Pan pub. Clara had not yet arrived, according to William. Daric pointed out George Lusk and Fred Best to Rich; it wasn't hard to understand what Daric had earlier conveyed.

"What are the police doing? Have you seen any results yet?" Lusk shouted to the crowd that had gathered.

"It's been four days since that poor woman's murder and nothing, absolutely nothing, has happened," Lusk ranted.

The crowd was growing louder as Lusk stirred their distrust of the police. Most people still considered them a threat to their civil rights. They associated the police with martial law and the government's way of spying on and bullying them.

Best had planted this seed of animosity in Lusk and was thoroughly enjoying watching it blossom. Best was determined to get his sensational story even if he had to create it himself.

"Why don't they offer a reward for the capture of this murderer? Maybe that way we can finally get him off our streets and behind bars, and our women folk will be safe again." Lusk got louder as the encouragement grew in volume.

"Keep an eye on this situation for me, Daric. I'm going to give the superintendent an update. He'll want to know about this," Rich instructed, then left the pub and its volatile crowd.

136

"HOW ARE YOU feeling?" Mel asked Annie when they met outside Christ Church on the corner of Commercial and Church Street.

"Not any better than yesterday, I'm afraid," Annie replied wearily.

Mel noticed how pale Annie looked. She was wondering whether Eliza had really hurt Annie and Annie was hiding it from her.

"Have you had anything to eat today?" Mel asked. She was thinking maybe Annie was just a little malnourished. Maybe a hot bowl of soup would do her a world of good.

"Not even a cup of tea," Annie replied distractedly.

Mel was not going to let Annie's vague answer go unnoticed; something was definitely wrong.

"Here." Mel took Annie's hand, turned it over and placed two pence in her palm. "Go buy something to eat. And don't go spending it on rum, either. Do you hear me?" Mel warned. The Ten Bells pub was directly across the street and the Britannia pub was just one block down.

"Yes, I do, and thank you," Annie replied more clearly. Annie had a weakness when it came to drinking, but, at the moment, that was the furthest thing from her mind. "I may check myself into the hospital for a few days; see what's wrong with me."

"That's not such a bad idea," Mel agreed. She placed a peck on Annie's cheek before they went their separate ways.

Annie walked down Commercial Street and turned left onto Fashion Street. She had to stop and rest for a minute even though she had covered no great distance. She knew something was wrong with her, but she didn't know what. After a brief rest, she continued on her way, turning down Osborn Street, then left on to Whitechapel Road. She could see the large three-storey red brick building looming in the distance. *It seems so far away,* Annie thought. But she knew she had to keep going. The London Hospital was where she needed to be right now.

137

WHEN MARY HAD finished her shift, she went searching for Dani. It had been an extremely difficult and emotional day for Mary. One patient she had been taking care of over the past several weeks and had become quite close to passed away that afternoon. Mary was thankful, though, that she had been there to provide some comfort during his last few hours. Now, she was emotionally drained and exhausted and just wanted to get home.

Mary knew where to begin her search because Dani had been spending every spare moment she had in the same place. Mary walked down the hall until she was in front of a door at the end of the wing. She knocked twice. There was no answer.

Mary turned around, when she heard footsteps behind her, to find Dr. Treves coming down the hall.

"Mrs. Case, I believe you'll find them out in the garden," Dr. Treves offered, eyes sparkling with mirth.

"Thank you, Dr. Treves," Mary said.

"Mrs. Case. Mary?"

"Yes, Doctor."

"I want to thank you for letting Miss Delaney spend so much time with Joseph. I've noticed such a tremendous change in him.

It's like he's transforming from a hunted creature to a thoughtful, caring, affectionate man," Dr. Treves said gratefully. He believes, for the first time in Joseph's entire life, he was actually enjoying himself.

Dr. Treves had brought Joseph to the hospital and set him up in a couple of rooms at the end of a hospital wing where Joseph would spend the rest of his life. Dr. Treves noticed during the past two years that Joseph possessed a vivid imagination and had romantic ideals. He also had the curiosity of a child.

"Don't thank me, Doctor. You should be thanking Miss Delaney," Mary replied cheerfully, making her way back down the hall to the door leading out into the inner garden.

Dr. Treves was right. There, sitting in the shade of a large cherry tree, were Dani and Joseph. Mary observed for a moment, not wanting to disturb them.

"Just once, I'd like to be like other people: to be able to sleep lying down, to be able to settle my head into a nice soft pillow," Joseph said sadly.

"Why can't you?" Dani asked, even though she knew the answer.

"My head is too big and too heavy. I tried it once, years ago, and found I couldn't breathe properly. My head has only gotten bigger and heavier since," Joseph explained resignedly. "I have to sleep sitting propped up against a wall, knees drawn to my chest, where I can then rest my head."

"You never know what tomorrow will bring, Joseph," Dani reassured him. "Maybe Dr. Treves will find something that will help you. You have to think positively, okay?"

Joseph had always dreamed of being like other people: to have a normal life, to marry a beautiful woman, to have children, and to live in a real house. But they were all just dreams.

"I wrote a poem. Would you like to read it?" Joseph asked timidly as he quickly changed the subject.

"I'd love to." Dani beamed.

Joseph reached into his inner vest pocket and pulled out a piece of paper. He gently unfolded it and handed it to Dani.

Dani looked at the artistic penmanship. She marvelled at the fluid grace that seemed to dance along the page. The poem read:

> *"Tis true my form is something odd,*
> *But blaming me is blaming God.*
> *Could I create myself anew,*
> *I would not fail in pleasing you.*
> *If I could reach from pole to pole*
> *Or grasp the ocean with a span,*
> *I would be measured by the soul;*
> *The mind's the standard of the man."*

Dani tried subtly to hide the tear in her eye, reaching up casually to brush it away. *What a beautiful soul,* she thought. Dani knew Joseph's dream to be like other people would eventually be his demise and it saddened her.

"You don't like it." Joseph was crestfallen.

"No, on the contrary, Joseph. It's beautiful," Dani reached for Joseph's hand. Her melancholy thoughts were conveying the wrong message.

"Then, why do you cry? I thought you cry only when you are sad or you are hurt."

"There are also happy tears, Joseph," Dani explained. "Like when someone surprises you with something special that touches your heart. That's what you did for me."

"That's good, then?"

"That's extremely good," Dani said, smiling brightly and giving Joseph's hand a little squeeze for emphasis.

Thursday, September 6, 1888

138

THE DAY STARTED out with a ray of sunshine, but it only lasted a few minutes. Clouds rolled in, masking the light and throwing a damp misty rain upon all who dared to venture out. It was the kind of dark, damp, dreary day that echoed the sombre mood of those who had gathered to mourn the loss of a loved one. Or more accurately, those who had gathered merely to gawk.

Since the murder of Mary Ann "Polly" Nichols, the gossips, the loafers and the curious had come to see the crime scene for themselves. They had all hoped to find a small speck of blood they could point out to all who were present. They didn't realize that their morbid fascination only heightened the horror of this brutal murder.

The small funeral procession consisted of a hearse, driven by Mr. Henry Smith, the undertaker, and two mourning coaches. The mourners were Edward Walker, Polly's father, and William and Edward John Nichols, Polly's husband and son. The procession turned onto Baker's Row, passed the corner of Buck's Row and turned onto Whitechapel Road, where neighbors had gathered to pay their last respects.

The polished elm coffin bearing a plate inscribed with the words "Mary Ann Nichols, aged 42, died August 31, 1888" was buried in the City of London Cemetery, London. *The Times* later reported that the expenses for the funeral "were borne by the relatives of the deceased, her father, husband, and son".

139

THERE WAS A loud pounding on the front door at 22 Mulberry Street. Standing on the front stoop was a man of medium height and slight build, with a small mustache, side whiskers and grey hair, insistently hammering to get the attention of the occupants.

Samuel cautiously pulled open the door to see who was causing all the ruckus, only to be thrown aside by the man rushing past him into the house.

"Hurry, close the door!" the man ordered.

"John!" Samuel exclaimed, peering up and down the street before closing the door.

John leaned against the wall as he struggled to catch his breath.

"Have you seen the papers? They're looking for you, John," Samuel warned, as he escorted his unexpected visitor into the kitchen. After Samuel had gotten a drink for them both, they sat down at the kitchen table. Samuel pushed the latest edition of *The Star* toward John, plus some articles he had clipped out of other newspapers.

John Pizer, a.k.a. Leather Apron, was wanted for questioning by the Metropolitan Police. All the articles in front of him claimed Leather Apron was the prime suspect in the murder of Mary Ann Nichols. Several eyewitness reports recounted that he was known for bullying prostitutes at night. They said he would wait outside a public house and accost them when they left. The papers also claimed he kicked, bruised, injured and terrified his victims.

One article also said he sometimes threatened his victims with his knife, which he always carried and used as part of his trade. John Pizer was a slipper maker and was always seen wearing a leather apron; hence, the nickname 'Leather Apron'. Many only knew him by that name.

"But I didn't do it! I wasn't even here at the time of the murder," John cried.

"I know you didn't do it, but I think you should stay out of sight for a while. People are looking for someone to blame for the murder and, right now, you're their target."

John slumped down in his chair.

"Look, you're safe here and at least off the streets," Samuel stated. John was, after all, his older brother.

140

"THINK ABOUT IT, Frank," Daric pressed, straddling a chair and leaning over the backrest. He'd been trying to get a point across to Frank for the past hour, with little success. Daric had finished at the pub and was waiting for Rich to return.

"I am, but I don't see what you're getting at." Frank never did quite follow Daric's logic.

"Okay, let me go over it one more time." Daric slowed the pace down so Frank's brain could absorb what he was about to say, again.

"You told me, before, that every constable on the beat had a specific route he had to cover. Correct?" Daric wanted to get Frank's confirmation of every point along the way. He hoped that, by doing so, he would finally get his line of thinking across to Frank.

"That's correct." Frank replied, stifling a bored-induced yawn.

"And you said that there was an expected length of time for a constable to cover his entire route. Correct?"

"Not anymore," Frank corrected, quite pleased that he had one-upped the smart-ass in front of him. "The time is no longer stipulated."

"Okay, granted. But it had been stipulated for years, correct?"

"Yes," Frank grunted, still not seeing where Daric was going.

The exchange had caught the attention of the other officers in the station. They were going about their business, but listening discreetly to the discussion, anxiously awaiting its outcome.

"Good." Daric was hopeful he was making progress. "So, let's use Constable Mizen as an example. Constable Mizen's beat is the region of Baker's Row and Hanbury Street, interconnecting with Constable Thain's beat from J Division. Correct?"

"Correct," Frank replied, shifting papers on his desk. Daric could see Frank's attention span was reaching its limit. He needed to drive his point home, now.

"Even though the pace at which a constable walks his beat is no longer stipulated, I've noticed that they still stick to the old time. They still cover their beat, making a complete circuit every ten to fifteen minutes."

"What did you do? Time them?" Frank grunted.

"As a matter of fact, I did," Daric replied. "And so could any criminal, or in this case, murderer. He would know how often a constable would appear at one point along his route and he could figure out that he would have ten to fifteen minutes to commit a murder and disappear before the constable completed his circuit."

"Are you serious?"

Sergeant William Thick walked past Frank's desk, pausing momentarily at Frank's outburst. Thick was a twenty-year veteran with the Metropolitan Police, having served the majority of that time in H Division. He was a stout man with a pleasant face that sported a drooping yellowish mustache.

"And, as a criminal, I could detect the approach of the constable by the distinct pace he walks and by the sound of his leathery footsteps," Daric concluded. He now waited to see whether Frank had followed his line of thinking.

"You expect me to believe a criminal can tell when a police constable is approaching based purely on timing and what did you say," Frank took a quick glance at Thick, but continued uninterrupted, "the sound of footsteps? Sergeant, tell me you think this lad's off his crumpet."

"If I agreed with you, Frank, we'd both be wrong," Thick replied, resuming his duties. Frank just huffed in response.

141

QUINN WALKED TO the back of the gazebo, flipped the cover plate and inserted his USB key. The lower level access panels opened. "Follow me," Quinn said, as he started to descend. Richard didn't have to be told twice. He jumped out of his chair and followed Quinn.

"Whoa, where did all this come from? This is amazing, Quinn," Richard remarked. He needed to act surprised by what he was seeing. After all, this wasn't his first foray into this level, but, as far as Quinn knew, it was.

"This is where the real work is done," Quinn continued indifferently. He was standing in front of his computer console. With one wave of his hand, the console came to life.

Richard stood beside Quinn. He looked at the complex series of equations projected on the wall. Richard was very skeptical, but intrigued at the same time. "So, are you trying to tell me you built a time machine? An actual *DeLorean* time machine, one with its own flux capacitor?" Richard mocked.

"It's nothing like the *DeLorean*," Quinn retorted. "That was pure science fiction in those old retro movies. This is real science. Science based on quantum physics."

"Go on," Richard encouraged.

"I won't bore you with the headache-inducing mathematical equations. Suffice it to say, those old science fiction movies got one crucial piece right . . . the extreme power source required for time travel," Quinn disclosed. "Quite simply put, in the past, we lacked the technology and the ability to generate enough power to make it happen. Until now, that is."

"Explain yourself," Richard demanded.

"While Sandra and I were cave diving in New Zealand four months ago, we came across a mineral I'd never seen before. I took a small sample home to test its atomic structure. It wasn't until after I'd finished the testing that I realized I'd found something exceptional. This mineral contained an unusual combination of properties that could generate extraordinary energy, the likes of which I've never seen or heard of before," Quinn explained, barely able to contain his excitement. "I named it chronizium, after *Chronos*, the Greek god known as the father of time: empirical time, which is divided into past, present, and future. Not to be confused with the deity, *Aion*, the father of eternal time," Quinn prattled on. Then he quickly refocused. He didn't need to waste time spouting trivial details to Richard.

"With the chronizium, I now have the required power source. And with today's post-silicon computers and unlimited access to information, technology is no longer the issue it was in Einstein's era."

"Are you trying to tell me you found a new energy source?" Richard asked condescendingly.

"By programming the chronizium's properties into the computer, I could build the necessary algorithms for Hermes to solve the problem that had defeated physicists for decades: quantum gravity, the amalgamation of general relativity and quantum mechanics," Quinn claimed proudly.

"Hermes?" Richard asked

"You called, Professor?" Hermes popped into full view on the five-by-five-foot platform.

"What the hell is that?" Richard cried, jumping back at the sight of a toga-clad hologram.

142

"NO, HERMES, I didn't call you," Quinn muttered in frustration. "But, now that you're here, I'd like you to meet a colleague and dear friend of mine. Hermes, this is Richard Barak Case. Richard, this is Hermes, my artificial intelligence," Quinn completed the introduction, rather awkwardly. He sometimes found it difficult to remember Hermes was simply a program and not a real person.

"So, that's what the platform is for," Richard mumbled, not realizing he had put voice to his thoughts.

"What?" Quinn asked.

"It's a pleasure to meet you, Mr. Richard Barak Case," Hermes interjected. "I must say Barak is a very unusual name." He was fully aware of what Richard had just uttered, but kept that information to himself, for now.

"It's been handed down through our family for generations," Richard pronounced. "Its origin is . . ."

"Hebrew and means flash of light or lightning," Hermes finished.

"That's correct," Richard said. "How could he know that?" Richard glared at Quinn.

"Hermes is a second generation cognitive computer designed to mimic humans. He learns, he senses, he adapts. I don't program him, so much as I teach him how to learn; as a result he is much more efficient than computers where you have to type in millions of lines of code just to get the computer to do what you want."

"Are you trying to tell me he's human?"

"Close, but not quite," Quinn said proudly. "Humans are more efficient in how they interact with their environment, compared to a computer. It's this fact that drove me to change the architectural premise of how Hermes runs."

Richard walked around the hologram, admiring the attention to detail. "He looks so real," Richard said awestruck.

"He's been linked to the most sophisticated and most respectable sources of data with his primary objective being time travel: from Einstein's theories, to quantum physics, to cosmic strings, black holes, and, of course, wormholes," Quinn said with pride, as a father would, talking about his accomplished son.

"Let's, for argument's sake, say, I believe you. How does our time travel device work exactly?" Richard asked skeptically.

"Have you ever wondered whether bridges or portals to the past or the future could exist within the laws of nature?" Quinn asked.

"Can't say I've ever given it much thought," Richard replied nonchalantly, but he couldn't help but be very intrigued.

"Well, there are. These bridges or portals are essentially tunnels through time, shortcuts between two points. They're called wormholes."

"Yeah, I've heard of wormholes. But they're found in outer space," Richard said tersely.

"Wormholes exist all around us. They're just too small to see. They're smaller than a molecule, even smaller than an atom. They exist in a place called the quantum foam." Quinn realized, based on the glazed look on Richard's face, that he was getting too detailed again.

"What if it were possible to capture a wormhole, then expand it to be large enough for a person to pass through?" Quinn asked, anticipation creeping into his voice.

"That's a pretty big 'what if'," Richard jeered.

"The wormhole would virtually be a bridge between two points in time," Quinn explained.

"And you're telling me you've actually built a machine that will do all that, will enable you to travel through time?" Richard couldn't believe what he was asking.

"Not a machine, per se, but a device. Here, let me show you."

Quinn walked to the small metal table where he picked up one of the two small bands. He held it up so Richard could see it.

"This is what I call a travel band. You wear one on each wrist. In the simplest terms, when the bands touch the chronizium particles imbedded in the bands react to generate sufficient energy to capture a wormhole from the quantum foam. The wormhole expands and pulls the traveller through the opening, along a tunnel in time and out the other end, collapsing upon the traveller's exit."

"Kind of small for your wrist, isn't it?" Richard said sarcastically, still trying to digest this incredible story.

"These two bands were for Bear," Quinn explained, pointing to the other small band in the container on the table. "I was going to test them on her first." Quinn placed the small band back in its container and picked up the two larger ones.

"These contained the travel bands I was going to test. But, somehow, Daric and Dani got in here and now they're both in London," Quinn said sadly.

"So?" Richard wasn't following Quinn.

"They're in London, England, in 1888," Quinn stated. "I have to get them back."

"Oh my God!"

143

THE WEATHER TODAY was worse than yesterday. There was still no sunshine and heavy squalls were expected to roll in from the north. It seemed that everyone was out to get their errands run before the worst of the storm hit.

Annie had returned to the Crossingham's Lodging House, entering through the back kitchen door. She ran into Timothy Donovan, the house's deputy. "Where have you been, Annie?"

Timothy Donovan had a thin, pale face and was a dour-looking man for his young age of twenty-seven years. Ill humour usually came from hardships endured through the years; Donovan wasn't old enough to bear such a grim countenance.

Timothy Donovan had known Annie for sixteen months as a prostitute and four months as a lodger. And never in that time had she ever been an offensive soul, except that one incident with Eliza Cooper. Annie was still sporting the shiner Eliza had given her.

"I haven't been feeling well, so I checked myself into the hospital for a few days," Annie replied weakly. She reached into her pocket and pulled out a pillbox. It fell apart, scattering pills all over the floor.

Annie bent down to retrieve her pills. Donovan stooped to give her a hand. He had to admit, Annie didn't look well at all. Annie picked up a torn piece of an envelope she found near the fireplace. She placed her pills in the envelope and folded the side inward to keep the pills from escaping a second time.

"Why don't you rest here a spell?" Donovan offered. Annie nodded her acceptance and then Donovan carried on with his business.

After about an hour, Annie thanked Donovan as she prepared to leave. "I haven't sufficient money for a bed, but don't rent it. I shall not be long before I am in."

"You can find money for your beer, but not for your bed," Donovan replied coldly. He was convinced Annie was drunk.

"Never mind, Tim. I shall be back soon. Don't rent my bed," Annie said firmly. And with that she left the premises in search of her doss money.

The rain was driving hard, and the temperature had dropped by the time Annie left the warmth and the safety of the Crossingham's kitchen.

144

DARIC WALKED UP quietly behind Clara, who was vigorously scribbling notes in her notebook. Her last interviewee had just left, giving Daric the perfect opportunity to stop by to say hello. He had been trying for hours to talk to Clara, but she had set up back-to-back interviews in the pub all day. There had been no break in the flow of traffic until now.

Clara was so engrossed with what she was doing she didn't hear Daric's approach. "Hi."

"You scared the Dickens out of me," Clara chastised, placing her hand over her heart.

"I'm sorry. I didn't mean to startle you," Daric apologized.

"You're forgiven. Besides it was my fault. I was just too focused on my work and wasn't aware of my surroundings."

"That's not a good thing, especially around here."

"What's that supposed to mean?"

"Daric," Mr. Farrow hollered. "I need you to bring a keg up from the basement—now!"

"Don't leave. I'll be right back." Daric took off to complete his task as quickly as possible. He knew it was late, and it was around this time that Clara made her way home, alone. But not this time. Daric was determined to accompany her. He was going to do his damnedest to keep her from any harm.

By the time Daric returned upstairs, his task completed, Clara had gone.

"When did she leave?" Daric asked Mr. Farrow.

"Who?" Mr. Farrow grunted.

"Clara Collet," Daric snapped. "She was sitting over there," he added, pointing at the empty table by the front window.

"Oh, her; nice little thing, she is," Mr. Farrow sneered.

"When?" Daric demanded.

"Steady on," Mr. Farrow growled. "She left not more than five minutes ago."

"Okay." Daric rushed behind the bar and snatched his coat and hat.

"But I think you're too late, lad," Mr. Farrow said.

"No, I'm not. I can still catch her."

"No, I mean you're too late, 'cause she left with another man," Mr. Farrow grinned. "Well, not really left with, but he headed out right after her."

With that, Daric flew out the door and down the street in pursuit of Clara.

145

CLARA HAD TO admit, she had been a little unnerved by Daric's remark. She knew she was working in a rough neighbourhood, but that was part of the job. She had accepted that risk when she took the position. The research work she was doing was extremely important, not only to her, but to the women who lived and worked in the East End.

Clara had been lost in her own thoughts when she abruptly stopped. She thought she heard footsteps behind her. She turned to find the dimly lit street empty. She shrugged and continued on her way. *Damn you, Daric; you've got me spooked.* There it was again. Instead of stopping and turning around this time, she stepped up her pace.

When Clara turned the next corner, she could have sworn that she heard running footsteps. They were rapidly coming up behind her. She was beside herself; she wasn't sure what to do. Thank goodness she always carried her sturdy brolly. She turned it around in her hands and held it like a baseball bat, with the thick handle at the opposite end. She pressed herself against the wall, listening as the runner rapidly approached. She had to time this perfectly; she thought.

One . . . two . . . three . . . She swung the brolly with all she could muster, striking out at waist level, catching the runner right in the mid-section, just as he rounded the corner. He doubled over, grabbing his gut. She raised the brolly for another blow to the back of his head when . . .

"Wait, it's me," Daric barely got out between gasps for breath.

"Daric, what are you doing here?" Clara said, reaching down to help Daric straighten up. He was still clutching his mid-section.

"I asked you to wait. I wanted to walk you home," Daric said raspingly.

"I think you witnessed, first-hand, that I can take care of myself," Clara teased.

"Apparently," Daric conceded. He gently clasped Clara's hand. "Now that I'm here, allow me the honor of escorting you home."

"I'd be delighted." A faint smile edged Clara's lips. She leaned in and placed a conciliatory kiss on his cheek.

* * *

Hidden behind a corner within earshot of the couple, but cloaked in darkness, was the stranger from the pub, the man who had left directly after Clara. He was wearing an Inverness coat, a deer-stalker hat and carrying a Gladstone bag. He wasn't thrilled with the events that had just unfolded. He had had plans for this evening and they had been ruined by that damned Daric.

I'll get even, he thought. He turned around and retraced his steps. He had to make other arrangements for the evening.

Present Day

146

"YOU'RE ACTUALLY ASKING me to believe that Dani and Daric have travelled through time and are now in 1888, in London, England?" Saying it out loud made it sound even more ridiculous, especially to Richard's ears.

"Yes, I am. I was so focussed on completing my computations for time travel to the past, because it was the more difficult of the two, that I haven't completed my computations for time travel to the future, yet," Quinn said, somewhat embarrassed to have left something unfinished. He was meticulous when it came to ensuring he had every 'T' crossed and every 'I' dotted.

"But you said it works. What does it matter which way you go: forward in time or backward?" Richard asked pointedly.

"I have to finish my work in order to bring Dani and Daric forward in time, to the present day—to bring them back home. Right now, every time they travel, they go further back in time," Quinn explained.

"What do you mean, 'every time they travel'? How many times have they traveled?"

"Twice. First to California in 1937; then to London in 1888," Hermes disclosed.

Richard had forgotten Hermes was even there. Richard glanced over at Quinn, who nodded solemnly. Richard then turned his focus back to Hermes and asked, "How do you know where they are? Or when, for that matter?"

"There is a chronometer built into the travel bands that registers time. And a directional finder, similar to a GPS, that registers longitude and latitude. I use these coordinates to pinpoint a location using topographical information from that era," Hermes explained.

"Fascinating." Richard was truly impressed. Turning his attention back to Quinn, he asked, "So, how do Dani and Daric determine where they're going?" He wanted as much information as he could possibly get about Quinn's breakthrough in quantum physics.

"May I, Professor?" Hermes asked politely.

"Be my guest," Quinn assented.

"I expanded on the research that was done years ago by Dr. Bin He, at the University of Minnesota. Dr. He created an electroencephalography or EEG-based, non-invasive brain-computer interface known as BCI. This interface allows the user to interact with the computer system using thought only. The EEG records and decodes a particular brainwave called the sensorimotor rhythms or SMRS; the SMRS communicates with the computer. The computer, in turn, reads the SMRS as an executable command or more specifically in this case, as a different spatial location," Hermes explained, matter-of-factly.

"The bands were designed to be worn by one person, not two," Quinn interjected. "I can only surmise that the stronger of the two brainwaves will dictate the travel destination. But I'm not one-hundred-percent sure. Herein lies the problem: Dani and Daric don't know how they travel from one time period to another, so they can't control their journey through time," Quinn uttered despairingly.

"Time travel—that's incredible, Quinn!" Richard exclaimed in utter astonishment.

"I'm hoping to send Bear back in time, with a message in a

collar, to let the kids know how the travel bands work. At least they would be able to control when and where they travel next. That is, until I'm able to bring them home. And in order to do that, I need to kinetically link these two small bands with the ones Dani and Daric are wearing. Then, the next time they travel, Bear will join them in that same time period. The message Bear delivers will let them know what's going on," Quinn added optimistically.

"And, when I finish my work, I can use my remaining supply of chronizium to initiate time travel from here to bring Dani and Daric back home." Quinn finished his explanation while reaching under the table, grasping at empty air. He bent down to get a better look.

"It's gone!" Quinn cried out.

147

A RATHER FRAIL-LOOKING elderly man of fifty-six years of age left his residence at 29 Hanbury Street promptly at 6:00 A.M., according to the chimes from the Christ Church bells. John Davis lived on the third floor, front room, with his wife, Mary Ann, and their three sons.

John Davis was a carter and started work early every morning. When he went downstairs, he noticed the front door was open, as it often was. The back door leading to the yard, however, was closed. *Odd,* he thought. He walked over and opened the back door. What lay on the ground to his left, between the steps leading into the yard and the fence, sent him running in terror.

James Kent and James Green, who worked for Bayley's packing-case manufacturers, at 23-A Hanbury Street, were on their way to work, when they were almost bowled over by the hysterical old man who looked like he had just seen the devil himself.

"What's the hurry, old man?" Green asked, while grabbing his shoulders to stop him from toppling over.

"Come here!" Davis implored Kent and Green.

Skeptical, they followed Davis along the passageway. "There." Davis pointed. Kent and Green looked into the backyard and quickly realized what had sent the old man into a panic.

Henry Holland, a co-worker of Kent and Green, had followed them when he heard the yelling. He peered over their shoulders. What he saw almost made him lose his breakfast.

After a few moments of stunned silence, Holland said, "We need to get help."

"You don't need all of us. I'll go open the shop," Kent said, as he turned and left the scene.

"I'll go find a constable," Holland said, following Kent down the street from Davis's residence.

On entering the shop, Kent went directly to his desk, opened a drawer, and pulled out a bottle of brandy. He pulled off the stopper and took several deep gulps, to settle his nerves.

"I could use a belt, too," Green said as he snatched the bottle from Kent.

"Do we have an old tarpaulin around here?" Green asked unsteadily after another swig from the bottle. "I want to cover the body."

"Yeah, over in the corner," Kent replied, taking back the bottle and having another gulp. He replaced the bottle in the desk drawer while watching Green leave with the tarpaulin.

Holland headed toward Spitalfields Market in search of a constable. Davis took off, as fast as his old legs could carry him, to the closest police station, on Commercial Street.

Inspector Joseph Chandler was at the corner of Hanbury and Commercial Streets when he noticed several men running along Hanbury. He intercepted one, who told him, "Another woman has been murdered." Chandler went immediately to investigate and to secure the crime scene.

148

RICH AND DARIC were at the station early in the morning as they had been almost every morning since the Nichols' murder. Rich was checking on the progress of the investigation and handing out the day's assignments when a sudden commotion drew his attention to the front entrance. He saw an old man bursting through the front door of the station. "I need to speak to a senior officer," John Davis panted, trying to catch his breath.

"I'm Inspector Case. How can I be of assistance?"

"There's . . . been . . . another . . . murder . . . ." Davis said, still trying to slow his heart rate. It wasn't a long run to the station from his place, but he was out of shape.

Within minutes, several officers were following John Davis to the murder site, where they found Inspector Joseph Chandler, who had been first on scene.

"What do you got, Joe?" Rich asked.

"Over there," Joe replied grimly, indicating the tarpaulin to his left. "I sent for Dr. Phillips and for reinforcements and an ambulance. I also sent word to Scotland Yard."

Inspector Joseph Chandler had joined the Metropolitan Police in 1873. Rich had known Joe Chandler for many years, but he had never seen him this rattled at a crime scene before.

Rich walked over, bent down, and reached over to pull back the tarpaulin. "It's not good, Inspector," Joe warned.

Rich paused for a moment to take in the morbid scene. A crowd had gather and was rapidly growing. "Let's get these people back and clear that passageway," Rich instructed his team. Once the crowds had been pushed back, Rich slowly drew back the tarpaulin and beheld the mutilated body of a woman. He tried to take a calming breath as he viewed the victim. He had never witnessed this kind of brutality in all his years as a police officer and prayed he never would again. It was unthinkable. *What kind of sick creature could have done this to another human being?* he thought.

"I'll take it from here, Inspector," Dr. Phillips said. He had come up behind Rich, startling him and pulling him from his thoughts.

Dr. George Bagster Phillips was H Division's Police Surgeon and conducted or attended post-mortems on behalf of the station. He was an elderly man of fifty-four years of age, highly skilled, and incredibly modest. His busy life had contributed to his brusque and quick manner. Nevertheless, he was extremely charming and as a result, very popular.

Dr. Phillips knelt as close to the victim as he could, avoiding the pool of blood on the ground above her right shoulder. It was more than apparent that this woman was beyond medical help. After completing a cursory inspection of the wounds, Dr. Phillips ordered that the body be removed and taken to the mortuary.

"Wait," Rich said. He reached over and closed the victim's horror-filled eyes. He dug into his pocket and pulled out two coins, placing one over each eye.

"I never understood that custom," Frank mumbled.

"It's to pay the ferryman to take your soul across the River Styx to the land of the dead," Daric explained. "If you cannot pay him, you are doomed to remain a ghost and forced to wander forever between the two worlds."

"Whatever," Frank replied.

After the body had been removed, Rich noticed several items neatly arranged where the victim's feet had been. There was a folded piece of coarse muslin, a comb and a piece of an envelope with the Sussex Regiment coat of arms on it and bearing a London postmark dated August 20, 1888. Nearby, he saw two pills; they must have been the contents of her torn pocket, he reasoned.

"Hey, look at this." Daric called their attention to a wet leather apron. It was laid out and drying on a water spigot, not far from where the body had been found. A bucket of clean water was sitting below the water spout.

Rich and his colleagues spent the next few hours searching the crime scene. They noted several blood-stained areas, all in the backyard. They determined there were no stains in the passageway, in any part of the house, or in any of the adjoining yards.

149

"HEY, YOU, STOP!" Detective Walter Dew yelled and took off in pursuit. The police had been trying to locate this guy for a week, ever since that stone-throwing incident.

The man Dew was chasing was about twenty-five years old, with a muscular build. He had a rag wrapped around his right hand and a paper clutched in his left. He ran through the streets, desperately trying to increase the distance between himself and the police on his tail.

The man ran down Commercial Street, dodging carriages and cabs, diving between the legs of horses, trying to evade capture.

"Stop!"

People who had been standing outside watched the chase down the street intently. One bystander made the somewhat reasonable deduction that, if the police were pursuing this man. "It must be the murderer," he yelled. No one will ever know for sure who yelled, but his yell was the catalyst for the events that immediately followed.

The crowd joined the chase. As it grew in numbers, so did the cries of, "Lynch him" and "Murderer." Soon hundreds were racing down the street. Several other police officers joined in the pursuit, only igniting the crowd further. The result was like throwing gasoline onto a raging fire. The situation exploded into a frenzy and it was no wonder: especially on the day of another murder.

The man being pursued realized what was happening. He could tell by the cries of the mob they were ready to lynch him for a murder. He knew there was no way he could reason with them in their frenzied state. If they got their hands on him, it was game over. There would be no judge, no jury, no trial. As far as the mob was concerned, he was guilty, and they would exact their kind of justice. He had only one hope.

150

RICH, DARIC, FRANK and Inspector Joseph Chandler returned to the Commercial Street station to review their notes. They also needed to allow Dr. Phillips enough time to perform the post-mortem, before they headed to the morgue for an update.

"Don't you find it odd that at both murder scenes there were no footprints?" Daric pondered aloud.

"Why is that odd?" Frank asked.

"With all that blood, you'd think the murderer would have gotten some on his boots," Daric said. "But, there were no footprints or tracks leading away from where the bodies were found. I find that rather odd."

"So do I," Rich concurred.

The station door flew open. A man ran inside screaming, "You've got to help me!"

Detective Dew was the next one through the door, panting. "Barricade the door, quick," he yelled.

"What's going on?" Rich asked, gesturing a few officers toward the front door.

"Inspector, there's a mob out there. They think this guy is our murderer. There have to be hundreds of them. They want his blood," Dew said, as the officers slammed the door shut and threw the bolt to lock it.

"Hey, I'd know that ugly face anywhere. That's the guy who tried to mug me," Daric exclaimed.

"Well, well, if it isn't Mr. George Cullen, better known on the streets as Squibby," Rich explained.

"We know he's in there and we want him," a voice yelled from outside.

"That sounds like Lusk," Daric said.

"Yeah, and he'd be the one to stir up this crowd," Rich added.

There was a loud sound of shattering glass followed by a dull thud. Someone had thrown a brick through one of the station windows.

"We want him, now!" was punctuated by another shattered window.

"Duck," Frank yelled, diving under his desk, just as another projectile sailed by his head.

"Lock Squibby in a cell," Rich said to Barrett. "That should keep the mob away from him."

"You, you and you, come with me," Rich ordered. *I don't have time for this nonsense,* he thought, heading for the front door.

Barrett grabbed Squibby's arm and led him to a cell. Before locking the door, Barrett pulled the paper out of his clenched fist. It was a section of *The East London Advertiser.* It read:

The murderer must creep out from somewhere; he must patrol the streets in search of his victims. Doubtless he is out night by night. Three successful murders will have the effect of whetting his appetite still further, and unless a watch of the strictest be kept, the murder of Thursday will certainly be followed by a fourth.

And it was, but the paper was today's early morning edition. How could they have known?

It took the better part of an hour to settle and disperse the mob outside the station, without further incident. Rich had assured them that Squibby wasn't the murderer, but had been arrested on a prior assault charge.

151

ON SATURDAY AFTERNOON, Dr. Phillips was scheduled to conduct the post-mortem examination at the Whitechapel Workhouse Infirmary Mortuary. It was nothing more than an unsanitary shed and completely inadequate for his purposes, but he would make do with what he had.

Upon entering the mortuary, Dr. Phillips discovered that the body had already been stripped, partially bathed and laid out on the table awaiting his arrival. The only clothing left on the body was a handkerchief. He remembered that, back at the crime scene, it had been tied around the victim's neck. They had tossed the rest of her clothes into a corner.

"I left specific instructions that this body wasn't to be touched until I got here," Dr. Phillips snapped at one of the nurses.

"Doctor, we were told to prepare the body for you. No one said not to touch it," the nurse explained.

"What's the name of the man in charge here?"

"Robert Mann, Doctor," the nurse said.

Dr. Phillips grunted. *That's the same buffoon who mishandled the other victim,* he thought. *Well, what's done is done.* Dr. Phillips would talk to the constable who was supposed to be in charge of the body, to find out how such a simple order could be so misunderstood.

"Dr. Phillips, this is Mel Palmer. She believes she knows who the victim might be," Constable Barrett said, having brought Annie over from the station.

"One moment," Dr. Phillips said, as he reached for a blanket. "Okay."

Mel stepped forward and peered down at the body laid out on the table. Dr. Phillips had covered the horrific wounds; only the head was uncovered. He felt no one needed to see the handiwork of the merciless butcher, especially one of the weaker sex.

"Oh, Annie," Mel said desolately. "That's Annie Chapman," Mel moaned.

"Thank you, Miss Palmer, for coming down," Barrett said and accompanied her out of the morgue.

* * *

Several hours later, Rich, Frank and Daric arrived at the morgue.

"So, what can you tell us, Doctor?" Rich asked.

"She was eviscerated," Dr. Phillips replied acidly. "And some of her organs are missing."

Dr. Phillips paused a moment and then stepped away from the table to face his visitors. "I'm sorry, Inspector; I didn't mean to bite." Dr. Phillips sighed. "It's just such a horrendous act of brutality, the likes of which I'd never want to set eyes on again."

"I understand, Doctor, and I agree with you," Rich admitted. "What can you tell us about Annie Chapman?"

"At the time of her death, she was undernourished and suffered from chronic diseases of the lungs and brain membranes. It wouldn't have been long before those diseases would have killed her," Dr. Phillips said sadly.

"There was bruising over her right temple and there were two distinct bruises, the size of a man's thumb, on the forepart of the upper chest. All of these are older wounds that occurred days ago. There are abrasions on her ring finger, indicating the murderer forcibly removed her ring or rings," Dr. Phillips said.

"We found no rings at the crime scene," Frank offered.

Doctor Phillips continued with his findings, going into great detail as he outlined the number and types of wounds inflicted on the body of Annie Chapman. He also provided, with itemized accuracy, how he believed the murderer extracted the organs and how much time it would have taken him to do so.

"Doctor, are we looking at the same type of murder weapon as was used in the Nichols' murder? Could we be looking for one suspect?" Rich asked.

"The instrument used to cut the throat, and the abdomen was the same. It must have been a very sharp knife, with a narrow blade at least six to eight inches in length. The method in which the knife was used seems to show great anatomical knowledge," Dr. Phillips concluded.

152

PARENTS WANTED THEIR children off the streets. Mothers worried about their working daughters coming home after dark. Husbands were worried for their wives. And prostitutes still had to make a living.

The women of Whitechapel were angry. Their rage was driven by terror. They feared that the killer would strike again. "Thank God, I needn't be out after dark!" exclaimed one woman.

"No more needn't I," chimed another.

"But my two girls have got to come home latish, and I'm all of a fidget till they comes," cried a mother.

A little woman with a rosy cherub face summed up the general view thus: "Life ain't no great thing with many of us, but we don't all want to be murdered, and, if things go on like this, it won't be safe for nobody to put their 'eads out o' doors."

* * *

"Terrible, it is; simply terrible."

"What is?" Martha asked, catching Elsie in the kitchen muttering to herself again.

"Those poor souls, killed that way and left out on the street." Elsie shivered at the thought. "Terrible it is."

"What is?" Mary asked when she entered the kitchen.

"Elsie's been goin' on about those murdered women," Martha said.

"I agree with you, Elsie. It is terrible. Tragic, actually," Mary said.

"Missus, your seamstress, Mrs. Wilson, dropped off that package you've been expecting. I put it on Miss Delaney's bed, just like you asked," Martha said.

"Great. Thank you, Martha." Mary left the kitchen to open her much-expected package. First, however, she had to find Dani. As she passed the drawing room, she saw Dani talking with Daric, quite animatedly, too.

"Dani, if you could spare a moment. I want to show you something," Mary interrupted.

"Coming," Dani replied. "We'll finish this later," she muttered quietly to Daric. She took off after Mary, who was taking the stairs two at a time.

In Dani's bedroom, laid out on the bed, were some of the most practical clothes Dani had seen in this time period. When Mary had asked her seamstress to make a couple of outfits for Dani, she had let Dani describe how she wanted them cut, because Dani couldn't get comfortable in any of the clothing that were fashionable in this era. And what lay on the bed suited Dani perfectly. She just hoped they would be appropriate enough to please Mary. She wouldn't want to cause her any embarrassment.

"Try them on," Mary invited eagerly.

Dani picked out an outfit and put it on while Mary waited anxiously. When she was finished, Dani turned around and asked, "What do you think?"

Dani was wearing a long pale-blue, narrow skirt with a matching blouse. She projected the image of feminine beauty: tall and slender, with a voluptuous, yet not lewd, bosom and shapely hips. She was statuesque, conveying ease and style. Dani had also pinned her hair into a knot at the nape of the neck, a chignon or waterfall of curls.

Mary was totally taken in by Dani's beauty, accentuated by the style of the clothes she had designed and was modeling. She couldn't believe how practical they seemed. No more bustles or crinolines or layers of heavy material. Mary loved them.

"Do you think I would look as fantastic as you do in those?" Mary asked hesitantly.

"Most definitely." Dani grinned.

Sunday, September 10, 1888

153

IT WAS SHORTLY after 8:00 A.M. Sergeant William Thick knew exactly what he had to do.

It had been in all the various newspapers. The police were looking for a suspect by the name of Leather Apron. He was being sought for questioning in connection with the recent murders in Whitechapel.

The East London Observer gave a rather uncomplimentary description of the man known as Leather Apron. It said, *His face was not altogether pleasant to look upon by reason of the grizzly black strips of hair, nearly an inch in length, which almost covered his face; the thin lips, too, had a cruel, sardonic kind of look, which was increased by the drooping dark mustache and side whiskers. His hair was short, smooth and dark, intermingled with grey. His head, slightly bald on top, was large and fixed to his body by a thick, heavy-looking neck. He appeared splay-footed and spoke with a thick guttural foreign accent.*

It's always harder when it's someone you've known for years, he thought. Thick made his way down Commercial Street, turning left onto Whitechapel Road. He was in no hurry. He had known Leather Apron a.k.a. John Pizer for eighteen years and had immediately volunteered to bring him in for questioning.

Thick turned off Whitechapel Road, walked a block, and then turned onto Mulberry Street. He walked to the front door of Number 22 and knocked.

John Pizer pulled open the door. He knew immediately that the man at the door had come for him. This wasn't a social call.

"You are just the man I want," said Thick.

Thick escorted Pizer to the Leman Street station for questioning, with Pizer proclaiming his innocence, the entire way.

Pizer told the police that, on the night of Mary Ann Nichols' murder, he was staying at the Crossman's Lodging House on Holloway Road. He said he spoke to a policeman about the fire at the Shadwell Docks that he later went to see. He told them the fire broke out around 8:30 P.M. and was under control around 11:00 P.M. Although it wasn't fully extinguished for several hours, he left and returned to Crossman's Lodging House, arriving around 2:15 A.M. He didn't wake until 11:00 A.M. that morning and that's when he learned of the murder. Pizer couldn't have committed the murder. He wasn't anywhere near Buck's Row.

* * *

Later that morning, the inquest into Annie Chapman's' murder started.

154

DANI HAD LEFT for the hospital, alone this morning. Mary hadn't been feeling well and had elected to stay home. She had been throwing up all morning and couldn't seem to keep anything down. Dani suggested that some dry crackers might help. She was almost certain that Mary was experiencing morning sickness. She felt for her friend's suffering, but knew, in the long run, Mary would be elated.

Upon her arrival at the hospital, Dani had informed the duty nurse of Mary's absence. As a result, many of the nursing staff had to handle the duties previously assigned to Mary.

The day had turned out to be a long and tiring one. By the end of it, Dani was eager to get home and see how Mary was faring. Before heading home, however, she had to stop in to say good night to her friend.

Dani knocked on the door. The customary response for her to enter came back almost immediately. She opened the door and found Joseph sitting by the window reading a book which he immediately put down.

Joseph couldn't get enough material to read. He read every issue of the daily newspapers, which kept him well informed on the happenings of the real world outside his room. His greatest passion, however, was reading romance novels. He adored the chivalry he read about in his books. He often fantasized that he was living in the stories he was reading.

"Are you departing, my lady?" Joseph asked in greeting.

"Yes, my gallant gentleman. It is time for me to bid you adieu." Dani instantly picked up on Joseph's role-playing. She had studied drama in school and loved to play along with Joseph's imaginative scenarios.

"Does your chariot await?"

"Not tonight, dear one. I thought I'd enjoy the leisurely stroll. I'm to meet up with my kin. That I shall say good night till it be morrow," Dani recited, quoting a small, but notable, piece from Shakespeare, as she left the room.

"Till it be morrow," Joseph muttered, but Dani was already out of earshot.

Dani made her way out of the hospital. It was only a couple of blocks to the Frying Pan pub.

What Joseph had been reading in the papers of late caused him great worry. He picked up a paper and read: *Finding that, in spite of the murders being committed in our midst, our police force is inadequate to discover the author or authors of the late atrocities, we the undersigned have formed ourselves into a committee and intend offering a substantial reward to anyone, citizen or otherwise, who shall give such information as will be the means of bringing the murderer or murderers to justice.* It was published on behalf of the Whitechapel Vigilance Committee.

The thought of Dani being out on those dark and dangerous streets, alone, especially at night, drove Joseph nearly mad. He had to do something. He grabbed his coat, hat and cane and disappeared through the garden door.

Joseph was grateful that Dr. Treves had made a long-standing arrangement to have a cab at Joseph's disposal, whenever he needed one. There was always one parked outside the London Hospital's front entrance.

"Meet me around the corner by the Frying Pan pub," Joseph

instructed the cabbie. "I'm going for a walk." The hansom cab drove off in the direction of the pub.

Dani walked along Whitechapel Road, turning left onto Osborn. She was enjoying the fresh air or, what she had considered to be fresh air in London. Dani paused. She thought she heard footsteps behind her. She turned to investigate, but no one was there. *It must be my imagination,* she thought, continuing on her way.

Joseph had kept to the shadows as he followed Dani through the dimly lit streets. He had caught sight of a stranger moving toward Dani. Joseph quickly moved in to intercept the stranger who took one look at Joseph and ran in the opposite direction.

Dani entered the Frying Pan pub, safe and sound. Joseph knew her brother would see her home safely; he had completed his task for the night. He turned the corner onto Thrawl Street and entered his waiting cab.

"Home, please," Joseph said, relieved that his fair maiden was no longer in danger.

155

"OH MY GOD, it's gone!" Quinn cried out again.

"Quinn, what is it? What's gone?" Richard asked warily. He knew exactly the cause of Quinn's anguish.

"The chronizium; it's gone. It was in a chest on this shelf. Now it's gone."

So that's what's in there, Richard thought greedily.

"Are you sure? Maybe you forgot where you put it?" Richard was trying to provide a rational alternative. He had stolen Quinn's chronizium supply on his previous visit to the lab and he now possessed the new and powerful source of energy. He just didn't know what he could do with it, yet.

"I'm sure," Quinn stated, unequivocally. "The kids must have taken it with them. Not that it will do them any good. Even if they knew what they had, they'd never be able to get the chest open."

Quinn turned from his futile searching and stared, pleadingly, at Richard. "I need your help, Richard."

"With what?" He hated to be inconvenienced in any way and that included demands on his time.

"I have to find some chronizium. Without it, I don't have the power to initiate time travel from this end; I won't be able to bring the kids home," Quinn explained.

"Of course, I'll help you. Anything you need, it's yours," Richard said eagerly. His mind was already awhirl with endless possibilities: he would be famous. He wanted this incredible scientific breakthrough all to himself. He just needed a little time to put a plan into place; sticking close to Quinn right now was the first step.

"I need to go back to New Zealand and find more chronizium."

"How can I help?"

"I need your private jet. I'd rather not advertise this trip to anyone. Besides, the chronizium will not be easy to find, let alone take out of the country without having to answer a barrage of awkward questions. All of which I would prefer to avoid."

Richard's greed was steering him down a path where many would never venture. His common sense and intellect were playing a game of tug-of-war: *You can't be serious—time travel? Get a grip. But what if Quinn has actually perfected the ability to travel in time? The opportunities would be endless.*

"Of course, but on one condition," Richard offered.

"Name it."

"I'm going with you . . . and before you say no, hear me out. You just told me the chronizium would be difficult to find, so you will need my help. You also said you wanted to keep this trip under the radar, right?"

"Yes, I did."

"So, give me a couple of days to get my affairs in order and I'll fly you to New Zealand. No one else needs to be involved. We can be there and back before anyone even knows we've gone."

"It's a deal," Quinn agreed, knowing he had no better options.

Quinn returned to his console. "I have to get back to work. Hermes and I have to link Bear's bands with Dani's and Daric's. And then we have to finish the computations for travelling to the future," Quinn stated urgently. "You go make the necessary arrangements and then call me when you're ready." Quinn turned back to his equations, not waiting for a response.

Richard showed himself out. He almost ran back to his car. He jumped in and sped down the driveway, spitting gravel in his wake. He couldn't wait to get home.

156

"I'LL BE RIGHT with you," Daric said, upon seeing Dani enter the pub. Daric delivered the drinks he was carrying and picked up the coins.

"I'm off, Mr. Farrow," Daric yelled to the back room. William Farrow had been revelling in Daric's extra hours at the pub; indeed, he had decided to take some long overdue and much needed leisure time for himself. It was the first he had taken in years and, even if it involved nothing more than sitting on his duff in the back room, he was relishing it.

"All right, Daric. See you tomorrow," Mr. Farrow said, coming out to take over the running of the pub.

* * *

"I feel like Cassandra," Dani muttered.

"What?" Daric was lost in his own thoughts as they walked along Commercial Street to meet Rich for a ride home.

"I said, I feel like Cassandra," Dani repeated.

"Cassandra?"

"Yeah, Cassandra, from Greek mythology. She was a princess

of Troy who served as a priestess in the temple of Apollo during the Trojan War. She was given the gift of prophecy; she could foresee the future. But at the same time, she was cursed, because her prophecies would not be believed," Dani explained.

"So, why do you feel like her?"

"Because we know who Jack the Ripper was, but, because of our situation, we can't tell anyone what we know. Even if we could, how would we explain how we came to know?" Dani asked despondently.

"Who was he?" Daric asked eagerly.

"Come on, Daric," Dani chided. "Remember, back about five years ago? It was all over the media."

"No, I don't remember."

"They knew he was about five-foot-seven and quite muscular. He had a pale, brown mustache."

"So does half the male population, from what I've seen," Daric muttered.

"With advanced forensics and with routine DNA testing in our time, they could finally identify who Jack the Ripper was. Don't you remember?" Dani said teasingly.

"No, I don't. Just tell me," Daric urged in frustration.

"It was . . ."

"Look out!" Daric screamed, hurling himself at Dani.

When their bodies collided and crumpled in a tangle of limbs on the ground, their bands touched. Dani and Daric instantly vanished from under the wheels of the thundering carriage that suddenly came upon them out of nowhere.

Author's Notes
Part II

What can one write about Amelia Earhart that hasn't already been written? As a fellow pilot, I can understand her infatuation with being able to move three-dimensionally, being free to go where you please, just like an eagle. But that's where our similarities end.

When I was thirty-eight-years-old, I was taxiing my single-engine Cessna 150 along the apron toward the hangar when the flight instructor said, "Stop here." I pulled over as requested and applied the brakes. The instructor removed his headset, opened the door and got out of the airplane. He said, "It's time for your solo. Do one circuit and bring the plane back here. I'll meet you inside." He shut the door and left.

There I was, all alone in the cockpit. I was both terrified and exhilarated. I had been wondering why we had spent most of my lesson that day doing 'touch and gos'. For those not familiar with the term, 'touch and gos' are circuits of an airfield where the pilot lands the plane and, then, immediately retracts the flaps, applies full throttle and takes off again.

So, as I sat there, alone in the cockpit, my mind raced over all the things I had to do: call the tower for clearance, taxi as instructed to the hold position just off the active runway, move into position for take-off, check all panel instruments, and then, with just the right amount of pressure on the rudder pedals, apply full power and slip the *surly bonds of gravity*.

With one circuit of the field almost completed, I was now on my final approach for landing. My heart rate was exploding, even more so since I always found landing more challenging than taking off. My mind raced with the myriad of items that needed attending to: lower flaps, reduce airspeed, keep the nose up, line up with the centre line of the runway, easy now . . . easy, look straight down the runway, flare and touchdown. It was over—I had done it! And all by the age of thirty-eight! What an accomplishment. I felt so proud of myself.

In contrast, on January 11, 1935, when Amelia Earhart was thirty-eight-years-old, she became the first person, not just the first woman, but the first person, to fly solo from Honolulu, Hawaii to Oakland, California. Later that same year, on April 19, she flew solo from Los Angeles to Mexico City. Then, on May 8, she flew from Mexico City to New York. A few months later, Amelia contemplated one last fight that would set her apart from all others: to circumnavigate the world at its 'waistline'.

I couldn't, even in my wildest imagination, ever dream of undertaking such an extraordinary task, even if I had the years of flying experience. And let's not forget that, in 1937, they didn't have the technology we have today.

Thinking back to Amelia's second attempt at her world flight; Amelia, Howland Island and the three Guard ships were all operating with their own individual clocks set in five different time zones and their calendars on two different days and dates. It was no wonder there was a problem with communications. It was because of Amelia's world flight that Greenwich Mean Time (GMT), also known as Zulu, was adopted for all distress communications.

The more I researched Amelia, the more she seemed to be calling out to me. Not in the cryptic sense, but more through the coincidence of dates. For instance, Amelia departed on her around-the-world flight on Saint Patrick's Day; that was the day my parents were married. She was last heard from and disappeared over the Pacific Ocean on her way to Howland Island on July 3rd; that was the day I started my career and my days of youthful innocence ended. And while surfing through the television stations, I stumbled across the movie *Flight of the Phoenix*, the original version with Jimmy Stewart. At the end of the movie, the following message appeared:

*"It should be remembered . . . that **Paul Mantz**, a fine man and a brilliant flyer, gave his life in the making of this film . . . (Died July 8, 1965–also called Hollywood's best known daredevil)."*

July 8th also happens to be my dad's birthday! Coincidence or something else? You decide!

I would be remiss if I didn't acknowledge the debt of gratitude I owe to those who have spent years and, in some cases, decades, researching, analysing and documenting Amelia Earhart's life. I have tried to honor their work by adhering to historical fact, while interweaving my characters—the Delaneys, Richard Barak Case and others—into the fabric of history. Of note, Paul Mantz and Terry Minor left Hawaii on March 20th with the others and the Electra was shipped back to the mainland on March 27th not the 22nd.

I hope you enjoyed the journey . . . ***Until Next Time.***

Author's Notes
Part III

When I first had the idea of writing a book, which quickly morphed into a trilogy, I knew I'd have to navigate my way through a sea of information. What I didn't realize was how much water a sea contained. Nor did I realize how many interesting things exist in the sea. I soon learned. I also realized that I had to stay truly focused on my goals, if I was going to reach my destination. Every time I lost my focus and veered off course, I was at risk of losing my way or being swamped in the vast sea of information.

Let me try to explain, so you can appreciate my journey.

In my story I introduced a fictional couple: Rich and Mary Case. Now, I needed to find a home for the Cases, so I started searching for 19th century dwellings. I discovered there are many different kinds of dwellings. I decided that Mr. and Mrs. Case were going to live in a terraced house, a style of housing that was, and still is, common in London. I also discovered the usual characteristics of a typical middle-class terraced house: the layout, the types of rooms, the décor, etc.; I settled on the characteristics that would grace the Cases' home. So far, so good, but I still needed to address a key question: where was the house going to be located? So, using the internet (I don't know how writers ever did any of this without the internet!), I ventured forth, using various mapping tools to find the perfect neighborhood for the Cases. Sounds pretty simple, right?

Not quite. I now had to consider where the Cases were going to work, taking into account the location of their house and then factoring in the various modes of transportation. So, after another plunge into the unfathomable depths of overwhelming data, I determined that the Cases would have to work within a two-mile radius of their home. But, I still haven't figured out what they'd do for a living. Thinking . . . thinking . . . I'd make Mrs. Case a nurse—oh wait—was there a hospital nearby? Let's dive deeper.

Great. There was the London Hospital—oh wait—what's that? Joseph Merrick lived at the London Hospital during our story timeline. Maybe I could work him into the plot. So, off I go, jumping into Joseph Merrick's story. Several hours later, I resurfaced . . . now, where was I? Oh yeah, looking for a location for the Cases' house. It had to be in a fairly upscale neighborhood and within a two-mile radius from the London Hospital and—oh wait—I still didn't have an occupation for Mr. Case!

Think . . . think . . . think . . . I've got it. I'd make Mr. Case a police inspector. I'd have him work in Whitechapel, close to where the Ripper murders occurred. Okay, now let's find the police division where he will be assigned. After another leap into the digital world, my research revealed twenty police divisions. Thankfully, only H Division and J Division were heavily involved in the Ripper investigations. I also found reference to the City Police, but after further research I realized their involvement in the investigations occurred after the period covered in my story.

Now, where was I? Oh yeah, Mr. Case. I'd made him a police inspector and I assigned him to H Division.

Good, I was making headway. I found a job and a workplace for Mr. Case. Now, I needed to understand what policing was like in London's East End in 1880's—oh wait—what defined the East End? Better figure that out. Hey, look at this. The police weren't even issued fire arms.

Okay, I finally knew what encompassed the East End and what the police did. So where was I? Oh yeah, looking for a place of residence for the Cases. Maps . . . maps . . . more maps. Wait. What's that? There were two White's Rows, three Church Streets, two John Streets, two Montague Streets, and three Devonshire

Streets, all within close proximity to each other. There were also three George Streets; two of them ran parallel to each other and were just three hundred yards apart. Confusing, to say the least. How did the police ever know where to investigate a complaint or, for that matter, a murder?

Are you exhausted yet? I am. The saying 'up the proverbial creek without the metaphorical paddle' doesn't even begin to echo the level of frustration in trying to reach my destination.

But street names were not the only befuddlement. People in the late 19th century didn't carry any formal means of identification—and they were often known by several different names. For example, a witness at Mary Ann Nichol's inquest was cited in the police report as Ellen Holland, but was listed under other names in various newspapers: as Emily Holland, in *The London East Observer* and *The Illustrated Police News* of September 8, 1888; as Jane Hodden in *The Manchester Guardian* of September 4; and as Jane Oram in *The Times* of the same date. Amelia 'Mel' Palmer, a friend of Annie Chapman, also went by her surname: Farmer.

Even the police had trouble with names. Several newspapers had reported that Inspector Spratling's testimony at Mary Ann Nichol's inquest had stated that Spratling had directed Constable Cartwright to examine the neighbourhood where the deceased had been found. No Police Constable Cartwright has ever been identified. So, who was this Constable Cartwright?

All this stuff about names was interesting, but it wasn't really helping me get to my destination. I adjusted my bearing: I needed to get back to finding a place for the Cases' home. Okay, I found one: a perfect neighbourhood directly across the street from Victoria Park. Wow. What a beautiful fountain. And hey, look at this: Baroness Burdett-Coutts, the wealthiest woman in England, dedicated her time and wealth to philanthropic causes including, co-founding with Charles Dickens, a home for young women who had "turned to a life of immorality". This was all great stuff, but it took me off course again.

Focus . . . focus . . . so, we know that Mrs. Case is working as a nurse at the London Hospital and—oh wait—what did nurses wear in 1888 and what was their role? I veered off on another tack that took me through all kinds of uncharted stuff. Look who was there—Florence Nightingale. Not only was she influential in establishing training for nurses, but her concern over sanitation, military health and hospital planning resulted in practices that still exist today. Wow. Pretty impressive stuff, but not what I was looking for. Through my diving into depths unknown, I came across another very remarkable woman: Clara Collett. Her vast collection of statistical data, accumulated as part of her work for Charles Booth, led to her working for the Board of Trade. For over thirty years, Collet was involved in a variety of important studies that greatly influenced reforms concerning the working conditions and wages for women. Both these women significantly influenced the future, but unfortunately their monumental achievements were clouded by the autumn of terror. Focus . . . focus . . . and so it goes . . .

It was never my intention to become an expert in Ripperology, but it was so easy to get swamped in the waves of information that were endless and often in conflict. So, after spending months reading everything I could get my hands on regarding the Ripper murders, I realized the current was taking me in the wrong direction. I didn't want to write about the murders or the investigations or, least of all, even pretend to think I could solve a century old mystery. I wanted the Delaney children to experience what it was like to live in the late 19th century.

I knew throughout my voyage on the sea that I could never stop the waves; at the same time, I was confident that I could learn how to surf! It was a great ride.

I acknowledge my debt of gratitude to those who have dedicated so much of their time and effort into the relentless quest of identifying Jack the Ripper. I also acknowledge my gratitude to those who have meticulously documented every remaining and known fact about the period from August through to November 1888 in the East End of London. I have tried to respect historical facts, while at the same time, interweaving my characters: the Delaneys, Richard Barak Case and others into the fabric of history.

I hope you enjoyed the journey . . . *Until Next Time.*

Bibliography

1. **Time Travel**

   - Gott, J. Richard. Time Travel in Einstein's Universe: The Physical Possibilities of Travel Through Time. Mariner Books, 2002.

   - Kaku, Michio. Physics of the Impossible: A Scientific Exploration into the World of Phasers, Force Fields, Teleportation, and Time Travel. Doubleday, 2008.

   - Magueijo, Jaao. Faster Than the Speed of Light: The Story of a Scientific Speculation. Basic Books, 2003.

   - Nahin, Paul J. Time Travel: A Writer's Guide to the Real Science of Plausible Time Travel. Johns Hopkins Univ Pr; Revised ed. edition, 2011.

2. **Amelia Earhart**

   - Branson-Trent, Gregory. The Unexplained: Amelia Earhart, Bermuda Triangle, Atlantis, Aliens And Ghosts . New Image Productions, 2010.

   - Long, Elgen M. Long and Marie K. Amelia Earhart: The Mystery Solved . Simon & Schuster, 2009.

   - Purdue University Library e-Archives, George Palmer Putnam Collection Of Amelia Earhart Papers. n.d. http://earchives.lib.purdue.edu/.

- TIGHAR, The International Group for the Historic Aircraft Recovery. n.d. http://tighar.org/Projects/Earhart/AEdescr.html . 2012.

- Matson Ocean Liners https://ssmaritime.com/malo-lo-matsonia.htm

3. London 1888

- Casebook: Jack the Ripper. n.d. http://www.casebook.org/index.html . 2015.

- Cornwell, Patricia. Portait of a Killer: Jack the Ripper Case Closed. G.P. Putnam's Sons; 1st edition, 2002.

- Eddleston, John J. Jack the Ripper - An Encyclopedia. CreateSpace Independent Publishing Platform, 2015.

- Flanders, Judith. Inside The Victorian Home. W. W. Norton & Company, 2006.

- Paul Begg, Martin Fido, Keith Skinner. The Complete Jack the Ripper A to Z. John Blake , 2010.

- Treves, Sir Frederick. The True History of The Elephant Man, Appendix 3. British Medical Journal, Dec. 1886, and April 1890

Acknowledgements

Thanking the people who were most important to *Lost in Time* seems like an impossible task, considering I started this book so long ago, being the first of three in a series. If your name is not listed below, it could be in one of the other two books. If not, it's probably because I've forgotten and I am terribly sorry.

First and foremost, I give a heartfelt thank you to Hugh Willis. I'm sure you never thought, when you agreed to go on this *Next Time* journey with me, you were committing to a trip that would last five years! I thank you for your patience with my typos, your determination with trying to improve my grammar and your never-ending encouragement. I honestly believe your kind words helped me to make this journey through to its final destination. I'm grateful that you took this trip with me.

Thank you to Rose Lythgoe, you were my first reader of the entire series and you flattered me with your enthusiastic feedback. I am also grateful to Kerry Mills, Lori Sullivan, Joyce Dennis, Sandy Riddell, Arlene Douglas, Wendy Cathcart, Carolyn Nixon, Cameron and Mary McBain and Joyce Wiltshire. Your reassuring words were heartfelt and appreciated.

I would also like to acknowledge Lynda Orrell, Emergency Room Nurse (retired) for her technical assistance and for your encouraging words. Thanks to a dear friend Michael Brier for your aviation and navigational expertise.

And finally I'd like to thank fellow authors Cathy Marie Buchanan and Rosemary McCracken for sharing their writing journey with me and for providing some valuable advice to a debut writer.

The adventure continues with

NEXT TIME BOOK 2

RUNNING OUT OF TIME

Read on for an exciting glimpse into the next book in the Next Time series coming out soon.

Part IV

*In the Wrong Place
at the Wrong Time*

1

"THAT WAS HIM!" Dani shrieked. "That was Jack the Ripper!"

"I know," Daric barked back. "And that bastard will never pay for his crimes."

"Where are we?" Dani asked, trying to orient herself.

"Look out!" a child screamed from somewhere over Daric's left shoulder. Daric's prone form looked up. The front hooves of a reared horse were plummeting downward, directly toward him. He instinctively rolled away, taking Dani with him.

"That was close," Daric muttered.

"Grab them!" a man's voice bellowed from above.

Two men among the crowd gathered at the side of the road rushed forward and seized Daric's arms. They pulled him up onto his feet and wrenched his arms high behind his back.

"Hey, take it easy," Daric protested, unable to mask the grimace on his face.

Another man from the opposite side of the road bent down and pulled Dani to her feet, pinning her arms as well.

"Hey!" Dani objected. As she peered over her shoulder to see who was holding her so tightly, she let out a gasp. She was looking into a pair of wide-set brown eyes that were staring out at her from a shadow-draped face under a wide-brimmed black hat.

"Don't you be givin' me no evil eye, witch," he snapped.

"Where did they come from?" a woman asked worriedly.

"They must be witches!" cried a young woman from the back of the crowd.

"Here," the cart driver said as he tossed some rope to the men who were restraining Dani and Daric and who made quick work of securing their hands behind their backs.

"Can we get on with it? We'll deal with these two later. They're not going anywhere," a man on horseback shouted.

As the cart slowly past, Daric looked at Dani to make sure she was okay. As he did, his eyes met those of the man holding her. At first he couldn't believe what he saw: a face with thin lips, a broad nose, and a thrusting pointed jaw. He would know that face anywhere, no matter what kind of clothes its owner was wearing.

Daric mouthed the words. Dani acknowledged with a nod of her head. Another Uncle Richard.

Present Day - Saturday

2

RICHARD'S MIND WAS Awash with the possibilities. Time travel: could it be true? To be able to travel through time. He would be famous, the envy of his profession; hell, he would be the envy of everyone. "Quinn actually did it!" he muttered. "The things I could do with those travel bands." There was only one problem: the bands were in England, in 1888, the last he knew.

Richard was annoyed that Quinn had been reluctant to share his incredible breakthrough with him. At the same time, Richard knew he would not have understood the endless equations involved in Quinn's achievement. They gave him migraines.

Although annoyed, Richard would bide his time. He would leave Quinn to work out the still unresolved details. Once Quinn was finished with his work, Richard would make his move.

After parking his Abruzzi in the garage, Richard entered the house. He immediately proceeded to the north wing where he had previously installed a fingerprint scanner locking device. Unlocking the door, he entered, yelling, "Hey, Eddie, I'm home!"

"You can't keep me here," a timid voice muttered back.

"Of course I can, you worthless piece of shit. Nobody even knows you're missing, or cares, for that matter. Besides, you have a roof over your head, a comfortable suite of rooms, and decent meals whenever you want them. A far cry from where you were two months ago when I scraped you off the street and kept you out of the hands of the law. So, be grateful," Richard spat.

Edward "Eddie" Jonathan Keys was a young man, small in stature compared to Richard. Weighing one-hundred-fifty pounds, with narrow shoulders, he stood six feet. He had sad jade-green eyes behind thick black-framed glasses. His short brown hair was a little longer on top. He had a small mole just above the left corner of his mouth.

Eddie had been in the Foster Care system since he was five-years-old. That was when he had lost both his parents in a terrible car accident on their way home from a party one stormy winter's night. His life had been turned upside down in a matter of seconds when the police had come and told him the news. Learning that he had no living relatives who could take care of him, the police immediately delivered him to the local child care authorities. When old enough, he had left his last foster family late one night, and had been taking care of himself ever since. Until two months ago, that is, when he was hacking into a convenience store's ATM and was caught by Richard.

"I have a little job for you," Richard sneered. He had known he had a good thing when he caught Eddie breaking into the ATM. Richard had stood in an obscure corner of the store and watched the young man. He was immediately impressed by the self-made gadgets the kid pulled out of his pockets, all designed to access the cash in the machine. He would have succeeded, too, if Richard hadn't grabbed him and hauled him away. So far, the kid hadn't disappointed him.

"See this little box?" Richard asked, holding up the small metal chest he had taken from Quinn's lab. "I need you to open it."

"Why don't you open it yourself?" Eddie said defiantly, seated comfortably in his desk chair.

Before the pain could register, Eddie found himself sprawled on the floor, his overturned chair beside him. He had not seen the abrupt backhand slap coming his way.

"Because, smartass, it has a very special lock. Open it!" Richard demanded, as he pitched the small box onto Eddie's chest. "Buzz me when you're done."

Richard stormed out of the room, locking the door behind him. He made his way to his office where he poured himself a stiff drink. Richard knew he had to get back into Quinn's lab to get access to his work. But Richard would need a distraction first, something to draw Quinn's attention away from the lab. *What would possibly bring Quinn out of his lab?* Richard thought deviously. He took another deep belt from his glass when an idea struck him. A sinister smile edged across his pencil-thin lips. Tomorrow: all he had to do was make one quick phone call.

The pure genius of it, he thought.